JUNE RAIN

JUNE

RAIN

Denfield Dowdye

Trafford Publishing

Order this book online at www.trafford.com
or email orders@trafford.com

Most Trafford titles are also available at major online book retailers.

Note for Librarians: A cataloguing record for this book is available from Library and Archives Canada at www.collectionscanada.ca/amicus/index-e.html

Printed in Victoria, BC, Canada.

ISBN: 978-1-4269-2093-6 (sc)

ISBN: 978-1-4269-2094-3 (dj)

Library of Congress Control Number: 2009940292

Our mission is to efficiently provide the world's finest, most comprehensive book publishing service, enabling every author to experience success. To find out how to publish your book, your way, and have it available worldwide, visit us online at www.trafford.com

Trafford rev. 03/1/2010

 www.trafford.com

North America & international
toll-free: 1 888 232 4444 (USA & Canada)
phone: 250 383 6864 ♦ fax: 812 355 4082

Acknowledgments

Thanks to those who provided information, advice, and encouragement. They include Karen Y. Brown, Cecilia Martin, BMK, Anita Doreen Diggs, Michael L. Miller, Michael Stephens, Ed Jackson, Mia K., Ricky Johnson, Tip, and great teachers at Morgan State—especially Nina Tassi—and at Baltimore City Community College, such as Karen McClaskey and Harold Levin. Double thanks to editor Bill U'Ren.

PROLOGUE

As Harry Wade and Floyd "Juney" Stubbs entered Washington, D.C., in an old Plymouth late on a Saturday night, neither sensed the presence of death as a backseat passenger starting to stir. Wade, struggling to control his well-known temper, looked at Stubbs, who was steering with one hand and talking into a cell phone with the other, even though they'd recently passed a sign banning just that. Wade saw Stubbs as unpredictable and unreliable, the type of black man to avoid. But on this trip, he'd had no choice.

At forty-one, Wade had long thinning hair, sideburns, and for the last two days, a leather patch over his leaking right eye. He'd lowered his cigarettes to one a day but remained a heavy scotch drinker. Nick Rowe, a man Wade had met eight years earlier while one of the few white men on the yard at Rikers Island Prison, had offered him five grand to drive the Plymouth from the Bronx to Miami, no questions asked, but a sudden eye infection fouled things up. Wade had to get Stubbs to drive at the last minute, but the past three hours, complete with a non-stop stream of low-volume 70's r&b from the car's CD player, had made him regret it. Both ex-cons knew that the trunk contained something, and Stubbs wanted to call the shots even though he was just a driver.

Stubbs ended his conversation and slipped the phone into his pocket. "I got a buddy right up the road," he said in a rumbling voice. "We can head on over there and use his garage. He ain't got to know what we doing." His hand went up to a toothpick sticking out of his mouth.

"How many times I gotta tell you," Wade replied, his fists clenched. "We follow the plan. If we need to stop, there's a house before we get to Charlotte. Otherwise, it's one straight shot on down to Florida, and we deliver the car. That's what we gettin' paid to do."

Stubbs, a bigger, older, gray-haired man with freckles on a medium-brown complexion, sucked his teeth. "Listen. It's every man for himself out here. We find out what's in the trunk, sell it, split the money. We ain't got to go fifty-fifty. I know you the man, I know you the man. The guy who gave you the car and the guy pickin' it up, you think they give a shit about us? C'mon, now. Get real."

"You talkin' bullshit," Wade said. "I know the dude gave me the car. I don't know no buddy of yours. Why should I trust him *or* you?"

Stubbs knew that he was here only because of Wade's vision problem. He rolled the toothpick to the other side of his mouth and said, "Man, you known me for years. I ain't settin' you up."

"I known you on and off. That don't mean I gotta trust you. Who the fuck you think you are, anyway, tellin' me what to do?" Wade said, fumbling with the CD player. "How you turn this shit off?"

Stubbs ignored the question. "Look, I got experience in this here game. Florida's a long ways off. Cops be pullin' people over on the way down there. You know it. Got dogs sniffin' all up in the car, sniffin' your drawers, all kinds of crazy shit…"

Wade shook his head. "You so worried about cops, why don't you slow the fuck down? You know something's in the trunk, and you been speeding the whole way. What the fuck is wrong with you? What I bring you for anyway?"

"They'll stop you for goin' too slow just like they'll stop you for goin' too fast," Stubbs said.

Wade lost it. "That don't mean you gotta be settin' speed records and shit! Pull over. I'm drivin'."

Stubbs said, "Man, you can't see. You don't know where my buddy at…"

Wade slammed the dashboard. "Shut the fuck up! I told you to pull over!"

For some reason, Rowe had said to avoid the normal 95 South to

Virginia and take a roundabout route at D.C., so they'd just left 29 South and were on Georgia Avenue. The car turned left onto nearly deserted Jarvis Street and cruised past several closed shops. Stubbs slowed down and pulled into a small vacant lot that led to a dark alley. He cut off the engine. "I'm tellin' you," he said as he opened the door to get out and switch seats, "you makin' a mistake..."

Stubbs' feet hit the ground, and he heard Wade sliding over into the driver's seat. As he walked around the front of the car, he visualized Wade, younger, smiling, arm outstretched, when they'd been introduced a few years previously at an upstate New York racetrack, and he heard Wade's voice, barely audible on a bad cell phone signal yesterday, asking if Stubbs wanted to make a little easy money for a run down to Miami.

Muttering, he started to get in on the passenger side, thinking about how nobody had respect anymore, and saw Wade pulling a small pistol from under his shirt. The motherfucker looked like he wanted to shoot him!

Adrenaline flooded Stubbs' brain and body. Within a second, he yanked a switchblade from his waist, clicked it open, and lunged toward Wade, who raised the gun and fired. The "Bang!" stung their ears. Stubbs slumped onto Wade's knees, a .22 caliber bullet having penetrated one lung, clipped the other, and lodged near his right collarbone. His five-inch blade had cut into Wade's throat, sliced his windpipe and larynx, and come out the side of his neck. Blood sprayed the dashboard and windshield as Wade gagged, stiffened, and pitched forward. His chin smashed into the horn and split open. With the knife's handle sticking from his adam's apple, he started convulsing. An elbow hit the gear stick, causing the car to shift into neutral and roll forward.

Stubbs fell out onto the pavement and lay there, grimacing. He heard Wade's body thrashing involuntarily as the car came to rest gently against a utility pole, both doors open and Roberta Flack's "Killing Me Softly" floating from within.

After half a minute, Stubbs struggled to his feet. He couldn't move his right arm, and every breath caused searing pain in his chest and shoulder. Looking skyward, his back arched, he lurched around in a circle, then staggered toward the driver's seat. Wade lay still except for a twitching left index finger, his gun beside him.

Stubbs leaned into the car, turned off the music, and pulled the knife from Wade's throat. He reached under the driver's seat and pressed the button to pop the trunk, but nothing happened. After wiping the blade slowly on the dead man's shirt, he slipped the knife into his own pocket, removed the keys from the ignition, and went to the back of the car.

With blood drooling from his lips, he realized that he could breathe only by dragging air in loudly through his mouth. The key wouldn't open the trunk, so he used the knife. When he finally popped the lock, no light came on. After groping around inside and finding nothing, he lifted the floorboard and pulled out the spare, which he dumped on the ground. He felt along the tire's surface and found a small section that had been cut out and carefully replaced. Inside was a small green plastic bag circled by a band of duct tape. It contained powder. Stubbs took the bag, closed the trunk, and tottered toward the alley, trailing thick red drops.

He began to feel cold despite the comfortable, spring temperature. Weaving along the dark alley, he tried to slip the bag into his waistband, but pain and a wave of dizziness overwhelmed him as he approached Jarvis Street. He leaned against a dumpster, lightheaded, each attempt at breath sounding like a rusty, closing hinge. Still clutching the blood-smeared parcel, he choked on warm liquid that rose up within his chest and flowed out through his mouth and nose. More than a million dollars worth of uncut Thai heroin tumbled from Juney Stubbs' hand as he groaned for the last time and fell forward…

CHAPTER ONE

FREEMAN'S CHOICE

Until his death from an aneurysm thirty-nine years later in a Hawaiian hospital, Freeman never figured out what made him look to his left that night as he crossed an alley in northwest D.C. It was early June. He'd been taking a long stroll home along Jarvis Street after a late-night dinner and a couple of glasses of Chianti alone at a nice little Mexican restaurant. He'd stopped at a supermarket to pick up green peppers, paper towels, and hot sauce, which he carried in a plastic shopping bag. Freeman had a list of things to do the next day, starting with a ton of laundry, so he was walking faster than usual while singing in a fine tenor "Vote for Me," a song he'd almost finished for his group's next CD: *Yes, he's a big-time politician, been trained for it since . . birth/Next step up the ladder, to be most powerful man on . . earth . . .*

Someone above clapped, and Freeman looked up to see a smiling Hispanic girl, about ten-years-old, wearing a white nightgown and peering down at him from the window of a second-floor apartment atop a discount mattress store. Freeman smiled back, waved, and continued on.

Bearded, dark-skinned, and sporting long dreadlocks, he stood six-foot-two and weighed over two-hundred-and-sixty-five pounds, big enough to deter nighttime assailants, though a lack of physical courage belied his imposing appearance. He made ends meet by singing and playing rhythm guitar and horn for Vortex, a locally popular reggae band, and over the years, his vocals had acquired an authentic-sounding Caribbean accent; he also worked at a used CD shop called Sound Value in northeast.

His pace quickened as he passed a small furniture outlet with a rusting, old-fashioned metal gate across its darkened entrance, and a liquor store that seemed dwarfed by the amber neon sign above it, which said simply, "Liquors." No one was in sight, and the only traffic was an occasional car on a cross street in the distance.

His girlfriend, Simone, a free-spirited junior at the University of Maryland, had left for the weekend to visit a friend up the road. Funny, they'd been together for years, but whenever she was away, he still found himself a bit suspicious and uneasy. For one thing, the way she looked meant that she couldn't cross the street without some guy trying to make a move on her. And she'd do anything. She liked trying new things and taking chances. But, he knew that those qualities, plus the fact that she was white, made the relationship different and more exciting than others he'd been in.

A quarter mile short of Delham Parkway, a major road that led to Route 29, he started to cross an alley and, for whatever reason, glanced to his left. There, a man in a black shirt lay face down, arm outstretched, his torso protruding from behind a dumpster.

Freeman froze in mid-step. Faint light from the other end of the alley shone on a small green plastic package near the man's fingers.

"Do Not Enter" signs stood on either side of the alley. A brick wall faded into shadow on the left; to the right, sheets of plastic wrapping lay across three tall wooden crates that glistened with moisture although no rain had fallen in weeks. Further on, several cardboard boxes lay in a heap, and beyond them stood the dumpster.

Freeman looked all around to make sure that no one saw him. He took two steps into the alley and paused. The man could be injured or dying, or maybe it was some kind of a trap. He didn't want to get involved in anything, but with few people walking this route at one o' clock on a Sunday morning, he decided to see whether or not he could help. He held his breath and walked toward the body.

Something small shuffled among the boxes and scurried across the alley, causing Freeman to jump. He continued, his movements in slow motion as he reached the dumpster and crouched. The middle-aged black man lay spread-eagled in a pool of blood. He appeared dead. Fear gripped Freeman. Again, he noticed how light fell on the green, duct-tape-wrapped package that looked to have fallen from the man's grasp. He leaned down toward it but stopped; in a lot beyond the alley, a white car with its front doors open and its lights on rested against a utility pole. Two feet stuck out of the driver's side.

Trembling, Freeman walked through the semi-darkness to the car. Inside it, blood was everywhere: a blood-soaked white man wearing an eye patch lay still, his hand near a gun on the passenger seat. Freeman looked from one dead man to the other and back. He couldn't believe it. How long had these corpses been here?

But whatever had happened, he wanted nothing to do it, and he turned back toward Jarvis Street. He stepped over the black man's arm, but once more, the green package caught his eye. He stopped and stared at it. It had its own aura, as real as the bag itself; surrounded by a circle of light, it seemed almost to speak to him: *Here I am. Take me. I'm yours.* Freeman stood, hypnotized. The situation had trouble written all over it, but he saw no harm in taking the bag. Maybe the contents were worth money, and if not, he could just throw it away.

He looked around one last time, saw no one, and picked up the package. The feel told him drugs. A lot of it. He hesitated for a moment, started to drop it into his grocery bag, reconsidered, and slipped it into his pocket. Hearing distant sirens, he began running toward home, but after half a block, he realized that he looked suspicious—and that he was way out of shape—and slowed to a walk.

———

Twice a week or so, Freeman's girlfriend stayed with him at Gersi Place, a quiet semicircular little strip of rowhouses where he lived alone, three blocks south of Jarvis. Once he got in, he lay the package on a table in the living room, turned on a lamp, sat in an old armchair, and gazed at the green bag. But seeing two dead bodies in the street and finding whatever he'd found had him on edge; he went upstairs to get some weed from the bedroom, came back down, rolled it in pistachio-flavored paper, and lit up, hoping to relax and figure out his next move.

He took a drag and stared at the package through a slim swirl of smoke that snaked slowly to the ceiling. The bag contained strong-smelling white powder. Even though Freeman had tried coke a few times, he couldn't distinguish it from heroin or anything else by sight or taste, but he knew that he'd found one or the other.

The smoke soon took effect. He went upstairs to the computer, turned it on, clicked to the Internet, and tried to find out how much a pound of cocaine and a pound of heroin were worth. The second number made his mouth fall open. He ran back downstairs and eyed the bag again, hands on hips. Who could identify its contents? Vaughan Chandler, Vortex's bassist and singer and the star of the group, was supposed to have tried many drugs, but he was touring somewhere with a bigger band and wouldn't be back for a couple of weeks. Plus, Chandler was unreliable, and Freeman didn't trust him because of a money dispute they'd had years back.

Freeman had friends and acquaintances who had "experimented" with drugs, none of whom he could trust with this kind of secret. He thought of his girlfriend; Simone wasn't a druggie, but she'd been around different types of people and seemed to know about a lot of things. She was in Laurel, visiting a former classmate, but he couldn't remember when she'd be back, probably because of the weed and wine.

The DVD player's clock said 1:51 am. She might still be up. Freeman headed for the kitchen and picked up the phone.

—

After a vigorous session of hashish-and-champagne enhanced sex, Simone Seacroft lay beside Henry, her other lover, in the bedroom of a small cottage he'd rented by a stream near Conklin, Virginia, a town eight miles southwest of D.C. Across the room, a forty-inch-screen beamed a muted replay of an old Mike Tyson fight. Henry watched it, his head propped on a pillow, a half-full bottle of Moet in an ice bucket on his nightstand.

"Nothing here to eat, right?" Simone asked, her dilated, green eyes blinking heavily.

"No. Hold on a minute. We'll go get something."

On the screen, black-clad Tyson swung away at his opponent, a taller, magnificently muscled, bald-headed fighter who had "WARRIOR" written across the waistband of his purple and white trunks.

Simone looked at the ceiling and thought about what she considered her biggest character flaw, her inability to respect boundaries, and how it had affected her love life. She'd been with Freeman for almost two pretty good years when she met Henry on a plane headed south from New York's Kennedy Airport. She'd barely made the flight and had to squeeze past him to get to her window seat. His was one away, by the aisle. Soon after takeoff, she pulled a paperback from her bag and started reading.

"Good book?" he asked.

She looked up, and he smiled with his eyes only. "I used to read a book a week," he said, "but business keeps me busy."

"What do you do?" she asked.

"I'm with a waste management firm based in Florida. You?"

"I'm a student. I have a part-time job with a small publisher in Virginia."

"Where do you go to school? What do you study?"

"University of Maryland. I switched from psychology to graphic art."

"Psychology can be a tough field to work in," he said. "The money's not bad, but you have to deal with other people's issues. Usually, life gives you enough for yourself to try to work out. You've got to be good to handle your stuff plus other people's."

"You're right. People just fascinate me, though, the way their minds work. But I'm into art, too. I think art and psychology have similar functions. Art heals."

"I know what you're saying," he replied, smiling. "Art used to be my thing, too. One time I had to write a long paper on *La Guernica*."

"Picasso's painting. If I could meet anybody from the past, it'd be him."

He nodded and continued, acting as if he were more interested in her major than he was in her tits. He thought for a second and remembered that he was traveling under his real name. "My name's Henry," he said.

They spoke for much of the hour-long flight to Washington National Airport, during which his eyes rarely left hers, and when he asked for her number after disembarking, she'd given it. The well-groomed, impeccably-dressed Cuban's direct, mature demeanor contrasted with that of laid back, carefree Freeman; she guessed that that was why, as they spoke over the next few weeks and eventually got together for drinks, she became drawn to Henry.

But she liked Freeman, too—no, loved him, in her own way. He was warm hearted and kind, and even though he looked like a big rasta-thug, he treated her the way a gentleman should treat a woman. That was a breath of fresh air, but sometimes, to her, the relationship lacked something. Plus, she'd juggled two and three boyfriends in high school and enjoyed it, as she did now.

Henry lived in West Palm Beach and traveled constantly—not the settling down type, but wicked in bed. They always had a good time together. Dealing with two men who had opposite appeals exhilarated her, and guilt never entered the picture. Maybe she'd always be that way. She just didn't want to hurt Freeman by having him find out about the other man. That was the exciting part.

"We should go somewhere together," she said now, struggling with a craving for warm apple pie with chocolate chip ice cream.

"Like where?" he replied.

"You're always traveling. I'd like to go sometime."

He tilted his head slightly toward her but kept his eyes on the TV. "What would your boyfriend, whatsisname, say about that?"

The sweet-smelling smoke, drink, and intense sex had her tingling down to her toes, and words felt odd coming out of her mouth. She liked Henry's accent the first time she'd heard it, but tonight it sounded more appealing than usual, like soft, orchestral music, gentle but suggesting hidden strength. She looked at him. In the dimness, shades of blue and red beamed from the television and flickered across his black hair, his sideburns, his almost hypnotic eyes, and the elaborate tattoo that snaked across the right side of his chest, around his bicep, and back to his shoulder blade.

She knew that it was just sex for him, that he probably had many other women. During their fifteen-month affair, he'd told her his age: forty; that he'd worked for the Cuban government, defected, and taken another name; that he'd left a family behind; that he now worked for a waste management firm that had branches along the east coast and more coming out west. She didn't know what to believe, but that was okay; she liked mystery. She *did* know that he had great magnetism. He made love better than anyone she'd been with in her twenty-two years, and, unlike Freeman, he had no problem with money.

"I'll take care of my boyfriend. He's not an issue," she replied, drawing a pattern with her middle finger across the tattoo on his chest. "Where are you headed on Monday?"

"Tuesday. Vegas." He smiled at something on the screen, and she turned toward it. There, the boxing match had been stopped, with the taller fighter literally hopping with pain and rage, and Tyson, his head lowered, beckoning him with both hands to come on. She realized that this was a replay of the fight in which Tyson had bitten off part of his opponent's ear (she couldn't remember the guy's name). It seemed crazy, seeing it.

Naked, Henry stood, turned off the TV, and headed for the shower. "C'mon," he said. "Let's go."

Simone noticed the sound of nighttime frogs and the stream fifty yards from the cottage. It took her a while to find the digital clock. Aware of her neck muscles stretching and contracting, she turned her head toward the clock's turquoise numbers: 1:19 a.m. She got out of the bed and, swaying before getting her balance, ran her hands through her hair. She joined Henry in the shower, which was illuminated by a series of pink-tinted bulbs above the mirror. The warm water's soft pressure created an indescribable sensation against her skin. "Where are we going?" she asked.

"I want to show you something."

———

Twenty minutes later, they were headed toward Old Town in his rented BMW on North Fargo Lane, an empty, birch-lined, two-lane blacktop. A three-quarter moon high to Simone's left bathed the foliage and road with its pale radiance. Her high hadn't begun to wear off.

At a dark side street, Henry made a right and pulled off the road and onto a wide gravel path. Simone tried to read the street sign, but it was in heavy shadow. Henry cut off the engine and motioned for her to follow him toward a gap in the line of trees. She hesitated. She'd never had any reason to distrust him, but it was *dark* out here; he could do anything to her, and no one would know. But there'd been many times when they'd been alone together in different settings, situations in which he could have harmed her if he wanted. She reached for a small can of Mace that she always carried in her bag, uncapped and pocketed it, and followed him to the end of the line of trees.

The air smelled of leaves and rich earth. Framed by the moon's glow, Henry turned past the last tree and stood still, his arm extended for her to join him. She did and held her breath. Ahead lay a large, shimmering lake surrounded by trees, low hills, and a few distant buildings, all suffused and outlined by moonlight.

"Look at that," he said. "Like a painting."

"It seems unreal," she replied after a while.

He took out the small pipe they'd been using at the cottage, held a lighter to the bowl, inhaled twice, and passed the hashish to her. Simone took two puffs and returned it. She focused again on the lake's dream-like beauty, which, combined with the drug's effects, made her feel as if she'd been magically transported to some other world…her cell phone went off: Freeman.

"What you up to?" he asked.

"On my way to get something to munch on," she answered. "What are you doing?"

"Something crazy happened here tonight."

"What?"

"I found something. I want you to check it out." He sounded serious.

"What do you mean, you 'found something'?" She could feel Henry's stare.

"It's not something to talk about on the phone. When you coming back?"

"Tomorrow," she said. "Tomorrow afternoon. Tell me. What's going on?"

"I'll tell you when I see you. Just let me know when you get in, okay?"

"Freeman. You always do that. Why start to say something and then leave people hanging? I hate when you do that."

"Trust me, baby. You'll understand."

"All right. I should be there about seven. I guess I'll see you then."

She clicked off too soon to hear him say, "Don't mention to anyone what I just told you."

Simone and Henry remained at the lake for several more minutes, then returned to the car and drove to an all-night eatery in Old Town. She kept wondering about what Freeman had found.

—

The next day, Freeman scuttled most of his plans and stayed home. At around 5:45 in the evening, he was sitting in the shaded part of his front porch when Simone's old black Volvo pulled to the curb. She got out and walked toward the house, smiling.

Freeman's five-foot-nine-inch girlfriend always drew attention but even more so in this mostly black area. Wearing a light-colored blouse that accentuated her shoulders, which drew almost as much attention as the rest of her voluptuous figure, and a short skirt that showed her long, athletic-looking legs, she walked up the front stairs. She had shoulder-length auburn hair with blonde streaks, sensual lips, and green eyes that drew people into them. Seeing her excited Freeman, and he smiled back at her.

She kissed him, sat, and lied about her weekend, saying that she and an ex-college roommate, had gone bowling, eaten at a Chinese restaurant, and watched two DVD's, *Drumline* and *Supersize Me*, at the friend's house in Laurel. "So what happened on Saturday night?" she asked. "What's the big secret?"

Freeman stood and led her inside the house. He accumulated things without realizing it, and as they went through the living room, they passed a thigh-high stack of old newspapers tied with twine amid his worn furniture. Once in the kitchen, they had to share space with two trash bags filled with glass jars and water bottles that he'd been meaning to recycle for weeks. Even though the house looked no worse than usual, he waved his hand casually and said, "Excuse the condition of the place."

"What condition? It looks better than it did last time I was here."

The green package lay in the middle of a business page from the previous day's *Washington Post* on a table in the middle of the room. She went to the refrigerator and poured herself a glass of grapefruit juice while he described walking home from the restaurant and seeing a dead man in the alley and another in the car, with a gun on the seat. He spoke about how the package seemed to be sitting there, "waiting for me to take it," and mentioned how nervous he'd been coming home, sensing that the bag contained drugs and knowing that he'd just left a murder scene.

"It's got a strong smell," Simone said. "You said you didn't touch anything?"

He shook his head: "I was too shocked. Whatever went down happened just before I got there. If I'd been a minute earlier and seen something, I'd probably be lyin' right there with them. You ever seen someone who'd just been killed like that? Plus I'd been drinkin', too? I'm tellin' you. Freaked me out. I just wanted to get the hell away from there."

"And no one saw you?"

"No, I made sure."

"Seems like if someone fired a gun, the sound would draw attention."

"Nowadays, people hear shit all the time. They just want to mind their own business. They might be used to it around there, just trying to get their sleep. Besides, it's more shops on Jarvis than anything else."

Simone looked from him to the package. "What about security cameras? You know they got them all over the place now."

"I didn't think about that. I didn't see any. But those cameras are in the rich areas, more. You don't see them in this part of D.C."

Simone grasped the duct tape-wrapped bag and moved her hand up and down as if weighing it. "Feels like it's about a pound, right?"

"That's what I figure," he said as she put it down. He nodded toward the green package and said, "I guess we're never going to find out what's in it just staring at it." Freeman took a boning knife from a drawer next to the stove, cut a tiny hole in the bag, and withdrew a few grains of white powder on the knife's blade.

"It could be anything," he said. "Poison. Anthrax. Anything."

Simone looked at him from the corner of her eye and finished her juice. "If it was anthrax, I don't think you'd still be breathing." She smelled the powder and said instantly, "This smells like heroin. I've never used it, but that's what it smells like to me."

"Okay, but how can you tell?"

"Smell it."

He did, and the pungent, clinical, almost antiseptic odor made his nostrils tingle. "I see what you mean," he said, nodding. "I haven't done it either, but if I had to guess what it smells like, that would be it. That would exactly be it."

He put a few grains on his finger, touched them to his tongue, contorted his face, and said, "Taste it."

Simone nodded; the powder had a strong, bitter flavor that soon started to burn. She twisted her face and said, "Whew." They spat it out in the bathroom sink and returned to the kitchen.

He stared at the powder without blinking, the same way he had when he'd first seen it. If she were right, it was good for at least half-a-million wholesale and a million on the streets according to what he'd read. Freeman didn't know what to think. He'd spent much of the day wondering about the wisdom of taking the package and getting the feeling that whatever its contents, it could bring trouble. "I don't know," he said, scratching his scalp. "Maybe I should just turn it in. This shit might be worth a lot of money, but I don't feel like doing thirty years behind it, y'know what I'm saying?"

"You don't have to sweat it if you play your cards right, darlin.' I know what I'd do. I'd sell it. Tomorrow. It's up to you, though."

He stared at the package as if hypnotized. Freeman had always seen her as being materialistic, odd considering that while she wasn't wealthy, her parents were, at least by his standards, and eventually, she'd get something through them. But he'd learned to leave the subject alone.

Simone asked, "Have you seen anything on TV about any of this?"

"Uh uh," Freeman said. He looked at the clock on the wall above the sink and said, "The news is coming on in a minute. Maybe there's something on there about it." They returned to the living room, where he switched on the TV. A six o'clock newscast relayed the latest list of local, national, and international chaos but mentioned nothing of the previous night's nearby double murder. When the sports came on, Freeman and Simone went back into the kitchen and stood in front of the package.

"You know anyone who knows about this type of thing?" he asked.

"Not off the top of my head. You don't know anybody?"

He mentioned Chandler, Vortex's lead singer. Simone knew the band and knew that Chandler was out of town. She walked toward the stairs that led up to the bedroom and said, "We'll figure something out. Right now, I'm going to lay down. I'm tired." She started up the steps and glanced back to find him looking at her body. Soon, he followed.

———

The next day, Monday, Henry Ramos found a parking spot in southwest D.C. after twenty minutes of trying, and walked two blocks south in dry, mid-day heat to talk with millionaire defense lawyer Ephraim Barzey over lunch. Despite being fifteen minutes early, he knew that the veteran barrister—one of the few people who knew the truth about him—would probably already be there.

Enrique Osvaldo Guzman Ramos—"Henry"—was one of the best, and one of the most elusive, counterfeiters and forgers in America. He'd begun at sixteen, in Cuba, where such activity was rare; those who dared usually forged "convertible" currency, which the authorities focused on because despite being much harder to duplicate they were easy to pass to unsuspecting tourists. Despite the brutal consequences if caught under Castro's regime, Henry had used an uncanny talent for hand-drawn and hand-painted reproduction to forge non-convertible pesos—blue twenties, purple fifties, and ochre hundreds—that looked authentic down to the watermark. His mother's cousin taught him to use the bleached pages of a certain type of sketchpad bought in a nearby province to ply his trade, which he did for pleasure, not because he needed the money. His talent as a liar supported his skill, and no one caught him.

Just before his eighteenth birthday, Henry came to Florida with his father on the Mariel Boatlift. He worked in a stationery store, where he saved (and learned much about paper). He enrolled at a community college but spent more time reading about printing and counterfeiting than about history or economics. After two semesters, he dropped out, but by then, he'd met and befriended a maintenance worker there, an old gringo with faded jailhouse tattoos on his forearm. The man introduced Henry to a government worker who disposed of surplus items and who sold Henry a small offset printing press.

Henry modified it, set it up in an abandoned shed outside the city, and, with rag "paper" dipped in a twenty percent solution of penathrytil tritalanomine (to make a test pen's mark yellow) used it one Sunday night to make eight-thousand fifty-dollar bills. He then broke down the machinery, buried the parts, and sold his paper to a Russian mob-connected, cash-strapped owner of a waste management firm for thirty-five cents on the dollar. Walking from that first sale with the proceeds in innocuous duffel bags, getting into his beat up station wagon, and driving to his West Palm Beach apartment filled Henry with once-in-a-lifetime satisfaction.

Henry bought a bigger press and printed about once a year. He made millions. He learned that in America, cash—and a little charm—bought access to anything. He operated covertly, researched the criminals to whom he sold his goods, and let no grass grow under his feet; his innate need for variety—locations, climates, women, even cars—kept him moving and away from anyone with questions. He usually operated out west: L.A., Phoenix, West Palm Beach (his base, where forged papers had secured a small, monthly disability check, which helped keep him a legal resident), and, especially, Las Vegas.

Now and then, he'd dabble in various other schemes introduced by any of the fleeting contacts he made during his travels. He'd killed twice—once in response to a verbal threat that may or may not have been serious, and again to save his life. Murder didn't mean much to him one way or the other, as long as he didn't get caught—which he wasn't. But he *had* been arrested three times for other things: wire fraud and possession of stolen goods in Florida, and a weapons charge in New Jersey. He believed that the government knew about him but couldn't make counterfeiting charges stick, so they'd tried to nail him on bullshit. But Ephraim Barzey had always gotten him off with no problem.

Despite his success, though, Henry had started to want to do something different. A couple of years ago, restlessness led him to become a shadow investor in the Reno- based waste-management firm owned by the man who'd bought his first set of bills and who sought an alternative to loans to help finance expansion. Henry continued to profit from that; he'd even attended two meetings—all the while continuing to draw disability under his real name in Florida.

Still, his vague unrest continued. Barzey had called unexpectedly on Friday and suggested that they meet to discuss an unspecified matter. Now, Henry's curiosity increased as he entered the air-conditioned restaurant.

Flanked on the east and west by newly-built condos, Howie Tom's restaurant in Georgetown offered some of the finest Chinese dishes in the city. Its comprehensive menu and quick, efficient service made it popular; on warm, sunny days like this, lunch and dinner crowds filled the interior and occupied all outdoor tables, each of which had an oversized umbrella that created welcome shade.

Barzey, a tanned, fifty-six-year-old, second-generation defense lawyer, sat outside near a potted ficus, reading *The Washington Post*. Henry had known him for fourteen years. Of average height, like Henry, with longish gray-white hair reminiscent of a lion's mane, his red-and-gray polo shirt, white slacks, and tasseled loafers suggested an afternoon of golf. He folded the paper and gestured for Henry to join him.

"Good to see you, good to see you," the lawyer said patting the table. "Haven't spoken to you in a while, not since the I.R.S. thing a couple of years ago." A waiter appeared; Barzey ordered a gin and tonic and Henry a Bacardi on ice. "Can't stay long," the lawyer said, glancing at his Bulova. "Got a foursome at 12:45 at Belle Haven."

Once the drinks arrived, Henry leaned forward and asked, "So what's going on?"

"You know I look out for my people," Barzey said.

Henry nodded, and the lawyer continued: "I went to law school in Connecticut with a guy who works in the Treasury department. Real good guy. Anyway, he knows who some of my longtime clients are. He knows your name. I'm not saying he knows your business or anything like that, but he knows your name." He paused. "People have been looking for you. Secret Service and FBI. Up in Jersey."

"Since when?"

"It's recent. Part of a task force. Exactly what it's about, I'm not sure. You know, you've got to be careful about how you talk on the phone nowadays. Real careful." Barzey downed half his gin. "Anyway, if it's a Secret Service agent, it could be money-related. I don't know what you do or what you've done or anything. As far as I know, you're a respectable, hard-working, law-abiding businessman. I'm just telling you what *I* hear."

"When did you find out?"

"The day before I called. Thursday."

"Secret Service *and* FBI?"

"I believe they're looking at that weapons charge that got dismissed up there."

Henry thought back to the night someone had broken into his rented apartment while he was there, asleep, and he'd chased the guy down the stairs, into the street, onto the highway, and northwest from Atlantic City at 125 m.p.h. He'd fired and missed twelve shots, and the guy had gotten away. "They can't try the case again, can they?"

"That's the thing," the lawyer said. "They didn't try it the first time. If I remember correctly, a girl was with you that night. They tried hard to find her as a witness, but they couldn't. That's what happened, right?"

Henry nodded, staring intently at the lawyer.

"If they've got new evidence, they can present it and ask for a trial."

"Petty bullshit," Henry said, sipping his drink.

Barzey shrugged. "You know what it is. You're a target. They can't hook you on anything big, so they're just throwing stuff at the wall and seeing what sticks."

And costing me a fortune in legal fees, Henry thought. "Who are the agents?" he asked.

The lawyer pulled a folded sheet of pink, unlined paper from his breast pocket and passed it to Henry. "Royce" and "Oberhauser" were written in pencil. Henry slipped the paper into his pocket and asked, "Which one's FBI? Where are they now?"

Barzey shook his head. "Everything I know about them's on that paper. They could be anywhere. That could be them sitting right behind you."

Henry resisted the urge to look around the outdoor area and asked, "What about the statute of limitations?"

The lawyer smiled, finished his drink, and stood, ready to go. "Funny you should ask. Going back to the date of the alleged crimes in question, it expires at the end of the week, Friday. Maybe you should lay low for a few days."

Henry murmured "Thanks" as Barzey patted his shoulder on the way out.

The counterfeiter sat back and lit a Dominican cheroot. The lawyer had no apparent reason to lie. Did the government have something on Henry? Had someone rolled over on him? What was the 'task force' about? Henry had rented the cottage in Virginia under one name and bought a train ticket here under another, so he'd be hard to find. As a precaution, he'd always tried to keep track of paper that he passed and had heard nothing to indicate that anything had gone wrong, and, besides, he hadn't printed in two years.

He decided not to worry about it. If the government wanted him, let them come and get him. Fuck 'em. He'd intended to head out west the next day anyway and saw no need to change plans. He finished his rum, reached for Barzey's discarded *Post*, and scanned the front page. Within seconds, someone tapped his shoulder.

The unexpected touch shot an electricity-like charge through him, but he showed nothing. He took an instant to compose himself and turned slowly to face a twenty-something-ish, casually dressed white couple. They'd been drinking.

"Excuse me," the smiling woman said, tucking her brown hair behind her ear defensively. She wore black-rimmed glasses and a thin pink sundress. "We were just wondering. We noticed you sitting here talking to your friend, and we just started discussing you. You know, how you look."

Why me, Henry wondered. He thought about the two agents Barzey had told him about. These two and any number of the restaurant's other "patrons" could be here to arrest him. He wished he had the .45 that he occasionally carried holstered in the small of his back, but he'd left it in Florida, taped behind his refrigerator.

The woman's companion spoke: "Not to be nosy, but we just started guessing about you, what you do. She thinks you're some type of a businessman, advertising or something. I think you're more the artsy type, an actor or photographer or maybe a painter. We were just wondering. We made a little bet."

Henry put away the newspaper so that they wouldn't see what he'd been reading. He smiled politely and said, "Por favor, no hablo ingles. No comprendo."

The woman leaned forward and said in a terrible Spanish accent, "No . . so . . .tros ...estamos ..."

"Let's go," the man said, steering her away. "He doesn't want to talk. Let's leave him alone." He looked back at Henry and said, "Sorry."

Henry put out the rest of his cigar, paid the tab, and walked to his car, glancing back over his shoulder three times along the way. He rarely analyzed his actions, but he hadn't responded right to the woman's unexpected touch. He needed a change. He wanted something to happen—some kind of new challenge—but he didn't know what.

As he sped across the Key Bridge toward Virginia, the girl, Simone, came to mind. He called her on his cell and asked if she was at home. She said yes.

"Why don't you come over to where I'm staying?" he asked.

"I've got to be at work in half an hour."

"What time you get off?"

"Seven."

"How about then?"

"I don't know. I'll have to see."

"Listen. You said you wanted to go out of town with me sometime," Henry said. "How about tomorrow? I'm headed out to Vegas. Ever been out there?"

"I can't just drop everything and take off like that. I've got a boyfriend, remember? I don't want him to know anything."

"Yeah, right. What's his name again?"

"I told you before. If you don't remember, you don't remember." The fact that Henry often acted as if Freeman didn't exist bothered her.

"It would be just a couple of days," he said. "I'll take care of things. We'll have a good time."

"Yeah, but something's come up. I need to stick around for a while."

"What's the problem?"

"I can't talk about it. But I'll call and let you know if we can get together later. Bye."

Henry slipped the phone into his pocket. He enjoyed the girl. They saw each other once every two months or so, depending on his location, and he really didn't know that much about her. Sometimes, he couldn't figure Simone—a disciplined student who did well with her classes but who loved to party and have fun; she had expensive tastes and liked swimming, tennis, and horseback riding; she listened to rap and reggae. Henry usually couldn't remember the boyfriend's name, but he knew that she seemed protective toward him.

She was the right age, she had a killer body, and she knew what to do in bed. Plus, she had an upbeat, spontaneous quality, and didn't ask too many questions.

When they'd first met, he'd asked for her number as they left the airport terminal, and she wrote it on a scrap of paper beneath her name: Simone Seacroft. He'd read it out loud and said, "Pretty name."

"Thanks, but I can't take credit for it," she replied, smiling. "Somebody gave it to me."

To Henry, women were fun, a release, a diversion not to be taken too seriously. But steering southwest at Seven Corners, Virginia, he wondered about this one. He'd bet that her not coming with him to Vegas was related to her phone conversation at the lake, when the boyfriend had said he'd found something. As he'd done often since then, Henry tried to figure out what he could have found.

CHAPTER TWO

BLUES FOR TOMAAS

Three thousand miles away, in South Beach, Miami, Tomaas DeShields sat at a white wicker table on his fourteenth floor condominium's balcony. He had a hash brown, bacon, and egg breakfast in front of him, but, despite having not eaten since early the previous afternoon, he wasn't hungry. After tasting the food, he stood and went to the railing on this, his third straight day without sleep.

Something had happened to the package from Brooklyn—at least, that's how it looked. Another problem, a big one. But he'd known from the beginning that this might happen; it was just more of the chaos that had ruled his life since his mother had died when he was a kid.

His girlfriend, Gabrielle, had just come down from the rooftop pool. Wearing a yellow bathing suit, she walked out through the living room's sliding glass doors to stand next to him in the eighty-five-degree heat. "Still no sleep?" she asked.

Squinting, he shook his head. She shaded her eyes as they looked down. Depending on which window they used, their loft condominium in this building, which was off Clayton Avenue and around the corner from the Royal Palm Crowne Hotel, offered views of the city or the Atlantic. The ocean scenery was calm now but held the not-distant threat of the season's first hurricane. "You standing here thinking again," she said. "I told you, you think too much, sometimes."

"You know how it is, baby. It's a lot to think about out here. You think a lot, too. That's why you smart." His forced smile flashed gold incisors.

"Right, but you got to keep it positive, always." She rested her hand on his shoulder.

"The people out here I got to deal with," he said, gritting his teeth and shaking his head. "Black, white, yellow, brown, red, all of them—I got to be expecting the worst, 24/7. That way you know how to deal when you get it."

Quick-witted and observant, Tommy, at twenty-seven, was slim and lithe and had smooth, medium-brown skin and hair that was thick on top and faded on the sides and back. He had ropy muscles and little body fat even though he ate too much junk food. Today, he wore only a white tank top and black shorts; a miniature, Morocco-made stiletto, its blade and onyx handle inlaid in twenty-four-carat gold, glittered on a chain hanging from his neck.

Gabrielle Baptiste, twenty-three, was pretty and dark-skinned. Her short, straightened hair was slicked back from her forehead. She had an almost regal bearing—back straight, head held high—and was a dancer at The Lotus, an upscale strip club just up the road, where, on a good night, she'd clear over a thousand dollars in cash. Her quick tongue had sparked many rows with Tommy during their three-plus years, but her femininity helped douse them.

She poured a drink from the pitcher of orange juice on the table and drank it.

"Edgar's on his way up," she said. "I'm going to meet Trish, then I'm going to get the car washed."

Tommy nodded, and as she disappeared inside, his thoughts returned to the prospect of losing a million dollars' worth of dope.

A minute later, Edgar, Tommy's twenty-eight-year-old friend from detention center days, arrived and came out to the railing. He was a home improvement contractor who'd ventured into real estate, and he added to his income by working with Tommy sometimes; he'd driven the shipment from New York on Tommy's second run, and Tommy trusted him more than anyone. Six-feet-tall and sturdily built, Edgar had flat eyes that suggested seriousness, a man who focused intently on one thing at a time. Tommy had never worked, but he was listed on Edgar's payroll for tax purposes. "How'd it go?" Edgar asked.

Tommy told him what had happened. "Nick Rowe called me from New York Saturday night, said Harry Wade had just left with the bag in the car, was on his way here. That's the last I heard."

"So you got to go up to Brooklyn, right?"

Tommy nodded. "I wanna go now, but I gotta wait," he said, with clenched fists. "I gotta take a piss test tomorrow morning. I missed the last one."

Edgar exhaled loudly. "Something like this, every second counts, man."

"No shit, yo."

"I could go up there with you."

"I'll let you know."

"Anyway," Edgar said, "you got that adapter you borrowed last month?"

Tommy got the appliance and let Edgar out. He was walking toward the bathroom when his cell phone, which was out on the breakfast table next to the orange juice, started ringing. He walked back out to the balcony, where a seagull stood on the railing, eyeing his breakfast.

It was Monet, his cousin Vonetta's seventeen-year-old daughter calling, and Tommy sensed more trouble. For the hundredth time, he thought about leaving Miami, with its uncles and aunts and cousins and endless headaches. But he'd made a small fortune and a name for himself here by moving whatever came his way by land or sea. This was home. Still, as he picked up the phone, it seemed as if the city was starting to drive him crazy.

"Tommy, I'm worried about my mom," Monet said. "She's having a real hard time with what happened with Anthony. She's just different. The doctor gave her some pills, but that just seemed like it made her worse, so she stopped taking them. Her pastor's been out here a couple times. I don't know what to do."

Tommy squeezed his eyes shut and ran his hand across his forehead several times. "It's been about a year since Anthony died, right?" He tried to avoid this touchy subject.

"Yeah. It happened December, year before last," Monet said. "The trial was the next May."

"Where's your mom?" Tommy asked.

"She's out back, watchin' TV."

Tommy didn't have any answers, but he said, "I'll be there in twenty minutes, all right?"

"Thanks, Tommy," she said. "I'm on my way out, so just come around the back. She'll be there." Tommy clicked off and turned around; two gulls now stood on the railing, waiting for the right moment to steal his breakfast. "Even the goddamn birds," he thought. He wanted to shoot them.

———

As Tommy rode his Kawasaki ZX motorcycle along the MacArthur Causeway and north toward Vonetta's house near Hialeah, Gabrielle, in a blue and gray outfit, and her friend Trish, in white and green, were jogging side by side on treadmills at a gym that patrons crowded at lunchtime. Located on an office building's fifth floor, this room's tinted glass wall offered a view of bright, bustling 28th Street below; Sade's *Stronger Than Pride* played quietly from a speaker above the door.

At thirty-seven, Patricia Hartley was older than most strippers, but a six-day-a-week exercise regimen kept her in top shape. She was a bleached-blonde two-time divorcee, engaged to a fifty-four-year-old Japanese-American investment banker who'd left his wife to marry Trish. She'd become Gabrielle's confidante.

"I been wanting to sign up for some college classes," Gabrielle said, "but time's a problem for me. I got other things going on."

"You should go ahead and do it if that's what you want. You're not getting any younger. You think time's a problem now, I want to see what you do if you ever have a kid. I know something's going on with you, though. I can tell."

Gabrielle didn't respond.

Trish said, "You got the brains for college. I took classes when I lived in Indiana. I stopped when I came down here." She paused for breath, then continued. "I worked in an office for three years. But it was the same type of bullshit we have to deal with from ownership, management, customers, whatever, at the Lotus, just not as much money." Another pause. "So I've pretty much been dancing since then. People look at me, they don't know how old I am."

"No, you look young."

"Well," Trish said, upping the treadmill's speed, "this is how you do it."

"I been dancing since I was seventeen," Gabrielle said. "So that's six years. It's good money, but I don't want to be shaking my ass for the next fifteen years, you know? That's why I think about school. Tommy says I should keep doing this for a while."

"You better think for yourself," Trish said. "Guys come and go." She stopped talking, to catch her breath. "Make a plan. Figure out what you want to be doing ten years from now and take steps toward it. And whatever you do, don't start getting high."

Sweat covered both women; they were breathing through their mouths as their feet thudded on the treadmills' rubber. "Most of the time Tommy and me do all right, sometimes we don't," Gabrielle said. "He loves me. Something's going on with him, though. We been together three years. He's always been kind of moody, but it's getting worse. Sometimes he'll go for days without sleeping. And he tries to cover it up."

Trish asked, "Is that what's bothering you so much? Tommy?"

Gabrielle said nothing.

"Whatever it is, you're wound up nearly as tight as he is," Trish said. "Sounds like he's bi-polo. I used to date a guy who was bi-polo. He was in advertising. Flipped out just from the stress."

"Can't tell Tommy about seeing a doctor," Gabrielle said as her machine started to slow.

"I know you love him, and that's fine. Just don't forget to do what's best for you."

Gabrielle started to tell the older woman about another, bigger problem, the one that was distracting her and delaying her school enrollment but decided not to. She ran in silence until the machine stopped. "I'm heading upstairs to work with the weights," she said, wiping her forehead with a towel.

As Gabrielle started to walk away, Trish, still running hard, smiled and said, "Angels are here."

Gabrielle thought for a while and asked, "For how long?"

"Tonight *and* tomorrow. Know what that means, right?"

"And I got to work both nights." One of the Los Angeles Angels' outfielders liked the Lotus in general and Gabrielle in particular. He stopped in once or twice a year when his team visited southern Florida. The club's manager granted the high-profile, free-spending client special liberties and had encouraged Gabrielle to comply.

"I don't feel like putting up with any of his baseball-player bullshit," she said.

"Don't worry," Trish said, still smiling. "I've been there. Just stay focused on the bottom line. You can handle it."

———

For no apparent reason, maintenance workers had blocked off one side of Bearden Lane in solidly working-class Woodbridge, just west of Hialeah, so Tommy had to park his bike across the street from 4901. He removed his helmet with its heavily tinted visor and squinted, blinded momentarily by the sunlight's glare. In the back of his mind, he still wanted his cell to ring with a call saying that the package had arrived, but he knew that it wouldn't. His cousin's dark red, two-story clapboard house, overflowing inside with nicknacks and mementos, stood forty feet back from the street; it had a palm tree on the sidewalk, one on the front lawn, and another out back. As he unlatched the gate on the wire fence surrounding the property, Cassius, Vonetta's retriever, known for chasing mailcarriers and passers-by, barked and emerged from beside the house, wagging his tail but struggling with the heat.

The dog followed Tommy along a foot-worn path past the mailbox and hedge in front of the house to the rear, where Vonetta sat in a heavily shadowed, plant-filled enclosed porch. She didn't see him until he walked up the stairs and tried the door handle. Tommy's relatives knew that he dealt in something secretive and illegal, but they didn't know what; "Like father like son," they said. (All were on his dad's side. His deceased mother, a Haitian, had no kin in the U.S.) An uncle and an aunt were cordial toward him while another uncle said as little as possible. His cousins treated him as a regular cousin. He remained closest to Vonetta, who was ten years older, maybe because she, too, had grown up in dysfunctional circumstances. They'd been friendly since his early childhood.

She smiled but avoided his eyes as she let him into the glass room. The well-tended plants made the air smell fresh. He sat to the side on a wicker stool, and she in a rocking chair. Between them, a large jar of lemonade and an empty glass were on a green-cloth covered table. In the half-light, she looked the same: medium-brown skin, glasses, hair in short braids, no makeup or jewelry, maybe a little thinner, young for her age, attractive. Although her appearance suggested modesty and shyness, she'd never had a problem speaking her mind.

The TV was on, and he asked what she was watching.

"A DVD. It's got William Petersen, the guy used to be in *CSI*," she replied.

Tommy had never heard of either. He asked, "Oh yeah? Any good?"

"Everything he's in is good." She got up, went inside, returned with another glass, and poured him some lemonade. Plants filled the place. They were on tables; in pots on the floor; in baskets hanging on golden hooks and chains suspended from the ceiling. "Perennials," she said. "It's good to watch them grow." They talked about Monet, who'd graduated a year ahead of schedule from Du Bois High and who'd been offered two scholarships, and about Vonetta's beloved Florida Marlins, buried in last place in the N.L East (Tommy knew little about them; he liked football).

Reluctantly, he mentioned his dead nephew: "How about the thing with Anthony? You doing any better with that?"

Vonetta bit her lip. Her son had been a tall, rangy seventeen-year-old honor student and baseball player at DuBois High who talked of joining the Marines. A boy named Mark Wilkerson had lost a fight with him, gone home, returned with a gun, and shot him four times outside a recreation center on a Saturday afternoon. Mark was a troublemaker from a family of troublemakers who exerted enough influence in the area to intimidate witnesses from testifying.

His acquittal on all charges changed Vonetta, a high school geography teacher. People who knew her could sense the difference; it was as if a surgeon had operated and removed something basic to who she was. Soon after the trial, her daughter said, "Her whole vibe is different." Everyone was waiting for a sign that she was returning to normal.

Vonetta looked Tommy in the eye when he mentioned her son. "I'm really proud of Monet. She'd be the second one out of all of us, after me, to go to college. But Anthony was my heart." She cleared her throat. "You know how he was. Losing him like that, just all of a sudden, was bad enough, but seeing that boy who killed him get not guilty and hugging everybody in the courtroom and his family all happy, as if something great had happened..." She hesitated, then continued. "It's real hard for a mother to accept something like that..."

Tommy resisted the urge to pull out a cigarette; instead, he drank some lemonade. "Von," he said, "you gonna have to find a way to move on. There ain't nothin' you can do about Anthony. Sittin' here thinking 'bout it just gonna make it worse than it is. Trust me, I been there..."

Vonetta leaned back in her rocking chair. "I know what you're sayin' Tommy. I'm gonna move on. But I'm gonna be carryin' this with me the whole way. The whole way. My son's gone, and it's not right for that boy to do what he did and not have to pay for it. The system's not right. They only care about rich people. This whole world isn't right." Her anger and frustration resonated as she paused. "You know him, right? The boy, Mark? He's out there still carryin' on. Right in the same neighborhood where he shot my son. Monet saw him a few weeks ago. Gonna kill somebody else's baby, you watch, now he know he can get away with it. He ain't no good. You just watch."

Tommy finished his drink and looked from her to the TV to the back yard, where Cassius got up from the palm tree's scant shade and came to the house, his tongue hanging out. When Tommy opened the door, a huge orange and black butterfly fluttered in with the dog, which went to Vonetta and lay down beside her feet. Tommy returned to his seat, but he had nothing more to say, and after a while, he picked up his helmet and started to leave. He told her to take it easy and that he'd see her later. She said, "You know it ain't right, Tommy." She said it as if urging him to do something about her murdered son. When he turned to look at her, she looked right back and started nodding her head.

Walking to his motorbike, he pictured his cousin sitting alone in the porch's cool, clean air, devastated by a death while surrounded by life—beautiful plants, exotic butterflies, a well-manicured yard with finely-trimmed hedges, lush palm trees, and loyal Cassius. Tommy sat on the black bike, looked back at the house, and stared at the window of the second-floor room that had been Anthony's for all of the boy's seventeen years. Tommy thought about him, his potential, his funeral, the trial, the lawyers, the missing witnesses, the verdict, Mark Wilkerson, Vonetta. He hadn't been close to his nephew, but he'd shared some of Vonetta's anger about the trial's outcome. He thought about his dead mother...

Tommy blocked it all out. He looked at the road ahead and focused on his current task. He flipped open his cell phone, and called Edgar. "Where you at?" he asked.

"Home."

"Meet me out front in twenty." He then called Miami International and checked flight schedules to New York. He put on his helmet, started the bike, and headed south.

—

Ten months earlier, the mother of Edgar's second and third children (he'd had an earlier one as a teenager) had taken them and moved out, leaving him alone in his 2,300 square foot house in Larchmont, near Wynwood. When Tommy arrived there, he found Edgar in the palm tree-shaded driveway checking a white 4Runner's engine. Outkast boomed from the speakers. As Tommy approached, Edgar turned down the sound, got inside, and motioned him into the passenger seat. They sat there with both doors open. "What's goin' on, yo?" Edgar asked, chewing gum.

Tommy lit a cigarette. "This thing up in New York. I need to get up there, but I can't move 'til one-thirty tomorrow. You got time to go? There's a flight in ... " he checked his watch, ".... two hours and fifteen minutes."

"You mean, go up there *now*?"

"Hey, this an emergency situation for me, yo, straight up."

Edgar tapped his fingers on the steering wheel, thinking. "I need to be here Thursday morning," he said. "We start rehabbing a store not far from where you at in the city."

"All right, that's cool. See, Nick Rowe arranged for the dude to drive down here Saturday night and bring that package. You met Rowe when you made that run for me beginning of the year. You just go up there, talk to him, tell me what's up, come right back tomorrow night."

Edgar asked, "You ain't call him since Saturday?"

Tommy shook his head. "No. It's like this: if everything's smooth, Rowe don't hear nothin' from me. Somebody's supposed to see him Friday, give him the other half of his money. This way, whoever go up there and talk to him—me, you, whoever—he won't be expecting it."

Edgar shook his head. "I don't know, yo. You say he cool and everything, but, to me, he sound like he might've did somethin.' If he did, he probably ain't gonna be at his place when I get there..."

Tommy turned away and blew a thin line of smoke out the open door. "Let me worry about that, yo. You ain't payin' for nothin.' I know he might of did somethin.' And if he did, he made the biggest mistake of his motherfuckin' life. That's what you goin' up there for. Find out for me." He passed Edgar a slip of paper that had Rowe's address and phone numbers.

Edgar looked at it and nodded. "Who's the guy supposed to be drivin' the shit down here?"

"White boy named Wade," Tommy said. "I never met him, but I known Rowe since I was a kid. Dealt with him a bunch of times, never had no problem. It looks like Wade took off with the package. But I don't know for a fact. I want to look Rowe in the eye when he talk, but I can't wait 'til this time tomorrow, y'know what I'm sayin'?"

Edgar asked, "He black or Spanish? I couldn't tell when I met him."

"Rowe? He's mixed. His dad's from Germany, or his mother's from Germany, one or the other. He was born there and came here when he was real young. Was in the army. Did a dime up at Riker's Island for armed robbery. Did the whole stretch, didn't rat nobody out. He old school."

"Wade drive down here for you before?"

"Nah," Tommy answered.

Edgar said, "Maaan, I say squeeze Rowe from jump. Whatever happened to the package, it's on him. He the last one had it. He responsible. You got to press that nigga to find out where your shit at, yo, for real."

"I'm gonna find out what happened. Don't worry 'bout that."

They sat quietly for a few seconds. Edgar, tapping his foot to Outkast's beat coming low from the speakers, asked, "What's the weather up there?"

"It's June, nigga. It's hot."

Edgar laughed.

Tommy said, "Find out what's goin' on, let me know. That's it. I be there tomorrow afternoon, about five."

Edgar said, "All right. But if Rowe or anybody else give me a problem, I gotta handle it."

"Do what you gotta do, but you representin' me in a business deal. Like I told you," Tommy said, "Rowe old school. You play it right, you ain't gotta carry no gun when you see him." He looked at his watch. "You got a plane to catch, yo." He ground his cigarette out in the ashtray and asked, "You got money?"

"Yeah, I got this. You hit me when I get back." They bumped fists, and Tommy left.

———

He rode home to his air-conditioned condo, set his cell to recharge, and tried to sleep but wound up staring at the ceiling, his hands clasped behind his head. He wanted to smoke some weed but had to take a drug test in the morning.

He thought about all the things that could have caused the New York shipment to disappear, and about what to do about each. He thought about how, despite misgivings, he'd gotten into this situation. He thought about his fifty-seven-year-old father, Leon, now dying of AIDS near Savannah, Georgia, who had spent more than half of his life either in prison or as a so-called drug "kingpin" on the street...

Tommy had tried to avoid that scene for more than one reason, but after being in a detention center from ages sixteen to twenty-one and lacking a formal education, he'd landed on a similar path. He'd made good money with hijacked cigarettes and hijacked liquor and, using false customs entries, with stolen DVD players and pirated Ipods. He multiplied his money with bootlegged laptops, and, after listening to his father, come up with a strategy to import heroin in five small shipments (rather than one big one) from Asia, clear three-and-a-half million dollars, and walk away from drugs.

He spent fourteen months planning and setting things up, using his father's and his own connections. He made two trips to the other side of the world to establish contacts in Bangkok, Ankara, Calais, New York, and Atlanta. The operation had gone perfectly the first two times: from Thailand by road and train to Turkey and France, then by ship to New York and down here to Florida. Each trip's profit went into a bigger buy on the next one, and the lure of higher paydays motivated couriers to deliver on time. But he'd learned long ago that no matter how well things had been set up and no matter how well-funded the operation, personnel would always be the weak link; people had flaws, and only the man on top was committed to getting it right.

His dad had connected him to cops in Manhattan, D.C., and Charlotte who could give information, but he wanted to involve as few people as possible. Last week, he'd paid a D.C. officer named Tracy Whitlock five hundred dollars through a middle man for telling him that on Saturday, the night the package disappeared, 95 South was going to be under heavy surveillance from southern Maryland to Virginia, and he should find another route. The driver, Wade, was supposed to have gone through Washington, not around it.

Tommy knew that things often went wrong due to developments no one could predict. A buyer was waiting for the heroin; Tommy had committed to pay for tons of equipment stolen from a Louisiana military depot next week. He needed the money from the missing bag of dope, but it looked like the whole thing was falling apart.

Suddenly, while lying on the bed, Tommy's body tensed; he clenched his fists and held his breath as a panic-like surge came over him. He squeezed his eyes shut, then relaxed them and forced himself to breathe deeply and loosen up. After struggling that way for several minutes, he opened his eyes and checked the clock; Edgar should be on his way to the airport. Tommy could only wait.

He continued to inhale and exhale, and after a while, began to feel tired for the first time in two days. His thoughts drifted—back to his father dying and refusing to go to a hospice, and to Vonetta and the last thing she'd said to him about her murdered son this afternoon in her greenhouse…

—

...**despite the room's coolness, Tommy** woke up from a dreamless sleep sweating and with his heart racing. He sat on the side of the bed and gripped the mattress tightly until he calmed down. Heavy depression had settled over him, but he knew he had to fight it. The clock said 7:04; Edgar would be in New York. He looked at his cell phone for several moments, then removed it from the charger. He switched on the TV and switched it right back off. He wanted to lie down; instead, he took a deep breath and forced himself to stand and go out to the balcony, where the air had cooled. He stood at the railing to the building's north end and lit a cigarette.

Vehicles and pedestrians flowed in all directions amid palm trees at the intersection below, and the sails of yachts harbored in the Marina gleamed in the distance. Tommy liked this place, but he was unsure about how much longer he'd be here. Gabrielle wanted to rent out the condo and buy a house, but he didn't even know if he wanted to stay in Florida. He'd decide what he wanted to do this year.

His thoughts returned to his predicament. After he'd finished his cigarette, he got his phone from the charger, returned outside, and dialed the cell number for the D.C. cop, Tracy Whitlock. When she didn't answer, he left a message: "Hey, this Tommy from Florida. My car went missing up that way over the weekend. See if you could find that for me." He gave the license plate number and clicked off. Leaning on the balcony railing, he looked down again at the early evening street.

He felt like seeing Gabrielle dance tonight. The club's management didn't want the girls' boyfriends or husbands there, but they didn't know him. He loved watching her onstage, where he'd first seen her. So, once in a while, he'd go to the Lotus unannounced and pick a spot at one of the bars or by the stairs or in the hallway that led to the bathrooms, where she couldn't see him. She usually looked surprised when he'd finally show his face.

His stomach's growling made him recognize his hunger, so he decided to grab some Chinese and go to the club. He finished his smoke and went inside to take a shower.

—

The Lotus Club was on Pearlstone Place, off Biscayne Boulevard. One of the city's most popular spots, it featured a unique set up. The first floor had four green plexiglass stages, each shaped like a giant lotus, with footlights, and a dancer under pink and white lights on each of four petals. After the dancer did her set, she'd go into the audience and mingle, trying to pick up extra tips and/or get patrons to buy more drinks from the house. As soon as she left the stage, another dancer would emerge from the lotus's center and replace her. A curved bar with a long, pink neon light ran behind the stage from one side of the room to another.

A spiral glass staircase led upstairs to another larger stage and "courtesy rooms," where clients would go for "private dances." The second floor had two smaller bars, and a door to the manager's office was near the stairs. No customer could initiate physical contact with a girl; rules prevented a dancer from discussing her private life, but any "personal arrangements" between her and a customer were up to them. At least two security men were on duty at all times.

When Gabrielle had arrived tonight, the club's longtime manager, a tall, slim, gray-haired Californian named Gus Buchannon, had told her to expect some of the Los Angeles Angels' baseball players and that while she might not like some of them, she had a duty to entertain and turn a profit for the club. "You're a professional," he'd said. Buchannon was terse and impassive, and he had an attitude toward her even though few of the dancers made as much money as she.

Gabrielle was the darkest of the Lotus's four black girls and the only one without long hair or a weave hanging past her shoulders. By nine, she'd made a good amount for a Monday with no conventions in town. She'd been working mostly downstairs since six and had over two hundred in her "tip purse." Two strawberry margaritas she'd drunk were having an effect as she stood in the small chamber beneath the upstairs stage, waiting to dance. Britney Spears' "Toxic" came on, and the lotus's center above her opened.

Wearing a short white outfit and yellow heels, she put on a smile and walked up the stairs to join the three strippers already under the lights in front of about forty-five patrons, including many women. She walked to her spot, leaned against a pole that went from stage to ceiling, and started to dance.

Gabrielle looked different from the Lotus's other girls. A light sheen of sweat and gold glitter made her chocolate-brown skin shimmer.

While performing, she didn't think about money; she tuned in to her own sexuality and radiated confidence while tuning her body's message to the instincts of particular customers, which she could feel, without being too obvious about which ones. Even though few girls made as much money, Buchannon didn't hire any other dark-skinned dancer.

As "Toxic" ended and Beyonce's "Naughty Girl" began, a petite teenaged dancer named Lina finished her turn and went to sit between a well-dressed thirty-ish black couple near the front. She seemed to know them; she kissed the woman and turned her attention to the man. To Gabrielle, the younger girls were much bolder than they'd been when she began.

Two black men came up the stairs to Gabrielle's left and stood looking at the stage—wait, was that Tommy standing behind them? No, just somebody going to the bathroom. After a while, they both stepped forward, and Gabrielle recognized Dan Evans, the baseball player who liked her. The man with him was bigger, bald, smoking a cigar, in oversized black and gray and wearing tinted, gold-rimmed glasses. Evans was carrying a drink and had on gold chains, bracelets, and a hooded, rust-colored silk jogging suit. When he and the other man came to sit in front of her, she thought, "Oh no."

Customers had slipped bills into Gabrielle's garters, and others had thrown them at her feet. She noticed Lina get up from between the couple she'd joined and sit on the man's groin with her arm around his shoulder. The woman with him said something to Lina, smiled, and crossed her legs toward them. Gabrielle, in bra and panties, kept dancing. She avoided looking at Evans but could feel his stare. She expected him to call her over to talk when the next song ended, as he had the other two times he'd seen her dance.

The music switched to Janet Jackson's "Anytime, Anyplace," and Gabrielle stripped naked for the last song of this set. She strolled from one customer to the next, with each slipping money into one of her belts. Meanwhile, in the audience, Lina started sliding herself back and forth rhythmically on the man's lap to arouse him as his companion stroked her shoulder.

Evans put a hand on the stage, leaned forward, and slipped a hundred into a belt while caressing Gabrielle's thigh. Above the music, she heard him say, "I'm here to see you, sugar. You know it," in a slight southern accent. With a cold glance, she nodded her thanks.

The song ended with her on her back, smiling, breathing hard, a foot on a front seat customer's shoulder. He, too, gave her cash, and as she looked up, Lina and the couple walked toward the booths on the other side of the room.

Gabrielle wanted to avoid Evans. She turned toward a white, executive type sitting alone at a table, who hadn't taken his eyes off her, but Evans held her wrist and pulled her gently toward him. Normally, she'd have signaled for security to deal with a customer who grabbed her, but Buchannon wanted her to go along with the program—at least to an extent—so, wearing only her shoes, she sat with Evans and his friend at their table.

Evans put his elbows on his knees, leaned forward, and said, "You look like you having a good night."

"Yeah, so far," she replied, smelling martini and cologne, along with the other man's cigar smoke. "I'm hoping it's gonna stay that way."

"Maybe I could help you have a good one. You move like a dream up there, sugar."

"Thanks. I know you ain't going to cause me problems like you did last time, right?"

"No problem here. But you lookin' good as I don't know what. I just want what everyone else in here who see you want." He smiled. "What I got to do for you to like me?"

"It's not that I don't like you, baby," she said. "But, like I told you last time, I don't swing like that. You ask me for something I ain't giving, and I'm thinking maybe you all big time and just forgot what 'no' means."

Evans laughed and asked, "What's your name, sugar?"

"Bree."

"I mean your real name."

"See, you know you ain't supposed to ask me that."

"Okay, okay. Bree. You know who I am, right? I'm a ballplayer. I'm Dan. You seen me on TV." Gabrielle looked from him to his friend, whom she assumed to be a bodyguard, sitting motionlessly a few feet away; she couldn't see the man's eyes through his glasses. "What you drinking?" Evans asked her.

Gabrielle hesitated, then said, "Strawberry margarita." Evans signaled to a barely-dressed waitress and ordered drinks.

Whether due to illness, fatigue, disgust, babysitter issues, or getting fired, whoever was supposed to follow Gabrielle onstage didn't, so as AC/DC's "Back in Black" started the next set, three girls were up there instead of four. Gabrielle turned away from Evans and focused on them: Nikki, a twenty-three-year-old white dancer whose recent implants had boosted her earnings, Sabine, a slim, lively French girl with words in her native tongue tattooed around her left leg (translated, they read "got it under control"), and Tina, a brown-skinned Puerto Rican whose beauty and statuesque physique made her as popular as any of the other girls, none of whom thought she could dance.

The drinks arrived soon after the music began. Evans gave Gabrielle hers and rested his hand high inside her thigh while he sipped his. Gabrielle set her margarita on the floor, stood, and stared at him. She heard movement to her left and turned. Tommy approached, his replica stiletto bouncing on its gold chain.

Stunned, Gabrielle knew what was going to happen but resisted an urge to call Tommy's name. She tried to grab him and said "No!" Tommy shook her off.

With surprising quickness, Evans' bulky friend put down his drink, stood, and reached inside his breast pocket. Tommy, hardened by dozens of fights in and out of detention homes, lowered his head and landed a solid right to the man's chin. The man's head snapped back and his glasses went flying. Tommy threw a left to the temple that staggered the man. Tommy's stiletto and chain flashed as he swung a right as hard as he could that smashed the man's teeth. As the man fell, Tommy connected with a left and right.

Tommy whirled toward Evans. The ballplayer raised his fists and bared his teeth. Tommy stepped forward, but a three-hundred-and-forty-five pound security man in a black t-shirt grabbed him in a bear hug from behind, picked him up, and carried him downstairs and out to the street.

Evans straightened. He wiped his mouth and, not eager for this type of publicity, yelled, "No cops! No cops!"

Gabrielle could've killed Tommy. What was he thinking, starting a fight in a strip club—while on probation? The situation with Evans had been manageable, and Tommy knew that something like that drew negative attention to her and served no purpose. She looked around. Buchannon, the manager, standing outside his office, removed his glasses and glared at her. He said nothing as she walked past him and went downstairs to prepare for her next set.

The music continued, and Evans and his bloodied bodyguard left. Within thirty seconds, the entertainment picked up as if nothing had happened.

—

The club's lights went out a few minutes before two. Fifteen minutes later, Gabrielle went to the bartenders and "tipped out"—gave them ten percent of her earnings as calculated by the house. She didn't mind; she'd netted eight-hundred-and-eighty-five dollars, tax free. As Gabrielle walked toward an exit with her gym bag over her shoulder, Buchannon came from a side door and stood in front of her in the dimness.

The fifty-ish manager, dressed in maroon and black, removed his reading glasses and stared at her for a moment. He pointed the glasses at her and said, "See that kind of shit, what happened upstairs? That's bad for business. The ballplayer's got a platinum card. He's got privileges. You know what he paid for that card, right? He *pisses* away money when he comes here. Can't get rid of it fast enough. And he brings other guys who do the same fuckin' thing. Think he'll be back soon? Huh?"

Gabrielle looked people in the eye in a way that made some uncomfortable. She turned that stare on Buchannon as she said, "He got whatever card he got, but that don't mean *I* got to go along with everything he wants. Some girls go home with clients and some don't. It's up to the girl." She pointed at the manager. "That's what *you* told me when I started here, remember? I'm one who don't. I'm telling him, and he's acting like what I say don't count. He can go fuck himself."

Buchannon exhaled loudly and said, "The boy upstairs with the fast hands. Boyfriend? Husband? If he is, you know he ain't supposed to be here."

"None of your business who he is."

"Bullshit. Anyone starting trouble in here's my business. I seen him before," Buchannon said.

"Okay, first thing, *he* didn't start any trouble. If your Mr. Platinum Card had respected the rules, *your* rules, nothing would have gone down..."

"Whatever. Whoever the hell he is, tell him next time he sets foot in here, I'm throwin' him right out on his ass," Buchannon said, "and he's probably gonna get something broke on the way. Tell him that."

Gabrielle looked him up and down. "*You* ain't doin shit. You get one of these go-rillas you got working here to *try* and do something."

Buchannon's voice got louder. "Who the fuck you think you are? You walk around here like you're Queen Shit, I should throw *your* ass out on the street right next to your raggedy-ass pimp..."

Gabrielle's tone remained even. "Bitch, stay right here. Let me go get him and you tell him that to his face. And as much money as I bring to this rat hole, you ain't doin' a goddamn thing. I don't miss days, and I don't show up late. Who else you got here like that? When I go, it's when I feel like it."

"You got some fuckin' nerve, some fuckin' nerve..."

"You better kiss this." She turned and walked out the exit door, along a trash-strewn alley, and onto Pearlstone.

She knew that she'd pushed it, but she believed what she'd said; Buchannon loved money more than he loved air and food put together, and as long as she drew the kind or regulars—like Evans—that she did, and as long as she made the kind of money for the Lotus that she made tonight, he'd take that and more. Plus, if he *did* fire her, she'd probably have another job within a day.

Tommy owned a green Land Cruiser, and she had a red Mustang, but after a few months living together, they'd realized that they liked each other's vehicle, so she usually drove his, and when not on his bike, he drove hers. The truck was thirty yards ahead, and Gabrielle clicked the remote to unlock the doors. She got in and started the engine, thinking that, considering Tommy's latest sleep problems, he'd probably still be awake. She wanted to give him a piece of her mind too, but she knew that something was stressing him and decided to wait until morning.

When she arrived, he was sitting in the living room, his head back, snoring so loudly that she turned on the lamp and stared.

—

After a bumpy flight to New York, Edgar rang the buzzer at his cousin Chuck's brownstone in Brooklyn's Clinton Hill-Bedford Stuyvesant area just before eight. Chuck opened the door, wearing tan shorts and a black Eddie Palmieri t-shirt. He was short, bespectacled, and thirty pounds overweight. Like Edgar, he had braided hair. They hugged, and Chuck said, "C'mon in, bro," with a New York accent.

Before leaving Miami, Edgar had called and said that he'd stop by this evening. Thirty-five-year-old Chuck drove trucks to deliver bottled water. He loved his house, where he lived with his wife and two daughters.

The building's dark cool interior smelled of recently cooked food and musk incense. The sounds of a TV game show came from a closed room as they passed. They walked by a kitchen and went downstairs to the basement that had a pool table, mini bar, and big-screen TV showing a Yankee game. Chuck muted the volume. On a counter stood a bottle of Corona and a partly-eaten meal of sausage and Spanish rice. Edgar declined Chuck's offer of food, and they spoke for a few minutes about their families, wages, and taxes. Then, Edgar said that he needed a favor. "I'm up here on business, yo. I need a gun, just for tonight."

A child ran across the room above their heads. Chuck nodded slowly and said, "See, I don't roll like that no more. Plus, I got to be real careful what I keep in the house with the kids here and everything. A few years ago, it wouldn't be no problem," Chuck said. "But I was younger, know what I mean? Now I got responsibilities." He put too much rice in his mouth and had to take his time chewing while looking at the TV.

After a while, he took a long swig of beer and asked, "You want something to use, or you just want to scare somebody, or what?"

Edgar shrugged. "Just to carry, that's it."

Chuck nodded again and spoke with his mouth full: "Hold on a second. Let me see something." He went upstairs for a few minutes, and returned with a small satchel that he gave to Edgar. ".38 Special, oiled and clean, bro. And it's got a little what-you- call-it you wrap around your ankle."

"Holster."

"Yeah. So bring it back when you finished, unless you use it. If you use it, wipe it and throw it in the river. You use it, don't come back here, bro. I don't know you. Yo, I'm serious about that bullshit."

Edgar nodded and said. "I ain't seen one of these since I was a kid." He removed the weapon and examined it from every angle. "I don't need the holster. I carry right here." He patted the small of his back, then spun the .38's chamber.

Chuck said, "6:30 in the morning, I'm outta here. You finish your business by then?"

"I figure I be back here," Edgar checked his watch, "around midnight."

"I'll be 'sleep." Chuck reached into his pocket and flipped a key to Edgar. "Whenever you get back, you could crash right there," he said, pointing to a black leather couch." He finished his Corona and asked, "Sure you don't want none of this food, bro?"

Edgar shook his head, thinking beer and guns, same old Chuck.

———

Nick Rowe was bald, lean, and muscular. He had a small silver hoop hanging from each ear and a graying goatee on an expressionless face. His nine years-plus for armed robbery at Rikers Island Prison had left him with scars under his left armpit, on his left shoulder, and on his left forearm from getting shanked.

At forty-three, he lived alone in a narrow, two-floor Harlem rowhouse. He owned an old Cadillac that he'd bought partly to help take care of his mother, who was recovering from a heart attack and who lived twenty-one blocks north. He welded at a plant in Queens that specialized in fire extinguishers, and he did what he could on the side—legal or illegal—to help make up for the fact that child support and the length of his sentence had left him broke when released.

As often happened in New York at this time of year, the evening temperature had dropped almost thirty degrees from a blistering daytime high. Rowe was walking home with a bag slung across his back after a late workout at Junior's Tae Kwon Do, located above a clothing store on 125th Street, not far from the Apollo. No martial artist, he used the gym's equipment to stay in shape and to work up a sweat.

Earlier, he'd tried to call his one child, a teenaged son who lived in Newark, but the boy hadn't been in. Rowe planned to go there on Saturday to speak to him about recent disciplinary issues at school.

Rowe turned onto his block, 139th and Amsterdam. As he approached the house and reached for his keys, someone stepped forward from the shadowed doorway of the building next to his. Rowe turned, ready for anything; at first, he couldn't place him—good-looking, long braids in a ponytail, wearing an oversized navy-blue t-shirt, jeans, and tan boots. Then he did—the dude who'd made the run for Tommy down to Miami in January. He said, "Tommy D's boy from Florida. What's goin' on?"

Edgar said, "What's up?"

Thinking that Edgar had come to pay him the rest of his cut for sending the package down last Saturday night, Rowe said, "You all were supposed to call me first."

The guy kept watching him intently, as if looking for something. He said, "Nah, this ain't about that. We gotta talk, yo."

Rowe heard attitude in the voice and thought, "Problem in Miami and maybe a problem with this dude." He studied Edgar for a second and said, "Come on in." They walked up the stairs and entered the house.

Rowe switched on the overhead light in the first room on the left— bare white walls, three chairs, a coffee table, a TV, a small bookcase, and a couch, all on a worn wooden floor. Blue curtains covered the windows. Rowe sat on the couch and gestured for Edgar to do the same on the other side of the coffee table. The guy continued to stare at him. Rowe asked, "You want a drink?"

"Nah."

"Okay. So what's the deal?" Rowe asked.

"Tommy got a problem. The package you say you sent on Saturday never reached."

"Package *I say* I sent."

"That's what Tommy told me," Edgar said. "You say you sent it."

Rowe said, "So you here to do what?"

"What you think?'

"Trying to figure," Rowe said. "If I lost somethin' like that, I wouldn't send somebody else to find out what happened."

"Don't worry about that," Edgar said. "Tommy got somethin' else goin' on right now."

"Um hm. Must be somethin' big," Rowe said, as if he didn't believe it.

Edgar reached for his cell, flipped it open, hit a button, and held the phone forward. "Here. Ask him. Hit 'talk.'"

Rowe leaned back. "Everything went the same way it went the first two times," he said as Edgar put away the phone. "The same woman met me Saturday early at a bench in Riverside Park. She gave me the package in a shopping bag. I paid her. I tested it, made sure it was what it was supposed to be.

"Wade met me in a parking lot in a garage in the Bronx Saturday night, just like what happened with you. The same place. His eye was all messed up—swollen real bad, and he kept wiping it. Looked like he couldn't see out of it, but he said he was okay to drive. Anyway, the Plymouth was already there; I gave him the keys, plus his cut. Told him not to take 95 down around D.C. Called Tommy and told him Wade was on his way. Next thing, you're outside my house."

Edgar hadn't taken his eyes off Rowe since he'd recognized him coming down the street. He nodded, then leaned forward and said, "I hear you on that. Sound like you tellin' the truth. I figure if you was dumb enough to try to do something with that package, you wouldn't be around here, wouldn't have even let me in. But I don't *know* that. You understand? What I *do* know is you the last one had it. And if your boy Wade did something or something happened to him or whatever, you the one brought him in on the deal. *You* the one brought him in. That's what I know."

Rowe said, "Oh yeah? Well this what *I* know. I know Tommy. And he ain't sendin' you up here to come to my house and tell me what *you* think—he sendin' you to find out what's goin' on, and that's it."

"Know what? You right. Yeah, you right. But like I said, what's goin' on is you fucked up. Big time. Anybody could see that."

"Says you. The deal's between me and Tommy," Rowe said. "What you say don't count."

"What I say don't count, huh? Old broke-ass nigga, you better..." Before he could finish, Rowe's hand went down behind his feet and under the couch. Edgar reached back, lifted his shirt, pulled his cousin's

.38, and aimed at Rowe's head. Rowe came up with a Glock and aimed at Edgar's chest.

Neither fired; Edgar knew that they needed Rowe to get Tommy's package, and he hadn't come to New York to kill anyone. Rowe, older now and wanting to avoid unnecessary trouble, wanted no shooting in his house. So they sat for several moments, one false move from death. Finally, Edgar stood slowly, gun-arm extended, and backed toward the door.

"You better just get the fuck on back where you came from," Rowe said, following, his pistol on target as Edgar backpedaled out the room, through the front door, and down the stairs. Rowe stopped halfway down the front steps, but they remained in each other's gunsights as Edgar walked backward to his rented Chevy across the street. Edgar lowered the revolver as he unlocked the car door; a white pickup truck coming down the block skidded to a stop and backed up quickly, its driver not expecting to see two men with guns in the street.

Rowe kept his weapon at his side as Edgar's red car passed and disappeared around the corner. He went inside to re-place the Glock under the living room couch and came back out into the deserted street. He sat on the top step, pulled out his cell, and called Tommy.

CHAPTER THREE

HENRY'S RAP

When an apprehensive Freeman woke the next morning, Monday, at his house in Washington, he had almost four hours before he was due at the CD store, which opened today at ten. He'd looked at Simone sleeping beside him and decided to go for a walk, an activity that he enjoyed because of the creative freedom that it lent to his thoughts, so, with rush hour traffic still a ways off, he dressed and went out.

A steady westerly breeze helped him awaken fully. Freeman couldn't stop wondering if he'd made a mistake when he'd picked up the green package in the alley on Saturday night; he'd thought of little else since. For one thing, he didn't have much money, but he didn't need much. He had no problem covering his bills and mortgage. Beside that, only he knew that his parents had set up a trust fund for him that he'd be eligible for at thirty-five, and that would end any financial burdens, at least for the foreseeable future. But that was a ways off.

Freeman entered Roberto Clemente Park and wound up sitting for a few minutes on a bench beside a pond, staring absently at ducks. The day looked as if it were going to be bright. The sun blazing just above the horizon made the eastern sky almost white and tinged the few clouds and much of the empty park's shrubbery with gold.

Whatever he did with the dope, the consequences of getting

caught with it were so disastrous that his mind shut down whenever he dwelled on them. Being arrested with that kind of weight wasn't like, say, shooting someone, where you could plead temporary insanity or something. No, they treated drugs pretty much as black and white—either you had it or you didn't. And if you had a pound of it, not even God could help you, at least not in D.C.

The band had a practice scheduled for this evening, and he tried to switch his thoughts to music and did, for a while. But after a few minutes, restlessness made him get up and resume his walk.

Back at Gersi Place, he picked up the *Washington Post* from the front porch and entered the house. Simone had left, surprising considering that she didn't have to be at work until one. Freeman found himself thinking that perhaps he should not even have told her about what had happened in the alley. The previous evening, after she'd come over and he'd described finding the package, they'd gone to bed, made love, dozed off, awoken, and lay on their backs in the dark, talking for over almost an hour about what to do with the duct tape-wrapped parcel. She wanted him to sell, but he had doubts.

"I hear you," he'd said, "but if I just turn it in, that's a whole lot of stress off me. Plus, it's heroin. You know what that shit does to people's lives? You know the kind of pain it brings to families? Better to just get it off the streets. I mean, I been thinking about it, and..."

Simone interrupted, "Thing is, people who'd be using it are going to get high whether you make money from it or not. Trust me, there's more than enough of that stuff out here to go around."

"You sound like a damn drug dealer, justifyin' some bullshit."

She ignored him. "And if you wanted to turn it in, you shoulda done that as soon as you got in that night. Now, they're gonna ask you all kinds of questions. You're going to have to get a lawyer. Remember, you'd be putting yourself in the middle of a double homicide investigation in Washington D.C. Or maybe that would be good. Yeah, maybe you should go to the cops; you'd be on the six o' clock news and the newspapers. You'd get a lot of publicity for your band, right? To have pictures of yourself in handcuffs all over the city? That's what they say, right? Any publicity's good publicity? Just don't lower your head or cover up when the cops lead you out of the courtroom to the squad car, like a lot of guys do. Hold your face up for the cameras and try to make sure they spell your name right and the name of the group. Smile. Make sure you wear a Vortex t-shirt." She went into an official-sounding TV-newscaster voice: "Freeman McNeal, guitar player for Washington-based reggae group, Vortex, and already implicated in a record heroin possession case, was charged today with two counts of murder here in northwest D.C. in what authorities are calling one of the worst cases of..." She stopped talking and chuckled.

He said, "Okay, but remember, we don't really know what it is. I mean, we think we know, but we really don't."

"You can smell what it is," she replied, "plus the circumstances when you found it, it's got to be what we think it is. There's a way to find out for sure."

"You say sell it, but to who? I don't know nothing about drugs. And you sure as hell don't unless you been doing a whole lot I don't know about. I don't know anyone who knows shit about this kind of thing. Just the one guy I told you about, and he's out of town."

"The singer in your group?"

"Yeah, Vaughan. But I don't trust him a hundred percent," Freeman said.

"I told you," Simone said. "Let me ask around. Just give me a couple days."

"That's what I'm tryin' to tell you. You go out there asking those kinds of questions, you draw attention to yourself. And to me, indirectly. Right now, I just want to get rid of it. Like, by any means necessary. Probably shoulda left it right there in that alley, be honest with you. I'm thinking about just flushing it down the toilet."

"Freeman, you can get half-a-million dollars for that, and it's worth twice that on the street! Baby, listen to me. I'm not tellin' people, 'Hey, my boyfriend's holding a million dollars worth of dope, do you know anyone who's interested.' Nobody's gonna know anything about you."

Freeman said, "The fewer people know anything about this, the better my chances of staying out of jail. You're all out there asking questions, you ain't the one gonna get locked up."

"No one's getting locked up, honey. Give me a couple days. Look, we're gonna have to have to take some kinda risk one way or the other. At some point, you're gonna have to trust someone to some extent. You trusted me enough to tell me, right? Tell you what. If we don't have a plan by Wednesday, you flush it or whatever else you want to do with it. How's that?"

"No, Simone, just chill. Don't do anything. Let me handle this."

That reminded him of another issue, that vague but constant question of trust regarding her, still there after three years together. Freeman had no idea what caused it, but experience had taught him to listen to his instincts ...

In the shower before going to work at Sound Value, the CD store, he decided to hide the million dollar parcel, so after breakfast, he wrapped it in two plastic shopping bags and wedged it into the back of an old broken boom box he kept in a dark corner of the basement. Not an original spot but not the first place anyone would look, either.

Before heading off to work, he glanced at the newspaper. An article in the Metro section caught his eye:

> Two men were found dead on Sunday morning in an alley in Northwest. A white man in his forties was stabbed while in a white 1998 Plymouth. The other victim was an older black man who had been shot. Police suspect a carjacking gone bad and are seeking witnesses. Identification is being withheld pending notification of next of kin.

The story surprised Freeman. He hadn't seen anything on the previous evening's newscast and assumed that the local media had overlooked the two murders, as they did most that took place in the city. The article indicated that investigators had few leads, but you never knew how true these stories were. After reading it three more times, he muttered, "Carjacking," folded the paper, and left for work.

—

As usual, few customers came first thing on a Monday. Having recently finished inventory, Freeman and the store manager had plenty time to contemplate the posters and photos on Sound Value's walls—The

Roots, Dizzy Gillespie, Joni Mitchell, Tupac, The Yellowjackets—and to think. What Simone had said about getting involved in a double homicide if he tried to turn the package in made some sense, although he knew that she'd been exaggerating. Still, he didn't feel comfortable with Simone's "plan" of "asking around" discreetly. If she said the wrong thing to the wrong person, anything could happen; people got killed in D.C. every day for a whole lot less than what that bag was worth, a whole lot less.

What she'd said about having to trust someone at some point made sense, too, although he realized that he'd hidden the stuff in the basement from her as much as for any other reason.

He thought about Vaughan Chandler, Vortex's front man. Freeman would probably get some ideas if he could talk to him and not tell too much. He wanted to do *something*, and the more he considered talking to Vaughan, the more it felt right. But he wanted to discuss it in person; he could either wait until the singer returned next week, or visit him. Thinking about the second option turned his anxiety into enthusiasm. He didn't feel like spending too much money on a plane ticket, but if he could find something under a couple of hundred dollars...

Like an omen, Judah Wilson, the group's keyboard player, called and postponed tonight's practice until Thursday.

"Judah," Freeman said, "Where's Vaughan?"

"Spoke to him a couple days ago. He's in Chicago until Sunday, touring with Triple Threat. Then he's headed back here."

"What's his cell number?"

Judah gave it to him, and Freeman said, "Thanks," and hung up. Chicago. Jumpin' town, from what he'd heard. During his lunch break, he went to the computer in the back office and checked flight prices and schedules on the Internet. Later that afternoon, he called Simone and told her that he'd be heading out of town until tomorrow.

—

Freeman left at 5:55, went straight home, and threw some clothes into a bag. He didn't own a car, and while he walked toward Georgia Avenue to catch a cab to the airport, his neighbor from two doors down drove up and asked him where he was rushing to. He told her, and she gave him a ride.

He smiled as he got his bag out of her car, said thanks, and entered the terminal. At that moment, Edgar was approaching Chuck's house through Brooklyn's congested streets to borrow the .38, Tommy was eating at the Szechuan Oasis before heading to the Lotus and a fight with Dan Evans' bodyguard, and Simone was cozying up to Henry Ramos at Dudley's, in the St. David Hotel near Alexandria, Virginia.

Situated at the entrance to a park, the spacious, gleaming restaurant had mini-floodlights amid azaleas outside its tinted glass walls, a forty-foot ceiling, and plush maroon carpet. A widescreen TV remained turned off above several patrons who sat at the polished oak bar.

Patrons sat at most of the restaurant's tables, but no one was near Simone and Henry, who were sitting side by side in a corner on a mini "couch," their dinners on small shiny black tables. Both of them were wearing all white. They'd drunk most of a bottle of Burgundy, and Henry waited until they were splitting an oversized slice of apple crumb cake topped with vanilla ice cream to ask, "So what's going on with your boyfriend?"

Simone said, "Nothing. He's just real hardheaded sometimes."

"Well, who's usually right?" Henry asked, digging into the pie.

Simone just shook her head as if mildly disgusted.

Henry pressed the issue: "What's the problem?"

She drank some wine. "I don't want to talk about it, Henry."

"I can understand that, if something's personal. But the thing is, the issue you're having with him is affecting what's happening with us. So, in a way, I'm involved too, even though I don't know what the situation is."

She turned toward him. "How's it affecting us?"

Finishing a mouthful of ice cream, Henry said, "I like for us to be together. That's why I asked you to come with me out west for a couple of days. You said the other night that you wanted to travel with me. Now, all of a sudden, you can't make it. It's got something to do with what's his name. I can tell."

Simone sipped her wine and said sarcastically, "What, you're going to act like you're jealous now?"

"Maybe I am, a little." He surprised himself by saying that. "Just tell me what happened that changed your mind from Saturday to Monday morning."

"Freeman. My boyfriend's name is Freeman."

"Right, Freeman. So what's going on with you and Freeman?"

She leaned back, stretched her legs, hesitated as if making a judgment, and shook her head. "It's something crazy. You couldn't relate."

"Try me. I'm pretty good at relating," he lied, lighting a cheroot.

She said nothing for a long while, then raised the glass to her lips as if the wine would help her decide how much to tell him. "He found something the other night, the night you and me went to the lake real late. That phone call I got, remember? That's when he was telling me about it."

Henry nodded.

"Anyway, what he found, it's illegal to have, and," she hesitated, "we're deciding how to handle it. It's like an ongoing discussion."

"Okay," Henry said, "so he found something. So what's the big secret?"

"It's illegal."

"Okay." Henry finished his drink and took a puff from his cigar.

"I mean it's real illegal."

"You mean like a gun illegal or drugs illegal?"

Simone said, "Something like that."

Henry signaled for the check and pressed the issue. "I don't get it. Why does that stop you from coming with me?"

When Simone didn't answer, they sat quietly until the check came. Henry paid in cash, and, full from the meal, they stayed seated a while longer.

Henry had always been secretive with her, so she didn't feel that she owed him an explanation for changing her mind about going to Las Vegas, but she remembered what she'd said to Freeman about having to trust someone at some point, and her instinct told her to give Henry a general idea about what had happened. She didn't know much about his background, but she sensed that he'd had a wide range of experience, and his opinion would count for something. But Freeman wanted her to keep quiet.

Conflict showed in Simone's eyes. Drawing on his cigar, Henry stood, put on a white Panama hat, and cradled her elbow as they left the restaurant and waited outside for his valet-parked BMW. When it arrived, they got in, and he said, "You don't trust me?"

"Henry, don't talk to me about trust, okay? It's been two years, and I don't know shit about you. You want to keep your business or whatever you're doing to yourself, fine. Just don't talk to me about trust."

He said, "Put on your seat belt."

The alcohol had her head spinning as Henry drove away from the hotel. Henry soon threw the stub of his cigar out the window and then did something that later, he couldn't remember having done before—he told the truth about himself. In his accented English, he said, "Listen, as far as illegal and legal are concerned, you've seen me use phony names, right? Once was at a hotel in Philadelphia. You asked me about it, and I told you it was for business reasons. Remember? It was, in a way. But I don't do any work *for* the company I'm with. I'm just an investor. I use phony names because I break the law. All the time. That's my real job. That's what I'm going to say, okay? I break the law for a living. As far as I'm concerned, there *are* no laws. The world is every man for himself. Unless you have a strong—what do you call it—" he searched for the right word. "...a strong conscience or some kind of religious hangup, there's no reason for anybody to follow any law except for being scared, scared of getting caught. If you're not scared or if you can figure out a way around the cops, you grab every goddamn thing you can for yourself and your family. That's how the old boys on top do it. That's how they get to the top, and that's how they stay there. They say 'fuck law.' They pay lawyers millions to tell them how to get around it. As far as they're concerned, that's why lawyers exist."

As the car sped south toward his rented cottage outside of Conklin, he continued: "Legal and illegal only exist for them to get more money for themselves, to make the gap between them and everybody else bigger. Even in my country, the system is supposed to be set up so everybody's treated the same. Castro said "Equality" while he re-built Cuba, but it's all just theory. A few on top run things, and everyone else does what they say. It can't be any other way. It's human nature. It's nature. The strong take from the weak, and you do what you have to do. I've been breaking laws since I was a kid, and I sleep better because of it. If you or your boyfriend is worried about breaking law, the only thing to worry about is getting caught. You tell him that."

Simone leaned her head against the headrest, thinking that perhaps she'd just gotten her first glimpse of who this man really was.

No one spoke further until they'd reached the cottage ten minutes later. The car pulled into the driveway, and Henry switched off the engine. They sat still, staring absently at the cottage through the windshield.

He noticed her breasts rising and falling with each breath. He couldn't wait to get her inside. He was about to touch her nipples when she leaned back further and closed her eyes. Partly because his revelation made her feel a bit closer to him and partly because she was drunk, she said, "He found a pound of heroin, pure. That's what it looks like and smells like. And tastes like. And the way he found it ...it looked like two men killed each other over it, in an alley. We don't know what do with it."

Henry stared at her for a while, then touched her elbow. "Come on," he said, unlocking the car doors. "Let's go inside and relax."

———

Freeman slept through much of the flight to Chicago's O'Hare Airport, which landed a few minutes before eleven. While walking through the terminal, he called Chandler: "Where you at, man?"

Loud music at the other end almost prevented him from hearing the response, which Chandler had to repeat: "A club near the lake. East Illinois Street. It's called The Green Light. Come on over. We got you covered."

The air outside felt cool enough to make Freeman wish that he'd brought a jacket. He caught a cab to the club and got into a heated argument with the cabbie about the thirty-eight dollar fare, which he eventually paid. When told at the Green Light's door that he'd have to pay another twenty to enter, he called Chandler's number again.

"Meet me around the side," the singer said.

Freeman walked around the front of the club, past the ticket taker and a glowering bouncer, and into an alley, where he stood next to an old service door, and waited. From inside came an infectious beat that became clearer once the door opened. Out came the man whose voice a D.C. music critic had described as one that "danced with melodies the way Fred Astaire danced with Ginger Rogers." Of average height and forty-five pounds overweight, he wore loose, light colored clothing. A white kerchief covered the bearded Chandler's short dreadlocks as he propped open the door.

Canadian-born to Jamaican parents, he spoke in either American English or Kingston slang, depending on his mood; tonight, he sounded like a West Indian. He looked at Freeman through bloodshot eyes and said, "What a go on, boy? What you doin' out this way?"

Freeman wanted to get information without hinting that he had illicit goods. "I got an uncle in Peoria. I was out this way visiting, and I said, 'Let me give Vaughan a holla. I heard you were here on tour.'"

"Yeah man. We just winding it down." Chandler smelled of alcohol and cigarette smoke. "Come on in, man, come on in. Me know the owners. They not goin' say nothin.' Come meet the crew."

Freeman followed him inside. The increasingly loud music—a catchy organ hanging tightly to a strong bass hook; perfectly timed bass drum, snare, and high hat; and slow, insistent shaker—grabbed both men. Without even realizing it, their shoulders, arms, and steps shifted to the beat as they walked along a dark hallway, through a green curtain, and past a bustling kitchen to the main floor, where three hundred people were moving to the sound. Feeling the music from head to toe, Freeman went out to the middle of them while Chandler pulled a young redhead in skin tight blouse and jeans from a crowded corner booth, presumably where he'd been sitting, and came out, too.

Mirrors lined the walls. Green and white spotlights crisscrossed the crowd, which rolled in unison, like a wave. Freeman whirled and stepped, back and forth and from side to side in time to the beat. His arms went up, down, out, around, and his hips and feet shifted with those of all the other dancers. The spotlights turned to strobes as a subtle, sweet-sounding rhythm guitar joined the instrumental, injecting itself immediately into Freeman's blood and keeping him moving, with eyes closed, until...

The song ended, and the Terror Squad's "Lean Back" came on. Freeman, Chandler, and Chandler's partner danced off the floor and to a dark, crammed booth. Freeman, sweating and smiling, took a chair from against the wall and sat facing seven twenty-somethings who were talking to each other. They were three males and four females, three black and four white, each squeezed against the next on a U-shaped, black leather settee that curved around a wooden table covered with beer bottles, glasses, and plates. Chandler started to introduce Freeman to his friends, but no one could hear him.

Freeman turned toward the dance floor and nodded to the track. When he turned back around, some space had opened next to Chandler, so he got up and sat next to him. He raised a foot up to the couch, cupped his hand to Chandler's ear, and leaned toward him. "I got a situation back home," Freeman yelled.

"What's that?'

"I know a guy found something and don't know what to do with it. He asked me, but I don't know either. It's crazy, man."

Chandler asked, "Oh yeah? What he found?"

Freeman wanted Chandler to know as few specifics as possible; if Vortex's star performer were returning to D.C. at the end of the week, he might hear something, somewhere, that might connect Freeman indirectly to a double homicide. But then, Freeman realized that he was being too cautious; he had no reason to think that anyone even knew that the package existed. The morning paper had the cops suspecting a carjacking that had turned into double murder. Freeman had no idea what had happened in the alley that night, but he figured that if anyone else had been involved, the person probably would have taken the package, which, after all, had been sitting right there, out in the open.

He said loudly, "It's a big old bag of dope, yo."

They continued shouting into each other's ear over the music. "You sure that's what it is? A lot of beat bags out there, Freeman. You know?"

"The guy says so, man. The way he found it, it's got to be the real thing. Looks like it and smells like it."

Chandler smiled and looked at Freeman. "You seen it?" he asked.

"Oh yeah." The pretty black girl squished next to Freeman passed him a spliff. He took two good drags, passed it to Chandler, and said, "Yeah, dog. I seen it. I say it's legit. Got to be."

Chandler nodded, took a hit, looked at the spliff as if appraising it, took another puff, passed it, and asked, "Where you boy at? Him you come out here to see?"

"He back east."

"So what your boy lookin' to do?"

"Sell. I told him to think about turning it in," Freeman said, trying to hide the truth from his bandmate, "but he say he tryin' to make some paper off it."

"How big the bag?"

The smoke hit Freeman's system, and suddenly, everything looked, sounded, and felt dreamy. He took in the scene on the dance floor before returning to the conversation. "About a pound. I say it's pure."

Chandler widened his eyes as if shocked. "Freeman, why you tell him to turn it in? Tell him sell it, man. That's money right there. It's money make the world go round—you don't know? Listen, he goin' to get about half the street value. Whoever he sell it to goin' mix it with something else and sell it on the street. If it's a pound or a kilo, he goin' get about five-hundred-thousand. That's how that work."

"Yo, I hear it's worth twice that."

"That's the same thing I'm tellin' you, man," Chandler said. "Street value and first buyer price is two different things. If the shit's real, street value make it worth more than gold. For real. You know uranium, the shit them use to make a nuclear bomb? Serious dope worth more than that. Check it. Price so high 'cause it illegal. Them legalize it, price come down. But them not goin' do that. Too many o' them makin' money—judges, lawyers, cops, wardens, probation officers. Criminal justice system big, big business in America. You know it. Billions o' dollars every year."

Chandler continued to shout into Freeman's ear over 50 Cent's "So Seductive": "Me know somebody definitely be interested in that. Let me talk to him, see what him say. I get back to you real soon, hear?" Then, he remembered that Freeman fell far short of the upper income tax bracket and added, "Might can work out a little finder's fee for you, you feelin' me? But you got to make sure it's what your boy say it is. Anyway, we can find that out easy enough."

Freeman shouted back, "Don't mention my name to anyone you talk to, all right?"

"What I'm goin' say your name for?" Chandler asked.

The spliff came around again, and Freeman took in so much smoke that he choked. Somebody passed him a beer, which helped him regain his composure. He asked, "How you find out exactly what it is, or exactly what it ain't? It's some kind of test, right? Chemicals?"

Chandler nodded. "I know couple people got it. That ain't no problem."

"You know how to do it?" Freeman asked, smoking again and passing the weed to Chandler.

Chandler inhaled deeply, held it in his lungs, and nodded. After finally exhaling twin white streams through his nostrils, he said, "But if it's pure, like you say, you can tell it easy, man. It's a smell, like you said. But don't worry. I talk to you when I get in. I catch you sometime Monday."

Freeman nodded. Chandler's red-haired companion returned from the bathroom and ended the conversation by wedging herself between them. Chandler passed her the spliff, shut his eyes, and swayed to the sound.

Freeman drank more beer and focused on the crowd dancing under strobe lights. He'd gotten some of what he'd come for—information—but Chandler didn't respect time, plus Freeman didn't want to sit still for a week; he remained unsure about his next move.

Chapter Four

The Professional

At around eleven on Tuesday morning, Gabrielle woke with a headache. Sunlight passing through the bedroom's yellow curtains caused her to squint. Finally, she got up and checked her phone. Tommy had sent a text:

> have 2 go 2 NY. B back tomorrow but not sure when. hope I didnt cause a problem for u at the club last night. i know u told me not 2 go there 2 often. the dude in the sweat suit was all out of line with u. i know u had it covered. sorry if I caused a problem. it wont happen again. will call soon.

Gabrielle stared through the balcony's glass doors. She knew that Tommy sold different things on the black market, but he usually didn't discuss specifics with her other than when he'd sworn to her early in the relationship that he didn't sell drugs. When they first met, she didn't care what he did. To her back then, life was a hustle, and Tommy was a good hustler; that helped draw her to him at first. She'd always liked guys who were aggressive enough to challenge the law. To the younger Gabrielle, black men in white shirts and ties were sellouts. But what he did had a downside, too, one that she was finding harder to overlook.

Sometimes Tommy would be there, sometimes he wouldn't. Because he himself didn't know where he'd be from one day to the next, she couldn't rely on him. Plus, he could be arrested—and had been twice since she'd known him—at any time. And worst of all were the times when he'd be away, and the phone would ring, and she'd get a feeling that someone was calling to say that he'd been beaten, or kidnapped, or shot or anything. It had taken a while for her to admit it to herself, but after three years, even though Tommy loved her and had money, the uncertainty of what he did, combined with his unstable nature, was stressing her and making her unhappy.

She lowered the air conditioner's thermostat, poured a glass of orange juice and sat at the kitchen island. As soon as she'd finished drinking, the phone rang.

"Hey girl. I just spoke to Nikki." Gabrielle recognized Trish's voice. "She said your boyfriend started a fight and got thrown out. And she heard you cussed out Buchannon at closing."

Gabrielle said, "Yeah, well, that's about what happened."

Trish laughed and asked whether or not Gabrielle wanted to get together with her for lunch. They agreed to meet in thirty minutes.

—

They sat across from each other in a booth at Sonya's Corner, by a window that faced 21st Street. Sonya's did mostly takeout, so even though it was lunch time, few people were in the small, simply furnished eatery. Having described the fight and her argument with Buchannon, Gabrielle said, "I'm sick of the shit. I think about quitting every week. I mean some parts of it are fine. Like, I always liked the dancing."

"Yeah? A lot of girls do it, but they don't like it."

"No. I like it. I feel free when I'm up there, like I'm in control. Some nights are better than others, but I like the feeling. And the money's good. But sometimes I wonder what it would feel like to have a job where you have benefits, you know? And I like some of the girls I've met. But you always got to put up with assholes like Buchannon and that goddamn baseball player last night. It's always some fool who's a nut or who's had too much to drink or who can't control himself or needs some attention. What the fuck is wrong with guys, anyway? Are they all crazy, or just the ones who come to strip joints?"

"Honey, trust me" Trish said, "If I knew what was wrong with them, we wouldn't be sitting here getting ready to go back to the Lotus. I'd be a millionaire by now."

"A lot of times it seems like they don't understand shit that's staring them right in the face." Gabrielle shook her head and looked out the window.

"Well, your man couldn't control himself last night, but he's not so bad."

Gabrielle replied, "Girl, Tommy got issues. Tell you the truth, I don't even know if it's worth it, sometimes. I mean, I don't have to worry about him cheatin' on me or catchin' something and bringing it back to me. At least I don't *think* I do. I care about him a whole lot. But carin' about him's startin' to be a problem. You heard them sayin' about how black males in their twenties are an endangered species? Tommy fits those statistics. I didn't worry about it when I was younger, but you look at things differently when you get older."

Trish said, "As far as him cheatin', you never really know. I mean, if you say he's not, you're probably right, but you never know for sure. Love him, but always keep a part of yourself for yourself."

Gabrielle bit her taco and said, "I hear you. But I'm the type, I love my man completely, you know? I can't do things halfway; I'm a Scorpio. But, just like we never know for sure what they're doing behind our backs, they don't know about us, either. I've seen women do some crazy shit soon as their man's not around."

Trish winked at her and said, "No shit. You got something going on with a guy, right?"

Gabrielle shook her head, and Trish said, "Okay, it's not another man, but *something's* happening with you. I can see that much."

Gabrielle swallowed her food and started to speak, but the words got caught in her throat. She turned her head toward the window again, and a tear fell from each eye simultaneously. Trish reached across and covered Gabrielle's hand with one of hers. Neither woman spoke for almost a minute as Gabrielle struggled with her emotions. Finally she said, "I've been running from something, for years, just caught up with me. A child. A daughter, Jasmin. She's five-and-a-half. I gave her up for adoption when she was born." Tears resumed, and she lowered her head.

She cried quietly for a while; then she dabbed her eyes with a napkin and continued. "You're the first person I've told. Ever."

"Tommy doesn't know?"

"Tommy, my mom, nobody. I was confused, ashamed. I moved out on my own right when I turned sixteen because my mom and my stepdad limited me too much. I thought they were too controlling. Next thing, me and this boy are shacking up in Fort Lauderdale. He thinks he's making money, nine dollars an hour. I'm still in school, working at Wendy's in the afternoons. We used protection most of the time. I was like, I knew getting pregnant would just really slow me down, and I sure as hell didn't have money for daycare and babysitters. But, you know, we were just kids, and we weren't careful. It just happened. All of a sudden, I'm pregnant. I'm in shock, I'm scared, I'm terrified. I'd seen a lot of girls get pregnant, get trapped—I see some of 'em still trapped...

"Anyway, he's going crazy, tellin' me to get an abortion. I went to the clinic and set up the appointment, but I couldn't go through with it. Just couldn't do it. He said he didn't have money to raise a kid and left. No note, nothing. I come home from the clinic one day, and he's gone. Haven't heard a word from him since. I was kind of desperate. I saw a poster on a bus about adoption as an alternative, and I called the number. The people at the agency said I could do it so I could keep in contact with the couple that adopted her and maybe see my child when she got older at some point, but I just wanted to get it over with. I felt relieved but real, real guilty at the same time. I told the agency people I didn't want to know anything about her.

"But all of a sudden, I started thinking about her. A lot. Early last year, I called the agency and asked them if they could help me see her. It was like, I was thinking about it so much I didn't have a choice. A counselor said she'd see what she could do. I've spoken to the parents. I met them last week. Told them I'm a waitress."

"Does the counselor know what you do?"

Gabrielle nodded. "I told her in a roundabout kind of way. Anyway,

I'm supposed to see Jasmin next Tuesday, but she won't know I'll be there. We'll just see how it goes."

Trish said, "She's five. She doesn't know anything about being adopted."

Gabrielle shook her head.

"That connection between mother and daughter is strong," Trish said. "The guilt falling out your eyes and rolling down your face, you got to let it go. A lot of people stay mad at themselves for things they did when they were kids and didn't know better. Teen years are temporary insanity. Whenever you feel bad, you got to look at it that way." She'd been holding Gabrielle's hand to show support the whole time. Now she let go and asked, "You gonna tell Tommy?"

"Not now. Like I said, the way things are with him, you don't know what's goin' on from one day to the next." Gabrielle signaled for the check and paid it. They stood and walked away from the booth. "This the first time I've spoken about this, so I'm asking you to keep it to yourself," she said as they walked out into the noon heat.

"Don't worry. That's not a problem. I talk a lot, but I *can* keep my mouth shut about some things. But it'll all work out," Trish said, putting on her sunglasses. "I told you before, you're smart, and you look as good as any girl out here. I hope you don't mind how I'm always giving you advice. I know you're grown and I'm not your mama, but you got a lot going for you. You can do something with yourself, do the kind of things I wish I'd done. Maybe you can even do something for your girl, too, even though she's not with you. Down the road, you never know. Everything's open nowadays. Kids and birth mothers reconnect with each other all the time."

"Yeah, just take it one step at a time, I guess. You're off yesterday and today, right?" Gabrielle asked, her mood more serious since her revelation.

"That's right, honey. You can have The Lotus Club all to yourself. Let me give you a lift home. It's midday. No shade."

"Yeah, I guess I'd better. I sweated enough for one day just walking down here."

Trish checked her watch, then pointed at her car and said, "I'm parked right across the street. I got about five minutes on the meter."

Once inside her silver Camaro, she turned a switch on the dashboard, and Norah Jones's voice filled the car as they drove east.

Trish parked in Gabrielle's building's underground garage, turned toward her, and asked, "You gonna be okay?"

Gabrielle smiled brightly and said, "Yeah, I'm gonna make it."

Trish leaned forward and kissed her on the cheek. Then, she kissed her on the lips. The second kiss surprised Gabrielle, but it felt good. She kissed back, then leaned away and looked deeply into Trish's brown eyes; they were warm, loving, filled with desire. Trish held her and kissed her again more urgently. Gabrielle's lips parted, and she raised her hands to Trish's shoulders...

After several moments, she again leaned back and looked into Trish's eyes. She reached for her bag, got out of the car, and stooped to look at Trish once more. Then, she turned and walked to the elevator.

All the way up to the fourteenth floor, Gabrielle thought about this, her most intimate contact with a woman. How did it connect to the secret she'd just shared? She started to wonder about why she'd liked the kiss but then decided that it wasn't that big a deal and that she shouldn't analyze too much or worry too much; the future would take care of itself. She entered the condominium apartment and remembered that she had to go grocery shopping and that she had a dental appointment. She looked at the phone. Tommy had called but left no message. She picked up the receiver and started to call him back but changed her mind. She didn't have time.

—

Hazel Royce, one of two black female Special Agents at the Hoover Building in Washington D.C., left her second meeting of the day at the complex and yawned the yawn that she'd been stifling for twenty minutes. A woman who added to her five-day-per-week swimming-tennis regimen by walking whenever she could, she took the stairs up to her fourth floor office, and as she sat at her desk, a fellow agent poked his head in and asked if she wanted to join him and another agent for lunch.

"Not today. I'm backed up here," she said, gesturing toward files spread across her usually tidy desk. She activated her computer, then went to the refrigerator and pulled out a brown bag that contained last night's leftovers—today's lunch—which she popped into the microwave. She returned to her chair. Someone had left a voicemail message, and she listened to it:

"Ms Royce, this is Carl Oberhauser in Miami. I've got a possible I.D. on Enrique Ramos at a rental cottage outside Conklin, Virginia, from last Wednesday. It's 8712 Edgemere Lane. Again, this is a possible, not a confirmed, but we got surveillance footage from Union Station up there in D.C. on Wednesday afternoon that looks like it could be him. I'm sending you the film."

Royce checked the time. This task force on which she and Oberhauser had been working had not had good results, mostly because higher-ups seemed not to realize how much agents like her already had on their plates. These days, her main focus was a case on which she, two other F.B.I. agents, and a Justice Department lawyer formed a team investigating accounting irregularities at Solstice Incorporated, a multi-national retailing company that sold food and household goods at discount prices. She had so many e-mails, invoices, tape transcripts, background checks, and memos to collate and analyze that she thought the amount of LEAP, or overtime, that they'd have to pay her might worsen the federal budget deficit. Let them worry about it.

But she hadn't forgotten about Enrique "Henry" Ramos, the chameleon-like counterfeiter to whom she'd been assigned as part of a collaborative, inter-agency effort to apprehend long-time law-enforcement targets. Five years earlier, New Jersey prosecutors had indicted him on weapons and reckless endangerment charges that were later dismissed because of a missing witness, a girlfriend of his. That witness was now a mid-level figure in a Nevada bribery case involving a public official and had been arrested recently in Las Vegas; the girlfriend was looking at a plea bargain and had agreed to provide information against several people, including Ramos.

Royce, along with Secret Service Agent Oberhauser, who'd been working on Ramos for months, had been assigned to the case. Ramos presented a major problem: no one could find him. He had printed millions in high-quality counterfeit notes over the last twenty years, but whenever his paper would show up, he would vanish. And he covered his tracks so that no one could trace anything back to him. But even without enough proof to convict, the government *knew* what he did and would settle for any kind of a charge that would stick. If they could get their hands on him, they could pressure him, no matter how good his lawyers, and maybe get him on something bigger.

The government had only a few more days to serve Ramos papers on the weapons charge. She and Oberhauser had followed several false leads on him, and she suspected that this possible sighting at the train station would be another. She turned on her computer and opened the file that Oberhauser had sent. It showed black-and-white footage of a slim man carrying a bag in each hand. He had short black hair combed back. He wore a dark sports jacket, white shirt, white slacks, black slip ons. At the bottom of the screen in small white letters was the time and place of the film and the name under which the subject was traveling: Carlos Rodriguez.

Royce watched the footage five times. She slowed it and zoomed in on it. She froze it and sat staring, drumming the eraser end of a pencil on her desk. Finally, she printed stills from the screen and went to a bulletin board covered with charts, pictures of missing persons, maps, crime scene photos, wanted posters, and all kinds of memos and messages. She pulled down a mug shot of Ramos taken in New Jersey the night he'd been arrested for emptying an unregistered handgun at someone and compared it to the images taken at Union Station a week ago. It looked like it could be him, but there were so many men who did, and, as she'd learned, so many Enrique Ramoses; a bureau database listed one-hundred-and-fifty-one in the U.S.—and those were just the documented ones.

Royce wanted to follow up on the lead, but she had much work to do regarding the far bigger Solstice case. She returned to her desk, called a junior agent in the basement's enormous computer center, and said that she needed contact numbers on the rental agent for a cottage at 8712 Edgemere Lane outside Conklin. The information came within a minute—a woman named Emily Peters whose phone numbers had an Atlanta area code.

An answering machine picked up Royce's call to Peters' office, so she tried a cell number. Ms Peters answered, sounding efficient and polite. Without identifying herself or the nature of the call, Royce asked for information on the cottage. Emily Peters referred her to a northern Virginia property manager-rental agent, Alex Kirby.

Royce called Kirby, identified herself as a federal agent, and arranged for an afternoon meeting at his office.

She clicked off and turned to an open Solstice file, looking for an affidavit that she wanted to check against a graph that was now on her computer screen.

—

Tommy finally left the Ledgemont Clinic near Fort Lauderdale an hour before his flight was scheduled to depart from Miami International. In ten months, this had been by far the longest he'd had to wait to take the urine test. He'd gotten there at 10:15, forty-five minutes before his appointment, and been surprised to find eleven people waiting in the small first-floor waiting room. Usually, he'd have to wait behind two or three people who were there for various reasons before he'd step into an examination room, sign a form, and piss into a plastic jar while a technician watched to make sure that the test was legit.

Fourteen months earlier, Tommy had agreed to do a favor for a Chinese guy he'd done business with before who said he thought cops might be watching his North Miami Beach house. The Asian, also named Tommy, needed a place to store stolen TiVo players. Not knowing what kind of heat the Asian was facing, Tommy said no, but his namesake needed help, and Tommy owed him a small favor, so late one night, a couple of people unloaded the merchandise into a storage unit that Tommy rented long-term. He charged $150 per day for no more than a week, the maximum time he could stand holding on to an eighteen-wheel tractor trailer's worth of stolen electronics.

Miami P.D. raided the unit the next afternoon. A fuming Tommy thought he'd been set up until Chinese Tommy got seven years in federal lockup for hijacking, and transporting stolen goods across state lines. Tommy wound up with six months' home detention reduced to three, and random piss tests for a year-and-a-half, and the judge had ordered him to miss none of them or risk a charge of violating probation.

While waiting at Ledgemont Clinic for his number to be called, Tommy tried to relax—dozing, reading magazines, calling Gabrielle and getting no answer, even talking to a little girl whose mother was sitting next to him; as he sat in the waiting room, watching his flight time approach, and with each patient seeming to take longer, he had to restrain himself from walking out the door, getting into Gabrielle's Mustang, and driving straight to the airport.

But he'd missed the last test three weeks ago while out on a yacht trying to straighten out details on selling the now-missing package from Thailand. He'd stayed home for much of the next day, half expecting to be arrested. He couldn't risk missing another one.

Today, no one asked about the test he'd missed. But everything was taking so long; he had a plane to catch…Finally, Tommy took the test, left the clinic, and ran to the Mustang. He started the engine at 1:24, cursing to himself and thinking he'd probably miss the 2:25 flight. It would take half-an-hour to get there—if traffic went okay—plus he'd have to wait for the bus from the airport parking lot to the terminal. Once there, he had to check in; then he needed to get to the gate. The whole thing was turning into a disaster. Edgar's ticket had cost $378 round trip, plus car rental. Tommy had to pay $270 one way; once in New York, he'd have to pay for a car and who knows what else. Until he found the package, he didn't have money to throw away.

He'd talked to Rowe and Edgar separately on the phone last night. He'd told them to limit what they said; still, they'd described a mess that made him want to get up to New York and speak to Rowe even more.

Traffic flowed smoothly along 95 South. Tommy got to the airport parking lot at 2:03, just in time to catch a shuttle to the terminal, which he entered at 2:13. He got his ticket and ran to the security gate, where he stood in shock: a line stretched as far as he could see. He tried to tell a uniformed airport worker that he was about to miss his flight, but she seemed not to speak English. He walked to the front of the line and cut in front of a business executive type, explaining to him and the security officer at the gate that his flight was due to leave in four minutes. He showed his ticket to prove his point, and they let him through. A minute before the plane's departure time, he sprinted down a long corridor toward Gate H14, his bag swinging from his shoulder.

He got there at 2:26, panting. When he told a woman behind a desk that he was trying to catch Flight 137 to New York, she said that its takeoff had been delayed. He sat, caught his breath, and waited until the plane left thirty-five minutes later.

—

Tommy got a window seat near the back of the plane. Once the flight had taken off, he closed his eyes to try to ease the stress that, in recent months, sometimes overwhelmed him, but he couldn't help thinking about the two phone conversations he'd had the previous night. The fat-ass bouncer had just thrown him out of the Lotus, and Tommy needed to wind down. As he drove Gabrielle's red Mustang to The Billiard Palace in Kendall, Nick Rowe called.

"Tommy? Nick."

"Yeah, what's goin' on?"

"You sent some kid up here?"

Tommy heard anger in Rowe's voice and knew that something had gone wrong. He asked, "What happened?"

"Okay. So, he was being straight with what he said about your shit?"

"Well, I ain't gonna talk about that now, but I guess you got the general idea, yeah."

"Look, man," Rowe said. "I understand if you gotta problem. But how the fuck you gonna send some punk kid to my house actin' like he think he King Kong and shit? I'm serious with business. I don't fuck around with niggas like that."

Tommy shook his head. "I know you serious. That's why I brought you in. That's what I told him when he went up there." Tommy's phone clicked twice, signaling an incoming call. He checked the caller I.D.: Edgar. Tommy told Rowe to hold on and clicked over.

Edgar said, "Yo Tommy. I just left his house. Yo, that nigga ain't right..."

"What you mean he ain't right?"

"That nigga shaky like shit, yo." Edgar sounded angry and tense.

Tommy asked, "He lying?"

Edgar said, "Nah, I ain't sayin' all that, but you can't . . ."

"Let me call you back." He clicked back to Rowe and said, "Yo Nick. What happened, man?"

"I don't know where you found that boy, but you need to check him. Tell him stop watchin' gangsta videos on cable. He gonna pull a gun on me after I let him in my house? Somebody else woulda took his ass right the fuck on out. He act like that's what he lookin' for."

Tommy said, "Look, I got a situation. We gotta talk. I'm comin' up there tomorrow. I'm gonna holla at you."

"Like I told him, as far as your deal goes, everything went smooth on Saturday, just like it did the first two times. The last thing I knew was when I called you right after the driver left. That's it. Anyway, I get off work at 3:30. Far as I'm concerned, I appreciate you puttin' me down in the first place. But don't send that kid near me again. I'm serious."

"All right." Tommy clicked off and called Edgar back: "What the fuck happened, yo? Didn't I tell you don't be carryin' nothin' in that man's crib?"

"What, you spoke to him? Swear to God, Tommy, he pulled on me first. Swear to God. For real, yo, if I wasn't representin' you, you woulda had to find some other kind a way to figure what happened to your shit 'cause I woulda smoked his motherfu…"

"Where you at?"

"West Side Highway headed down to Brooklyn, down by my cousin, the one with the house in Bed-Stuy."

"You can stay up there 'til Wednesday night, right?" Tommy asked.

"Yeah. But I gotta be back in Miami Thursday morning."

Tommy said, "All right. Sit tight. Lemme holla at you tomorrow, early."

Now, cruising above the clouds, Tommy thought that he didn't want to hear any bullshit about cowboy games and who said what to who. He wanted to know what had happened to the missing package, and he thought that he had everything in place to do that. But he had to move fast.

Half an hour into the flight, he found himself getting sleepy. He thought about Gabrielle and how she seemed to be thinking hard about something lately. He regretted what had happened at the Lotus last night. The fight had involved guys at her table, so whether or not club employees knew of his connection with her, that situation would draw negative attention to Gabrielle; who knew what might have happened if he'd been around when she woke up this morning. She was hell on wheels when she got mad, but he loved her through all of her tantrums and had from the beginning. Tommy thought back to how their relationship had begun...

He was twenty-three, a hoodlum living fast and hard in southern Florida, running with three others: Brandon, a big, strong intimidator; Skinnon (short for "skin and bones"), who took only one thing seriously—money; and Ralph, a quiet, daydreamy type who had a crazy temper. They called themselves "The A-Team," and they planned to stick together until they'd made enough cash, then go their separate ways. Tommy organized, more or less. He set up hijackings, robberies, and any other kind of ripoff that would turn a profit, except drug dealing, which he associated with his mother's death and which drew too much attention from cops. He'd gotten some inside information from an ex-girlfriend who worked as a waitress at a club in Vero Beach and had gone there twice to check it out. It looked easy enough.

So on a Friday night, the A Team sat waiting in a blue 2000 Firebird in a lot across the street from the spot, Smoke and Mirrors, Brandon behind the wheel as usual, Ralph and Tommy on dexedrine, all dressed for a night on the town. A few minutes past midnight, Tommy lit a cigarette before he and Skinnon left the car and walked to a vacant lot behind the club, where they checked three mattresses piled on top each other that had been placed there earlier. They then approached the club from the east and paid twenty dollars apiece to enter. Ten minutes later, Brandon approached from the west and went in. Ralph followed five minutes after that.

About nine hundred people packed the place, making it steamy despite dozens of whirling ceiling fans. Smoke and Mirrors was all shiny black surfaces, polished wood, and glass, and featured large, tropical-looking plants along the walls. Tommy sat at the bar, sipped a Bacardi on ice, and kept an eye on the shadowed second-floor area that housed the office while the other three danced along with everyone else to Buju Banton's "Spectacular." Already, Skinnon was all over a shapely dark-skinned girl, and Tommy hoped that his homeboy hadn't forgotten why they'd come...

At 12:40, their inside contact, Roxie, who'd been paid thirty-five hundred dollars, came out of a second-floor bathroom, stood at the balcony railing, stared down at Tommy, and patted her head: time to move. Tommy downed his drink. He looked to the dance floor and made eye contact with his crew members, tugging his ear toward each.

One after the other, with Tommy last, they went upstairs and walked past the office and bathrooms to a storage closet that stood in near darkness and had been left wedged open. Each one reached inside and pulled out what Roxie had just put there—one of four .357 Ruger revolvers that Tommy had bought at a South Carolina gun dealer three weeks ago under a false I.D.

They walked in line back to the office, where Tommy knocked, not too hard but hard enough. A slender Hispanic man in a cream-colored suit opened and said, "Yes?" The lamp-lit, teak-paneled room contained only one other person.

Tommy pushed the gun firmly against the man's navel and forced him into the office. Brandon followed and aimed his weapon at a tall middle-aged white man sitting at a large desk in front of an open, cash-filled briefcase. Knowing that the music would prevent anyone else from hearing, Brandon yelled, "Get away from the motherfuckin' table! Move or I'll blow you goddamn head off!" The seated man looked angry as he raised his hands above his shoulders and slid his chair back.

Skinnon and Ralph entered, closed the door behind them, lifted their shirts, and, with 50 Cent's "Get Up" playing on the dance floor, unwrapped large plastic bags from around their torsos. Skinnon went to the desk and emptied the case's contents into his bag. He left the office and walked to the men's bathroom, which was locked from inside. Skinnon knocked five times. Roxie opened and let him in. He went to the window, which faced a vacant lot, threw the bag outside, and jumped twenty feet down onto three mattresses piled on top of each other. He then walked to the car.

In the office, Ralph aimed at the white man's head and said, "You the manager, right?" The man didn't answer. Ralph said, "Open the goddamn safe." The man didn't move. Ralph went around the table and hit him on his head. He fell, and Ralph pressed the gun against the man's right eye, saying, "The safety's off. Open the goddamn safe or I'll pull the trigger and let your boyfriend over there do it."

The manager said, "There's nothing in there but some papers, nothing that you'd use."

Ralph, his eyes dilated by the speed he'd taken, shouted, "If there ain't nothing in there, just open the shit before I make a mess up in here!"

The man flinched and said, "You've got to move the desk. It's under the desk."

Tommy said, "The desk ain't hooked to no alarm, right?"

"No, no alarm," the manager said.

Tommy came around the desk, kicked the man in the ribs, and yelled, "The desk ain't hooked to no alarm, right?"

"No! No alarm! No alarm!"

Somebody knocked on the door. The crew looked at each other. Brandon opened it and aimed his gun at a stocky, bearded Hispanic in a blue suit who had long hair drawn back in a ponytail. He looked like Security. Brandon gestured for him to enter and stand near the smaller man, and closed the door.

Ralph said to the manager, "Anybody else knocks on that fuckin' door, that's the last sound you ever hear. You understand? I don't care who it is or what they want. I feel like lettin' you have it, anymotherfuckinway." He stood back to cover all three men, paying particular attention to the security guy, who looked like he wanted to try something.

The oak desk weighed a ton. Tommy and Brandon tucked their weapons in their waists and strained to drag it back a few feet. It had stood on a gray and red rug, and they rolled that back to reveal a marble tile floor.

The phone rang. Ralph, Brandon, and Skinnon looked at each other as it kept ringing, five times…six times…seven…Tommy told the slim man in the fancy suit, who'd let them in, "Answer. Whoever it is, get rid of 'em. Fast."

The man's hand shook badly as he picked up the receiver and spoke in weak but perfect English: "Yes …. This is Omar…. No, he just went downstairs. He'll be back…. Okay, I'll tell him."

He hung up, and Tommy asked, "Who was that?"

"A woman calling for him," the well-dressed man said, pointing at the manager with his chin.

Ralph told the manager, "Open it. I ain't gonna say it again."

The manager used his fingertips to pry loose a tile.

It covered a combination safe. He went through the combination twice and opened the small door. Brandon took Ralph's bag and reached inside the recessed safe. He pulled out documents, a videotape, and several stacks of cash in wrappers. He put the papers and video back and dropped the money into the bag. He went out the door, to the men's bathroom, and jumped through the window to the mattresses laying in the alley.

Meanwhile, back in the office, Ralph took a roll of duct tape and a straight razor from his pocket. He taped the manager and the other two men to two chairs and taped their mouths while Tommy aimed his gun at them. Once Ralph finished, he and Tommy walked out of the office and left the club the same way as Skinnon and Brandon. They all met them in the Firebird, which they'd parked two blocks east, away from the parking lot's surveillance cameras.

Drinking rum and laughing, they sped back to Miami with Outkast on the CD player. At one point, they took an exit ramp, pulled under a bridge, and used the trunk light for Tommy to count the cash—over $57,000.

When they reached the city, the robbery's adrenaline rush had them wired, so they went to the Cheetah, a strip joint on Embrey Terrace. Brandon drove the car home to drop off the money and said he'd be back in thirty minutes.

Despite the late hour, customers occupied most of the old club's seats. Tommy bought a beer. He lit a cigarette and sat in the middle of the room. Among six women on stage, his attention went immediately to a chocolate-skinned girl on the left. She had short, streaked black hair combed straight back, big eyes, high cheekbones, full lips, and a dimpled chin. She had an athlete's body, and she moved like no other dancer he'd seen. She removed her bra and panties as the song changed. Tommy couldn't take his eyes off her, and although she hadn't looked his way, it almost seemed as if she knew he was there, that she was dancing *to him*.

At the next table, Skinnon said to Ralph, "Hey yo, check Tommy hard on shorty. Check Tommy on shorty. Yo, Tommy man, you like that, or what?" He cupped his hands around his mouth and said in a nasal voice, "Earth to Tommy, Earth to Tommy, do you read me? Can you hear me? Over." They both laughed. Tommy did, too, but his eyes stayed on the girl until she left the stage.

Tommy returned to The Cheetah almost every week after that. He told her his name and spoke to her when he could without pressing too much. She gave him a name, Bree, and said that she didn't date clients. She wouldn't tell him her age or whether or not she had a boyfriend or a kid or anything. He gave her his number, but he didn't expect her to call, and she didn't.

Then, one Friday night after he'd been going for about six weeks, she wasn't there. When another girl said that Bree didn't work there anymore, he left. The next Thursday, she called him and said that she'd moved to a club called The Lotus in Downtown Miami. He said that he'd see her there and checked his caller I.D. He asked, "Is this your cell number?"

"Yeah. But don't use it, okay? You not supposed to have it in the first place." Tommy saw her the following week and most Fridays after that, all the while struggling with a nearly irresistible urge to call her number.

Sometimes she'd sit with him for a few minutes after she'd completed a set. And on one of her nights off, as if rewarding him for respecting her wish that he not dial her number, she surprised him by calling, and they spoke for over an hour. They spoke again a few times after that, and eventually, he invited her to dinner and to a Nas concert. She accepted. Within six months, they were living together, and a year after that, they moved into the Miami Beach condo.

The A Team had broken up a long time ago; Brandon, now a Muslim, worked in a Tampa barbershop, Ralph had died in jail mysteriously (authorities said "heart attack"), and Skinnon just disappeared. Tommy and Gabrielle's three-and-a-half years as a couple had been bumpy but good, at least for him, and he thought that she'd have said the same thing. But he could see her changing as a person, and that was going to affect their relationship one way or another. Every aspect of Tommy's life was stressing him, and the resulting tension was changing him, too. He squeezed his eyes shut and tried to relax until, eventually, he dozed off.

A jolt woke him; the plane had landed in New York.

—

At 2:00, Hazel Royce got into her government-issued Mercury sedan, which was parked in the Hoover building's sub-basement. She checked herself briefly in the mirror—short afro neat, medium-brown skin clear, teeth clean, string of pearls straight—and put on sunglasses as she drove out onto crowded 4th Street and south toward property manager Alex Kirby's Virginia office.

Royce had wanted to join the F.B.I. since the age of fifteen. The idea of spending all day tracking the nation's worst criminals fascinated her while she'd been growing up an only child in a solid middle-class family in a Cincinnati suburb, so she earned an AA degree in accounting and then a Bachelor's in English at Drayton State in Ohio. She went straight to law school, which she worked her way through during evenings as a clerk in a nearby drug store. After she finished in the third percentile of her graduating class, she joined the Bureau at the age of twenty-seven.

Within a year, the agency transferred her from the Cleveland branch to an old field office in Washington, where she found herself amid a firestorm of racial turmoil. Her previous location had had racial problems, but they'd been simmering for so long that the few blacks and other minorities considered it part of the terrain. Tensions at and around the almost exclusively white male D.C. office had burst into the open, and many organizations, including the NAACP, issued a series of press releases drawing attention to issues such as favoritism, questionable dismissals, and hiring and promotion policies.

As a newcomer, Hazel tried to keep a low profile; the unsettled climate affected everyone in the bureau, but D.C. in particular. Adverse publicity and talk of class-action lawsuits brought matters to a head. As one result, black women, previously at the low-end of the notoriously conservative agency's totem pole, suddenly received promotions at a rate far greater than before—until the fuss died down. Certain inequalities remained—not enough emphasis on recruiting Hispanic and black male agents, for example—however, Hazel benefited from the "new" order and found herself at the Hoover Building, moving up the ladder and with more flexibility in setting her daily schedule. Not that she had a problem with time; single, she loved her work and eagerly put in as many hours as necessary to finish her assignments.

Now, in her thirteenth year with the bureau, Hazel Royce had built a solid reputation. To keep doing what she was doing, she'd turned down two supervisory offers that would have required her to move to Michigan or back to Ohio. Her conscientiousness caught the eye of her supervisor, who recommended her for the Priority Apprehension Task Force, which had been developed to foster—and publicize—co-operation among intelligence agencies, such as DEA, FBI, and ATF, after 9/11's terrorist attacks. Her main responsibility had been to work with Secret Service Agent Carl Oberhauser in trying to apprehend known but unindicted counterfeiter Enrique "Henry" Ramos, but all efforts had failed. Ramos would just vanish from the radar for months at a time—periods when he'd almost certainly assume at least one false identity—and their job had been hampered by his having such a common name; three times, teams of federal and local agents had raided buildings—in Reno, Milwaukee, and Sunnyvale, California—only to find that they had the wrong Enrique Ramos. Like Royce's assignment to the task force, Ramos caused more of a headache than anything else, but she took his case seriously as she did everything that crossed her desk.

So, twenty-five minutes after leaving FBI Headquarters, she pulled up in a business park in front of Alex Kirby's second-floor office. The mid-afternoon heat had her sweating lightly by the time she got upstairs and entered a suite. An attractive Hispanic secretary in an olive-green dress informed Kirby, and Royce walked into the property manager's office a few minutes later. He was a tall, well-groomed black man in his mid-forties. His hair was combed back, and a finely trimmed mustache outlined his upper lip. He wore a starched white-on-white shirt, a red tie, gray suspenders, charcoal slacks, and burgundy wing tips. Like the man, his office was stylish, all brown, gray, and white; behind his desk, a large window offered a view of treetops that went off into the distance.

Kirby straightened his tie, smiled, and said, "So, Ms Royce, what can I do for you?" Royce heard a Southern California accent.

"I have some questions about 8712 Edgemere, or rather ..."

Still smiling, he said, "The cottage by the stream, right? Nice location. Fine, fine property. Beautiful. Like you, if you don't mind me saying it. Five rooms, phone and TV in each, all amenities ..."

"Actually, Mr. Kirby," Royce reached into her purse and produced her badge, "I'm with the F.B.I.. My questions are about the man who's been renting 8712 since Wednesday. What can you tell me about him?"

"Oh." His smile faded as he turned to the monitor on his desk and tapped his keyboard. "Let me see. 8712, 8712, 8712 ...That's out in Woodbridge. Here we are. Enrique Ramos. Yes. In on Wednesday, out this morning . . ."

"Out? What time?"

"His lease elapsed at 11:00."

Royce pulled out a mug shot and laid it on the desk. She asked, "Did you see him at any time?"

"No. We conduct our transactions electronically, pretty much. Most of our initial arrangements are made over the phone, but we usually don't see our guests, no."

"So your secretary wouldn't have seen him either."

"Right." Having noticed no ring on Royce's finger, he added, "Have we met before, Ms Royce? You're an attractive woman. You've got the kind of face a man would remember, and you look familiar."

"Mr. Kirby, thank you, but I'm here on important business, please. Could Ramos still be at the cottage?"

"I don't think so. He'd have to pay an additional fee. It does happen sometimes. But when it does, the cleaning agency notifies us right away."

Royce asked, "How would you know whether or not he's stayed past his limit?"

"We give our guests an hour's grace period. We use a cleaning company, Preston Finishing Services. They'll show up no later than, say, twelve-thirty. The property's supposed to be vacant, with two sets of keys outside in the lockbox. If the tenant's still there, the cleaners tell us. That's part of their contract."

"So you got no call from the cleaning company today," Royce said.

Kirby shook his head. "Ms Royce, I can see you're no joke. Believe me, if we had, I'd have told you."

Royce asked, "Can I speak to Preston? I'd like to speak with whoever was assigned to 8712 today."

"Sure, why not." He whistled a tune while punching buttons on his computer's keyboard, then said, "This man you're looking for, what is he, a bank robber? Murderer? I watch that show sometimes—*America's Most Wanted*. Crazy the things people do nowadays, isn't it? Well I guess I don't have to tell you . . ."

"Part of a routine investigation, Mr. Kirby, nothing to worry about. Be honest with you, your guest probably isn't the man we're looking for..."

"Here it is, Caldwell and Tanner. They work sort of as a team. Here's their number," he said, handing her a slip of paper from the rolodex.

Royce called the number on her cell: "Hello, is this Caldwell? Tanner? .... Yes, Ms Tanner, I'm a federal agent. My name is Hazel Royce ....No, nothing's wrong. I'm calling from Alex Kirby's office.... Yes...Have you been to 8712 Edgemere today?"

The cleaning woman said that neither she nor her partner had seen anyone nor had they seen anything unusual at the cottage.

"....Okay....Okay, that's fine," Royce said. "I might have to contact you later on, but that's fine. Thank you."

She clicked off, thought for a few seconds, and asked Kirby for the cottage's phone number. When he gave it to her, she stood and said, "I appreciate your time and co-operation, Mr. Kirby. I have to tell you, if this were to turn out to be the man we're trying to find, your records on this rental could be subpoenaed. It's unlikely, but there's a chance."

As she started to leave, Kirby stood and said, "Ms Royce, Cassandra Wilson's singing next weekend at the Park Pavilion. I can get tickets."

She opened the door, looked back over her shoulder, smiled, and said, "Thanks, Mr. Kirby. I'd like to, but right now, I'm much too busy."

He smiled back and said, "You know what they say about all work and no play, right?"

"Yes," she said. "I know what they say. But our job carries a pretty heavy responsibility. Remember the people on the TV show you watch, Most Wanted? Somebody's got to find them."

Just before the door closed, Kirby straightened his tie again and said, "Let me know if you ever get your man."

—

Royce had learned early that most people became tense when they heard "F.B.I.," so, occasionally, she didn't identify herself as such initially, as rules required, when on bureau business. But, tense or not, the two cleaners hadn't sounded quite right on the phone, and as Royce left the property manager's office, she considered going to the nearby cottage just out of curiosity.

Once inside her car, she called the number to 8712 and got no answer. She waited for a couple of minutes and tried again but got the same result. She had a fingerprint kit, and a copy of Ramos's prints, along with other forensic equipment, in the trunk, and if Caldwell and Tanner hadn't yet done their duty, which Royce suspected as a possibility, she might have been able to come up with something. But then she thought again. Based on experience in this case, this probably wasn't even the right man, and if it were and by some outside chance he were still there and something went wrong, she'd be violating all kinds of policy by confronting him alone. So she drove back to her D.C. office and left Oberhauser, the Secret Service agent assigned to help her find Ramos, a voice-mail message describing what had happened.

But her first instinct had been right. The cleaners, Felicia Tanner and Ann Caldwell, didn't mind their job, but they resented their supervisor, an ex-military man who thought that he could bully his workers' best work out of them. In response, Tanner and Caldwell worked at their own pace. They got away with it because around the clock, Preston Finishing Services had so many people cleaning at so many locations, business and residential, that the supervisor often couldn't keep track of who was where despite all of the facts, figures, and charts in his ever-present laptop.

So, when Tanner and Caldwell were supposed to have been at 8712 Edgemere, they were at a Pizza Hut in Alexandria, and when the highly-educated-sounding sister called saying she was F.B.I., they were at a mall, shopping for clothes for Caldwell's newborn granddaughter.

In fact, if Royce *had* gone to the cottage, she would have arrived as Henry Ramos was leaving. This being the third time he'd stayed there in the last six years, he knew that he could ignore the 11:00 checkout time, so he did; he hadn't even woken up until 11:15. When he opened his eyes to another sunny day, Simone had already gone. As soon as she'd told him the previous night about her boyfriend's bag of heroin, he decided to cancel plans to fly west this afternoon. Henry wanted to know as much as possible about it, but he decided not to press her; he could get specifics, like the package's location, by showing helpful interest without being too pushy. So he'd driven to Conklin to eat a late breakfast and pick up clothes from the dry cleaners. When he got back, he checked D.C. for a good hotel and booked a room through Sunday at the Van Nostrand.

Henry paid attention to the news, but he didn't like music much; his time on Edgemere Lane was mostly very quiet, the way he liked it, so when the phone rang as he got ready to leave, it startled him. He thought it might be Simone; only she knew his location. He didn't want to miss a call from her, so he reached for the receiver, but she thought that he had left hours ago, so he hesitated with his hand in mid-air until the tenth and final ring. He then continued packing, being careful to leave the cottage untidy, as most people did, but not so much so that it would bring attention to him, when the phone rang a second time. Again, he resisted the initial temptation to answer, while counting the rings; for whatever reason, something seemed odd about these two calls. After another ten rings, the sound stopped, and he hurried up and left.

CHAPTER FIVE

OLD SCHOOL

That day, Tuesday, Simone had woken up next to Henry at 8:20, thinking about men. The night before, she and Henry had made love in a way that had her feeling relaxed this morning. He wasn't romantic or sentimental, but she couldn't resist his passion, which heated her up just thinking about it. Beside that, he knew what to do and when, and she had the feeling that he was starting to see her differently, to value her more. Or was she just imagining it? But as much fun as they had together, she could never consider him for a real relationship. His mysteriousness turned her on but only as far as the way things were now, and she recognized that he had some other quality that she couldn't put her finger on—just as she couldn't identify what had kept her with Freeman for the last three years.

At first, she'd found Freeman to be cute, funny, affectionate, reliable, kind, considerate, a passionate lover. She liked his band. He was the first black guy she'd been with in a meaningful way, and she enjoyed the differentness that the racial factor added to it. But she'd liked all of her boyfriends in the beginning, only to get bored eventually; at least, that's the way it usually went. Generally, she could get what she wanted from Freeman, but that had been true in most of her dealings with males, going back as far as she could remember; it was one of several reasons why she liked dealing with them more than with women. In fact, she planned to use her femininity to get something from a guy today...

Simone thought about money. Freeman had scheduled a trip to Illinois but hadn't told her why. She assumed that it was related to the green bag; she'd find out soon enough. She turned her head on the pillow toward Henry, who lay on his stomach, sleeping beside her, the first man she'd been with who didn't snore. After he'd surprised her last night by admitting that he broke the law for a living, he'd wanted to know more about what Freeman had found and hinted that he might want to buy it himself.

Now, in morning light that filtered through the bedroom's blue and tan curtains, she saw him as more enigmatic, more dangerous, more exciting. She imagined him as some kind of international arms merchant, brokering deals between buyers and sellers from different continents. Or a mercenary, hired by multinational corporate entities to dispatch high-ranking third-world political figures who didn't fit into the broader scheme of things—he had that kind of air about him. But for some reason, even though she normally loved taking a chance, she had mixed feelings about the idea of him getting involved with the package.

She grabbed her phone and went out into the sunshine that beamed onto the wooden cottage's front porch. She looked up Hassan Salim, a two-time classmate and former study group partner at the University of Maryland, in her list of stored numbers and called him. She'd flirted with Hassan, a studious, good-natured chemical engineering major, until he started taking things too seriously and she had to distance herself a bit. But whenever she saw him, they'd chat, and she could tell that he still liked her even though she'd heard that he had a fiancée.

He usually took summer classes, so she figured he should be still in town. He answered her call on the second ring, and after a minute of small talk, they arranged to meet at 11:20, after his biochemistry class.

———

Simone was waiting at the library checking her watch when Hassan arrived a few minutes late, on crutches, with his right knee in a brace, wearing headphones, his books in a backpack. They sat away from others enjoying the weather, on one of several benches in scant shade provided by a row of yellow poplars.

He turned off his music, and Simone touched his knee lightly, asking, "What happened to your leg?"

"A car crash three weeks ago coming back from Pittsburgh on a Sunday night. A young guy, probably drunk, was speeding in and out of traffic. I saw him coming. He forced me off the road into a ditch and didn't even stop. I had to have surgery for a torn meniscus, and I bruised some ribs. My car got totaled."

"Wow. Sorry to hear that. Anybody else get hurt?"

"No, I was by myself. Hurt like hell, but I'll be okay. Everything's insured. Anyway, so what's new with you, Simone? I'm surprised to hear from you. It's been a while."

"Just stressed."

"Classes are over for you. You should be relaxing, traveling."

She leaned toward him so that her tits were almost touching his arm, which was draped across the back of the bench. "I need some help with a problem. I wouldn't call unless it was kind of important. I know you stay busy. But you've got to swear you're going to keep it to yourself."

"Don't worry. I can keep my mouth shut. I'm a male."

"What's that supposed to mean?"

He smiled and said, "Just kidding. What's wrong?"

"I've got a cousin visiting from L.A. She's young. She's been in a little trouble out there, nothing too heavy. But over the weekend, I found some white powder in a matchbox in her bag, and I'm worried she's into something. I'm scared it's heroin. If it is, I'm telling her parents. I want to know if there's a way to test it. I figure you'd be a good person to ask. You know a lot about chemistry and stuff."

Hassan whistled and said, "Heroin? Wow. How old is she?"

"Seventeen," Simone answered.

"Going through your cousin's bag, huh?"

"Can we just say it fell out?"

Hassan said. "Hey, you can say whatever you want. Well, it could be heroin, coke, it could be anything..."

Simone, winging it, said, "See, the reason I said heroin is we've been hearing rumors about that on and off for months. I say 'we,' I mean her parents. She's been hanging out with the wrong crowd at her school. They think they're all grown up, and they don't have to listen to what grownups have to say because the world's so much different now, and adults can't relate, and yadda yadda yadda ... They're real close to my mom. Her mom's my mom's sister. I mean, there's only so much I can do, but I'm just trying to help. I want to know for sure."

Hassan just looked at her for a while as if figuring something. He said, "For heroin, there's a test. You drop two solutions, acid mixes, on the powder. A positive sample turns bright green, then like a bluish-aqua color.

"You don't have it, do you?" she asked.

"What, the test? No," he said, "but I can get the chemicals."

"When?"

Hassan shrugged. "I don't know. Few days. Are you sure you want to do this? Sounds weird."

"She's my cousin!"

"All right, all right. Let me call you, okay?"

They talked a little about classes and instructors and ex-classmates until the conversation ended a few minutes later; then, she watched him put his headphones on and struggle to his feet. As he hobbled away, Simone felt a twinge of disappointment because he hadn't shown the same kind of interest that he had previously. She spent a moment wondering about his fiancée's name until remembering that she had other things to worry about. She got up and walked to her car.

—

Mount Witley Park in Brooklyn was quiet and peaceful. Tommy walked to an empty softball field, stood behind a fence at home plate, and lit a cigarette. Within ten minutes, Nick Rowe approached on foot from the street on which Tommy had parked. Originally, they'd met through Tommy's father, Leon. About fifteen years ago, between leaving the army and being arrested for armed robbery, Rowe had been Leon's driver-bodyguard-bagman-enforcer. Tommy's father still spoke well of him, and while setting up his Thailand to New York to Florida connection, Tommy had followed his father's advice and recruited Rowe without meeting him face-to face.

Now, Tommy compared the mixed-race Rowe's appearance to what it had been when Tommy was a kid: about fifteen pounds lighter, hair gone, same goatee but turned mostly gray, small silver hoop in each ear instead of a tiny gold cross hanging from one, work shirt and Dickey's instead of silk suits and designer shirts, same blank facial expression—not riding high but solid, still a man to take seriously.

They shook hands; Rowe's eyes showed no trace of deceit, but they never showed much of anything. Tommy said, "Good to see you. It's been a few."

Rowe said, "Yeah, Tommy, same here. Same here. How's your dad?"

"Well, not good right now, but it's ups and downs. Haven't seen him in a while, either. Spoke to him last week, though."

"Been a long time since I saw him, too. I got to go check him out. He's in Georgia, right?"

"Savannah. Got a little house there. I'll get you the address," Tommy said.

"Yeah. I got to do that. But first things first. What happened to your shipment?"

Tommy shrugged and said, "That's what I'm here to find out. Your man Wade left New York with it Saturday night. That's the last I heard."

"Man. I known Wade for years. You can never be 100%, but he's not the type to do somethin' stupid."

Tommy said, "Well, somebody did *somethin'.* Tell me about him again."

"He's from out west, Oakland or someplace out there. No folks up this way. Met him while I was inside. He was there for extortion and assault. I didn't ask too much about it. From what I heard, he'd got involved with a married woman, her old man found out, Wade had something on the guy that the wife had told him about and tried to shake him down. They got into a fight in the street, and Wade left him there in a coma. That's what they say. Quiet, keeps to himself. Likes his scotch. He old school, like me."

"Kids? Wife?"

"Not that I know of."

"You had said he don't get high, right?"

Rowe shook his head. "Like I said, he drinks. That's it."

"You know where he lives?"

"I ain't bringing him in unless I know where he's coming from."

Tommy squinted and looked around the park. "So, Saturday night, he didn't know what he was carryin'?"

Rowe shook his head. "He got paid to drive the car to Florida. Told him to go around D.C. I didn't say why. I told him everything I'd told him before, like about the house in North Carolina if he needed a stop, but he said he'd gotten plenty rest. He had the address for the place he was going to in Miami. Didn't say a whole lot more to him than that. He had a map. Two maps."

"So you gave him the car keys, and everything went smooth."

Rowe said, "Yeah." Then, as an afterthought, "He had something wrong with his eye."

"Something like what?" Tommy asked.

"It was all swollen up. Like some kind of infection."

"Could he handle a car with his eye like that?"

Rowe replied, "I asked him, he said it wasn't a problem."

"Yeah, but could he handle a car? What do you think? Would it affect his driving? Would you drive to Florida with your eye like that?"

Rowe nodded and said, "Yeah."

"But he could have got into an accident, run a red light, gone off a bridge, hit someone crossing the street, anything," Tommy said, turning away and putting his hands on his hips. "If he can't see right, you ain't supposed to let him go, Nick. You didn't say nothin' about that on Saturday."

Rowe said, "His driving was good enough to get him to meet me to pick up the car, and he looked fine leaving. From what you told me, everything was on a set schedule, right? It's eight o'clock Saturday night, with him there in the garage, what am I supposed to do? If I could have driven it myself, I would have from the beginning. But the record I got, I ain't takin' a risk like that at my age. Look, I'm me, you're you, he's him. Maybe you wouldn't drive with your eye like that. Maybe you would. If I was him, I could have made it. He said he could. I took his word for it and let him go."

"You didn't just take his word. You took a risk with my goddamn money."

Rowe said, "You talkin' a lot of shit. You don't know what the fuck happened. Find out first, then get pissed off."

Anger flashed through Tommy like a lightening bolt. He stepped toward Rowe until their faces were inches apart. "Who you tellin' don't get pissed off? I know what happened. That's *my* shit gone. You know how much I had riding in that car?"

Rowe said, "Back off."

Tommy radiated anger. He balled his fists and remained still, then, remembering his goal, turned and walked to his car.

Rowe called after him, "Don't step to me like that again, hear? I don't give a shit *who* your dad is. And you still owe me half my money."

Tommy kept walking. Rowe watched him until he'd left the park, thinking conflict last night, conflict now—a lot of tension in the air. He wouldn't have tolerated what Tommy had just done from anyone else, but he understood Tommy's frustration. Still, on Saturday night, he'd thought that he'd made the right call in trusting Wade.

He went to his car and drove to 1273 Delancey Street, a five-floor tenement on the Lower East Side. It took twenty minutes to find a parking space, but once he did, he went to a bar, got something to eat, and had a beer. He returned to his car and called to check on his mom; she needed tea, and he said he'd pick some up and drop it off for her early in the morning.

Rowe then sat for about an hour until just before the sky turned dark. When the street had relatively few pedestrians, he opened the trunk, got a glass cutter and a length of nylon rope, which he tucked under his shirt, and walked to 1273. He stood on the front steps, looked up and down the street, and went inside the front door. He pressed apartment 4-D's buzzer twice and got no response. He waited for a minute and tried again; still no answer. He checked the street a second time and picked out a skeleton key on his overcrowded key ring. He opened the lock quickly and entered the building.

—

Earlier that day, Freeman had awoken thirsty, groggy, and still lit up from hanging out with Vaughan Chandler the previous night at The

Green Light. Alone, wearing only his shorts, in a large windowless furnished space with little light, he groaned and looked around; he was on a wide, fold out couch, and someone had slept next to him. He had no idea who. He also didn't know his location or how he'd gotten there. After a few minutes, he got up and walked around, looking for a clue to his whereabouts. He couldn't find a light switch, so he stumbled in the darkness until he located a staircase and realized that he was in a basement.

The steps led up to a bright, spacious kitchen filled with shiny pans and utensils. On the clay-colored island sat a huge glass bowl filled with various fresh fruit, including mangos, papayas, and a pineapple. It took a while for his eyes to adjust to the change from downstairs' dimness. A wall clock showed 10:43, so he had five hours before his flight back to D.C. Next to the sink was a door with a window that gave a view of several acres of flat grassland that ended at a row of tall trees. Freeman opened a six-foot-tall stainless steel refrigerator containing all types of food, grabbed a glass from a cabinet, and poured some cranberry juice.

After drinking it, he took an apple from the bowl, walked through the kitchen, and turned right to a sunken living room that had everything—leather couch and seats, lamps, coffee table, wall to wall carpet—done in white. Two big paintings—one of an eagle swooping past a waterfall in a valley, and one of a distant yacht in a harbor, with long blades of grass overlapping from the sides, both in white frames—dominated opposite walls. A wooden African sculpture stood in each corner, and Freeman realized that he was in a mansion, a big one. He crossed to the other side of the kitchen and tried a solid-looking oak door. It opened to a large den with a high ceiling and glass cases filled with hardcover books all around except for a transparent wall across from him, which provided a view of a field that led to far away trees.

He closed the door. Standing next to a broad, spiraling staircase, he looked up and yelled, "Hello!" Within seconds, a heavyset young woman with long, braided blonde hair came down. She was wearing a dark, flimsy, multicolored gown, and Freeman remembered her vaguely from last night. She said, "Hi."

"Hey," Freeman said. "Where is this place?"

She sat on one of the bottom steps. "This is Doug Weitz's house.

You know Rick Weitz, Triple Threat's producer? Doug's his brother. You're in Oak Brook Hills, just outside Chicago. Vaughan said you and him are in a band. He said you're from D.C."

Freeman bit into his apple. He didn't get embarrassed easily, but he felt a little self-conscious talking to this barely dressed stranger while wearing only a pair of boxers. "Yeah. I'm in his group. It's called Vortex. We play mostly along the northeast, down Virginia. Vaughan sings and writes."

She nodded and said, "Vaughan's voice fits with Triple Threat's music. "

Freeman said, "Um hm. He can sing, no doubt." He looked around again and said, "So this is Rick Weitz's brother's place, huh?"

"Have you met Rick?" she asked, leaning forward and revealing more-than-ample cleavage.

"Not in person. Our band nearly signed a contract with him a few years back. I spoke with him on the phone a couple times," Freeman said.

"Yeah. His brother's big in the business. He's got this house and another one in North Carolina. He probably doesn't even know we're here," she said. "You were out of it last night."

He said, "I remember leaving the club and getting into a car. That's it. That's what you get hanging out with Vaughan. Two things he can do, sing and party," he said, nibbling his fruit.

"Yeah, we got back here late." She extended her hand, smiled, and said, "I'm Elise. I sing with Triple Threat. Everybody else went out already."

Freeman shook her hand and introduced himself. He said, "I got into town yesterday. Came to visit an uncle in Peoria. Vaughan's the only person I know in Chicago. I'm supposed to catch a plane back east this afternoon."

He excused himself started to go downstairs to see if he could find his bag and/or some clothes when the doorbell rang. As Elise went to answer, Freeman ducked into the kitchen and to the steps that led down to the basement. On the way down, he heard her open the door and say, "Oh. Hello."

Back in the basement, he found a light switch, flipped it on, and looked around. Like the rest of what he'd seen in the house, the room was luxurious with its matching chairs filled with throw pillows, thick rug, big-screen plasma TV, teak side tables, brick fireplace, and maple paneling. Freeman finished eating his apple. He didn't see his bag or any of yesterday's clothes. He looked beneath cushions, under the bed-couch, behind a chair. Standing with hands on hips, he heard the man upstairs shout angrily. Freeman listened, heard nothing further, and continued looking for his belongings, but after a minute, the man started yelling again.

Freeman stood still and listened to the muffled, one-sided quarrel. He couldn't make out the words, but the man sounded furious, and Elise wasn't responding. He resumed his search but slowed down once more as the man's voice got louder and he started to pound something.

If the man hit Elise, Freeman would be in a dilemma: he didn't want to do nothing while someone assaulted a seemingly nice woman, but walking into this situation while practically naked with no one else in the house could make things a whole lot worse.

Urgency quickened his search for his bag. He began to root around between, in, and among furniture, while the man's bellowing got louder. Finally, he stood with hands on hips. He'd already checked the bathroom and had run out of places to search. He opened that door again and this time looked behind it; there, he found the shirt, pants and shoes that he'd worn from D.C. hanging from a hook; his bag was in a corner.

Freeman threw on his clothes and hurried to the stairs, but he hesitated once he got there. He had more size than courage, and he had no idea what he was walking into. Maybe the man was jealous and would get angrier at Freeman's appearance; perhaps Freeman should stand here and intervene only if the man became violent. He stood with one foot on the bottom step, unsure.

After a while, the man stopped yelling. Freeman heard a loud noise followed by sounds of heavy footsteps and a door slamming. He went upstairs and through the kitchen. Elise was sitting on the spiral staircase's steps, where she'd been before, looking downcast. A brass ornament had been thrown to the floor near where she sat. He approached her and asked, "You okay?"

"No," she replied.

Freeman heard a car start outside and drive away. He didn't know this woman and her troubles didn't particularly interest him, but he felt sorry for her. "What's wrong?" he asked.

"My ex-husband. I'm trying to get an increase in child support, and he doesn't want that. He got a big pay increase at his new job, and I think his daughter should get some benefit. I'm not breaking any laws. He's like he wants to kill me or something."

Freeman said, "That's one of the reasons I'm not married. You got to be lucky nowadays. You think you know someone, and next thing, you're caught up in some kind of nightmare. I've seen it. It's real easy to get with the wrong person, and..."

Still looking at the floor, Elise said, "Baby, you don't know." She started to tremble. Freeman shook his head. He looked down too, thinking about the marriages he'd seen go bad, beginning with his parents.' He started reliving that until Elise's shaking became more pronounced, and her left arm started jerking up and down. He stepped back and looked at her. She'd lost control of her movements; she raised her head and arched her back, and her body's tremors were lifting her off the step on which she sat. She shuddered so hard that she fell off the step and onto the floor, where she writhed, her arm thrusting wildly.

Freeman stood in shock as her nose started to bleed. Her eyes turned up, and she banged her head against the brass ornament on the floor. He thought about wrapping her in a bear hug, but as he neared her, she seemed, somehow, to have the presence of mind to raise her right hand in a gesture to ward him off.

Whitish liquid trickled from the corner of her mouth. She was lying on her side with her knees bending and straightening violently, almost in tandem with her arm. Her gyrations had carried her away from the stairs and toward the door. Her body shook some more and then, as suddenly as they had started, the convulsions stopped, and she went rigid, about half a minute after it had all begun.

Freeman stared at her. She lay still trying to catch her breath for several moments, then started to compose herself. He regained his wits and went to the kitchen for paper towels and some ice water. When he returned, she was sitting on the floor, knees up, coated in sweat. Breathing heavily, she pulled herself up to the same step she'd been sitting on before. He handed her the tissues, and once her breathing became more regular, she said, "Thanks. Epilepsy. I still get them like that once in a while."

Shaken, Freeman hesitated, then slowly sat next to her and asked if she was all right. When she said yes, he gave her the water and started to ask about her illness, not because he was interested, but because he wanted her to feel some sense of normalcy even though, from what she said, she'd been having seizures for almost twenty years. Later, he'd look back and think that he probably wanted the feeling of normalcy for himself, not for her.

"You got kids?" she asked.

"Not yet."

"That's good. I know what just happened probably shook you up," she said, hunched over and looking at the floor, "but remember I told you this: be careful who you have your kids with. You get with the wrong person, it'll mess up your whole life, for the rest of your life. Remember I told you that."

She offered to prepare breakfast for them both, which he accepted. While she cooked, Freeman took a quick shower and got his things ready to leave. He had plenty of time before his plane's scheduled departure, but he'd had enough of the Windy City to last for a while.

He went back upstairs and enjoyed a meal of eggs, sausage, French toast, and orange juice with Elise. They discussed music for a bit, and when he picked up his bag to go, she offered him a tour of the house, which he declined. He got the address from her and called for a taxi.

It was a nice day, so he said goodbye to Elise, who smiled as if nothing had happened, went outside to wait for the cab, and walked along a curving driveway for over two minutes before he got to the street. When he did, he realized that he was still kind of high from last night. He looked back at the house, Colonial, all blonde ash, glass, and stone against a cloudless sky with no other building in sight. The cab arrived on time, and the driver took Freeman to O'Hare, where they got into an argument over the forty-four dollar fare. Angry at the cabbie and still shaken by Elise's seizure, Freeman waited for his flight.

—

Simone shared a third floor apartment that was seven minutes from the university with another student, a music major named Anna, who was usually elsewhere. Driving there after leaving Hassan, she called Freeman. He was on his way to the airport in Chicago. He said he'd discussed things with Vaughan and gotten a reasonable response.

"I might be able to get things rolling in a few days," he said. "But the way he is, you got to stay on him to get him to do anything. He forgets a lot."

"I know the type. I might have someone interested, too," she said, trying to hint at something without letting him know that she'd gone against his wish to keep quiet.

Freeman said, "Simone, I told you. I'll handle the selling. You're not supposed to say anything to anybody. We agreed on that, right?"

"Well, we sort of did. Anyway, it's no big deal. Don't worry, baby. Things'll work out."

She'd be getting off work too late to pick him up from the airport, so they arranged to meet late at his place. Simone didn't think he'd approve of what she had in mind regarding Hassan's test, and she'd hoped that Freeman wouldn't be back until later, maybe even tomorrow. She hit the gas and hurried home.

At a minute before noon, she entered her building, rushed upstairs, and began looking for the key that Freeman had given her a couple of years ago that opened his front door. She used it sometimes but had a habit of misplacing it, like now. She looked everywhere, and after twenty-five fruitless minutes, she stood in the middle of the apartment, cursing in frustration.

She wanted to get to the package and take a tiny sample of its contents as soon as possible because Hassan could call ready to test at any time. Freeman hadn't liked the idea of her asking people she knew about testing for heroin. He was indirectly mixed up in a double homicide and didn't want anything to happen that would even remotely connect him to the green bag, but, to her, he was being too cautious. "Sometimes, you got to take a chance," she'd said as they lay in bed on Sunday night. "Scared money never wins."

"Yeah, I know that's what they say, but scared money doesn't wind up doing fifty to life, either," he'd replied. "Like I said before, you talk all big and bad, but if something goes wrong, you're not the one gonna wind up doing jail time."

She stroked his shoulder and said sincerely, "No, it's like I told you.

No one's doing any time. Everything I'm saying's in your best interest, baby. I'm trying to look out for you. See, you're real easygoing. That's what I like about you. You're a lover, not a fighter. But something like this needs some initiative, some creative thinking. Someone's got to push this envelope. You see what I'm saying?"

Freeman reached into a drawer, pulled out some matches and a blunt, lit it, took three good drags, and passed it to her. "I understand what you're saying," he said. "But I don't see it that way. This is my deal. I'm gonna call the shots on this one."

He'd surprised her with the way he'd said that last bit. And she didn't mind following his wish—except for the part about the test. The sooner they did that, the better, and he didn't even have to know about it—at least not until after. If she got it tested, she'd tell him the result as soon as she knew. He'd probably be mad at first, but they needed to find out what they had—or what *he* had, so even though they pretty much knew already, once she'd confirmed it, he would see that she'd been right. But they needed to test it.

Right now, though, she couldn't find the key to his goddamn house! The clock on the living room DVD player said 12:32; she had to be at work in thirty minutes, and she hadn't eaten. She stomped twice in frustration and went to the kitchen to grab something to eat, thinking that she'd try to come back during her break and look again, just in case Hassan called.

—

Eight hours later in New York, Nick Rowe entered 1273 Delancey. He walked past the elevator and took the stairs to the top floor, checking the apartments' numbers to get the lay of the building as he went up. Nobody saw him. He climbed the last flight and examined the lock on the door to the roof. He popped it with an illegal pick within fifteen seconds, then stepped onto the roof as the sun's last embers were dying a hazy death on the horizon to his left. He treaded lightly to the building's defunct-looking chimney and tested its sturdiness. Satisfied, he removed the rope from under his shirt and tied one end to the chimney twice and the other around his waist.

Rowe went to the edge of the roof that bordered the back of the building, leaned over, and looked down to a square courtyard six floors below. Four other buildings' rear sides faced the courtyard, from the east, west, and north. He could hear a girl talking loudly inside an apartment; some tenant was watching a sitcom, and another was listening to the all-news radio station's weather forecast. He eyed all windows. No one was looking out.

Night had fallen; the only light shone from two lamps at courtyard level and from occupied rear apartment windows. It was enough for him to see. Rowe clutched the rope, climbed backward over the roof's edge, and lowered himself down the side of the building step-by-step, using the wall for footing, like a fireman. He descended silently, past the fifth floor to the fourth. He stopped at the apartment that should be 4D; there was no indication of life beyond the curtains. He got next to the glass and wound the rope tightly around his left hand. With his right, he took out the glass-cutter and marked a rectangle in the lower pane. He pushed in the cut portion, reached inside, and undid the window's latch. He then stood on the sill and lifted the window.

Rowe entered a kitchen. He untied the rope from his waist, stood still, listened, and heard no sign of an occupant or a dog. He turned on lights as he walked slowly through Harry Wade's apartment to make sure its three rooms were empty and began searching.

—

Tommy's phone rang. He woke up startled, disoriented, wondering where he was. He sat alone in the driver's seat of a car parked on a tree-lined street. It was getting dark out. The phone stopped ringing as he removed it from his pocket; Edgar had called. Tommy looked around and realized that he'd fallen asleep outside Mount Witley Park in Brooklyn after talking to Nick Rowe. Fallen asleep!

Worried, he got out of the car and stood in the road, looking around. He'd had sleep problems and stress before, but falling asleep in the street in this situation meant things were out of control. The situation...he had a situation to deal with. He took a deep breath, wiped his eyes, leaned against the car, and looked at the phone.

It was 8:58 p.m. He'd dozed off almost two-and-a-half hours ago. Edgar hadn't left a message, but two others had. Tommy wondered whether he'd slept through the calls or his phone hadn't rung because it had been out of range to pick up the signals. The first number seemed familiar, but he couldn't place it. It had come at 7:01 p.m. It had no name and a seven-five-seven area code, which he didn't know offhand; he listened to the second, a call from Gabrielle at 6:57:

"Hey, Tommy. I got your text this morning. I was still asleep when you called before. I worry about you when you're not here. You know that, right baby? I'm just checking to see if you're okay. Anyway, miss you, and I hope you won't be up there too long. I'm at the club, but you can give me a call back when you get the chance. All right. Later."

Gabrielle turned off her phone when at work. He started to dial her number and leave a message but checked the other voicemail instead. The D.C. cop, Tracy Whitlock, had called:

"D.C. police found the car you're looking for on Sunday morning. It was involved in a carjacking that resulted in two homicides. Anyway, it's here in the District."

Her words stunned Tommy. Carjacking? Homicides? He listened twice more. She'd said nothing about the small green bag hidden in the trunk. He tried to imagine the scenario, but all kinds of possibilities ran through his mind. Tommy called her number; the phone went straight to voicemail, meaning that she was probably on duty. He had to get to D.C.

He got into the car, started the engine, and drove until he hit 95 South fifteen minutes later. Rush hour had passed, but traffic crawled once he'd crossed into New Jersey. He picked up the cell and started to try Whitlock's number again, but he got an incoming call from Rowe before he could finish. Tommy clicked to it.

"It's Nick. I'm at Wade's place."

"All right, go 'head."

"He ain't here, your shit ain't here. But he didn't mean to take off with it. He meant to make the run and come right back. He got all his clothes here, pictures of his parents, suitcases, some kind of medication he's taking, everything he owns still right here. And yesterday was the last day he had to pay his rent. He meant to make the run to Florida and come straight back. He knows I know where he lives. If he planned to rip you off, he would've stayed away from here. He'd have taken his stuff with him. At least some of it."

Tommy paused for a second and thought about Wade planning to turn around in Miami and drive directly back to New York, where his apartment contained his belongings and he could have paid his rent on time. He said, "They found the car in D.C., carjacked. They got two dead bodies."

Rowe whistled. "He one of them?"

"I'm goin' there to find out. I don't know what they found, who they found, nothin.'"

Rowe said, "Okay, man, I'm here. Let me know what happens."

Tommy thanked him and clicked off. He had to wait for another fifteen minutes before traffic eased, but once it did, he pressed the gas pedal until the needle touched eighty-five.

CHAPTER SIX

FOR MONEY

Simone's frustration showed as she left her job at Lapham Brothers, a huge, warehouse-like home improvement store, at 10:00 p.m. on Tuesday. Earlier, she'd had to deal with two rude customers on the phone and two more in person. Then, she'd returned to her apartment during her five o' clock break and finally found the key to Freeman's house—it had fallen into a shoe on the floor of her clothes closet. She called her job to say that she'd be a bit late getting back due to car problems and drove to Freeman's place to look for the bag of heroin. On Sunday night, after they'd sampled its contents in his kitchen, she'd seen him reseal it and put it in the back of a cabinet next to the dishwasher. But when she'd looked this afternoon, it wasn't there. She searched the kitchen and started to look in the living room until she checked the time; she'd abused her evening break enough and had to get back to the store. Her anger made her kick over a chair on the way out.

But finding the bag would have made no difference because Hassan hadn't called to say that he had the chemicals. So while driving toward Freeman's on this beautiful evening, Simone was considering telling Freeman about Hassan's test and asking for a sample to check.

She parked near Freeman's house, and as she approached it, her phone rang. It was Henry, saying that he'd decided to stay over for a couple of days and wanted to see her, now.

"I want to see you, too, but I made plans to go over to my boyfriend's tonight, so..."

Henry asked, "Have you told him that you know someone who might be interested in what he has?"

"Well, in a way..."

"See, I've got to know what I'm dealing with. I can't do anything with 'We think' or 'We're pretty sure.' You understand."

"All right. Look, I can't talk right now," she said in a hushed tone, stopping two doors away from Freeman's house.

Henry spoke in a heavy voice: "I want to see you. Tomorrow. Tomorrow night."

"All right. Look, I gotta go." She clicked off and turned toward Freeman's, where the living room light was on.

—

At ten minutes to midnight, Tracy Whitlock turned in her daily activities report in to her sergeant, and got off duty. Her tendency to try to get by with less than the five hours of sleep that she needed had caught up to her; she felt exhausted as she got into her dark red Wrangler and started the twenty-five minute drive to the house that she shared with her lover in Prince George's County.

Before starting the engine, she checked both her cell phones. She recognized Tommy DeShields' number. He'd called three times since 9:50, most recently half an hour ago, when he'd left a message. Her vehicle's tires scrunched against the parking lot's gravel as she listened to Tommy's voice: "We got to talk. Give me a call when you can." Tracy noted urgency in his tone as she rolled down the windows so that the night air would help keep her alert on the road. She thought about calling him back but needed sleep badly and decided that she'd contact him tonight or tomorrow morning, depending on how she felt while driving home. She merged onto I 50 and thought about how she'd gotten mixed up with Tommy.

Tracy was thirty and an eight-year veteran of the streets who'd already seen enough to understand why so many cops regretted having joined the force; she did too on bad days, but for the most part she liked her work. She'd known that law enforcement often burned people out. Friends and relatives in southern Maryland, where she'd grown up and gone to school, had tried to change her mind, but she'd made her decision, and she rarely changed her mind, no matter what anyone said.

At five-foot-three, she was one of the shortest officers in the city. She was smart and considered herself to have a strong mind—except when in came to love; in that area, she followed her heart. She exercised whenever her schedule allowed and wore her blonde hair in a ponytail. During her second year, she'd been assigned to ride once or twice per week in a patrol car in northeast with an older, respected officer named Brian Beck, who'd twice been cited for valor in the line of duty.

While with the colorful, dark-haired Beck, Tracy learned more about policing than she did during her year in the police academy and her previous year on the streets combined. He showed her how to handle equipment, get information, read the urban environment. He loved being a cop, and she looked forward to being partnered with him. He'd built a solid reputation within the department; none of the politics, bureaucracy, infighting, tensions, frustration, paperwork, or danger of the job seemed to bother him, and, whether dealing with a crack fiend or a high-end lawyer, talking was his most effective weapon.

Against regulations, they started to fraternize. An always stylishly dressed, divorced father of two, Beck quickly took to the plain-spoken young officer who had a touch of sunshine in her smile. His charm drew her to him, as did the casual, unshakable authority with which he carried himself, especially when on the street; she couldn't imagine a better beat cop. Tracy's boyfriend was stationed in Kuwait with the army, and she grew close to Beck. Three months after meeting, they slept together at the start of what would become an intensely sexual affair.

Depending on their shifts, they spent much of their free time in each other's company once she'd moved from her apartment into his three-bedroom house east of the city. They made love like charged-up teenagers—in their vehicles, during daytime motel rendezvous, once in a public bathroom; sex sometimes ended their arguments. She thought she understood his character until a chilly March night near the end of her third year as a policewoman when she received one of the biggest shocks of her life.

Twice while they were on patrol he'd parked near a bar called Hickock's Grill on the corner of Oregon and Lumley and disappeared into an adjoining alley. Both times he'd returned to the squad car within five minutes and driven away with no explanation. When he did it again two days into a new year, Tracy followed him and peered around the corner into the alley to see what he was doing. He knocked on a door that looked like the bar's fire exit. She didn't see who opened it, just Beck disappearing inside for a minute, then reemerging while slipping a small manila envelope into his jacket.

She was back standing next to the car when he returned. She didn't say anything, but it bothered her, and when he went down the alley a fourth time two months later, she followed again and stood across the street. A tall, slim, older black man with straightened hair came out of the side door that Beck had knocked on and handed something to him, which he slipped into his waistband.

A couple of weeks later, they went bike riding in northern Virginia on a worn trail that passed through a heavily wooded area. Cumulous clouds hid the sun, and temperatures were in the lower forties; a light breeze kept them refreshed even though leaves from last autumn formed a carpet that slowed them while crunching steadily under their bicycles' tires. After forty-five minutes they dismounted and walked their bikes up an incline. Tracy, strolling beside Beck, asked, "Brian, you know how we make those stops sometimes outside Hickock's, that bar on Oregon?"

He said nothing.

"What's going on in that alley?"

"Don't worry about that."

"Don't worry about it? We're partners a lot of times. What if you go down there one night and something happens? What do I write in my report?"

He said, "It's a C.I.," using the term for an informant. "I didn't want you in on it."

"Brian, I'm not stupid. I can see what you're doing."

He looked at her sharply and asked, "What the fuck you mean you 'can see' what I'm doin'?"

"Don't play games with me, okay? I know. You want me to know. That's why you're so fuckin' obvious about it."

They walked in silence except for the sounds of the leaves underfoot and their heavy breathing. Tracy never minced words, and after a while, she asked, "How long you been takin' money?"

He stopped on the narrow, tree-lined path and looked her up and down. "You wearin' a wire?"

She stopped, too. "What, you don't trust me, Brian?" She let her bike fall, removed her helmet, stripped naked, stretched out her arms, and turned in a circle.

He said nothing as she put her clothes back on. They resumed walking, with their heads down, and he said, "Look, Trace, I been carryin' two mortgages. I gotta get ready for two kids to go to college. The system isn't set up for people like you and me. The guy you're talking about? What I make in a year he might make in a week. All he wants is information once in a while."

"Drug dealer?"

Beck said, "Something like that."

"What's his name?"

"Why?"

"Why not? You told me this much."

Beck hesitated, then said, "Leon. From Florida. Most of the time, I deal with him through a middle man. I never took a dime from anyone else. I've done enough to make up for it. A hundred times over, I've done enough. You haven't been out here long, so you don't know. It's not always simple choices, black and white, good and bad. You'll find out."

"How long you been doin' it?"

"About three years."

She shook her head and said, "Every decision you make, you're choosing one way or another, one side or the other. Every decision. We're cops. If we don't do what's right, everything falls apart. Everything."

He snapped at her, "Who the hell are you to be lecturing me?" Then more calmly, "You haven't been out here long enough. You still think it's all a big TV show. I'm not makin' any excuses. I know it's wrong in a way, but being a cop in a big city, you're in a different world. Nobody backs us up, not the courts, not the politicians, not the assholes in the neighborhoods who call us as soon as one of them gets raped or stabbed or shot. Most of the time, not even our own fuckin' supervisors, even though we're the ones holding it all together. It's a different set of rules. All we got's ourselves and each other. There's good in the bad and bad in the good, and it gets real, real fuzzy sometimes, so you can't tell which is which. Sometimes a cop's got do something the outside world says is wrong so you can do what's right down the road."

"I thought you liked being a cop."

"Love it. Love it. Wouldn't want to do anything else. But for one thing, we don't get paid even half what we deserve. Us and teachers. Who gets the money? Lawyers." He spat.

Tracy said, "See, I kind of understand what you're saying, but we got a job to do, and..."

"Listen. I'm not gonna stand here and try to convince you of a goddamn thing. I'm just telling you what I've been living for fourteen years."

She said, "The guy giving you the money, he's got you by the balls. I mean, he could rat you out any time. You thought about that, right?"

The way Beck said "He knows better," gave her a glimpse of a side of him that she hadn't seen. She said, "Most cops who take get caught."

"Most guys get greedy. And sloppy."

"Sloppy? You mean like walking out of a side door and stuffing an envelope down your pants, like I saw you do?" He said nothing and she asked, "Anybody else know about it?"

"A lieutenant. He was like a mentor when I started. He introduced me to the guy you saw in the alley. The lieutenant retired right around the time I met you." Beck seemed to have unloaded a burden, and Tracy asked nothing more about it. Soon, they mounted their bikes and rode on.

In her eyes, he lost some of his luster after that, but despite her disappointment, they grew closer as time passed. Over the next eighteen months, they traveled to places she'd always wanted to visit—Paris, London, and the Bahamas. She wondered about the source of the money for the trips, which he paid for, but she enjoyed them too much to ask about or dwell on it.

Suddenly, after their last holiday, Beck was promoted to Detective, and within weeks, the district commander transferred him from Tracy's division to Narcotics, first with the tactical team, then to a citywide task force. No longer on the same shift, they spent much less time together; they missed each other, but clearly he enjoyed the constant raids, chases, and undercover buys and busts of his new assignment.

One late-summer Saturday afternoon soon after he'd been moved, they walked arm-in-arm through Georgetown, window shopping. Beck told Tracy that he needed a favor and asked her to get information from a hooker on her beat about the whereabouts of the girl's pimp. Just the way he asked made her think that it might be related to Beck's activities in the alley on Oregon, but she went along with it. The following Friday morning, she met him in a parked car outside a playground in northeast and gave him the information. He then handed her a newspaper with an envelope protruding from it. She asked, "Leon?"

Beck nodded. "Like I said, he's from down south. I usually don't deal with him directly. The time you saw him's only the third time I've met him. He's got a middle man, Jake."

"You give me all these details," Tracy said.

He shrugged and said, "Trust you, I guess."

She stared at the envelope for a long while and, without knowing why, took it. When she opened it in a McDonald's bathroom twenty minutes later, five one-hundred-dollar bills fell into her hand.

Fully-clothed, Tracy sat on the toilet seat, hunched over, and stared at the cash. After five years on the force, she still had her enthusiasm, but she'd become a bit more hardened and cynical, partly due to having seen too many judges free suspects for reasons that seemed to make no sense, when she—and the judges—*knew* that the suspect was guilty. Dealers, thieves rapists, child molesters, murderers. And she'd come to understand what Beck had said about cops having to operate in a system that had a much looser set of rules than those that governed the society at large. She knew that he continued to be an effective, widely-admired officer—and a man whom she loved more than she had any other—even though he took money.

Plus, like many members of the D.C. force, she didn't like the fact that policemen just outside the city made more than urban cops although they had a much easier job. Her younger sister, Kathy, and Tracy's niece, Dana, had asthma. Co-pays, deductibles, and a list of medicines had been squeezing Kathy's middle-class family for years despite insurance. Tracy helped when she could but sometimes felt frustrated because she couldn't do more. She slipped the money into her pocket.

Tracy and Beck slept together two mornings later. Afterward, while she lay with her head on his shoulder, he explained that because he was working citywide and occasionally needed information from her sector, he might have to rely on her for it once in a while.

"What kind of information?" she asked.

"Kind of thing you just helped me with," he said.

She remained silent for a while before saying, "I ain't ready to be taking cash in envelopes outside bars in Northeast, Brian."

"No one's asking you to. Just let me know what's happening once in a while. That's all."

She snuggled closer and said, "Let me think about it."

Just before three that afternoon, Beck's unit went to a small, detached, two-story house in southeast to serve a search warrant on a young, upper-level coke dealer named David Griffin, whom they'd had under surveillance for five months. Their witnesses and audio and visual evidence formed a strong case against Griffin, and, according to an informant, the house contained guns, boxes of cash, and tens of thousands of dollars worth of drugs.

The team's leader, up-and-coming young detective Cisco Bermudez, had already checked outside the building and seen no cameras, which many drug houses used nowadays. Four men, including Beck, went to the front entrance, knocked, announced their presence, and immediately rammed the heavy wooden door, trying to get in before Griffin could destroy or flush the goods; the fifth member, Brad Holland, stood guard outside the back yard. All five of them wore kevlar vests. The cops smashing the front door kept yelling "Police!" so Griffin wouldn't think they were robbers and open fire.

The third try knocked down the door. Bermudez and Beck rushed in with Glock semiautomatics drawn, followed by the two who broke the door, Fenton and Leeds. A burst of automatic weapon fire exploded toward them from the other end of a dim hallway that led to the back of the house. Fenton and Leeds slipped back outside. With no cover, Bermudez and Beck hit the floor and, heads down, fired blindly in the direction of the chattering weapon until it stopped and the rear door opened and slammed shut. A child was crying hysterically in a room a few feet away. Beck looked up and muttered, "Jesus Christ almighty." He and Bermudez were unhurt. Bullets had tattooed the wall behind them and taken out a front window and its curtains. The whole first floor smelled of cordite. Fenton and Leeds re-entered, and Bermudez made sure that no one had been hit. He told Leeds to radio it in.

Gunfire sounded from behind the house as the cops ran along the hallway from which the gunman had just left. In a bedroom on their right, a terrified eight-year-old boy leaned against a bed, shrieking, tears on his face, and his hands to his head; a TV screen showed cartoon robots flying in outer space. Bermudez pointed at Fenton: "You and Leeds search the place and take care of the kid."

He and Beck rushed to the back and out the door. Holland, the one who'd been outside watching the rear, was sprinting toward the street, pointing and yelling, "He went around the front of the house! He went around front!"

Bermudez and Beck ran back inside, along the hallway, and out through the front door. Griffin, a slim, light-skinned young black man in boots, khaki pants, no shirt, and a bulletproof vest, glanced back over his shoulder while running toward a green, window-tinted Xterra. He carried an Uzi. Before getting into the SUV, he spun and sprayed shots at his three pursuers, who again fell to their stomachs and lay still.

Griffin entered the vehicle, started it, and sped down the street. Bermudez and Beck ran to their black Explorer and Holland to an unmarked Taurus. Bermudez yelled to Holland, "Call in the pursuit!" and jumped behind the Explorer's steering wheel. Beck got in, and they took off after Griffin's accelerating XTerra. As Bermudez attached a flasher to the roof and turned on the siren, Beck thought about department policy against cops discharging their weapons in residential or commercial areas. And rules forbidding high-speed chases wouldn't allow them to follow for long. But they couldn't just let him go.

A hundred yards in front, Griffin's SUV hurtled through an intersection, down a narrow two-way road, and past a high school; Beck thanked God that school was out for summer. The Explorer shot through a yellow light. Up ahead, from a side street, a cruiser emerged, obviously alerted by Holland's call. It stopped sideways in the middle of the road, blocking the XTerra's path. Bermudez and Beck looked for Griffin to stop, but instead, he picked up speed. They could see what was about to happen. Beck said, "Oh no. Oh no," and braced himself, as if for impact. The XTerra rammed the squad car at over a hundred miles per hour, causing a "Crash!" heard half a mile away.

The police car spun like a helicopter's rotor. It flew about thirty feet, slammed into a parked car, and landed on its side, smoke rising from its undercarriage. Anybody inside had no chance. Griffin's vehicle crashed into a car parked across the street and stopped, its front obliterated. Bermudez and Beck's Explorer skidded to a halt twenty yards short of the XTerra. They drew their pistols and started to exit. Before they could, Griffin kicked his way out of the wrecked SUV. Blood poured from his nose. He coughed, took shaky aim with the Uzi, and fired wildly at the Explorer while staggering toward it along the middle of the road. The Explorer's windshield shattered as Bermudez and Beck ducked back inside. Bullets peppered the chassis and roof. Holland arrived in the Taurus and almost slid into the Explorer as he stopped. He opened his passenger door and shot twice at Griffin, who returned fire while fleeing across the street toward abandoned housing projects.

Eerie, ominous silence descended onto the scene. Covered in shattered glass, Bermudez and Beck raised their heads. Bermudez had cuts on his arm and neck. He got out of the vehicle, grabbed his radio, and yelled into it, "Ten-thirteen! Ten-thirteen! Needs assistance! At Barrow and Sperling! Ten-thirteen!" while sprinting toward the demolished squad car. Holland ran forward too, and they pulled the cruiser down so that it rested on four wheels. Beck got there as Bermudez and Holland tried to open the driver's door, which had been pushed to the passenger side. Wedged inside the wreck was a black, gray-haired veteran whom Beck had seen many times but didn't know. Glass fragments covered him like a blanket. The angle of his head meant a broken neck; blood had flowed from his ears, nose, and mouth onto his nametag, which said "Witherspoon." Beck thought, "Family man." Still gripping his handgun, he ran into the projects after Griffin.

The District owned Selwyn Homes, dozens of two and three-story brick buildings covering forty-four acres, which had fallen into disrepair and been vacated three years earlier. No one walked here. All doors had been chained shut, and they and the units' windows had been boarded over with green-painted wood, but vagrants determined to find shelter had pried open a few houses' entrances, which loomed as gateways into blackness.

Trees lined the area's sidewalks. Beck quietly called in his pursuit as he followed Griffin's thick splotches of blood through afternoon shadows. They led along four blocks and turned into a lot that had two houses on the right, two on the left, and a wide one straight ahead. The trail of blood continued past a waist-high pile of trash someone had dumped in the middle of the lot, and into the dark interior of a building on the far left, the door of which hung loosely from one hinge.

Sweat dripped into Beck's eye as he tiptoed to the door and stood beside it for a moment. He circled the building and saw no blood was on the ground, so Griffin was inside. With far off sirens wailing, he crouched beside the entrance. If he looked in through the doorway to see inside, he'd be offering a target to Griffin. There was nothing available for him to use as a mirror to help him see inside. He waited, then stuck his head out for an instant to peep into the darkness. Weak sunlight fell from some upstairs opening and a little more from the building's rear. He hesitated, then peeped again. This time, he thought something was in the gloom, a man maybe, laying face down on the floor. Griffin? The bastard had just been in two brutal collisions, plus Holland, the team's best shot, had fired at him. Had he been hit? Was that him there, wounded? Dead? But, it didn't quite look like him. The sirens got louder; help was on the way. But if that *wasn't* Griffin on the floor, then he could hear the sirens, too, and like a cornered tiger, would probably come running out of there at any second. And if he did, Beck's Glock, with few shots left, didn't stack up against a machine gun. He had to act.

Still low, Beck peered into the house and aimed with both hands at the object or person on the ground. The building's interior smelled of rot and mold. His eyes started to adjust to the faint light, but he still couldn't be sure of what or who it was on the ground, twelve feet from the entrance. He straightened and stepped forward. Yes, it was a person, but Griffin? He could hear that the sirens had arrived at the scene of the accident. Beck stepped completely inside the house and was about to look up and around when his radio crackled.

Suddenly, pain exploded across the back of his head, and he lost consciousness.

—

"...he was in there, but it wasn't him on the floor. That was a wino, passed out. But I couldn't see anything because of the darkness. I guess Griffin saw me coming. He ran out of bullets when he fired at us on the street. He was waiting when I stepped inside. He got me with a lead pipe. Sixteen stitches, a grade three concussion, and a small skull fracture. Plus, I got this from the fall." He touched an ugly bruise near his bloodshot left eye. "They say they've got to keep me under observation for a couple days. First time I've gotten hurt. I hear a lot of guys say they go their whole careers without pulling their guns. Seems like I'm pulling mine every other week. Anyway, we got him, though, soon as he left the building. He broke his nose and got internal injuries in the accident. Bleeding all over the place. The wino slept through the whole thing."

It was a few minutes past eleven that same night, and Beck was sitting up in bed on St. Peter's Hospital's ninth floor, the back of his head shaved, stitched, and bandaged, talking to Tracy, who was standing beside the cot with her hand on his. Having answered the questions asked by investigators and supervisors, he'd asked her to leave the recessed fluorescent bulbs overhead turned off to spare his eyes; a faint glow entered the room from outside through parted curtains that showed the 11th Street Bridge's lights in the distance and those of the Navy Yards and their four piers. Visiting hours had passed, but her uniform, plus his request to a nurse, had gained her entrance to his room.

"It's gonna be a couple minutes before anybody sees him again," she said.

"Who, the wino?"

"No," she said, laughing, "the kid, Griffin."

"Yeah," he said, "but as far as the dead cop's concerned, it'll have to be a manslaughter charge, not murder. A murder charge wouldn't stick."

"Lieutenant Mervin Witherspoon," she said. "That was his name. He transferred from northwest a couple months ago. Wife and two kids. They say you couldn't get him off the streets. He was old-fashioned, never missed work."

They went quiet. After a while, he beckoned her closer and whispered: "Trace, I need a favor. I got a manila envelope in a briefcase in the closet near the dresser. I need for you to get it to a guy for me tomorrow morning."

She looked at him and asked, "The bar on Oregon Street?"

"The guy from there, Jake. But you'd meet him someplace else. You'd meet him in a restaurant called Eden in Alexandria. Know it?"

"I could find it."

"It's a small place, like a cafe. He'll be wearing a gray shirt, jeans, and a blue baseball cap. You just walk in, you don't have to buy nothing. Walk past the counter, make a left, there's a bunch of pictures on the wall, next to a pay phone before you get to the bathrooms. Stand near the phone. It's not crowded during the mornings. Just stand there for a second. He'll walk up to you. You give him an envelope, he'll give you one, you put it in your bag, get in your car, go home." He interpreted her silence as acceptance and whispered, "Be there at ten. There's a pre-paid cell phone in the briefcase at the house, just in case. His number's programmed in. But if you need to use it, watch what you say. Keep what's in the envelope he gives you."

The next day, Tracy arrived outside the Eden restaurant ten minutes early and sat, parked up the street. Within three minutes, the man in the gray shirt and blue Padres baseball cap walked past her car carrying a small gym bag and entered the corner restaurant. At ten, she went inside. Jake was sitting with his back turned, alone in a booth by a window, sipping coffee and reading a newspaper. She went past him, turned left at the end of the counter, and stood between the pay phone and the bathrooms.

She thought for a moment that if someone wanted to set her up, this would be perfect: here she was, waiting for somebody she didn't know to give her money for an envelope she was holding that contained God knows what. But Jake approached within seconds, and everything went exactly as Beck had said.

The envelope Jake gave her contained fourteen fifty dollar bills.

But that was only the beginning. Three months after Beck resumed his duties, he was recruited into the newly-formed Narcotics Probe Task Force, a team of eight detectives from across the city charged with investigating the highest level drug cases. Tracy, lured by the simplicity of making at least an extra fifteen thousand dollars a year by swapping envelopes with someone once or twice a month, gradually took his place as Leon's contact in the department. She kept giving most of the money to her asthmatic sister, whose gratitude touched her. And when Jake mentioned that Tommy, Leon's son, was taking over from his dad for a while but everything would stay the same, she okayed it after having discussed it with Beck.

So, Tracy found herself here, now, a year later, drowsy from lack of sleep, pulling into the driveway of the house she shared with Beck, who was probably snoring inside, dialing Tommy's number on a prepaid phone. He answered on the third ring and said, "We need to talk."

She replied with closed eyes: "Yeah, you already said that on your message. What's goin' on?"

"You're not working now, right? Where's a good place? I don't know D.C."

"It's gonna have to wait. How about tomorrow?"

He sounded impatient, almost manic: "Listen, I'll be there in about...thirty-five minutes. I'm in Baltimore. I'll be right there."

Tracy shook her head. "I can't make it tonight. Tomorrow morning. Early."

After a long pause, he said, "Okay. Where?"

She thought for a few seconds and said, "Wellstone Cemetery. It's in northern Virginia. There's an entrance on Aldridge Lane. If you follow the path in from there, there's a big tree a couple hundred yards in. Say, nine o' clock?"

Sounding disappointed, Tommy said, "All right," and clicked off.

———

Earlier, as Tommy had slept in his rental car outside Mount Witley Park, soon to be awoken by Edgar's phone call; and as Nick Rowe sat parked outside Harry Wade's apartment, waiting for darkness; and as a sleepy Tracy Whitlock cruised northeast D.C.'s streets alone in her squad car, Simone, still wound up from her day at work, used her key to enter Freeman's house. Freeman was sitting in a living-room armchair, shirtless, his feet up, watching old, Bob Marley concert footage. He turned his head toward her and said, "Hey." An empty plate and two empty beer bottles were on a small table beside his chair. When she stood in front of him, he got up and caressed her hips. Her arms went around his neck, and they kissed deeply; she felt him getting aroused. She leaned her head back and asked about Chicago. He started to tell her about meeting Vaughan Chandler but then he remembered something and asked, "Were you here late yesterday? This morning?"

"Why you asking, Freeman?"

They still had their arms around each other, but her face now looked quizzical. He said, "I got here an hour ago, and that chair was on the floor. I know I didn't put it there."

Simone thought about the chair she'd kicked over when she left after looking for the package a few hours ago. She hadn't wanted to say anything about having been there, but she'd decided to tell him about Hassan's chemical test and to ask indirectly to see whether or not Freeman might be interested in Henry as a possible buyer. She stepped back, out of the embrace and replaced his hands on her hips with her own. "I was here today, looking for it. The package you found."

He frowned. "Why? What you talking about?"

"I know a guy who can test it and tell exactly what it is or isn't. I know two guys."

"You spoke to them about it?" he asked.

"Just in a general way. I didn't mention you, or anything like that."

Freeman rarely got angry, but when he did, it showed, and people got out of his way because of his size. It showed now. He said, "You and your fuckin' guys. I told you. This is *my* deal. *I'm* the one with everything to lose. We talked about it the other night. *I'm* making the goddamn decisions now, not you. Shit. Why can't you respect that?"

Surprised, she replied, "It's not about respect, it's..."

"What you mean it's not about respect? The bag we're talking about belongs to me, right? That means it's my goddamn property, right? It's not yours. *I* make the decisions."

"I did it for you," she said. "I was trying to help."

"Bull*shit*! You just want to do everything *your* way and fuck everything else. All you're doing is drawing attention to yourself!" He paced to the other end of the room, to the small vestibule, and to the front door, where he looked out of a narrow window for a few moments before returning to stand in front of her. "This ain't no joke, Simone. This for real. See how you're runnin' your mouth? That's how people get caught!" He lowered his voice. "This a double murder. Police knock on that goddamn door right now, what you gonna tell 'em, huh? Nothin'. You just gonna point at me with both hands, get in your car, and drive home. You got money to give me for a lawyer? Two lawyers? Three? That's what I'd need to get me out of this."

He looked down and shook his head before continuing. "I never should've trusted you. I figured you had my back, whatever decision I made. But you gotta go and do what *you* wanna do. It's like, fuck what I say. Always gotta be all about you."

Simone usually controlled the situation between them. After the day she'd had, Freeman's outburst made something inside her snap: "What you getting all pissed off about? Nobody knows shit about you. You're acting like I'm telling people your name."

"It's not about does anybody know anything about me. It's about you not respecting my goddamn decisions!"

Simone folded her arms, and her head bobbed up and down as she spoke. "Mr. Large-and-in-charge, huh? All of a sudden, Mr. Large-and-in-charge. Where the fuck was Mr. Large-and-in-charge on any other decision we've made together, huh?"

"I ask for your opinion. I let you do what you want most of the time because that's just the way you are."

"Yeah, right. It just seems like most of the time, I'm the one calling the shots. You told me about finding your little bag in the alley, I felt like I had to do something, for your sake. Be honest with you, far as I'm concerned, you don't know what the fuck you're doing. You're putting all your eggs in that one basket—the guy in your band. You said yourself he's not reliable. I'm giving you options, tryin' to help, but all of a sudden, you wanna be the boss."

He took a step toward her and pointed. "It ain't about bein' the boss. I said, 'Let me do it my way.' That's what this situation calls for. At least now I know. Never did trust you any fuckin' way. That's why I hid it. You didn't find what you were lookin' for today, right?"

Simone said, "It's like that, huh? You think you're rich now, and all of a sudden you can't trust me? Fine!" She walked to the front door and opened it. As she stepped out, she turned back toward him and said, "You're a dumb ass, Freeman. Watch. You're gonna fuck it all up." She walked to her car, got in, and started it. Freeman followed her outside and yelled, "You no good! You know you aint no good! You rotten! You..."

Driving away, she glimpsed him out of the corner of her eye: dreadlocks down to his chest, shirtless and barefoot, shouting, his hands cupped around his mouth. She heard his voice but couldn't make out the words. As Simone turned the corner and drove south, she tried, and failed, to remember the last time they'd had an argument this bad. What did this mean for the relationship? She wondered for a moment, but realized that right now, she didn't care.

A few minutes later, she reached for her cell and called Henry Ramos. When he answered, she asked, "Feel like company?" He gave her directions to the Van Nostrand Hotel in southwest D.C., and said he'd meet her there around 10:30, meaning that she had a little time to kill. Simone wanted Henry tonight. She drove home, showered, and changed into an outfit that she thought he liked—black jeans and black and white shoulderless top, both tight, and black shoes.

She got to the Van Nostrand a few minutes early and was sitting in the lobby skimming through a newspaper when he entered. Desire flashed through his eyes instantly. They started to make love on the elevator.

CHAPTER SEVEN

FOURTEEN CARRYING NINE

F.B.I. Special Agent Hazel Royce lived alone in a duplex in a gated community in Silver Spring, Maryland, just north of Washington. She'd been waking early all week, and on Wednesday, she got up at 5:00, half an hour before usual and three hours before she was due at work at F.B.I. Headquarters. She dressed, grabbed her swimming gear, and drove fifteen minutes to a nearby gym that had an indoor pool and stayed open twenty hours per day. She tried to go every other weekday because as the earliest arrival, she found doing laps by herself relaxed her mind even more than it did her body.

She changed in the locker room and walked to the not-too-brightly-lit pool, which had jazz playing at a barely audible volume. She dove into the water, but, after a few minutes, her mind wandered to the assignment that had been consuming most of her time for over a month: her role in the government's investigation of Solstice International.

The Securities and Exchange Commission had found that Solstice, which had hundreds of outlets nationally, had been regularly overstating its earnings by tens of millions of dollars for years, a practice that, among other things, had inflated stockholders' dividends and provided upper management with lifetime financial security. Dozens of employees in the firm's accounting division appeared criminally liable, but wading through just some of an ocean of documents was proving to be a formidable task.

As she swam leisurely, she forced out thoughts of Solstice but then found herself wondering about what had happened yesterday regarding the house on Edgemere and her search for Henry Ramos. Something about that still nagged her. Had that been him in Virginia? If so, he might be anywhere, using any name. All she had was a list of nine possible aliases, all of them common.

But Royce hated unfinished business, so she decided that as soon as she got a chance today, she'd run a list of his "aka's" to see if anything came up locally. She had almost no chance of turning up anything because if Ramos had intended to stay in the Washington-Virginia area, he'd probably have remained at the house on Edgemere. But Royce's approach toward her duties was that no matter what the result, she wanted to know that she'd done everything that she could. If she failed, no one could ever say that it had been because of a lack of trying.

She pulled herself out of the pool and sat on the side, gripping the edge and kicking her toes in the water, to take a breather. She thought about another aspect of the previous day's work, her meeting with Alex Kirby. She'd thought about him last night, too—good-looking, professional (well, in a way), polite, nice smile...There were a couple of guys with whom she went out occasionally, but neither one excited her; she hadn't spoken to either in weeks. Kirby was attractive, and he seemed interested, but she'd told him the truth: right now, she had too much work on her hands. Still, she found herself thinking again about his invitation to the concert on Friday...

She stood and dove back in.

—

Tracy woke as Beck got out of bed at 7:03. She lay there in the dimness, listening to him enter the bathroom and turn on the shower. When he came back into the bedroom to dress, she said that she needed more facts about the car that had been found in the alley in northwest early on Sunday morning, the Plymouth that had a dead guy inside and another outside. As a member of an elite, citywide task force, he had access to a ton of information, and he told her what he'd learned after she'd made her request to him about the car yesterday afternoon. Tracy jotted down a couple of things that he mentioned on a pad near the nightstand. Once he finished talking, she reached for him, and they started to fool around, but he had to be in downtown D.C. by eight and couldn't spare time.

Tracy heard the door close and Beck drive away. She was still sleepy, but if she stayed in bed, she'd probably miss her meeting with Leon's son, Tommy DeShields. So she got up, put on a t-shirt and sweatpants, and went outside for a walk.

A gloomy sky signaled an end to the area's three-week unbroken string of sunny days. Having lived here for over four years, she knew the streets and enjoyed her walks around the quiet, picturesque, recently-developed community. This morning, she said hi to a well-dressed black couple leaving for work, briefcases in hand, and waved to an elderly man in a bathrobe, picking up a newspaper. Then, she did something rare for her; for some reason, despite needing more sleep, she ran.

—

First thing in the morning, Tommy arranged for an extension on his car rental. He arrived outside Wellstone Cemetery in Virginia twenty-five minutes early and took a good look around. He knew nothing about this area and had met Tracy Whitlock only once; the way he saw it, he could be walking into anything. He'd spent the night at a motel along Route 3, and an 8:00 wake up call had gotten him out of bed. At 8:49, having looked around thoroughly, he parked a hundred yards up Aldridge Lane and waited for five minutes; then, under a threatening sky, he walked past a sign prohibiting visitors after 5:00 p.m. and through the large cemetery's iron gates.

No one else was there. The oak that she'd mentioned, its trunk at least ten feet around, loomed up ahead on his right, along the broad winding path that had no end in sight. Scores of small dark birds flew as one from near the tree as Tommy walked toward it. They dipped and soared over his head, and he thought about how this and all cemeteries had a strangely peaceful atmosphere, each unique but each the same.

While waiting under the tree, Tommy wondered about his dad, Leon, who was bedridden in Georgia. A year ago, the last time Tommy had seen him, he'd appeared the same as usual—shrewd, alert, with a sly sense of humor—but as this year had started, right around the time Tommy's nephew, Anthony, had been murdered in Miami, Leon came down very sick. Relatives said AIDS. Tommy knew that Leon had used heroin as well as sold it, but he didn't think his father would be reckless enough to share a needle with anyone...

His thoughts shifted to his cousin, Vonetta, in Florida, still almost paralyzed by grief and wanting Tommy to do something about the boy who'd walked free after killing her son. When it had happened, Tommy would get angry whenever he pictured the boy standing over Anthony and firing into his fallen body. Time had passed, but enough bitterness remained for him to understand her continuing anguish. Reflecting on it now, it seemed right to do *something*; he just didn't know what.

Tommy lit a cigarette. He checked his watch: nine on the dot. This part of the cemetery contained dozens of ornate crosses and tall majestic angels, cast in stone and bleached white by decades of sun and rain, that watched over the dead. As he'd done several times recently, he thought about his mother, Rosita, and the way she'd died, killed in her kitchen by men seeking revenge on Tommy's dad, murdered in a way to make her husband suffer. Maybe Tommy was thinking about that more nowadays as he tried to look inward, seeking answers to his growing problems with his responses to things and sleep patterns and appetite and depression...

A burgundy SUV turned into the cemetery and crawled along the path that he'd just walked. It stopped thirty feet away, and Tracy Whitlock got out wearing a blue t-shirt and jeans, her eyes shifting in all directions. Seeing her for the second time, Tommy again noticed her shortness. The cop came to stand in front of him with her hands in her pockets and asked, "What's going on?"

Tommy looked around the cemetery again. He took a deep drag on his cigarette and blew twin streams of smoke from his nostrils before replying: "I got to find what happened to something I had in that car."

"They're checking the vehicle. First off, it's registered to an old woman who died six years..."

"Yeah, yeah, I know about the car. Tell me about Saturday night, when they found it."

Tracy shrugged. "You got an official version and an unofficial one."

"Give me the unofficial."

"Two small-time New York hustlers driving through town at one in the morning with something hidden in a spare tire under the trunk. A white guy and a black guy. They use a knife and a .22 to kill each other in a parking lot connected to an alley. Both weapons right there at the scene. Whatever you had in the trunk, it looks like the black guy took it. But it wasn't there when cops arrived."

"Right there, that don't sound right," Tommy said, frowning. From what Nick Rowe had said, Wade was supposed to have been driving by himself. He asked, "First off, who was the black guy?"

Tracy took a piece of yellow paper from her pocket and read what Beck had told her a couple of hours ago: "I got Floyd Stubbs, fifty-four, lived in Harlem, in and out of prison in New York doing short stretches since '74—burglary, statutory rape, extortion, arson, aggravated assault, possession of stolen goods."

Tommy said, "Sounds like one of your boys in blue showed up, one of the first ones who got there, found the bag, and took it."

Tracy didn't blink. "Nah. A scene like that, you got other cops all over the place, you got people gawkin' out their windows. You think about what happens if you get caught..."

"Them boys do any goddamn thing. You know how you all work. Shit. Look at you. Look what you doin.' " Tommy exhaled another long line of smoke and asked, "What's the official story?"

"Carjacking. The brother got shot trying to steal the white guy's car. When a perpetrator dies in commission of a crime, the case is closed as 'abated by death.' That's what this is. The car's in the lab. It's gonna be there for a couple weeks."

"So the case is closed."

"Um hm. It's too much goin' on down here. We got gangs comin' in from all over the country. Right now, it looks like they're comin' from all over the world. Whatever happened to your two friends in that car, we ain't got time. Nobody gives a shit about 'em, anyway. Just you."

Tommy dropped his cigarette butt, stepped on it, and asked, "So all this goin' on and nobody saw nothin'?"

"A couple people heard the shot and the car horn go off right after, so we pretty much got the exact time," Tracy said. "And somebody *did* see something."

"Who? Saw what?"

"A little girl, lives right there. The shot woke her. A couple minutes later, she looks out the window and sees a big black guy with long dreadlocks. She's seen him around there before. He looks right at her and smiles. She says he went into the alley carrying a paper bag, then came running right out. She says he might live around there, a few blocks up."

Tommy shifted his feet. "Talk to her. Find out about the guy with the dreadlocks."

Tracy said, "It's not that easy. That's not my turf, out that way. I mean, I know people work that precinct, but..."

Tommy said, "Just see what you could find out about him." He stared off into space for a long time, thinking; he stood there for so long that Tracy began to wonder if something had happened to him. Then, he said, "I need to know about the other guy in the car Saturday night, the black guy. You got his address?"

"Workin' on it."

Tommy said, "Look, you doin' all right. Don't worry, Jake take care of you next time he see you, hear?"

Tracy nodded again and walked away. Tommy watched her get into her Wrangler and back out of the cemetery. Once she'd gone, he flipped open his cell, dialed Edgar, and said, "Yo."

"What's up."

"You still in Brooklyn, right?"

Edgar answered, "Yeah. I'm still by my cousin. I didn't hear nothin' from you, so I was getting ready to head back. You know I got to be to work tomorrow."

"Sit tight. I might need you to do something real soon."

"All right," Edgar said.

Tommy clicked off. For almost a minute, he stood under the oak tree, his mind racing, in the cemetery's silent tranquility. He started to dial home but remembered that Gabrielle would probably not be awake yet, and stopped. He put the phone into his pocket and walked to the rental car.

—

As usual, Simone woke before Henry. She felt hungry. She lay still for a few minutes, then went to the hotel window and looked out at a mostly full parking lot, a large field, and trees that led off into the distance. She thought about last night's argument with Freeman and felt that something had changed between them. Usually, she'd have more say in their arguments, and she was still surprised by how forcefully he'd expressed himself. She attributed his assertiveness to fear—fear of going to jail—and she understood. She went to the bathroom, brushed her teeth, and splashed cold water on her face. Unexpectedly, Henry appeared in the mirror and stood behind her. Simone smiled as he put his arms around her waist and kissed her neck. She turned her head and kissed back. She felt him get aroused and responded as he locked his hands together while kissing her face, ear, and hair. Their passion heated the room. Holding her tightly, he did it to her right there, facing the mirrored cabinet above the sink, while she moaned with pleasure.

As they showered together afterward, preparing to go out for breakfast, he asked, "So have you talked to him yet, your boyfriend?"

"No, not yet."

"I'm ready, Simone. If I make a deal with him, you get something. You helped make it happen."

Simone said, "Oh yeah? What do I get?"

"It depends. I have to see what he has and what he wants to do. Right now, neither of you even knows what's in the bag. You're just assuming."

"No, I'm pretty sure what it is. When it's tested, you'll see."

Henry smiled and said, "Right, it's heroin. What makes you so sure?"

On the way to the hotel last night, even though Freeman had pissed her off, Simone had decided not to tell Henry everything about the green package, to say some things but to hold some of it back. This morning, she felt more hurt than angry. Still, she replied to Henry's question by basically repeating the details that Freeman had told her about the two bloody corpses in the alley. She also told him about smelling and tasting the powder while in Freeman's kitchen.

"So he's got it there in the house?" Henry asked as she turned off the shower.

"I don't know. I looked. I guess it's there. I don't know."

They stepped out of the tub and onto a thick white rug on the floor. Henry reached for a towel and wiped her shoulders and breasts. "Where does he live?"

"D.C."

"What part?"

Simone turned her head and looked at him. "Why?"

"I'm just asking. I want to talk to the guy, but you're my contact. If you won't set it up, I'll do it."

"All right," she replied, "I'll handle it. Just don't worry about where he lives."

He shrugged and said, "Okay, okay. But you sound as if you two had an argument. Was it about this?"

"Henry, don't worry about it. Let me take care of things."

She sounded defensive—defensive and protective. He started drying her upper back and thought, "That's fine."

—

A sound sleeper, Gabrielle almost always switched off her cell and her home phone before turning in. But, because she was so preoccupied, she'd forgotten to do so after getting in from the club early this morning. Alicia Keys' *Fallin'* on her cell's ringtone woke her. It was Trish, asking if she could stop by for a few minutes.

Not fully awake, Gabrielle's voice dragged as she asked, "You remember how to get here? I'm in fourteen east."

Trish said, "Gimme about ...forty-five minutes." They clicked off, and Gabrielle wondered what Trish wanted to talk about. She felt a bit weird about her coming to Gabrielle's place after what had happened between them a couple of days ago, but she shrugged her shoulders and got out of bed to go to the kitchen. Before she reached it, the phone rang again: Tommy.

"You still in New York?" she asked.

"D.C."

"How long you gonna be up there?"

"I don't know, I got some business. Probably be back by—what's today?"

"Today's Wednesday, Tommy. Yesterday was Tuesday. You okay?"

"Told you, I'm tired. That's it."

"And stressed out," Gabrielle said."

"Part of doin' business. You know that."

"You just don't sound right," she said.

Tommy said, "You all bent out of shape worryin' 'bout me. I'm cool. I'm wonderin' about you. How *you* doin?"

"It ain't easy, sometimes, Tommy. I mean, I don't know where you been, what you been doin,' who you been doin' it with…a situation like that, the phone rings, it's almost like I'm scared to answer. I mean, when am I gonna see you again?"

Gabrielle's tone made him uneasy; he tried to switch the subject: "Nah, that ain't your problem. Something been stressin' you, big time. Something heavy going on you don't wanna talk about."

Gabrielle started to hint that she had something important to say, but this wasn't the time to mention anything related to the daughter she'd given up for adoption. She said, "Nothin' else happening, Tommy. I just want to see you so we can work off some of that business stress you carrying around."

She heard the smile in his voice when he said, "That's sounding good to me. Look, I be back next couple days. I'm gonna holla at you tommorrow."

"Love you, Tommy."

"Love you, too."

She hung up and went to the kitchen. While fixing breakfast, her thoughts went to the subject that had preoccupied her in recent days, her daughter. She wondered whether or not Jasmin's childhood had been anything like hers…

…Growing up working-class with two older brothers, a mother, and a stepfather in Tampa, Gabrielle frequently had a hard time getting words out. Once she got going, she was fine, but she often struggled with those first ones, sometimes getting a heavy facial twitch when trying to talk. Kids teased her, but that didn't stop her from trying to express herself, in class or anywhere else. She developed a serious look that caused grown ups to utter the same refrain every few weeks: "You so pretty—why you look so mean?" "You so pretty—why you look so mean?" She got tired of it; she got along fine with her siblings and friends, and she didn't *feel* mean, so after a while, she'd respond to the question by shrugging her shoulders or just ignoring it. Her speech impediment faded as she reached adolescence, but the stubbornness that had made her insist on speaking up no matter how other kids mocked her began to cause problems with her stepfather and, especially, her mother. As the youngest of three, Gabrielle thought that her parents were too strict; they didn't let her do things her friends could do—go to the playground by themselves sometimes, watch movies on the Lifetime channel, wear earrings and dress the way they wanted—so she couldn't wait until she could make her own decisions.

That desire for independence made her move out as soon as she turned sixteen. Making it on her own hadn't been easy, but beneath her sensitivity, she developed strength and the confidence to overcome obstacles. At first, she wondered whether or not she'd left home too soon, but overall she'd had no regrets. At least not until now…

Gabrielle ate cereal and toast, and checked the time; Trish had said she'd be there any minute.

—

As usual, Special Agent Hazel Royce had to deal with heavy traffic on her way in to work at the Hoover Building. She called a colleague in the computer center in the basement, and said that she wanted a regional search on ten names for yesterday afternoon, highlighting airports and train stations. When she added that she wanted it done quickly, the colleague said that she was busy with three other assignments but would get the information as soon as possible. Royce read off Henry Ramos' known aliases. She then clicked off and continued her commute, thinking that she'd leave work around four this evening to visit a friend in a nearby hospital.

—

Passengers crowded the train that Freeman took to work, so he had to stand. He was still fuming at Simone, whom he trusted less now than ever. Chandler was supposed to contact him in five days, but Freeman didn't want to wait that long, not with that stuff in his basement. Earlier this morning, he'd thought about moving it someplace, but where? Plus, he didn't like the idea of carrying a million bucks worth of drugs through Washington's streets.

This whole situation was starting to get to him. Probably, the best thing would be just to flush the bag's contents down the toilet; within ten seconds, he'd be free of a major headache. But he still heard Simone's comment as she'd left last night: "You're a dumb ass, Freeman. Watch. You're gonna fuck it all up." He knew that he should ignore her and focus on doing what was best, but, after being reluctant to admit it at first, he recognized that her words had stung, and that he wanted to prove her wrong.

Freeman felt himself drifting into dangerous waters. He had no weapons. He'd thought about paying someone for protection; he knew a guy who'd do it, a couple of guys. He didn't know anything about this person Chandler was talking about as a buyer, and Freeman was going to have to deal with him—and maybe others like him—directly. Plus, Simone could be spiteful, and he didn't put anything past her in terms of what she'd say, who she'd talk to, or what she'd do. He didn't think she'd do anything *too* crazy, but, as he heard people say, stranger things had happened.

Although he knew that he shouldn't, he took Simone's words as a challenge that compelled him to handle it alone just to prove that he could. He had no idea what to do next, but, despite increasing unease about holding a million dollars worth of heroin, as he jostled his way off the train at Rhode Island Avenue, he decided that even though he had no idea where this was leading, he was going to play it out to the end.

———

Tommy lay awake on the bed in his motel room, staring at the wall, his hands folded behind his head, wearing only boxers. The curtains were drawn. He'd been there waiting for over an hour since leaving the cemetery and stopping at IHop for breakfast. Despite weariness, he'd been unable to sleep; his thoughts revolved around his predicament. Maybe this was what he got for giving in to temptation and getting involved in the drug game in the first place. He'd had his doubts, but his dad had convinced him that heroin's big time profits were just sitting there for the taking. "You aint got to do it thirty-five years, like me," Leon had said in his raspy, high-pitched voice, "but I seen plenty dudes get in, make their money, and walk away. Plenty dudes.

I'm talking millions. And you young, too. Set it up right with the right people, you can't lose. Old timers used to say it: 'You in like Flynn.' I'm tellin' you. I got the people."

Tommy bit. His first two shipments had been small, but they'd gone perfectly; he'd had the product in hand within seven days. This one had too, until—until what? He closed his eyes and decided to think about something else. His mind drifted back to a night when he was seventeen, a night soon after he'd been released from a year-and-a-half stretch at the Theodore R. Dorsey Home for Boys near Hallendale...

With Tommy's dad in federal prison, Tommy had been staying in Miami with his seventy-three-year-old grandmother Alice, who doted on him but exercised little control. He hung with a group of boys that included Brandon, the heavyset bruiser who'd join him five years later in a string of robberies, thefts, and hijackings across the state as members of "the A Team."

Now, Tommy and his friends drank, partied, smoked, chased girls, and tempted fate. This steamy night, they were in an unfinished basement rolling dice, smoking blunts and passing a bottle of wine, when the lights went out. After cursing and picking up their money, they went upstairs. Darkness filled the whole house. Tommy went outside, where all lights—house lights, street lamps, traffic lights—were out. It looked as if that entire part of the city, maybe all of Miami, had lost electricity. With everything in vague silhouette, they headed downtown, whooping and clowning around, with the only light coming from headlamps on occasional passing cars. On the way, they heard someone mention that a power failure had hit most of the city.

Near downtown, they came across a gang of young men who were using rocks, sticks, and garbage cans to try to break an electronics store's plexiglass window. Tommy's crew joined them. At one point, a police car arrived, but it backed off under a hail of bricks and bottles from the profanity-spewing mob.

Finally, the glass broke; the crowd flooded in and scrambled feverishly for CD players, Ipods, TVs, boomboxes, DVD players, and whatever else they could carry. Careful to avoid the jagged glass, Tommy climbed in through the broken window, unaware that, except for Brandon, he'd never see his friends again. He stood in almost complete darkness amid a store full of shadows colliding with, and stepping on, each other in a frenzied dance of chaos and greed. A couple of the men who exited the storefront carrying loot immediately got robbed of what they'd just stolen.

Bumped from all sides, Tommy started to move further in to see what he could find. He groped around low on a side shelf and found a large boombox attached to a rail by a thick cord, which he tugged at and loosened but couldn't break. He pulled again and got the same result. He planted the soles of his feet against the wall and pulled with all his strength; the cord broke.

As he reached down for the boombox, harsh light filled the place. Shading his eyes with his hand, he squinted and turned to the front. A police car and a police van had arrived, blocked the front window, and turned on their lights. Six cops with shields, helmets, flashlights, and guns entered and told everyone to stand still; two more remained outside. Tommy was standing near a counter, and he ducked behind and under it. He heard the cops take control. They told everyone to put their hands up against the walls and spread their legs. After a couple of minutes, they ordered their captives to leave the store, single file. Still crouching beneath a counter, Tommy found a big cardboard box. It didn't cover him completely, but he turned it upside down and hid in it under the counter, listening to the looters shuffling out through debris that covered the floor.

Tommy heard the cops line everyone up outside and order them into the van. Sweat-soaked, he remained in the wrecked store, curled up inside the box, waiting for the cops and robbers to leave. A vehicle arrived, probably another van, and the rest of his fellow thieves were shipped out. Tommy's lower back was hurting, but he figured he'd soon be able to get up and walk away.

Suddenly, he heard someone's heavy footsteps enter the store leisurely and start to walk around. Tommy thought it might be a cop but could only guess. Whoever it was would take several strides, stop, wait, then take several more. The man walked around the other side of the store. Tommy wanted to run, but that would be risky: although he thought that partitions might divide the interior into sections, darkness had limited his vision, so he didn't know whether or not anything stood between him and whoever was walking around, a man Tommy assumed was armed. For some reason, he started imagining that it was the store's owner.

It sounded as if the cops had left. Tommy wasn't sure, but after a while, the "Clok...clok...clok...clok..." seemed to be moving toward him. It stopped for a few seconds and resumed, slowly. Yes, the steps were in Tommy's direction.

Tommy's nervousness increased. He listened intently: "Clok... clok...clok...clok ...clok…" The person stopped just a few feet away on the other side of the counter and stood still for a long while. Tommy held his breath. He counted as the man took five steps and stopped, two feet away. Sweat ran from Tommy's brow onto the floor; his back and knees were killing him, but he ignored them. The man continued to the counter's far end, turned around it, and walked at the same pace toward Tommy's large, overturned box.

Tommy knew that it didn't cover him completely. He hoped that the man would walk past but knew that he wouldn't. He decided what he'd do if he were about to get caught. The footsteps stopped right beside him. The store remained silent for several moments before a man spoke in a low voice: "Knew you were in here somewhere."

Tommy leaped from under the box. He lunged for chest level, reaching for the firearm he assumed to be there. He couldn't see the man grappling with him, but he grabbed a rifle barrel as the two of them fell to the floor. The man was huge. They rolled around for a while, with neither letting go of the weapon, but Tommy's much bigger opponent wound up sitting on his chest.

That landed Tommy back in the Dorsey Home, where he did four-and-a-half of a six year stretch for several charges, including burglary, trespass, assault on a peace officer...The judge took it easy on him due to the way that his mother had died, and his father's background.

Now, laying on the motel bed, after reliving that painful memory, Tommy groaned and started to drift into sleep until his cell phone rang. Disoriented, he sat upright and answered on the fourth ring. It was Tracy Whitlock. She gave Stubbs's address on 121st Street in Harlem.

"You get anything from the girl about the guy in the alley, the guy with the dreads?" Tommy asked, rubbing his eyes.

"Not yet. Like I said, that might take some time."

"Okay." Tommy clicked off. When Whitlock had told him the details about Saturday night, it sounded like Stubbs had come along for the ride for some reason and tried a ripoff. From what Nick Rowe had said, Wade, the guy who was supposed to be driving, had been a loner, so Tommy couldn't figure why Stubbs would be there in the first place. And he wondered if Stubbs might have brought someone else; if he had meant to take the goods, that would make sense. Anyway, maybe Edgar could find out whether or not Stubbs had been alone when he went to meet Wade on Saturday night. It wasn't much, but Tommy had nothing else.

He'd thought about calling Nick Rowe and asking him to do it. Rowe knew Harlem; he lived there, and Tommy wouldn't be surprised if he knew, or at least knew of, Juney Stubbs. Plus, Edgar had a habit of getting into shit...But Rowe would be at work, and every second counted. Tommy called Edgar and told him to go up to Harlem and ask around about Stubbs, especially his movements on Saturday evening.

Edgar said, "Yo Tommy, New York ain't for me, man. It's always some crazy shit up here. I don't know this nigga. Don't know nothing about him. Don't know who is, who he hang with, where he be at... How I look goin' up there..."

"Listen," Tommy interrupted, "I ain't askin' all that. I need to know if he was hangin with anybody early Saturday evening, that's all. If you can't find nothin,' cool. I'm just sayin,' seein how you right there..." He paused, then said, "Look, if you want to do it and you find out something, holla back."

After Tommy clicked off, he sat on the side of the bed, elbows on knees. Whitlock's call had caused an electric-like current of anxiety to surge through him. He figured Edgar would go to Harlem. Maybe he'd learn something about Stubbs' activities on Saturday; maybe he wouldn't.

But Tommy was looking forward to Tracy Whitlock's next call, the one that would tell him about the dreadlocked guy who'd run out of the alley. Anticipation had him feeling antsy, but he was still drowsy, too. He lit a cigarette that he smoked halfway through before putting it out because he found himself starting to doze. He dreamed, briefly: *outside at night...he's damp from head to toe...dogs start barking at him from all directions ...a man dressed in white, with a white broad-brimmed*

alone at 11:47 when the phone near the cash register rang. Standing

hat, approaching, his head lowered...street lights go out unexpectedly...
fear...a nearby explosion in front of him in the darkness...
He woke suddenly with his heart pounding.

—

Freeman had arrived at the CD store where he worked twenty minutes before opening. Lynnette, the manager, should have shown up at 11:00, but she hadn't, which was odd. So, apart from two customers, Freeman was alone at 11:47 when the phone near the cash register rang. Standing behind the counter, he answered and recognized Vaughan Chandler's voice: "Hey man, what happening?"

"Hey," Freeman said, surprised.

"Everything cool?"

"Yeah, man. What's up with you?"

Chandler said, "I still out here in Chicago. I talk with the guy this morning."

It took a while for Freeman to understand that Chandler was talking about the man who might want to buy the package. When he did, he let this second surprise pass through him before saying, "All right. What's the deal?"

"He want talk to you."

"Okay," Freeman said. "I'll talk. Set it up."

"Me set it up already. I going call you later. Bring the thing, see if it's real, yes?"

Freeman said, "Okay, all right. Hey listen. This ain't no...this ain't no...I mean, this guy's legit, right?"

"How long you know me?" Chandler asked.

"A while," Freeman said. "That's why I'm asking. You didn't tell my name or anything, did you?"

Chandler sucked his teeth. "No, man. Me not going steer you wrong. Follow me, no?"

Freeman said, "Man, I just want to know who I'm dealing with, what I'm getting into..."

"You want me tell you over the phone?"

"Why's everybody so paranoid about the phone?"

"This the U.S.A," Chandler said, "U Suffer Alone. And beside that, you one the most paranoid cats around. What you want to do?"

Freeman checked his instincts. He said, "All right. You say you're gonna call me?"

"Yeah, man." Chandler hung up.

Freeman put down the phone and stared at it; hearing Chandler's voice had reminded him that the band had scheduled practice for tomorrow night. He was nervous, real nervous. But he also felt relieved about being able to do something. Apparently, the guy Chandler wanted him to meet had a test, so he'd have to bring a small amount of the bag's contents to sample. He just hoped it wasn't some kind of setup...

Finally, Freeman looked up from the phone, not expecting to see the two customers who were standing in line patiently, their arms folded, waiting for him. He smiled at them.

—

Trish wore a white blouse, a white, flowered skirt, and no makeup as she entered the condo. When Gabrielle offered a drink, she said she'd take a Miller Lite. Gabrielle opened the bottle, handed it to her with a glass, and poured herself some orange juice. It was too hot to be outside, so they sat in the dining room near the glass door that looked out onto the balcony and glaring sunshine. Gabrielle asked, "How's your little girl?"

"She's all right. I got her in this summer program for smart kids who have problems in school 'cause they can't sit still. It's working for her, so far. They got a specially trained staff. Guess you been thinking about daughters a lot lately, huh."

"That's all I been thinking about."

Trish had a smile behind her eyes. They both sipped their drinks, and she said, "Hope I didn't throw you off the other day."

Gabrielle shrugged, and said, "No, I'm cool."

"Never kissed a girl before?" Trish asked.

"No, not me," Gabrielle said, looking at her directly. "You have, though, that's for sure."

Trish laughed. "It's not a big deal. My first kiss was a girl. Cynthia Lewis. Eleventh grade gym class, in the locker room."

"Started early, huh."

Trish nodded. "Not really. Hormones didn't start kicking in 'til I was, like, sixteen. My folks kept me under control when I was a kid; then I reached that age, and I been breaking loose ever since. You know how that goes."

Gabrielle smiled. "Yeah, I know about the breaking loose part. But you wanted to talk about something, right?"

Trish nodded and took another sip of her beer. "I'm just telling you so you'll know. The club's in trouble. The manager's in trouble."

"Buchannon? What kind of trouble?"

Trish said, "You know The Lotus is part of a chain."

"Right. Stannos? Stennis...?"

"Yeah, Stannos. Stannos Incorporated. They've got a bunch of clubs."

Gabrielle said, "There's one in Georgia, Club 24 in North Carolina, Lark's Nest in Mississippi, Clio's in Nashville..."

"Right. And they're talking about opening more up north. They're all making money. Except for us. A guy from Stannos was here the other day talking to Buchannon."

"How can we not be making money?" Gabrielle asked. "We have a slow night once in a while, but a lot of times, the place is packed. No way we're losing money."

Trish replied, "The cub's making a profit, but not that much compared to the others. That's what the guy from Stannos was saying. Basically, he thinks Buchannon's been fucking around with the books."

Gabrielle said, "I don't know about that. Buchannon's all business. I mean, he loves money, but I don't see him stealing. He ain't stupid. The numbers are all computerized, right? Buchannon doesn't even handle that part of it."

Trish said, "No, but he could do something if he wanted to. Easy. The girl Tiffany heard the whole thing. The Stannos guy said Buchannon's the manager, so he's responsible. Said he didn't want to hear no bullshit. Buchannon and the guy almost had a fight, right there in his office. One of the bouncers had to go in and break them up."

"When was all this?" Gabrielle asked.

"Friday afternoon. Early."

Gabrielle frowned. "So they'd close the club?"

"The guy was pissed when he left, talking about how it's a business and he ain't got time for excuses. Said something about closing and reopening under different management," Trish said.

Gabrielle finished her juice and shook her head. "Doesn't make sense. First off, Buchannon makes me sick, but I can't see him taking money like that. It's like he takes pride in being Mr. Efficient Businessman. You know how he walks around, like he's managing IBM or some shit."

"I know what you're sayin,'" Trish replied. "But, see, I think Stannos is a cover, a front. I think it's, like, the Mafia, something like that, runnin' the whole thing. If there's money missing, I wouldn't be surprised if someone on their end was doing it, and making it look like somebody working down here."

Gabrielle nodded.

"Doesn't make me much difference what they do, though," Trish said. "I'm just letting you know. I'm almost finished with them, anyway."

"You got something else?"

Trish shrugged. "I don't need it, Gabrielle, not now. Joe, my fiancé? He's got everything covered. I mean, he's set. As long as I'm with him, I ain't got to dance or do any other damn thing if I don't want to. Soon as the time's right, I'm gone."

Gabrielle laughed. "You were just telling me a couple days ago about not relying on a man," she said. "You were saying about how a woman's got to keep her independence, remember?"

"Look," Trish said. "From the time he started coming to the club, he was like, 'You're the one for me.' You've seen him. He'd do whatever for me. He put me in his will a few months ago. His will! I didn't even ask him. He's thinking about quitting his job, too. This time next year, we might be living in Hawaii."

"How old is he again?"

"Going on fifty-five," Trish said.

Gabrielle smiled and shook her head. She asked, "Does he know you like to swing the other way sometimes?"

Trish chuckled. "It's not like an everyday thing," she said. "Just once in a while, if I see someone I like. It's not cheating as far as I'm concerned, not with another woman."

"Just once in a while, huh?"

They looked at each other for a few seconds; then Trish stood, went to Gabrielle, and kissed her fully on her mouth. Gabrielle sat still, surprised. This felt so different. She lingered on the kiss's softness and sweetness, enjoying even the beer taste on Trish's breath mixed with the orange juice on her own. She responded with her tongue while getting up slowly, and their embrace got hotter. After a while, Trish moaned with desire and gradually started removing Gabrielle's dressing gown; Gabrielle did the same with Trish's dress. They kept kissing as Gabrielle led her to the bedroom.

———

When Tommy had called, Edgar was alone at his cousin's house. He'd just gone to the basement, put his feet up, and turned on the satellite TV after being in the back yard, smoking weed that Chuck had left him. He didn't feel like going to Harlem. As he'd told Tommy, after hanging around Bedford Stuyvesant for a-day-and-a-half, he'd had enough and was ready to head back to Florida. Edgar didn't like New York and had no idea how to find out about Floyd Stubbs or anyone else up here. But he knew that Tommy was in a tough spot and would do the same for him if the situation were reversed.

If Edgar were going into unknown territory to find out about some low-level thief, he wanted a weapon. His cousin was at work, and Edgar didn't know where Chuck kept the .38 that Edgar had carried to Nick Rowe's on Monday night. So, he turned off the TV, went upstairs, picked a five-inch-blade utility knife from a drawer near the dishwasher, wrapped it tightly in yellow plastic torn from a grocery store bag, and slipped it into his pocket. Five minutes later, he was driving northwest toward Manhattan.

———

It took almost an hour to find Stubbs' building, which was on a row of brownstones off Lenox Avenue. Edgar planned to ask around casually and see if he could learn whether or not Stubbs might have taken anyone with him when he left New York on Saturday night; if he couldn't find anything, he'd drive to the airport and head home.

He got no answer when he knocked on the door of number thirty-seven. He waited and knocked again. Someone inside came and checked the peephole, but whoever it was didn't recognize him and went back in. Edgar turned around and looked up and down the block. Two boys were sitting on a stoop across the street. They'd seen him knock and get no response. He called to them, "Yo, main man, where Juney at?"

The boys didn't respond at first; then, one of them said something about, "...check the pool hall."

Edgar wanted to know where the pool hall was, but he didn't want the boys to know that he wasn't from around there, so he gave them a thumbs up and walked back to Lenox Avenue. He turned the corner and asked a man limping slowly with a cane, "You know where the pool hall at?"

The man pointed his stick: "Yeah, Rodney's. Four blocks down. Make a left. It's in a basement." Edgar continued to 117th Street and turned the corner. The pool hall had the words "Rodney's Billiards" in badly faded red and yellow letters behind rusty iron bars, painted onto a window that looked as if it hadn't been washed in fifteen years.

He went downstairs. The front door was open, and he stepped inside and walked along a dingy hallway. Cigar smoke and quiet r&b music floated from an open door on his left. Inside, two older men sat at a table playing cards. Edgar asked, "Anybody seen Juney?"

One of the men looked up briefly and said, "He ain't been in here in a while. He usually be in the back. Maybe they seen him. Who's askin?"

Edgar said, "He my uncle," and continued to another partly open door at the far end of the corridor. Beyond it was a hot, poorly-lit room containing ten pool tables and a bar. Three middle-aged men were playing at one table, and two younger guys were shooting across the room. They glanced at him and returned to their games.

A man appeared behind the bar and asked if Edgar wanted a drink; Edgar ordered a Jim Beam. When the drink came, he downed half of it and asked the bartender if Juney had been around lately.

"Don't know no Juney."

"I'm his nephew from Brooklyn. He told me to stop here and look him up if I came up this way."

"Don't know no Juney."

Edgar figured he was lying. He finished his drink, slid off his stool, and said, "I'll take table five and another drink."

He paid for his whiskey and set it on a shelf behind his table, which was near the two being used. Then, he racked up and started playing. After a couple of minutes, he asked no one in particular, "Anybody seen Juney?" No one responded, and he asked, "None of you all know my uncle, Juney? He say this his spot."

"Nigga, ain't nobody know no Juney." One of the two young men had muttered it while they continued their game. Edgar turned to face them: the speaker was a shorter, dark-skinned guy wearing a flashy dark-blue shirt, who had braids lining his head; the other was bigger and wore a white shirt. Somehow, he looked like he'd just gotten out of jail.

Edgar said, "Just lookin' for my uncle, yo. Ain't no problem."

The short one spoke to his friend again without looking up, but Edgar made out the phrase "'bama-ass nigga" as pool balls clicked together hard on the young men's table. Edgar stared at the short guy, wondering why so many New Yorkers were such dumb-asses. He was dying to say something back but held his tongue. He downed his drink and kept playing.

The second drink along with the weed he'd smoked at his cousin's place had him smoothed out. Months had passed since he'd shot pool. He'd been good at it when he was younger and was still better than average. He enjoyed playing, so he figured he'd stay here for a few minutes; maybe someone would come in who knew about Stubbs.

A few minutes into his second game, a nine ball from the young men's table came bouncing to his feet. He picked it up and handed it to the shorter man, who'd come for it. The guy took the ball without a word and returned to his game. Irritated, Edgar said, "You're welcome." The young man ignored him and leaned over the table to shoot, but the other guy, the bigger one, stood holding his stick, looking hard at Edgar. When his turn came to play, he stood, still staring. After a while, he said to Edgar, "The fuck you lookin' at?"

Edgar glared back. "Same thing you lookin' at, homeboy."

The heavyset man raised his cue and walked toward Edgar, who heard the bartender approaching from behind. Edgar tried to move so he could see them both, but before he could, the bartender grabbed him from the back, pinning his arms. The shorter man approached too, saying, "Hold him, Pete. Hold him." Unable to move his upper body,

Edgar was one against three. An older man playing at the table across the room said, "Oh shit."

Edgar struggled but couldn't break the bartender's hold. The big man swung the stick at his head. Edgar turned to the side so the blow landed in his hair, high above his left ear. He leaned back into the bartender's chest and kicked the big man in the stomach with both feet, sending him staggering into a table. Edgar squirmed enough to pull the knife from his pocket and shake off the plastic wrapping. The shorter man picked up a stool and stepped forward. He said, "Watch it, Pete. He got something!"

Edgar strained against the bartender's strong grip; he dipped and forced him backward, away from the short guy, who looked for an angle to swing the stool. Edgar slammed the bartender into a wall, causing his hold to loosen. Edgar lifted the knife and plunged it backward, beneath his left armpit, into soft flesh between the bartender's ribs. The man screamed, "Aaaaaagh!!" and let go. Edgar turned and watched him fall, then spun back to face the short man, who swung the stool as hard as he could at Edgar's head. Edgar dropped to one knee, causing the swing to miss. He rose forward and drove the knife into the guy's gut twice, fast. The young man inhaled sharply and fell back, his eyes wide. Blood seeped through his shirt and between his fingers, which covered his wounds.

The big guy lunged toward Edgar from the side and swung his pool cue. Edgar raised his left arm. The stick struck his elbow and knocked him down. The guy hit him again in the shoulder. Edgar rolled, sprung out of his crouch, and drove the knife's blade all the way into the man's side. The man yelled twice and dropped the stick. His hand went to his side; he winced, looked down with bulging eyes, and reeled backward. Edgar shoved him. The man fell onto the table and yelled again as he rolled onto his injury.

Edgar looked around: the bartender was on his knees, hunched over, grimacing, holding his side. The short man was laying on his back, cursing, knees up, his bloody hands across his belly. The big guy continued to moan while trying to get up from the table. The three older bystanders stood frozen against the wall.

Edgar wiped the knife on the big man's jeans. After re-wrapping it in the plastic bag and slipping it into his pocket, he left. He hurried along the hallway and past the two card players in the side room without looking at them. Once outside, he removed his blood-spattered t-shirt, wiped his face with it, and wrapped it around his waist so that the bloodstains didn't show. Wearing a blue tank top, he went upstairs to street level and turned north, away from busy Lenox Avenue, taking the long way back to where he'd parked. Before turning off 117th Street, he glanced back in case someone was following. The only person on the block was a kid cruising on a bike.

Edgar turned left and realized that he was still lit up from the smoke and drink. He'd stabbed three men in the torso in front of three witnesses; any of the victims could die. He thought about being busted for murder or manslaughter. He could say self-defense, but he'd have to answer questions about why he'd come to Harlem from Florida asking about Juney Stubbs. But now wasn't the time to worry. If it came to that, he'd let a lawyer handle it. Trying to appear calm, he continued along the street toward his parked rental.

When he reached the car, he looked around before getting in. Nothing appeared suspicious. He pulled out quickly, and headed south down Lenox Avenue, thinking that if he made it out of New York, he wouldn't be back. He stopped at a red light and removed the stained t-shirt from his waist. While bending to slip it under the passenger seat, pain where the guy had hit him with the pool cue—in his head, shoulder, and forearm—made him wince. Edgar sat up and looked at his elbow: it had an ugly bruise and would be sore in the morning when he went to work unless he iced it soon.

He stared up at the light, waiting for a change, and never saw a frail-looking parent-less fourteen-year-old named Rudi who rode up to the driver's side on a gray Huffy bicycle. The boy pulled a 9mm from under his shirt and fired eight times at Edgar's head from point blank range through the half-open window, then pedaled the wrong way down 119th Street.

Edgar slumped to the side. His foot slipped off the brake, and the car rolled forward until it hopped the center median and stalled. Four bullets had found their mark. None of the paramedics who arrived ten minutes later could save him.

Chapter Eight

Test Anxiety

Henry had planned to get Simone to come to Las Vegas for the next few weeks until her classes started. He enjoyed her as much as he had any of the many women he'd been with over the years, and for some reason, he showed more of himself to her than to anyone else. She was young, yes, but he could train her, guide her. She talked a lot—like most of them—but she didn't pry; she could see that he wanted to keep some things private, and she respected that. But the best thing about her, beside her body, which nowadays aroused him the second he saw her, was that when they were together, he stopped thinking about the recent urge to change his life somehow. Simone distracted him from that.

So he figured he'd fly out west, then call her and send a ticket; after she returned to D.C. in August, she could always get a rinky-dink job like the one she had now.

Then, she'd told him about what the boyfriend had found, and Henry's plans changed. His first thought: if the package was legit, he could rip the guy off, sell it right here in D.C., and be gone within minutes. He could do that with one or two phone calls.

But that would probably mean the end of things with Simone, and he didn't want that now. The boyfriend didn't have a clue about what to do with the dope. Henry could buy low, sell high, make a nice profit, and head out west, with the girl. After all, he didn't need the money; he just saw a chance to stay active and turn a quick, easy profit.

The best bet would be to meet the guy and play it by ear. One thing for sure: he was going to be out west in time to use the fifteen-hundred-dollar ticket he had for next week's heavyweight championship fight at the Mandalay Bay Casino.

Now, eating a late-morning meal under an iron-gray sky, he sat across from Simone at an outdoor table while surrounded by immaculately maintained gardens on the Van Nostrand Hotel's ground floor; twenty feet away, water flowed gently from all three tiers of a circular fountain. Beside two women at another table, Simone and Henry were alone. Having discussed wine and Cuba's climate, Henry asked, "How's your food?"

"It's fine." Without warning, she leaned forward and added, "So you've got this mysterious activity that you don't want to tell me about. It's illegal, and it's made you very comfortable, money-wise. Beside that, all you do is gamble? Is that what you do all day?"

He chewed his crepe thoroughly, swallowed, and drank some grapefruit juice before answering, "You know, you're getting a lot more curious lately."

"Well, we spend time together. I like you. I *think* you like me, too. It's just normal to want to know *something* about you, isn't it? I don't think I'm being nosy or anything."

Henry shifted in his seat and finished another mouthful. "You're not going to believe this, but you probably know more about me than anyone else. You know I like to bet on sports. That's my thing. And I like to read."

"About business and finance, biographies..."

"Right, and history," he added. "See, you know me."

"Is that true?" she asked. "Nobody knows more about you than that? You've got women friends, right? I mean, to me, you're this complete mystery, and you're saying that I know you best. You're right. It's kind of hard to believe. Over a year-and-a-half, and to me, it's like you're a shadow. You're real, but you're not real."

He shrugged. "You don't have to believe it. Maybe you know too much about me."

Simone said, "The things you've told me—the way you left Cuba, working for the government, leaving your wife and kid behind—was all that true?"

"I said those things when we first met, right?" He hesitated. "Some of it's true. But you've seen me do things, heard me say things, many things. We've spent a lot of time together. You've got a *sense* of who I am. That's what I mean. You know me a lot more than you think, but you just don't realize."

"You talk in riddles, sometimes. Yeah, we've spent time together, but . . ."

He raised his hand and said, "Let's not discuss this now. I don't like to talk about myself."

"You've always been that way?" she asked.

He said nothing.

Simone rested her elbows on the table, beside her almost finished French toast and eggs, and tilted her head. "Don't you feel alone? That's not normal. I mean, to me, anyone who just kept everything bottled up like that all the time would have problems after a while. People aren't made that way."

He finished eating, leaned back, wiped his mouth, and looked at her evenly. "I know you want to be a psychologist or psychiatrist or whatever it is, but you've got to realize, people are flesh and blood; not everyone's straight out of your psych 101 textbooks."

"Flesh and blood—that's my point. I guess that's part of whatever it is you do, keeping everything a big secret. I can understand it, but, like I said, it's got to put a strain on you sooner or later. It's got to create a kind of pressure. After a while, it would start to drive a person crazy."

"I haven't gotten to that stage yet." He stared at her for several moments and said, "Come with me when I leave D.C."

She leaned back and sighed. "So I'm supposed to just drop everything and go to Las Vegas with you now."

"What is it you'd be dropping? You can get a job like the one you have anytime. You start school again in August, right? Come with me until then."

She said, "I've got an apartment, a boyfriend..."

Henry sucked his teeth. "Who are you kidding, me or yourself?

The last week, who've you spent more time with? Who've you enjoyed more time with?"

She looked away and said, "It's like I was saying, Henry, I know you don't see it like I do, but I feel like I just don't know that much about you. It seems kind of weird sometimes."

"But you know you like to be with me, right? What else do you need to know for now? That's the thing about a young woman. One day they're one way, next day they're some other way. Just the other night, you said it: 'Let's go some place together.'"

Simone said, "You know how high I was when I said that? That was the night we stopped at the lake, right? I'm getting high right now just talking about it. Seriously. Yeah, I'd like to go someplace with you. It's been a while since I went anywhere. But you're asking me to just drop everything and leave, for months."

"Pretty much."

"Look at me," she said.

"What do you mean 'look at' you? I'm looking."

"No. Look at my eyes. What do you see in them?"

Henry stared and said, "A reflection."

Simone smiled. "A reflection of yourself, right? How about from now on, I share as much of myself with you as you share with me. How's that?"

Henry smiled back and finished his juice. "We're making deals now, huh?" he said. "Tell you what. Give me a little time. You'll learn more about me. I have to be very careful. Especially now."

Fascinated, she ran her forefinger across her lower lip and said, "I'll think about going to Nevada with you. Thanks for the invitation. I'd like to, but I've got to think about it."

He said, "Okay. But let me know. As soon as we get this little thing rolling with your friend Phillip, I'm gone. That's what I'm here for right now. I'll give it a couple more days, and that's it."

Simone said, "Freeman."

"Huh?"

"His name's Freeman, not Phillip."

Henry said, "Um hm."

Simone had the day off. She looked at her watch and said, "All right. Let me talk to him. I've got a 1:30 appointment, remember? I've got to get back to my place."

Henry put on his white Panama hat and signaled for the waiter.

—

Gabrielle got into Tommy's Land Cruiser after stopping for gas on Lansing Avenue. She was headed to the gym on one of those Southern Florida days when the sun shone so brightly that people's eyes hurt; even behind the SUV's tinted windshield, she wore shades. For the past hour, she'd been trying to figure out what had made her go to bed with Trish. As Trish had said, Gabrielle didn't feel particularly guilty; this had been the first time in four years that she'd lay down with anyone beside Tommy, but, because she'd been with a female, she didn't feel as if she'd cheated on him.

Had emotional pressure led her to do something so sudden and out of character? She was uncertain about her job and career (made worse by news of the club's problems), concerned about Tommy, and, most of all, anxious about seeing the girl she'd given up for adoption, but she'd handled more than this before.

Sex with a woman had been unlike any previous experience. She'd enjoyed it. Gabrielle had never been afraid to challenge boundaries and didn't care about what others thought, but that tendency had caused her trouble more than once...

The traffic signal ahead turned yellow. She started to accelerate but decided not to risk a ticket in Tommy's vehicle and stopped as the light turned red. She did a double-take to her right at a homeless person with an orange, metal lunch pail who was curled up in the shaded, dusty doorway of a gated storefront. Gabrielle pitied these lost souls. Starting in November, they'd flock to Florida from northern states to escape life-threatening wind, snow, and ice, and many just stayed here. This one had long blonde hair and was wearing a light blue jacket in ninety-something degree heat, probably a nut case, like most of them.

The person shifted in slow motion, and Gabrielle felt a twinge of sadness: it was a young woman. Gabrielle shifted in her seat and looked harder, thinking that the woman's face looked vaguely familiar... Gabrielle removed her sunglasses and lowered the right rear window to get a better look.

The driver behind her honked his horn, causing her to face front; the light had turned green. Gabrielle made an awkward right turn and looked in vain for a parking space. She cruised down the block and cut into a narrow alley. Ignoring "No Parking" signs on both sides, she drove the SUV's right side onto the curb, parked, got out, and hurried back to the storefront on Lansing.

The woman lay there, her arm covering her head. Gabrielle stooped and said, "Hey."

The woman moved her arm slowly, and Gabrielle studied her features: she looked like a dancer who'd been at the Lotus soon after Gabrielle had started there, a friendly girl from New York who seemed like she should be in a university studying science or something. Gabrielle couldn't remember her name, only that it was unusual and began with a "t" or an "r," but she remembered rumors about the girl having started to sniff coke. Then, like so many others, the girl had disappeared, replaced and forgotten within two days. This looked like her, but Gabrielle was unsure. She leaned closer and tilted her head to get a better look. The woman smelled musty, as if she hadn't bathed in days. Dirt streaked her cheek, and spittle had crusted in the corner of her mouth, which hung open. Gabrielle asked, "You remember me? I'm Bree. I dance at the Lotus."

The woman appeared disoriented, in a stupor. Her movements were sluggish, eyes unfocused. She lifted her head in acknowledgment that someone was talking to her but didn't turn toward the voice. She sat up, allowing a better look, but Gabrielle still couldn't tell; if it was her, she'd lost weight and her face had become bloated. Gabrielle rested her hand on the woman's shoulder. "What's wrong? What's happened to you?" The woman responded with a blank stare.

Gabrielle looked around, wondering how to help. She had credit cards but no cash to give; the woman's appearance made Gabrielle wonder whether or not she'd know what to do with cash. Gabrielle noticed a series of piercings in the upper corner of her right ear and remembered: the girl from the club used to have shorter, darker hair and six gold studs in increasing size lining her upper ear. This was her. Gabrielle looked down at once manicured fingernails now filthy and chipped, then again into eyes that appeared to exist in a vacuum.

The woman reached for her lunch pail and struggled to her feet, barely able to maintain her balance. Gabrielle stood, too, and noticed a coffee shop across the street, two blocks down. She said, "Wait. I'll get you something to eat. Stay here." She ran across Lansing. As she neared the coffee shop, she looked back; the woman was walking away in the opposite direction with a stiff-legged gait, holding the lunch pail. Gabrielle jaywalked back to the storefront and started to catch up to her but stopped. What could she do? Despite growing concern about Tommy's illegally parked SUV, she shielded her eyes with her hand and watched the woman show no sign of checking for oncoming traffic before crossing a street; as the blue jacket faded into the distance, Gabrielle wondered how someone like that made it from day to day.

Gabrielle rushed around the corner to the alley where she'd parked, hoping that this wouldn't be another time when doing good received punishment as reward. She approached the Land Cruiser expecting to see a ticket, but there was none. She started the truck, steered back onto Lansing, and drove in the same direction that the woman had gone. If she saw her, she'd call around, try to find some kind of organization that would help, and take her there. She looked all along both sides of the road and on side streets but didn't see her.

Gabrielle drove to the gym with a heavy heart, wondering about the ruined woman she'd just seen. While in the locker room changing into her sweats, the name came to her: Heather. Yes, that was it, Heather from New York. She spent the rest of the afternoon thinking that Heather had once been some mother's little girl.

—

Brian Beck ate lunch at The Golden Goose, a tavern frequented by black cops, which was just outside the city along a quiet strip in Somerset. Wearing a navy blue mohair suit and a white shirt, he sat in a darkened corner booth opposite Detective Jeff Lassiter, whom he'd patrolled with eleven years ago. For twenty minutes, they'd talked about their kids, the Washington Nationals, the mayor, and an upcoming championship boxing match in Las Vegas; then the discussion switched to race. Once he'd finished his steak, Beck, the only white face in the house, ordered his second cognac and lit a Monte Cristo cigar, a treat he enjoyed about once a week. He shook his head and said, "You're making race more of an issue than it really is. Same as usual."

"Bullshit," Lassiter said. "You gotta know that. The department's got problems. The country's split on racial lines, the city's split, the department's split." He was tall, broad-shouldered, handsome, lightly bearded, and he smiled often. "Your founding fathers made sure it was always gonna be that way."

Beck looked up, and released a mouthful of smoke. "Here we go again," he said. "You just don't get it. While black's pointing fingers at white and white's pointing at black, the fat cats on top look down at the middle-class and the lower-class fighting each other for crumbs and laugh. The battle's about class, not race. You got the haves pulling further and further away from the have nots. I don't know about you, but I ain't with the haves."

Lassiter dug into his salmon, popped in a mouthful, and said between chews, "I understand what you're saying, but I can't be worried about your old boys up top. I ain't gonna reach up there, and neither are you. I'm talkin' about real life, what you and I face every morning when we open our eyes and get out on these streets. This department's got race problems, man. For one thing, you got these cowboys ridin' into town, don't understand the folks who live here, don't know 'em, don't care to know 'em, see themselves as a bunch of John Waynes, with their sixguns and shit. Working the streets, you got to have cops who can relate. They can't be seeing the folks they're dealing with as 'those people' at best, and 'a bunch of animals' at worst. It's a respect factor. Nothing's more important than respect, the kind of work we do."

"Okay, but you just had a black chief," Beck said as drinks arrived.

"How independent was he, though? Bottom line, he had to answer to the same influences everybody else around here does, the business community. That's who's running everything. That's who's running the goddamn government. I ain't talking about all the white cops on the force, but a lot of 'em—too many of 'em—got no sense of the community, man. They're outsiders, and the folks who live here see them ridin' around like a bunch of cowboys. That's the attitude too many 'em got."

Beck drank half of his cognac, took a long drag on his cigar, and asked, "You know what some of the brothers used to say after I cuffed 'em? They used to say I treated 'em better than black cops. Heard it a bunch of times. You got a bunch of black cops out there out of control against their own, treating people like shit. You know it."

Lassiter said, "Oh, some of us got issues, no doubt. But the ones you talking about went from being in a situation where, before they got uniforms, most of the society's looking down at 'em; now, they got a badge and a gun, and everybody's got to do what they say. Some of them can't handle that kind of a change. But most can."

"Give me a fucking break," Beck replied. "You got to judge everybody as an individual. You got some race problems on the force. I'm not saying ignore it, but after a while, you focus on it too much, you lose perspective. Don't judge me by what somebody else does. Go by who I am."

Lassiter finished a mouthful of food. "You the biggest cowboy out here. I heard about you chasin' the boy with the machine gun in the projects a while back. You ride the same horse down here today you were on back then?" he asked, smiling. "You got your pistol, go charging after Menace to Society, get knocked out, get promoted. That's what happened, right? You got promoted right after? Let *me* try some off-the-wall shit like that. They'll have me cleanin' toilets in the 5th District Stationhouse the next goddamn day. Swear to god, I don't know how you get away with some of the bullshit..."

Beck said, "Yeah, but we caught the guy, right? He was right there when backup arrived."

Lassiter said, "That's right. The goddamn cavalry showed up, right on time. You John Wayne, for real, man."

Beck grinned. "Anyway, I'll tell you one thing—the promotion wasn't related to that." Beck puffed his stogie and said, "I'm still waiting for you to run for office, though. Aim big. Go for president. Then you get to tell all the fat cats up top what you think of them face to face. They'll have to do what *you* say. That'll straighten things out."

Lassiter smiled and drank some beer from the bottle.

Beck checked his watch and finished his cognac. "I got a meeting," he said. "Look, you get anything on that guy I asked you to keep an eye out for in northwest?"

Lassiter put on reading glasses. He pulled a small blue notebook from his back pocket and leafed through its pages before finding the information. He hunched over to see in the dimness and said, "Yeah, the guy runnin' from the murder scene in the alley. Big dude, right? Dreadlocks? I asked a couple cops in that area. One of them says it could be a guy he's seen catching a bus around there sometimes in the morning, about nine. Maybe. The bus stop's on Jarvis, near Gersi Place."

Beck stood. "I don't know Gersi."

"You know the Petworth area?"

Beck nodded.

"Gersi's a small street, shaped like a semi-circle, about ten, fifteen houses."

"Okay. Jarvis and Gersi. Thanks. I'll check it."

Still eating, Lassiter said, "No problem. I got the tab."

Beck started to leave and said, "All right. I owe you."

Lassiter looked up and smiled. "Hey, Beck," he said. "You always drink before a meeting?"

Beck puffed his cigar, looked back, and said, "It's mandatory, ain't it?"

—

Freeman was pissed off for the second time in two days. Customers had been in the store all day, and the phone had been ringing non-stop. Lynnette, the manager, was scheduled to be here, but she hadn't shown up or answered any of his calls; she could have gone on one of her too frequent vacations without telling anybody, or be tied up with an emergency, or anything. Bottom line: she owned Sound Value, and she could do what she wanted. But Marshall, the other guy scheduled to work that day, hadn't shown up either, so, despite growing hunger, Freeman had been on duty alone and hadn't had time for lunch.

A middle-aged woman bought a re-mastered CD, Quincy Jones' *Walking in Space*, on Freeman's recommendation. When she left, he started out from behind the counter to slip quickly to the bathroom even though a couple of people were browsing. As he did, the phone rang. Freeman froze; his bladder told him to ignore the call, but it could be Lynnette or Marshall explaining why they hadn't shown up and when they would. He glanced at the clock: 2:01. Freeman picked up the receiver and heard Chandler's voice: "What's goin' on, man?"

"You tell me," Freeman replied, surprised that Chandler had called back so soon.

"You ready?"

"Well, I'm at work right now." He spoke so that the store's patrons couldn't hear.

Chandler asked, "I mean you got a pen and paper?"

"Yeah," Freeman said. "Go ahead."

"All right. You at 387 Ellingwood Avenue at 10:00. Tonight."

Freeman wasn't expecting anything so fast. He got nervous immediately but forced calmness into his voice. "Okay. It's a house? Apartment? What?"

Chandler chuckled and said, "I here. I ain't there. How I'm supposed to know?"

"Look, who is this guy?" Freeman asked. "I mean, what am I looking at? It's a guy, right?"

"Can't talk about that now. You ask me to help you out. I told you already; I not goin' steer you wrong."

Freeman tried to get a handle on things. Earlier, he'd decided to be assertive in this business. He thought about what he'd just heard and said, "Wait a second. I've got something he's interested in, right? Why's he telling me where to meet? I should have some say-so."

"No, man. You got something he want, he got something you want. I tell you what. Here's a number. Y'all two straighten it out."

Freeman wrote the phone number that Chandler gave, and the conversation ended. Ten o' clock that night. Freeman's discomfort had just doubled, but he couldn't back out now. He had a couple of things to do before the meeting. In an effort to think about something different, he tried to call Lynnette and Marshall but again got no answer.

—

As Beck headed toward his meeting on the ninth floor at department headquarters in downtown D.C., he called the prepaid cell phone number that Tracy had given him to discuss "sensitive" matters. The call didn't go through, and his phone indicated that he was out of range. He wanted her to know what Lassiter had told him about the man she'd inquired about, the big, long-haired black singer seen near a double-murder in northwest early Sunday morning, a case that the department had closed as a failed carjacking. She'd asked him to find out the particulars of that crime almost since it had occurred. Beck wanted to know why, but he hadn't had a chance to ask for specifics. He decided to call again in a few minutes.

His phone rang seconds after he'd replaced it in his breast pocket. He answered and heard his ex-wife say, "Brian."

"Hey, Debbie, what's going on?"

"We got a problem," she said. "Something happened down here this morning."

"What is it? The kids? You?"

Debbie asked, "Are you driving? Maybe you should pull over."

She was strong and sounded calm, but obviously, this was trouble, big trouble. He said, "That's all right. Just go ahead."

She sighed and said, "Calvin's in trouble. He's in jail."

Beck's heart jumped, then sank through his feet as he pictured his elder son locked up. After a pause he asked, "For what?"

"Some kid he's been hanging around with. Cops went to the boy's parents' house this morning with a search warrant. They say the two of them been breaking and entering for months all over the neighborhood. They found stuff in the boy's attic, computers, jewelry, digital recorders. Cal was there when the cops showed up. He called here not too long ago."

Facing one of the most shocking disappointments of his life, Beck tried to focus on the road while dealing with the situation. His son, who knew better, had caused bitter disappointment, but also concern. The first thing would be to get a lawyer. "All right," he said. "Let me handle it. Just sit tight. I'll be there in a little over an hour."

"I already got a lawyer," she said.

"Who?"

"Otis Broadbent. He's supposed to be the best one around. I'm supposed to meet him at the station in an hour."

"Otis? What, is he black?"

"Yeah. He's supposed to be good. He got the congressman off a couple years ago. Remember, with the contracts going to the congressman's brother-in-law?"

"Debbie, don't do anything until I get there, okay? Just wait for me." He clicked off. He and his ex-wife remained cordial, an improvement from how things had been for a while after a bad split six-and-a-half years ago. She, Calvin, and Allan, the younger child, lived thirty miles south, near Garrisonville, Virginia, and while Beck hadn't been the most attentive dad, he'd provided. He called, visited when he could, and took the boys to ball games. But he could have done more, especially before they became teens; he wondered how much blame he deserved for his son's predicament.

Nearing headquarters, Beck decided to go to the meeting but mention the family emergency and excuse himself; the whole Narcotics Probe Task Force would be there, including Byron Reed, Commander of Vice and Narcotics. Would any of them know about Beck's son? Would all of them?

As Beck turned onto Indiana Avenue, anger began to overshadow disappointment and concern, and he forgot about calling Tracy with the information he'd just gotten about the big, long-haired singer seen running from the alley on Saturday night.

—

Working customer service, with its refund and information requests, kept Simone preoccupied throughout Wednesday afternoon, but the situation regarding the two men in her life remained not far from her thoughts. Henry's request for her to contact Freeman made her uncomfortable. She didn't feel like doing it. When Freeman got mad, he stayed that way for days, and after last night's argument, he wouldn't be too interested in anything she'd have to say. And, to make things worse, she'd be bringing up the issue that had caused the disagreement.

Simone wondered whether or not the relationship would—or should—continue. At one point, she took a break and went to the bathroom with a paperback novel about a female thief but wound up sitting in the stall, staring at the floor, thinking back to when she and Freeman had met three years earlier…

…that summer, she'd gone to a few of Vortex's concerts with her friend Renette, who was fooling around with Judah, the keyboardist. Simone liked the band; she also liked the way the bulky, smiling guitarist played and moved to music.

After a mid-July show, the musicians and their girlfriends, all red eyed from post-concert weed, went to a restaurant. Simone went and

- 149 -

wound up near to the guitar player, who introduced himself while pouring her a glass of wine. They started talking about reggae, and he mentioned that he'd always loved music, which even accompanied most of his dreams, like the soundtrack to a movie. They continued to talk, and when he asked about a boyfriend, she mentioned that she'd just broken up. (What she didn't say was that she'd been seeing three men simultaneously, and when one had found out, there'd been a fight, an arrest, and a restraining order among other things.) "A lot of guys I meet are immature or looking to cheat on their wives or just stupid or all of the above," she said, sounding innocent and reasonable.

"Yeah," he said, "guys can be wild, but you all women are getting kind of crazy, too. Especially the ones around your age."

She smiled and nodded.

As they ate, Freeman told her more about himself: "I turned twenty-five in May. From Boston, originally. My dad was military, and we moved around all the time when I was a kid. I wanted to do my own thing, though, so first chance I got, I came out here University of Maryland to study sociology. I didn't finish school, but I like D.C., so I just kind of settled here."

"You got kids?"

"Not that I know of."

"Girlfriend?"

Freeman shrugged. "Not now. When you're with a band, girls come and go. But it'd be cool if I met someone worth sticking with. That's what most people are looking for, right?"

Freeman dealt with black women, but Simone's body would catch any man's attention, and the blouse and skirt she was wearing that night meant that she didn't mind showing it off. He also noticed her blonde-brown hair and her eyes, which, with their thick dark lashes, flashed like emeralds in the restaurant's light. By the time everyone was ready to leave, he had her number.

They went bowling the next Friday and got together again after the band's concert the following night at a Virginia nightclub. She told him about her middle-class upbringing in San Diego as an only child and the rebelliousness that made her move out east to study at the University of Maryland. Unlike other guys, he listened and asked questions as if he was interested in who she was and not just how she looked. They soon became lovers, and she liked him that way, too.

When out together, they got disapproving stares from whites and blacks alike; despite Freeman's sometimes maddening passivity, one night, along with a waiter, Simone had to use all of her strength to steer him away from a fight with three white teens who'd made drunken remarks to them in a Falls Church pizza parlor. Although Freeman had been outnumbered, she'd always had the feeling that he'd have done serious damage that night, the only time she'd seen him more angry than he'd gotten during the argument at his house last night…

Simone stood in the bathroom stall and got ready to get back to work. Her other lover, Henry had to move quickly, and putting him in contact with Freeman would benefit them both—she hoped. She preferred to wait for a couple of days but couldn't. Freeman got off at six, two hours before she did; she'd call him when she left work.

—

The idea of going alone to Ellingwood Avenue gave Freeman the jitters, and as he ate a roast beef sandwich and potato chips for lunch at a nearby place called Home Cookin', he thought about an ex-paratrooper named Maurice Sturdivant, who'd been a professional bodyguard; he might back up Freeman—for a fee. But when he considered that, Simone's parting words from the night before rang through his mind as a challenge to be assertive, and he felt a need to act independently.

After eating, Freeman, who'd forgotten his cell at home, as he often did, walked four blocks to an Amoco station, which had two pay phones. The first didn't work. He fed two quarters into the second and dialed the number that Chandler had given. A woman with a pleasant voice answered and said, "Hello?"

Surprised to hear a female, Freeman paused, then said, "I got this number from Chandler."

"Oh. Hold on." After a few seconds, a man came on the line and said, "Yeah. You the guy Chandler was talking about?"

Freeman said. "He gave me this number…"

"Ten o'clock okay for you?"

"Ellingwood is out of the way for me. How about Risley Boulevard in northeast?"

"The place on Ellingwood is a good spot to talk. If it's a problem for you, I can pick you up and bring you there." The man spoke quickly, with an accent.

Freeman could make it to Ellingwood; he wasn't far from it now. He just didn't want the guy dictating terms and controlling things. But now that he thought about it, this was only a first meeting. And if he went along, he'd have a right to decide the location of the second one, which would be the sale—if there was a sale. "All right," he said. "I'll be there at 10:00."

"I'll see you then." The guy hung up. Freeman walked back to Sound Value struggling to stop his nervousness from turning into fear.

—

Hazel Royce had gotten a message from downstairs about Henry Ramos's aliases. It showed ten positives for the names that Royce had submitted, meaning that if by chance the man who'd checked out of the cottage in Virginia a day earlier was the person she was looking for, and if for some reason he'd stayed in the area, he could possibly be one of the ten men (assuming that no two on the list were the same person listed twice) identified on this list.

Considering how common the names were, she'd expected more than ten matches. Her eyes narrowed as she scanned them: two had left D.C by plane, one had arrived the same way, one was hospitalized after a car accident, one had checked into a hotel, one had received a speeding ticket, two had checked out books at libraries, one had applied for a government job, and one had filed a complaint against a police officer. Royce ruled out the first three and the last two, then spun her seat away from the computer and sat tapping her fingertips on the chair's armrests. She was looking for a needle in a haystack and almost certainly wasting time.

She stood, walked to the window, and stared at the busy street below. People had warned her for years about all work and no play; she'd told them about how much she enjoyed her work and that there was nothing she'd rather do. But maybe what they'd said had merit. Whenever she went on vacation, she returned to her job feeling renewed. Perhaps she would benefit from working a bit less and starting to develop more of a social life. Maybe she should have taken Alex Kirby, the rental agent she'd met yesterday, up on his invitation to the concert; whatever else happened, at least she'd have heard good music. Well, he seemed like the type who wouldn't have too much of a problem finding female companionship, so it was probably too late for that now.

Royce turned away from the window. She printed two copies of the alias list on her computer screen, slipped one into her bag, and put the other in a drawer. She shut down the computer and left the office. But while driving southwest toward Rhyden Memorial to see a retired ex-coworker who'd just undergone shoulder surgery, she thought again about Kirby.

Once she'd found a spot in the hospital's parking lot, she called his office, but he wasn't in. Royce clicked off and walked to Rhyden Memorial Hospital's main entrance. She stopped at the front desk to sign in, and as she looked up at a wall clock, a thought froze her for several seconds.

She put down the pen and rushed back to her car. She opened the trunk and thumbed through a leather valise until she found the list of positive ID's for Ramos's aliases from the previous day. There it was, the fourth one down: "...Jose Martinez, admitted to Rhyden Memorial Hospital at 5:08 p.m. after being involved in a three-car accident on Parkland Avenue in southwest ..." She'd looked at this list earlier, knowing that she'd be here; the fact that she'd missed the connection surprised her more than anything else. How could she possibly have made this kind of mistake?

Royce's thoughts returned to the matter at hand. She went back into the hospital, where she identified herself as an F.B.I. agent and asked for the nursing supervisor. A minute later, a dignified, elderly black woman wearing a nametag that said "Nurse E. Whitaker" came. Royce again showed her badge and explained that she wanted to know about Martinez. Nurse Whitaker made two phone calls for a doctor named Bowers, who arrived promptly, looking young, tired, and disheveled.

"How can I help you?" Bowers asked Royce.

"You treated Jose Martinez?"

"Yes. Yesterday. What's this ..."

"What does he look like?"

"Young, I think he's twenty-one ..."

Not Ramos. Royce said, "That's all. Thank you both. I'm sorry I took up your time."

She went back to the front desk, finished signing in, and visited her friend. When she left forty-five minutes later, she realized that missing the connection between Martinez and the hospital—not any possibility that he could have been Ramos—had caused her excitement about checking his name; as she'd decided earlier, she had practically no chance of finding the counterfeiter. So, as she drove home, she thought nothing of the fact that she passed within three blocks of the Van Nostrand Hotel, where Henry Ramos had checked in the previous afternoon as "Carlos Rodriguez," the fifth alias on her list.

—

Later that evening, Freeman got off the number twelve and walked to the three-hundred block of Ellingwood, a tree-lined, working-class residential street that was empty except for a distant pedestrian and cars parked on both sides. He was fifteen minutes early. He stood on the corner, thinking that anything could happen. If his upcoming meeting with the potential buyer went bad, only unreliable Chandler would know where Freeman had gone and whom he'd been with. He'd never fully trusted Chandler, who should have told him *something* about the man. But he tried to breathe deeply to control his nervousness in the hope that whoever it was wouldn't see Freeman as an amateur.

He thought that in this type of situation, his appearance would work to his advantage. He attracted kids and pets like a magnet but intimidated many adults. He used to wonder which of his features contributed most to that: size, dark complexion, beard, long hair, or somewhat serious expression, and he usually decided in that order. Whatever the reason, no one messed with him. Perception often dictated reality, and tonight he had to give the impression of strength and confidence. But first, he had to stop shaking.

He started down Ellingwood at 10:00 and noticed that sweat was making his shirt stick to his back. With the temperature in the mid-sixties, he attributed the perspiration to the anxiety that was weakening his knees and stomach with each step.

Freeman flinched as his cell vibrated in his pocket just before he reached 387. He ignored it and looked at the small row house, which showed no sign of life inside. He walked up ten steps and knocked on the front door. No one answered, so he tried again and got the same result.

Two car doors opened and closed across the street. Freeman's throat and gut tightened as he turned toward the sound. A man in his early thirties and a stylish woman got out of a blue van. The man walked in front, slowly, back straight and head high, staring at Freeman. Slim and of average height, he looked to be Middle Eastern or Mediterranean; he wore a gray suit, white shirt open at the collar, polished brown wing tips, and rimless glasses. The woman, in tight jeans, loose white blouse, and heels, followed. She had smooth, dark skin and short hair. As they approached, Freeman swallowed hard and clenched his bladder.

The man muttered "How you doing," while walking past him to unlock the front door. Freeman reminded himself one last time to be firm. The woman's perfume caught his attention as she nodded briefly while entering the house's pitch-black interior behind the man, who opened a door to a room on the right and flipped a switch.

The room smelled of varnish. It had walnut walls and a thick, wine-colored rug over shiny oak floors. A full, wall-length bookcase stood behind an expensive desk and high-backed burgundy leather chair. A large dark ceiling fan with brass casings gradually came to life in the middle of the room, twenty feet above the floor. Knees trembling, Freeman followed the woman in. She sat on a dark-red loveseat and leaned back. Slowly, gracefully, she raised her chin as she crossed her legs and stretched her arms along the back of the seat. The man stood squarely in front of Freeman with his back to the woman, under the fan. Like her, he appeared relaxed and confident. "So what's the deal, brother?" He dipped and gestured with both hands in an exaggerated imitation of a hip-hopper, smiling, "What you got?"

Freeman made himself step forward so that he was about two feet from him and said, "I got this," while pulling out the tin foil and handing it to him. Freeman glanced for a second at the woman, who stared at him without blinking.

The man reached into his breast pocket and took out an old silver coke spoon with a snake coiled around the handle and two small glass vials that were each one-third full of clear liquid. He scooped a little of the powder from the foil and dropped it into a vial, which he shook and held to the light. The liquid turned bright green. He poured half of it into the second vial, shook it, held it up, and watched it turn a clear blue-green. He showed the vial to the woman, saying, "You got the real deal here, brother."

"I know," Freeman lied, praying that his nervousness didn't show.

"How much more you got?" the man asked.

Earlier, Freeman had weighed the bag on a digital scale as soon as he'd gotten home from work. "Shade over a pound."

"We deal in kilos," the man said, turning toward the woman. She pulled a PDA from her purse, pushed buttons, and handed it to him. The man looked at it and said, "I'll give you four."

Freeman assumed that he meant four-hundred-thousand dollars and spoke without thinking, before his face would show a reaction. For some reason, he said, "I don't know. I got someone else interested."

The man slipped the vials into his pocket as he said, "That's good for you brother. I'm telling you what *I've* got."

"Let me get back to you," Freeman said.

"You won't get a better offer."

Freeman shrugged. "We'll see. Maybe we can work something out."

"We're here. Let's work something out now."

"Let me call you," Freeman said.

The man stared at Freeman, who thought he saw something wicked dart in and out of the man's eyes. The man turned and whispered something to the woman; she kept looking at Freeman as she whispered back. "Call me tomorrow," the man replied, "around noon."

Things were moving too fast for Freeman. And he didn't like the way the guy was trying to control everything. "Make it day after tomorrow," he said. "Let me call you then."

The man straightened and studied him for several moments, then shrugged and nodded. "Whatever. Call when you want. But remember, if I don't pick up, I took my money someplace else."

Freeman glanced at the woman, who continued to look back as if she knew him.

He said, "Okay," turned, and left the house, trying to place the man's accent. He almost tripped while going down the stairs, and once he reached the street, he realized that he'd been trying not to wet his pants the whole time. The deal had been too easy—about ten minutes. He had no idea what had made him say that he had another offer, but he was glad that he had. As he walked toward the bus stop, the idea of exchanging the green bag for nearly half-a-million dollars electrified and frightened him. He wondered about the way the woman had looked at him. Had she recognized him from some place? Freeman figured that if they'd met, he'd have remembered her.

He stopped in a Subway shop and had to buy a six-inch chicken breast sub just so he could use the bathroom. Instead of waiting for the next number twelve, he walked along the route that it would take back to where he lived, looking back repeatedly to see whether or not it was coming—and to make sure no one was following. He checked his cell. Simone had called and left a message, one that Freeman didn't feel like listening to. He put the phone back in his pocket and walked for nearly half-an-hour before the bus caught up to him.

—

The woman's name was Lucinda Williams. From the van's passenger seat, she'd recognized Vortex's guitar player as soon as he'd come down the street and gone up the front stairs to knock on the door; she'd seen the band perform twice and heard that he worked at a music store in northeast. Although her boyfriend, Redda, knew Vaughan Chandler, he'd never seen the group, so he didn't know the guy looking to sell him a pound of heroin. She didn't tell him what she knew about the musician as they got into the van. As Redda took the wheel, he asked, "What do you think of him?"

"Hard to say. But I think you like what he's got."

They drove north from Ellingwood, and Redda said, "I'd like to know where he got it. It's high quality, very clean. Did you see the colors?"

Lucinda said, "Um hm. But he says he's got another offer."

"That's what he says. That's what they all say. I think he's going to call and want to make a deal."

She turned toward him and asked, "For four?"

As they merged into traffic on eastbound New York Avenue, Redda said, "If he calls, I can get it for less. There's something about him...like he's trying to act tough, but I think maybe he doesn't know what he's doing." They drove quietly for a while, with Redda deep in thought. Lucinda assumed that his thoughts were related to the powder's purity. She hoped that he meant no harm; she'd known him to kill for money, then come home and accompany her to a banquet, and even though she'd never spoken to the guitar player, she liked him.

Chapter Nine

Predators

On Thursday morning, Gabrielle awoke with a burst of energy. The bedside clock read 8:49, meaning she'd slept for almost six hours. She got up and went out onto the balcony; it wasn't too hot yet, so she stood looking out beyond the beach to the sea. The Lotus had been crowded the previous night. She'd bumped into Trish in the bathroom and told her about Heather, the derelict woman on Lansing Avenue. Trish didn't know Heather, but the woman's condition lingered with Gabrielle in an odd way; she didn't see how someone in that condition could last on the city's streets.

She made a conscious effort to think about something else. Tommy had said he might be back today. She went back inside and got her cell; someone had left a message a few minutes ago—Ann Claiborne-Strauss, the caseworker who'd been helping with Gabrielle's effort to see Jasmin, the girl Gabrielle had given up for adoption. Gabrielle called back and identified herself.

"Yes, hello, Miss Baptiste," Claiborne-Strauss said. "Thanks for calling back. I wanted to tell you I heard late yesterday from the Briscoes. Mrs. Briscoe wants to talk to you again."

Gabrielle had met Clay and Erica Briscoe, Jasmin's adopted parents, for an hour-and-a-half ten days ago at Claiborne-Strauss's office for what was basically an interview of her by them. Gabrielle hadn't felt completely comfortable, sitting next to the middle-class, conservatively-dressed black couple, but she put herself in their shoes and could understand them wanting to know where she was coming from. Mrs. Briscoe did most of the talking. Gabrielle thought that they'd asked some questions just to test her patience, but she'd gotten through it, and she wondered now about the reason for this call from them. She asked, "You know what it's about?"

"It's best for you to talk about it with them."

Gabrielle didn't like the sound of that. "What, they changed their mind or something?"

"I just think they've got a few more questions."

"Questions about what?"

"They probably want to know a bit more about you."

Gabrielle started to get angry. "I'm not trying to contact Jasmin. I just want to *see* her. I answered everything they asked me last week. You were there. They asked me all kinds of stuff got nothing to do with anything, and I answered. What else they gonna ask me? They want to know what time of month I get my goddamn period?" Gabrielle almost lost it but controlled herself.

Claiborne-Strauss cleared her throat and said, "I understand how you feel, Miss Baptiste. I know you mean well, but there are two sides to this situation—three if you count Jasmin—and you've got to try to consider the Briscoes' point of view. Sometimes, things happen. A lot of times, people have unexpected reactions when they see children they've given up for adoption. It can be a very emotional experience."

"Look Miss Ann, I can't tell you how I'm going to feel, but I'm not going to do anything crazy, okay? I just want to know what she looks like. I've thought about their point of view. Like I said last week, I'm trying to do this the way that's best for everybody. Whatever way they want to set it up is fine."

Claiborne-Strauss paused and asked, "Can you make 1:30 today?"

Gabrielle sighed and said, "That's not a good time for me. I start work at 2:00." Then, she switched and said, "I can make it."

"So, 1:30, here?"

"Okay, Miss Ann." Frustrated, Gabrielle hung up and stared at the phone.

—

Freeman slept soundly, but, as had been happening all week, he woke earlier than usual. He thought first about the guy he'd met last night. How did people make drug deals? Was he just supposed to show up, hand over the green bag, and walk out the door with half-a-million in cash? It didn't sound right, but how else did you do it? What if they wanted to set him up? What was to stop them from pulling a gun on him, taking the bag, keeping their money, and doing whatever with him? Nothing. And if they did that, Freeman had no defense. He'd wanted to go it alone, but he needed help. He decided to call Maurice Sturdivant, the ex-bodyguard, before heading to work; he had his number around somewhere...

Freeman picked up the *Washington Post* from in front of the house and got ready for work. He skimmed the paper, then went downstairs to the living room, where he'd left his cell to recharge overnight. Before searching the phone's list of stored numbers for Maurice's, he listened to a message that Simone had left the previous night, in which she apologized for what she'd said when they'd argued the night before. She also said that she had to tell him something "real important"; Freeman wondered briefly what the hell she was talking about.

He scanned the phone's address book but didn't find Maurice listed, so he went upstairs and dug through various people's contact information written on scraps of paper that he'd collected over the years and stored in a small plastic box. After a couple of minutes, he found Maurice's number. It could have changed since he'd given Freeman this one, but, although it was early, Freeman called. A sleep-heavy voice answered on the fourth ring: "Yeah."

"Maurice?"

"Who's this?"

"Freeman. Freeman McNeal. From the band, remember?"

A long pause, then, "Yeah, yeah. What's goin' on? Damn. What time is it?"

"A little after seven. Listen, I got a deal if you're interested. Can you meet me today?"

"Depends. What time?"

"12:30-1:00."

Maurice yawned and said, "Yeah, I guess. Where?"

Freeman told him where he worked.

—

Standing on the second-floor balcony outside his motel room, Tommy breathed deeply to gather strength after twenty-one hours of sleep. Route 3 was fifty feet to his right, and apart from trees and cars there, everything was gray, including the sky. Grogginess dulled his senses and weakened his body. Once he'd opened his eyes and realized where he was, he'd checked his cell phone: neither of the people he'd expected to call—Tracy Whitlock and Edgar—had, which surprised him.

Tommy pulled up Edgar's number while directly below, a housekeeper in a gray shirt and jeans lollygagged across the motel's courtyard with a mop and broom. Tommy pressed "send." On the second ring, a white man answered: "Hello?"

Startled, Tommy clicked off, held the phone at arm's length, and stared at it. He checked; yes, he had the right number. Edgar would have called yesterday whether or not he'd gone to Harlem, and someone else on his phone meant that something was wrong.

Tommy re-dialed. Again, the man answered. Tommy asked, "Who's this?"

"Detective Ted Hammond. NYPD, Homicide. Who's this?"

Tommy frowned and started to ask, "Where's Edgar?" but changed it to "What's going on? How you get this phone?"

"Who am I talking to?" the man pronounced "talking" with a heavy New York accent, almost "*too*-orking."

Tommy said, "Bernard. Bernard Jones. How you get this phone, man?"

"The guy who was carrying it was found murdered on Lenox Avenue early yesterday afternoon. We're trying to find..."

Shock overwhelmed Tommy. He clicked off and looked around, but nothing registered. Maybe it was some kind of mistake—someone might have gotten hold of Edgar's phone, or maybe the guy he'd just spoken to was bullshitting. But he'd sounded serious, and if what he'd said was true, that would explain why Edgar hadn't called...

Struggling to think straight, Tommy walked back into the shadowed room and sat at the edge of the bed. Edgar knew how to handle himself.

How could he be dead? What had happened in Harlem? Who killed him? Why? Edgar had disliked New York and hadn't wanted to go uptown but apparently had—because Tommy had urged him to do a favor. He shook his head and fingered the gold-plated mini stiletto that hung from his neck. He thought about Monday, when they'd sat parked in Edgar's driveway in Larchmont Mills, and Tommy had asked him to fly up north. He thought about how they'd become friends after meeting amid the brutal chaos that reigned in the Theodore R. Dorsey Home's overcrowded halls.

Tommy lit a cigarette. He stood and paced around the room, barely able to contain his grief. But then he realized where he was and why he was there. Grief would only slow him. He remembered how much was at stake and that every second counted. He had no choice but to find out about and deal with whatever had happened to Edgar later.

After a shower, he went downstairs to the front desk to ask about the nearest restaurant. The clerk, who looked to be about a hundred years old, directed him to Miss Essie's, a quarter-mile down the road.

Half-an-hour later, Tommy sat alone in one of the diner's booths in front of ham, eggs, waffles, and orange juice. But, after trying for ten minutes, he found that despite his stomach's rumblings, he couldn't eat. He dialed Tracy Whitlock's number with a shaking hand. When she answered, he asked if she'd spoken to the little girl who'd seen the heavyset black man run out of the alley on Saturday night. She said that she hadn't but was working on it and would contact Tommy as soon as she did.

He said, "Stay on it for me, you hear?"

"I'm tryin.'"

Tommy clicked off, put out his cigarette, paid his bill, and left. He got into his rental and checked the map. While struggling to swallow his food, Tommy had forced thoughts about Edgar's death out of his mind long enough to decide that if Whitlock got information about the big dreadlocked guy he was looking for, he'd need a weapon. He had to go to Hickock's Grill at the corner of Oregon and Lumley to see Jake, the man Tommy, and his father before him, used to pay cops.

Tommy drove west, but he kept thinking about Edgar. He didn't realize that Washington, D.C., banned hand-held cell phone use while driving, so he called Nick Rowe in New York even though Rowe was supposed to be at work. Rowe picked up and answered quietly.

"Nick, it's Tommy."

"What's goin' on?"

Tommy said, "The guy I sent to talk to you Monday night? Somebody killed him yesterday. Up around your way, 121st Street, the oh-thirty block." Rowe said nothing, and Tommy continued, "Do me a favor. Check that for me, yo."

Rowe stayed quiet for a while, then asked, "That it?"

"Yeah."

Rowe said, "Okay," and clicked off.

—

Simone pointed to the left, and said, "There's a spot." Henry slowed, u-turned the green BMW across the street, and pulled into a space in front of a small furniture store. She got out and said, "Be back in about fifteen minutes." He reached into his pocket, handed her a quarter, and said, "Here, feed the meter for me." She did so and walked away. He watched her butt until she disappeared from view, and then he opened *The Financial Times*.

Several minutes later, Simone entered a store. She'd never been there before and thought the ceiling, walls, and worn carpet looked tacky, pretty much the way she'd imagined. A business type was browsing to the side, and a teenager wearing too much makeup was buying something at the cash register. Simone stood behind her and watched as Freeman took the girl's money, smiled, thanked her, and gave change and a receipt. The girl left, and Freeman blinked hard when he saw Simone. She leaned against the counter and said quietly, "Hey, Freeman. How's it going? You got my message, right?"

"I was real busy last night."

"So this is Sound Value, huh? This where you work?" she asked, glancing around the store's interior. "This my first time here. You all by yourself?"

"The owner's supposed to get here in an hour. Her mother's in the hospital. I was here alone yesterday."

"Okay. Hey Freeman, I got to talk to you about something."

"What's wrong?"

She lowered her voice further: "Don't get mad, okay? I know you're still pissed about the other night. I'm sorry about what I said. I was out of line." She bent forward. "I haven't said anything about you to anybody. But I've got a buyer for you."

Freeman leaned across the counter until their faces were less than a foot apart and whispered through gritted teeth: "Simone, I *told* you..."

Simone interrupted in a hushed but strained voice: "God, Freeman, what you so mad about? No one knows your name. No one knows anything about you. I'm just telling you. If you want to get rid of it, someone wants to buy."

Freeman started to respond, but he turned and nodded to a middle-aged black man entering the store. When he looked back at her, she shook her head and said, "Just think about it, okay? Call me if you want."

She left and walked the six blocks back to the parked BMW, thinking about Freeman's stubbornness. Henry folded his paper and started the engine. As she got in, he asked, "What's happening?"

"Let me work on him a bit."

"Yeah, all right. Just remember, I won't be around here much longer."

Henry dropped her off at her apartment and drove to Laurel Park racetrack.

—

Gabrielle sat at one end of a long desk across from Mrs. Briscoe, with Ann Claiborne-Strauss to Gabrielle's right, at the head of the table. Sunlight lit the room through a small gap in burnt-orange curtains behind Claiborne-Strauss and fell across the desk in front of Gabrielle and onto ochre-colored carpet. Ten minutes earlier, an apprehensive Gabrielle had decided to stay calm no matter what as Claiborne-Strauss led her into the conference room, where Mrs. Briscoe was waiting. Now, Gabrielle breathed deeply as Mrs. Briscoe tested that decision: "See, I'm not accusing you of anything, and we're not judging you. But my husband and I are concerned because you didn't tell us the truth."

"About what?"

"About what you do."

Gabrielle gathered herself and said, "I told you I sell drinks. That's what I do. I couldn't tell you what else I do there. You all would have walked out on me."

Mrs. Briscoe leaned forward. "What else *do* you do there?" she asked.

"I dance, I take off my clothes, I talk to the clients, men and women. That's it."

"You sure that's it?"

Anger blazed in Gabrielle's eyes, but she said nothing.

"No disrespect, but you hear all kinds of things about those type of places," Mrs. Briscoe said, peering at Gabrielle over rose-tinted glasses. "We just wish you'd been a bit more honest." She was a good-looking, neatly dressed, brown-skinned woman in her late thirties, someone accustomed to comfort.

"Bit more honest? Folks like you all look down at me because of what I do, but it's men just like Mr. Briscoe who come into clubs all day, all night, with their briefcases and fancy suits and shiny shoes. Middle-class married men like him keep clubs in business, make owners rich, and the wives don't know shit. Don't know or don't care. No disrespect, but I know how you all are. If I'd said I was a dancer, I would've never seen Jasmin."

"I'll tell you one thing," Mrs. Briscoe said, her voice rising. "My husband doesn't need your 'clubs' and whatever you all have goin' on in there. I'll guarantee you that."

"I never said he did, but I hate the hypocrisy. You talking about bein' honest..."

Claiborne-Strauss interrupted: "I think we should remember there's a little girl in the middle of all of this. Let's focus on that, shall we?" She turned toward Mrs. Briscoe: "Okay, so you learned about what Miss Baptiste does for a living. What's the concern about her seeing Jasmin? What is it exactly that made you reconsider?"

"It's not that we've reconsidered," Mrs. Briscoe said, patting her short perm. "We just want to be sure. We want what's best for our daughter."

"We all do. What is it you want to hear from Miss Baptiste? I'm sure you had something in mind when you said you wanted to meet," Claiborne Strauss said.

"Some questions came up after the last time we spoke," Mrs. Briscoe answered. "My husband was telling me about situations like this where the birth mother sees the child she gave up for adoption, and then she feels that she wants more and takes things into her own hands."

Trying to sound reasonable, Gabrielle said, "You asked me about this last week, and I told you. Jasmin's with you. I understand that. You all are what she knows. I'm not trying to find her or talk to her or any of that. Look, I'm grown now. I'm not the same person I was when she was born. I didn't know anything back then. It's only natural for me to wonder, you know, what's happened to her, how she's developed. I appreciate the fact that you all were going to give me a chance to see her. You don't get nothin' out of it. But being a dancer doesn't make me a bad person. I guess that's the stereotype that's out there because some people think it's not right for women to take their clothes off, but we're just people, just like you or anybody else. I don't mean any harm. I'm not gonna do anything...wrong."

"My husband and I understand how you feel," Mrs. Briscoe said. "No one's saying you're a bad person or looking down on you. But you've got to be extra careful nowadays, especially when you're dealing with kids. We don't want to take any kind of chance, for her sake."

Gabrielle struggled to keep frustration out of her voice: "That's what I'm trying to tell you. You won't be taking a chance. I just want to know what she looks like."

Claiborne-Strauss spoke: "Why don't we think things over for a couple of days? I'm sure we can come to some kind of agreement. Miss Baptiste, how about if we call you? I'm sure everything will work out."

Gabrielle hid her disappointment as she stood and said, "All right." She shook hands with both women and walked away.

—

Freeman left Lynnette, the store owner, alone behind the counter and went to meet Maurice Sturdivant for lunch. As soon as his earlier conversation with the bodyguard had ended, he realized that if Maurice signed on, Freeman would have to explain the deal—at least most of it—to him. Now, nearing the small restaurant, he began to feel that he was caught up in something bigger than he was. Home Cookin', the eatery near Freeman's job, had few available seats when he got there; he ordered fish and chips and a Pepsi and went to a table in the back.

A few minutes later, Maurice arrived, his torso filling the doorway. He'd worked security for Freeman's band for four summers in a row, when Vortex traveled along the east coast on annual six-week tours. At one time, he'd run his own security firm after having been bodyguard for the star fullback on Washington's pro football team and his reputation for providing protection spread throughout the city. Then, he'd lost his license after putting a photographer in the hospital and having video of the incident posted on the Internet. No longer able to accompany athletes and movie stars visiting the D.C. area to public events, Maurice's status declined.

Still, he managed to do all right for himself. In conversation, he watched and listened to people intently. He was clean-shaven and had medium-brown skin and short dreadlocks. An ex-bodybuilder, he was a couple of inches shorter than out-of-shape Freeman but weighed about the same; his weight was in his thighs and massive upper body, which, along with a thirty-one-inch waist, made him look almost cartoonish.

Wearing a white t-shirt and baggy black sweat pants, Maurice bumped fists with Freeman. A Korean waiter served Freeman's drink as Maurice grabbed a menu and scanned it, asking, "They got any vegetarian in this joint?" He ordered two mushroom burgers, then leaned forward, resting oversized forearms on the table and asked, "So what's up?"

"I could use some help, dog. Your type of thing."

"I'm listening."

Freeman said, "I'm looking to sell something, something I ain't supposed to have."

Maurice nodded and said, "Maybe we better talk outside, when we finish."

"That's what I was thinking."

Freeman paid the tab after they'd eaten; then he explained the situation to Maurice—leaving out the corpses in the alley and the bag's contents—without going into detail as they strolled toward Freeman's CD store along busy lunchtime streets.

Once he'd finished, Maurice asked, "A lot of money involved, right?"

"Like I told you, I'm negotiating."

"But it's enough for you to have to bring me in."

"I might have brought you in anyway," Freeman said. "This ain't my kind of party, for real."

"You said you got someone else interested."

Freeman said, "Yeah, but I ain't really looking to play somebody against somebody else, you know what I'm sayin'? I'm just looking to get it over and done with and come out in one piece."

"I understand where you're comin' from, but I wouldn't be surprised if the dude picked up on that," Maurice said, "and played it. Sounds like a pro to me. If a guy like that sees something about you he can take advantage of, he's gonna do it."

As they stopped outside Sound Value, Freeman asked, "What do you mean 'something about' me?"

"Don't get all sensitive, man. You new to this type of game. You inexperienced, he's not," Maurice said. He changed the subject: "Hey, you still mess with that white chick, chick who used to hang around the band?"

Freeman shrugged and said, "I don't even know. On and off, I guess. Gets on my goddamn nerves sometimes."

"Oh yeah? Well, they always gonna do that, believe it. That's part of what a relationship is. It wasn't on and off last time I saw you all together, though. It was on for sure. Anyway, you should check the other offer, definitely. Any kind of business, you always keep your options open. You know that."

Freeman said, "Yeah, right. So, you down or not? How much you charge for your services, bro?"

"We'll talk about that. Give me a call later. Let me know what happens." They bumped fists and Maurice crossed the street to his white Acura as Freeman returned to work.

—

Ed Luke's Garage specialized in foreign cars, and Simone had been there, seated in one of the waiting room's black vinyl armchairs, for over two hours while one of Ed's mechanics changed the something-or-other on her twelve-year-old Volvo's transmission. She'd been trying to read her mystery novel, but a customer who'd arrived and sat opposite her twenty minutes earlier was distracting her. He was staring, and when she looked up from the paperback, he smiled to show gold teeth.

Simone ignored him, but after a while, he asked how she was doing. Simone answered as briefly as possible, but he kept talking to her, and after several minutes, she lowered the book and looked at him. He was a good-looking young black guy with short, neatly cut hair. He wore a too big, peach-colored polo shirt, white capris, and expensive-looking tennis shoes; a gold chain hung from his neck and two cell phones from his hip. A middle-aged Hispanic woman was watching *Judge Judy* on the waiting room's small TV and an older black man thumbed through one of several issues of *Popular Mechanics* that lay on a flimsy coffee table; they looked at Simone when she said, "Excuse me?"

"Nice shoes," the young man repeated.

"Thanks."

"Cost a lot, right? At least about two hundred?"

"No, not really."

"They not D.C. style, though, more L.A or something." He spoke slowly with a pleasant voice. "Your boyfriend buy 'em for you?"

"Nope."

"You got one?"

"I got a boyfriend, yeah."

"I bet he treats you good."

"Good enough."

"He better. You fine as I don't know what."

Simone returned to her book, hoping that her Volvo would soon be ready. But the young man spoke to her again: "So what's wrong with your car?"

"Transmission." Simone started to ask him to leave her alone so she could read, but her phone went off. It was Freeman. She answered, "What's going on?"

Freeman said, "I can't talk long. I'm at work. You said someone might want to buy."

Simone said, "Right. But he's going to want to check it first."

"Okay. Who is it?"

"A guy who was in a class with me a couple of years ago," she lied. "We kind of kept in touch. He deals in that sort of thing. He's interested."

"In class with you? What's he interested in?" Freeman asked suspiciously.

Simone got up and walked outside before continuing. "What do you mean, 'what's he interested in'? He's interested in what we were talking about. He knows about, you know, that sort of thing."

"No, it's just the way you said it: 'He's interested,' like he's interested in you, or something."

Simone sucked her teeth and said, "You're paranoid. I been telling you that since I met you."

"No, it's the way you said it. You should've heard yourself. Anyway, how well you know this guy?" Freeman said.

"He's kind of a businessman," she said, half telling the truth about Henry. "I mean, I don't see him; I speak to him on the phone once in a while. I know him pretty well, though. He's a Latino. I think he's got loot." She had to speak loudly so he could hear her above the sound of passing traffic.

"You told him about it *over the phone?*"

Simone said, "Don't worry. I didn't use specific words or anything."

"'Kind of a businessman,'" he repeated. "How old is he?"

"I don't know, late thirties, maybe forty."

Freeman said, "The thing is, I got to know one-hundred-percent he's legit. I don't want to take chances. To me, sounds like this guy could be anybody."

Simone sighed and said, "Like I told you. Unless you dump the stuff in the river, you're gonna have to take some kind of chance at some point. You know that, right? You can't be sure of anything one-hundred percent, especially something like this."

"Yeah, but the fewer chances the better," he said. "You say you met him in one of your classes and you talk to him once in a while, but he could be a cop or anything, taking classes."

Simone said, "He's not a cop. He's in waste management. I tell you what. Why don't you talk to him? You don't have to do anything. He doesn't know your name or anything about you. He never has to. Just talk to him and see for yourself. See how you feel about it."

Freeman hesitated for a second, then said, "Waste management, huh? Okay, set it up. But don't give him my number."

"All right. Let me call you a little later."

They clicked off, and she called Henry. Because of background noise on his end, she had to speak even louder while telling him that Freeman was interested. He said that he'd call her back in a few minutes and clicked off.

Simone returned to the waiting room. As soon as she sat, the young man across from her smiled and said, "That was him, right, your boyfriend? Sounded like it. I could tell from how you were talking."

Annoyed, she asked, "Is it your business? God."

He put up his hands and got an offended look on his face. "Whoa, baby. Just tryin' to be friendly. What, you too good to talk to the black man?"

"Give me a break," she said. "My boyfriend's blacker than you are."

He acted shocked. "Oh yeah? You sure don't act like it."

"No, black men are cool. But I hate gold teeth."

Stung, the young man sneered, "Shoot, you ain't all that, snowflake."

"Yes I am. *Brother*," she said, crossing her legs so he'd see them and returning to her book. The old man beside her reading *Popular Mechanics* chuckled.

———

Cigarette, cigar, and marijuana smoke filled the large, shabby, fluorescent-lit basement in southwest where Henry stood outside a cleared circle, drinking rum from a flask and watching two snarling, muscular pit bulls tear at each other. The fight had just started when Simone called. Now, he checked his cell phone's stored numbers while again walking to the back of the crowd of almost a hundred men, all hypnotized by the gruesome spectacle.

He wiped sweat from his forehead and called the contact he needed to make the deal with Simone's boyfriend. The man answered on the first ring; Henry identified himself and said, "I might have a bargain for you if you're interested."

"I don't know. I got a lot going on right now. What you got?"

Henry could hardly hear him. After turning the phone's volume to its highest level and putting his finger in his other ear, he said, "You want to talk? I'm in southeast D.C. I'll be here for a couple of hours."

"All right. I'm not far. I'm in Virginia. I can meet you there."

Henry gave the address and asked, "You like watching dogs?"

"Not now. I don't have time."

"Okay. Call me when you get here."

"Give me about…forty-five minutes."

Henry returned to the ring, where a handler in leather boots and gloves was using an electric prod to get a scarred dog off another, which lay bleeding and helpless. Henry sucked his teeth; he'd just lost fifty dollars. A young white man with thick, sandy-colored dreads cursed and passed a spliff, as if in sympathy. Henry took two deep drags and handed it back while waiting for the next fight.

—

Forty minutes later, when his phone went off, the liquor and smoke had taken effect. The dogs' ferocity boosted his high, as did the way their aggressiveness and the crowd's energy fed off each other.

When Henry answered, his contact said, "I'm on the street. I'm coming up to the house now."

Henry said, "Okay," and went upstairs and out to a perfect June evening. A man in a burgundy shirt, a black baseball cap turned backward, and sunglasses signaled from the driver's seat of a dark-blue, late model Infiniti double-parked across the street with its engine running. Henry had known him for over nine years, and they shook hands as he got in. The car cruised down the block and turned right. Henry lowered the visor as they drove toward the sun.

"What you say, Henry?" the man asked.

Henry rolled down the window and lit a cheroot. "Somebody's selling something," he said. "If it's legit, maybe you want to buy."

"So you don't know what you've got. Is that it?"

"It sounds like it's dope; that's why I'm telling you. But I'll find out soon enough," Henry said.

"I don't know," the man replied. "See, I'm stretched kind of thin right now. Why don't you go ahead and make the deal yourself?"

"I'm not really into the drug game. You know what I do; I pass paper. Plus, I'm not from up here. It'd be easier for me if I was down south or out west," Henry said, "but I can't put my hands on that kind of cash in a few days. That's why I called you, see if you're interested."

They drove in silence for a while before the car made another right turn. The man asked, "How much weight?"

"He says a pound."

"A pound? What quality?"

"I don't know about all that. That's what I have to check. Right now, I just want to know if you'd put up the money if it turns out to be something."

The man asked, "Who is it you're dealing with, man?"

Henry explained about being told about the bag by a young woman who swore that it was heroin and that the seller was inexperienced—and working alone.

The Infiniti stopped at a red light, and the driver turned, looked at Henry, and laughed.

"What's going on?" Henry asked.

The man explained that it sounded as if he'd been looking at the same deal, that he'd met the seller last night.

"Hmm. That's weird," Henry said. He puffed his cigar and gazed out the window as the light turned green.

Redda remained quiet until they turned back onto the street where he'd picked up Henry. He double parked again outside the house and said, "So you haven't spoken to the guy. He's never seen you."

"No. I'm looking to meet him tonight."

Redda rubbed his chin and said, "You know what? We can make some money off this. We can both make money."

"I was thinking the same thing."

Redda nodded. Down the block, a car pulled out, and he drove to the parking space. Once he got in and turned off the engine, he said, "Okay. This is what *I'm* thinking..."

—

In a nearly empty pool hall three miles away, Tommy shot alone, unable to avoid thinking about the many times that he and Edgar had hustled in similar places in Florida when he was younger. Earlier, he'd had no problem getting a .45 at Hickock's Grill from Jake, who'd handed it to him saying, "You see all the cars in this city? That's about how many guns up here in D.C., especially the kids. It's crazy, man."

He played for a couple of hours, struggling with anxiety while waiting for Tracy Whitlock to call about the dreadlocked guy who'd run from the alley on Saturday night.

Finally, he started to feel hungry, so he went to a dim, window-less, nearly empty bar a couple of blocks down. Soon after he'd begun to eat a plate of pork chops, string beans, and Hopping John, with toast, his cell rang. He answered without checking the ID and heard Nick Rowe's voice: "Your boy got into some shit up here yesterday."

"What happened?"

"Got into a beef with three dudes in a pool hall and shanked all of them. They still in the hospital, all in bad shape. One calls himself a hustler. It's a gang of 'em 'round that way; they got your boy out on the street when he was leaving. Head shots. That's what I hear."

Tommy had questions, but he couldn't change the past, and he had enough to worry about. He thanked Rowe and said he'd talk to him later. Once he'd finished his food, he lit a cigarette, ordered a double shot of brandy, and nursed it, lost in thought. Depression started to weigh on him.

He checked his watch: Gabrielle would be at work. He called and left a message on her voicemail saying that he was okay and would be back soon. He returned to the pool hall to mourn and to wait.

—

Simone could tell that Henry had been drinking when she let him into her apartment around 9:30. He followed her into the bedroom and leaned against the open door as she made up the bed. His clothing had an odd smell, tobacco and something else. "I was waiting for you to call," she said.

"I'm not going to be able to buy what your boyfriend's selling. I thought I could get the money together, but it's too much. It would take me a lot of time, and like I said, I got to get back out west. I don't know enough people around here to make a deal like that."

"You mean after all this you're backing out of it?"

He shrugged. "I just can't do it right now. Things didn't come together."

"Maybe you should still talk to him. He's just looking for the best deal. It doesn't have to be done today or tomorrow."

"No," Henry said. "Let him go ahead. I'm not going to bother with it."

Simone was surprised and disappointed; for some reason, she'd liked the idea of Henry buying what Freeman had found.

"So you stayed over in D.C. for nothing," she said.

"What, are you disappointed?"

"It's just that I've been telling him for the last few days that I knew someone who was interested. I was just going by what you said. This makes me look kind of stupid."

"Don't worry," Henry said. "He'll get over it." He pulled out a cheroot and started to light it until Simone looked up and said, "Hey, don't smoke in here."

Henry said, "Sorry. I didn't see the 'No Smoking' sign."

"Don't get smart, okay?"

"You're pissed off at me."

Simone said, "No, I'm not."

"Sounds like it." Simone said nothing, and Henry said, "Come with me to Vegas."

Tucking in a sheet, she said, "Don't pressure me, okay? I told you I was gonna think about it. God. I don't have to do *everything* you say, do I? Just because you're some kind of terrorist or whatever the hell you do..."

"Be careful."

His tone made her look up at him; something cold and frightening, something she'd never seen before, crossed his face, causing her to straighten slowly and stare at him. They stood that way for several seconds before she spoke nervously: "Look, I didn't mean..."

Before she could finish, Henry turned and left.

Simone remained looking at the bedroom door at the spot where his face had been. She asked herself out loud, "What was *that* all about?" Then, she remembered his words from earlier: "Give me a little time. You'll learn more about me." She thought that the terrible coldness she'd just glimpsed was part of his truth. She nodded and finished tidying the room.

She'd intended to clean her bathroom; instead, she sat in silence in the living room and drank a glass of chablis.

—

Beck's bedroom had thick, navy blue carpet, white walls, and blue curtains; a fifty-five-inch flat-screen sat at the foot of a low, sunken bed that had at each corner a lamp with a pale-orange shade. Two of the lamps were on when Beck entered well after midnight. Tracy Whitlock was laying back, naked, watching an old black-and-white movie. She turned her head toward him and said, "You look tired."

"Try having kids," he said. The previous evening, he'd explained to her over the phone that he'd be staying overnight in Virginia, trying to get his son freed from jail on the boy's own recognizance.

"No sir, you can have the kids. That's not for me," she said now. "What happened?"

He removed his jacket and tie, lay on the bed with his feet crossed and his fingers interlaced behind his head, and said that after the lawyer's maneuvering, Beck's son had been remanded over to his mother's custody at an early arraignment. Apparently, things were going to work out.

"Good thing he's not a black kid in the city," Tracy said. "Cop for a dad or not, he'd be up shit's creek right about now."

"Whatever. One less headache. For now at least."

"Lawyer cost a couple dollars, right?"

Beck snorted and said, "Don't ask." They watched TV for a few minutes as young, handsome Paul Newman, in white cowboy hat, approached beautiful Patricia Neal; then Tracy remembered and asked, "Hey, did you get that information I asked about, you know, the guy running from the alley in northwest Saturday night?"

"Yeah. Damn. I meant to call yesterday, Trace, but I got caught up in this shit with my son. What's that all about, anyway?"

Tracy told him: how Tommy had set up a run through D.C. on Saturday night; how she'd told him to avoid 95 South; how the car had disappeared and he'd called on Monday wanting her to find out what had happened to it; how she'd met him yesterday in the cemetery; how he'd called, sounding almost desperate, earlier today, pressing for information about the big, young, dreadlocked guy seen running from the alley where cops had found two corpses Saturday night.

Beck had never met Tommy, but he knew the father, Leon. Beck looked much more alert when Tracy finished talking than he'd been when she started. He appeared to think for a while about what she'd said, then told her what he'd learned from Jeff Lassiter about a man fitting the same description catching a bus at Gersi and Jarvis in the mornings.

When he'd finished talking, Tracy went to the closet and got her prepaid phone from her jacket pocket. Beck lowered the T.V.'s volume so he could listen to what she told Tommy.

—

After leaving Simone's apartment, Henry walked down Warrick Lane. When he got to his car, he stood next to it with his hands in his pockets. He could have broken Simone's neck when she made the comment about him being "some kind of terrorist or whatever." He hadn't expected her to say anything like that, whether out of anger or anything else. Until tonight, she'd known what to say and what not to say; he'd revealed certain things about himself for that reason. What he'd told her about how he operated outside the law had been in strict confidence, not for her to bring up in a moment of passion; five years ago—hell, a year ago, before he'd curbed his temper—she would have paid instantly for having such loose lips. Typical American.

This early evening retained all of the day's heat, and a thin film of sweat formed under the brim of Henry's Panama hat as he stood watching traffic zip by in both directions. Letting her know too much about himself had been a mistake; he lit a cheroot and thought about what that meant. If she was stupid enough to throw his comments from the other night up in his face tonight, what else would she say, and to whom? That he even had to think about this showed that he was slipping; everything pointed to a change in direction for him, but where to go? What to do? After a while, he got into the car and drove northeast toward the Van Nostrand Hotel.

A red light at M Street stopped him, and he tapped the steering wheel in frustration. How best to handle Simone? Should he just overlook it? Could he? Maybe the weed he'd smoked and the half pint of rum he'd drunk at the dogfight had clouded his judgment. He'd decide how to deal with her later, after tomorrow's business with Redda and Simone's boyfriend. Yes, tomorrow morning—he looked forward to that.

From his right, a long-legged, gum-chewing streetwalker in a skin-tight, white leather outfit strolled across the street. Her hips shifted with each step, into and out of his headlights, and she turned her head and stared at him with smoldering, unblinking eyes. Henry stirred in response to her body's invitation. As if sensing that, she started toward him, not bothering to wait for any signal.

He liked how she walked and how she was built, especially below the waist. She reached the car; she was younger than he thought—nineteen, maybe twenty. Should he? As she rested her hand on the door and lowered her face to his level, the light turned green. Alcohol-fueled temptation pushed Henry toward her, but he'd learned long ago not to trust girls who walked the street.

"What's happening, sport?" she asked in a throaty voice.

Exercising some of the self-control that Simone lacked, his foot touched the gas pedal, and he continued toward the hotel. He wanted this girl but had to be up early in the morning to meet Redda. Besides, he knew another girl in this area, an Eastern European, he could call later if he had to.

But part of him regretted leaving the girl on M Street behind. That, along with lingering displeasure over Simone's remark, made him stop at the hotel's bar before he went to his room.

—

The pool hall had gotten smokier and more crowded as the night progressed, but Tommy continued to play alone. His game, rusty at first, improved as his cigarette butts began to form a small hill in an ashtray on a side shelf. As one o' clock approached, his phone rang. It was the cop, Tracy Whitlock, with news that jolted him: the guy he was searching for looked like a man who caught a bus around nine in the morning, not far from where the Plymouth had been found in the alley. "All right, all right," Tommy said, dropping his pool cue and striding toward the front desk to pay his bill. "Gersi and Jarvis? Where's that at?"

"Northwest, near the alley where they found the car." she replied. "You got a map?"

"Yeah. I'll find it."

"Hey, listen," she said, hearing excitement in his voice. "This might not be the same guy. You know that, right? It's a maybe, that's all."

"Yeah, okay. I'll go with a 'maybe' right about now. All right. I'll check you later." Finally, he had something to go on. He clicked off and hurried out into the warm night.

—

Vortex practiced at the home of the drummer, Charles. Afterward, Judah, the keyboard player, gave Freeman a lift home, and on the way, Freeman asked to stop on Palletta Road in southeast. There, he got out and went to a door next to Shane's Sporting Goods, the place where he'd worked for a few months before starting at Sound Value. He used a key to open the door and used it again to open an interior one. He climbed a flight of stairs and opened another door that led to a large room that was empty except for a chair and table, barely visible in the gloom. When he'd worked downstairs, management used this as storage space, and he hadn't returned these keys when he left.

A row of unshaded windows that faced the street let in just enough light to fill the dusty room with shadows. Freeman couldn't see much, but to avoid drawing attention to the place, he didn't flip the switch that would activate overhead fluorescents. He walked around on the wooden floorboards, thinking that if he got here early, before business hours, say, on Saturday, this would be a good place to sell the package. Hands on hips, he stood peering into the space's semi-darkness, picturing the sale, then returned to the car.

Once in his house, he went straight to bed and lay there, wondering about why Simone hadn't called to say that the deal had been set up. Who the hell was this guy she was talking about? If she and the guy were friends over the phone, as she'd said, why had Freeman never heard of him? And what was he doing going from taking a fucking philosophy class to buying hundreds of thousands of dollars worth of heroin?

Freeman didn't intend to call Simone to find out. Although part of him missed her, especially at night, he'd had enough of her bullshit.

They'd had arguments before, and this wasn't the first time he'd been mad at her, but other girls were out there, and he was better off without the drama and having to figure out what was going on with her.

He could do this without Simone. The four-hundred-thousand dollars that the guy had offered last night at Ellingwood sounded fine to him. Tomorrow morning before work, Freeman would call and arrange to sell the heroin—on his own terms. And he'd call Maurice.

Something about that last part troubled him, though...Maurice was a good guy and all, and some security would help in a situation like this; still, Freeman didn't feel a-hundred-percent comfortable bringing him in on the deal, and the older Freeman got, the more he saw the wisdom of following his instincts.

He decided not to worry about it. He'd figure out how to handle that later. Within minutes, he fell into his normal deep sleep. Loud furiously-paced African drums accompanied his dreams.

CHAPTER TEN

UNSEEN SHADOW

Inexplicable enthusiasm filled Hazel Royce when she woke on Friday, again, earlier than usual. The sense of well-being remained as she dressed, drove to the gym, and swam alone. Nothing outstanding had happened recently, and, beside a possible visit from two nieces on Sunday, she hadn't planned anything for the weekend. At work, she was still grinding away at the Solstice file, and she'd given up on finding Henry Ramos in time to serve him the subpoena.

Maybe that contributed to the good vibes, making the decision not to worry about that nonsense any more. Toward the end of the day, she would contact Carl Oberhauser, the Miami Secret Service agent on the task force with her, who'd also been assigned to find Ramos, and say that trying to trace the counterfeiter in this area had led only to dead ends. She intended to say what she'd thought from the beginning, that the Ramos case should be re-opened at a later date when federal agencies might have stronger leads.

Dawn was breaking as Royce got to the gym. She changed and cleared job-related thoughts from her mind as she dove in and enjoyed the sensation of water against skin.

—

Simone woke in her apartment and lay on her back with open eyes. Something that she couldn't identify was troubling her. She'd meant to call Freeman last night and explain that the deal was off, but after what had happened over the last few days, she'd have felt like an ass. She ought to tell him something, though.

She rolled onto her side and faced the first sign of daybreak, which appeared as the faintest glow between closed, multi-colored curtains. The thing with Henry last night was weird. She'd seen how, a few days ago, his ears had perked up like a wild animal's when she first mentioned the possibility of drugs for sale. He'd delayed his trip to Las Vegas, the city he loved, on the chance that he could make a deal. He'd urged her to set it up, and then, all of a sudden, he'd realized that he couldn't do it and had to leave. It didn't make sense.

And his attitude last night was off, too. She'd seen him drunk many times; whatever he'd been drinking before he came to her apartment and whatever he'd been doing, his vibe just wasn't right. And when she'd called him a...whatever it was she'd called him, he looked like he could have killed her. Was that what he did for a living, assassinate people? It might not be that, but Simone had a feeling that his business was something along those lines. Whatever he did, she'd known from the first time she'd seen Henry that he wasn't a man to fool with—and that was a big part of why he was so hard to resist...

She wondered how Freeman was doing making his sale. She was a bit worried about him even though he was ignoring her. He was in over his head, and despite their shouting match at his apartment the other night, Freeman had a charm and innocence that made it hard to stay mad at him for long. Simone wasn't mad at him now; she could tell just from talking to him yesterday at the dump where he sold CD's that he was still pissed at her and had probably gotten double-pissed since then because she hadn't called back last night with the information about the buyer. She owed him an explanation.

He'd still be asleep, so she got up, fixed and ate two tuna-on-wheat sandwiches, and started to clean the bathroom.

Half an hour later, she called Freeman, knowing that he'd be awake. When he didn't answer, she assumed that he was probably still mad enough not to talk.

Well, the hell with him. It was his loss, and Henry was just as interesting, anyway. Simone got up and went to finish her chores.

—

Freeman had been on his front porch with paper and pencil, breathing the early morning air when Simone called. He appeared calm, as usual, but he felt nervous. He'd written the names and locations of three places—a park amphitheater, a vacant space upstairs from a clothing store (the place he'd checked the night before on the way home from practice), and a junkyard—along with different times when he could use them to make the sale. He didn't hear the phone, which he'd set to ring at low volume, and when he went inside to eat and get ready to go to the CD store, he was too preoccupied to notice the message light. He'd have called her back, but he'd made up his mind that he wasn't going to sell to whoever it was she was talking about.

Freeman couldn't tell for sure, but the man he'd met at Ellingwood appeared reasonable enough. Considering that Vaughan Chandler had introduced him, he hadn't been what Freeman had thought he might be—a young, wild-looking hoodlum; instead, the man looked like a businessman, in gray suit and glasses. But what was his name? Shouldn't Freeman know that? He assumed that Chandler did, but you never could tell with him. And the chick who'd shown up with the guy...Freeman still couldn't figure why she'd be there. But each to their own.

He left for work thirty minutes earlier than usual, sure about one thing: *he* would determine where and when the deal would happen; the guy had no say in that. Freeman just had to pick a place and time. Actually, he'd pretty much picked the place, and he wanted to do it as soon as possible. And he still hadn't decided on Maurice's role; he couldn't until he knew the bodyguard's price.

Focused on those things, Freeman got on the number twelve with the usual dozen or so other passengers and thought of nothing else for the whole ride. He never noticed the slim man about his age, dressed in dark blue and wearing a gold chain with a miniature stilletto, who, as Freeman showed a bus pass to the driver and looked for a seat, dashed across the street to board the bus at the last second. The man sat in a rear corner and stared out the window. When Freeman got off, he followed.

———

Someone buzzed from the lobby as Gabrielle stepped out of the shower. Who would that be? Not Tommy. She'd gotten his message last night saying that he was okay and would be back soon, but even if he'd lost his keys, any of the desk attendants would let him up without buzzing. Maybe it was UPS with some package. Naked and damp, she walked to the hallway and touched a button above a monitor. The screen came to life, and a video feed from the lobby showed Trish downstairs at the front desk. The clerk's voice sounded on the intercom. "A lady to see you. She says she's a friend of yours."

Gabrielle wasn't expecting Trish. "All right," she said. "She can come up."

She ran a towel across her face and along her body and threw on a bathrobe before opening the door for Trish, who entered wearing a black t-shirt and black shorts and asked, "Your old man here? Is this a bad time?"

"No. He's out of town for a few days. Come on in."

"I was just driving past. I called about fifteen minutes ago, but nobody answered."

"I was taking a shower," Gabrielle said. "What's up?"

"Just want to talk."

Gabrielle nodded toward the couch, and they sat facing each other.

"Buchannon's stressed," Trish said, referring to the Lotus's manager. "Everybody's noticed it. It's like he's scared."

"Good for his ass. Let him see what it's like to get squeezed the same way he squeezes the young girls when they start out there. I don't give a shit what he does or what happens to him, as long as he stays away from me."

"So you're okay if they shut the club down for a while."

Gabrielle shrugged. "They ain't closing that place. Whether the owners been stealing or Buchannon been stealing or whatever, the Lotus makes money. I know it's making money. Shoot, if they close it, they close it."

Trish laughed. They each had an arm across the back of the couch, and Trish extended her fingers until they held Gabrielle's. They sat that way for several seconds before Trish said, "You know, what happened here between us the other day, I didn't plan for it or anything. It just happened."

Gabrielle said, "Tell you the truth, I haven't even thought that much about it."

"Didn't mean anything to you?" Trish's voice held a trace of loneliness.

Gabrielle said, "Girl, you know I got a lot on my plate right now. I got enough to worry about already."

Trish brushed her thumb across the back of Gabrielle's fingers. "I tell you what," she said. "You're good. Maybe it wasn't a big deal to you, but it meant something to me."

"I'm not gonna lie to you," Gabrielle said. "I liked it. But I gotta step back from that for now. We got to leave that alone for a while."

Trish nodded, then said, "Gabrielle, listen..." The house phone rang, and Gabrielle got up and answered. Ann Claiborne-Strauss on the other end asked whether or not it was a good time to talk. "I spoke with Erica Briscoe earlier," the adoption agency worker said. "She says they're willing to go ahead with the visit as planned. They'd thought about changing the location, but they say they're okay with what we planned last week."

Gabrielle closed her eyes, raised her face toward the ceiling, and smiled. She took a second to compose herself and asked, "You talked to them about it?"

"I gave her my opinion yesterday after you left. She and her husband thought it over I guess, and she called here this morning."

"All right, Miss Ann. Thanks. I appreciate it. I'll see you later, then."

Gabrielle hung up and returned to the couch. Once she remembered the topic of her discussion with Trish, she said, "I understand what you're saying. But that whole thing wasn't really me; I couldn't even tell you why I did it. I'm thinking maybe it was just something to do, or stress. I don't know. Like I said, I haven't even thought that much about it. But Tommy's gonna be back soon, and he's got stuff we're gonna have to deal with. Plus I got this other business going on..."

"No, that's cool, that's cool. I understand. But I was just saying, I like you a lot. I always did. There's something about you; anybody ever tell you that?"

Gabrielle smiled and shook her head. "Not really. But I like you too. It's just that..."

Trish reached for her hand and squeezed it once more. She stood and asked, "You just got good news about your little girl, right? That what you're so happy about?"

Gabrielle smiled and nodded.

Trish said, "As long as the people she's with take good care of her, that's the main thing. You'll be able to tell whether or not she's happy when you see her. You tell Tommy about it yet?"

Gabrielle shook her head.

Trish said, "Yeah, you got a lot goin' on." She looked at her watch. "I'm gonna head out. I'll see you at the club later, right?"

Gabrielle walked with her to the door and opened it, saying, "I guess so. If they don't shut it down by then."

Trish kissed her on the cheek and looked into her eyes before leaving.

—

Hazel Royce sat alone at Ruby Tuesday's. After ordering lunch, she called Alex Kirby's office on a whim even though she hadn't thought of him all morning. After she'd identified herself, Kirby said, "What can I do for you Ms Royce? I'm not in any trouble am I?"

"Not that I know of," she replied with a smile in her voice. "I tried to call you yesterday about that offer you made the other day."

"Oh, about the concert? You changed your mind about going?"

"In a way, yeah. I appreciated when you asked me. I mean, I like that kind of music. But I try not to mix business and pleasure, and I was in your office to talk about something serious. You understand, right?"

Kirby said, "Sure, sure, I definitely understand. You probably won't believe this, but I'm the same way. From eight-to-four, I'm usually all business. It's just that once you walked out that door, I probably wasn't going to see you again. So I just figured I'd take a shot."

"That's fine. Like I said, I appreciated it. So, are you still looking for company for tonight?"

"Well, I found someone to go with me. But how about tomorrow? Do you like plays? Movies?"

"Sure. Both," Royce said. "What's out there?"

"I don't know, but we'll find something. And we can get something to eat, too."

"That'd be fine, Mr. Kirby. You can reach me at this number if you have it."

"Sure. I got your number. And it's Alex, okay? Call me Alex."

The conversation ended, and a young waiter soon arrived with Royce's ginger ale and appetizer.

—

Freeman grew nervous as the morning passed. Before coming to Sound Value, he'd gone to the Amoco station's pay phone and arranged to make the deal at 7:00 the following morning above Shane's, the sporting goods store where he'd once worked; his anxiety began during that conversation.

"Fifties and hundreds," he'd said. "The price we agreed on. You couldn't do that by tomorrow morning, right?"

The man laughed. "Don't worry about me, brother. I'm going to do what I have to do, trust me. You just hold up your end, and everything's going to work out fine."

"Okay. You know the area?"

"Don't worry about all that. You want to call shots, go ahead. It doesn't make any difference to me," the man said. "But I work alone, you understand? Someone was with me the other night when I met you, but tomorrow, I'm by myself. I'm looking for you to do the same thing. If I see anyone else, the deal's off. If I *think* I see anyone else, the deal's off."

Freeman interrupted, trying to sound relaxed: "No, just me and you, man."

The man continued as if Freeman had said nothing: "I don't play rough, so no guns. We make the deal like two men and go ahead about our business. None of this gangster stuff like the young people do. I can do that, too, if I have to, you understand? But where I come from, business is business. I like to keep it that way. You look like you're about business too. That's why I'm dealing with you."

The man sounded calm and confident, and Freeman thought about what Maurice, the bodyguard, had said about the guy without having met him—"sounds like a pro to me." Freeman had his own ultimatum: "That's cool. I got no problem with all that. But I'm not gonna stick around. 7:05, I don't see you, I'm gone."

"Don't worry about that. Don't worry about any of that. You're about business, I'm about business. That's good. That's what I want to hear."

Freeman said, "All right. There's a gate covering the front of the store. Next to that's a door and another door inside. The doors stay locked, but I've got the keys. I'll leave them open. You just come in and go up some stairs. That's where I'll be."

As soon as the conversation ended, Freeman called Maurice.

—

At noon, Freeman walked outside into hazy sunshine and entered Maurice's Acura, which was parked nearby with its engine running. Maurice drove down the block, turned left at the first corner, and pulled into a space on one of the run-down neighborhood's side streets. He turned off the engine, and they experienced a rarity in the city: silence. Maurice stared straight ahead as Freeman explained how he saw the sale and Maurice's role in it.

Maurice nodded and said, "Makes sense. But you shouldn't have told him where you want to meet until just before the deal. That way he can't prearrange nothing. This D.C., man."

Freeman said, "Yeah, well, I guess that's why you're gonna be there."

Maurice looked at him. "You set a time?"

"I wanted to go tonight, but it's on for tomorrow morning," Freeman replied.

"Man, you movin' fast. Too fast. I couldn't have made it tonight. I got to be in Norfolk."

"You can make it tomorrow, right? Seven o' clock?"

"That's a weird time. Why so early?"

"Don't want to get caught. Not too many cops out then. And that's a good time, for the place I'm gonna be at."

Maurice said, "All right, seven o' clock."

Freeman asked, "So what's your price?"

"Fifteen."

Freeman had expected a higher number, but just to be contrary he said, "Fifteen? Thousand? Yo, that's grand a minute!"

Maurice said, "First off, you ain't tellin' me how much the shit you sellin's worth. Only reason you'd do that is if it's worth a lot. A whole lot. Second, whatever it is ain't legal. You told me that your damn self. That means if something goes wrong, I'm doing jail time. And you ain't gonna bail me out 'cause, for one thing, you broke. You still broke, right?"

Freeman said nothing.

Anger crept into Maurice's voice as he continued: "Plus, right after they lock *me* up, they gonna bury your ass *under* the goddamn jail 'cause you the one gonna be carryin' the shit. What I'm asking is standard for that kind of work. I could've said I wanted a percentage, and you would've gone along 'cause you don't know what the fuck you doin'. But I didn't do that." He shook his head. "You asked me to help you out, and I said why not, save the brother from himself. I mean, what else you gonna do, get some yo-boy off the street to watch your back? Go ahead. Or you want to go by yourself, use your ass to stop a bullet? Go ahead. For what you looking for, you ain't getting a better deal than what I'm offering. You know that. I'm worth more than fifteen."

Freeman got out of the car, saying, "Okay, okay. You want fifteen, fine. Fifteen." He held the passenger door open and leaned back in: "I'd have to pay you after."

"See, you supposed to give me something up front." Maurice shook his head again and said, "All right, man. Pay me after. You still ain't driving, right? How you gonna get there tomorrow, bus?"

"Um hm."

Maurice threw his head back and laughed. Then, he leaned forward and laughed some more. Finally, he stopped and said, "You serious, right? You taking the bus tomorrow morning?"

"Yeah, bus and train. Why not?"

Maurice wiped a tear of amusement from his eye. "You lookin' to get shot, for real. Let me pick you up. Say 6:15. Where you live now?"

Freeman gave the address and asked, "You gonna charge me extra for that?"

"Nah." Maurice reached across, shut the door, and started the engine. "6:15," he repeated, and drove away.

Freeman walked back along the quiet street and headed toward Home Cookin' for lunch, thinking that Maurice was right: Freeman knew of no one he'd rather have covering him tomorrow, and he'd have paid more—quite a bit more—if the bodyguard had asked. Still, something didn't feel right...

—

The white Acura at the other end of the block pulled off, and the big, dreadlocked man Tommy had been following all morning turned and started walking toward him. Tommy ducked around the corner and put out his cigarette, wondering if this meeting in the car was somehow related to the bag of heroin—assuming this was the right guy and that he still had it. But that was assuming a lot. He crossed the avenue and, from there, followed the man to a small restaurant called Home Cookin'. Tommy waited on a corner seventy-five yards away, his eyes fixed on the eatery's door.

Tracy Whitlock had told him last night when and where he might find the guy he was looking for, but when he'd arrived there four hours ago at 8:15 after a sleepless night, he'd found two bus stops, one headed east, the other west. About ten minutes later, the guy he was looking for showed up across the street—tall, heavy, with long hair and a beard. He was about Tommy's age and wore a camouflage t-shirt, black beads hanging from his neck, tan cargo pants, and sandals; he paced back and forth, stressed about something, at the stop headed east. Tommy never took his eyes off him and didn't see the man's bus coming; when it stopped, he had to race across the street to get on it before it left.

Tommy followed him off the bus, to a Metro station, onto and off a train, and through a dreary residential neighborhood to an ordinary-looking music store called Sound Value. When he realized that the guy—who had no clue that he was being followed—worked inside, Tommy entered the doorway of a four-story apartment building next to a bodega down the block and across the street. Once behind the closed outer door's glass, he watched and waited. After a couple of hours, he went to the CD store's window and peeped inside. The man was behind the counter, his back toward Tommy, writing in a ledger. Tommy resisted the temptation to go in and look at him up close, maybe even talk to him, find out his name, but whatever was going to happen later, Tommy didn't want the guy to be too familiar with Tommy's appearance. He walked back to the apartment building's doorway.

Hours passed. He called Gabrielle. She was getting a pedicure and sounded glad to hear him: "Hey. When you coming home?"

"I'll be back down there soon. You okay?"

"I'm fine. Just missing you. I want to ask you where you are, but I know you're not gonna tell me."

"Can't trust the phones. You know that. Say something on the phone, next thing, you're in court, and they're playin' tapes of what you said to so-and-so on such-and-such day at such-and-such time. The government got all the rights, and they done killed privacy a long time ago. Like I said, I'll catch you later on." He considered telling her about Edgar's death, but the words wouldn't come.

They spoke for a while longer, each glad to hear the other's voice. When the conversation ended, Tommy returned his attention to the CD store. Doubts about whether or not he was watching the right person increased; there was probably more than one man in the area of Gersi and Jarvis who fit this guy's description. But Tommy kept thinking about the man's body language at the bus stop and during the trip out here. Something heavy was going on with him; it could be money, a woman, a kid—or Tommy's package from Thailand.

Tommy's cell went off. It was Mingo, the man who'd bought the first two shipments and who was supposed to buy this one—this missing one—in Miami on Monday night. "Still on, yo?" Mingo asked in a low tone.

"No doubt," Tommy replied.

"Solid. Later." Mingo clicked off. He'd be pissed if Tommy didn't hold up his end, maybe pissed enough to do something crazy. But Tommy had enough to worry about; he returned his attention to the store across the street.

A white Acura stopped there around noon. Tommy looked at his watch and almost missed his target—who Tommy started to think of as "Dread" due to the hair—come out and get into the car, which passed Tommy and turned left at the first corner. Tommy ran from the doorway and turned the corner in time to see the vehicle park down the street near the end of the block.

Dread and the driver remained inside, talking. Tommy watched until Dread got out, talked for a minute, then headed toward Tommy when the car drove off. When Dread left Home Cookin' and returned to Sound Value, Tommy went to the doorway across the street, waiting for the right time to make a move but unsure about his mission.

———

"Hello. I want to talk to you for a minute."

Crouched in front of a cabinet inside Sound Value, Freeman was using a screwdriver to adjust the location of one of a set of stickers for sale when he heard the woman's voice next to him. He hadn't noticed anyone enter. When he looked up at the speaker, he did a double take. He put down the screwdriver and stood, shocked: it was the woman who'd been with the guy on Ellingwood Avenue the night before last— the man he'd be selling the heroin to for nearly half-a-million dollars the next morning!

Freeman guided her toward the door. He signaled to Marshall, the guy working behind the counter, and said, "I'll be right back."

Once outside, he stood in front of her amid passing pedestrians "What the hell you doing here?" he asked. "What's going on?"

She put on sunglasses she'd been holding and said in her pleasant voice, "I know who you are. I just want to tell you to be careful, for your own sake."

"You-you-you know who I am?" Freeman stammered. He raised his hand to shade his eyes and blinked several times while staring at her. Finally, he asked, "Who are you? How do you know me? How'd you find me here?"

"The man you're dealing with. Be careful."

So many questions came to Freeman's mind that he didn't know which to ask, and he stood there, staring. Finally, he spoke: "Why you telling me this?"

"You're not used to this type of thing. I can see it, and he can see it. I'm just telling you to watch your step, that's all. I can't say anything else."

Freeman started to ask her about the man he'd be dealing with, but, as suddenly as she'd appeared, she turned and left, glancing at him briefly just before she turned the corner.

His mouth hanging open, Freeman watched her until she disappeared. He didn't know what to think as he ambled back into the store.

Marshall asked, "Ex-girlfriend?"

"Nah, man."

"That's what it looked like. You look like she just told you she's pregnant with your kid. With your twins. You okay?"

Despite his stress, Freeman laughed and waved him off. As he resumed working, he tried to get past the strangeness of the woman's visit to figure out what to make of her warning.

———

A slim black woman in a maroon blouse and white jeans entered the store and, seconds after she'd gone in, re-emerged with the man Tommy had been following. They looked like two very different people—she classy and neat, he loose and carefree—probably not in a relationship. Whatever the woman said surprised Dread. She must have been what he'd been thinking so hard about earlier. Could this be related to Tommy's missing shipment? He didn't see how, and as the woman walked away, leaving Dread standing still, thrown off by whatever she'd said, Tommy thought again that he probably had the wrong person.

But he had no other lead. Tommy left the doorway, crossed the street, walked right passed Dread, and followed the woman around the corner in time to see her get into a blue van and drive away. As Tommy turned and walked back toward the doorway across from Sound Value, his cell went off: Iris, the woman who stayed with his father, Leon.

"Your dad's real sick," she said.

Tommy's hand went back and forth repeatedly across his forehead. He asked, "Is he there?"

"Yeah, he came back from the hospital day before yesterday, but he's not doing too good right now. He's got pneumonia, for one thing. He's not eating."

"Can you put him on the phone?"

"He's sleeping. But I just wanted you to know; he doesn't have a whole lot of time left…"

Tommy swallowed hard. "All right. Okay. I'm up north right now, but I'm gonna stop by soon." He thanked her for calling and clicked off, picturing his father in the last stages of a battle against AIDS. Tommy had mixed feelings about him. He'd been absent for most of the time when he should have been there as a parent. Right after Tommy's mom had been murdered, for instance, Leon was in and out of Tommy's aunt's house, where Tommy was staying, but then Tommy didn't see him for weeks. And that was the way Leon had always been, here one second, gone the next, always talking, always moving, always with ten different things going on. But because of the way his dad talked, laughed, and played with him when he *was* around, Tommy had always gotten the feeling that Leon loved him as his only son, in his own way…

Tommy hadn't seen him since Tommy's young nephew, Anthony, had been murdered in Miami a year ago, and he wanted to visit while there was still time. But first, he had to straighten this mess out. He returned his attention to the music store.

He was still watching when the big dreadlocked guy came outside during rush hour and, apparently finished for the day, took a moment to scan the street, suspicious. For an instant, he seemed to look right at Tommy, then walked to the Metro station. Tommy wondered what was going on with the man while following him by train and bus all the way to 67 Gersi Place. There, Tommy's unsuspecting target pulled out a bunch of keys, opened the front door, picked up mail from the floor, and went in.

Tommy got his car from where he'd parked it eleven hours earlier and drove back to Gersi. He cut off the engine, lowered the window, and eyed number 67. The .45 Jake had given him the previous day was wedged into a slot under the rental car's back seat. He wanted to ring the doorbell, press the gun into the guy's bellybutton, force him inside the house, and find out once and for all if this man knew anything about Tommy's merchandise. But uncertainty had increased all day, especially after the scene in the middle of the street with the woman. And if this wasn't the right person, Tommy couldn't just walk out of the guy's house and drive away after questioning him at gunpoint. The main thing holding Tommy back, though, was that he didn't know if anyone else was in the small row house. He'd have to wait just a little longer and watch closely for any sign of another person inside. Then, he'd knock on the door and see what was what.

But the odds were against Tommy getting his shipment back, and as minutes ticked by, dejection and weariness set in. Soon after he'd parked, he did what he hadn't done since early yesterday: his head went back to the headrest, and he fell asleep. Within minutes, a heavy raindrop—the first precipitation in nearly a month—splattered on the windshield.

—

Relaxation usually came naturally to Freeman but not tonight. The woman's visit to Sound Value and her unexpected warning continued to dominate his thoughts as he prepared a meal and ate. Afterward, he listened to a Vortex CD and drank a glass of red wine, but jitters remained, even when his married-with-three-kids sister called from L.A. and spoke with him for twenty minutes.

Later, as Freeman drew his bedroom curtains, he barely noticed the rain falling against the window. He set his alarm for five and tried and failed to fall asleep. He shouldn't have let the woman who'd warned him at the store leave without getting some kind of explanation. Had the buyer sent her? If so, why? To unnerve Freeman? If that was the case, he knew where Freeman worked. But no matter how Freeman looked at it, none of that made sense; she must have come on her own. Freeman wondered what he was supposed to be careful about. The guy sounded so reasonable, so legitimate on the phone. Freeman's constant shifts and turns on the bed reflected his inner turmoil until finally, nearly an hour after lying down, he fell asleep.

Apart from sometimes waking to pee, Freeman always slept straight through until six-thirty or seven, depending on when he'd turned in. Tonight he awoke, panic stricken, to the sound of rain at 3:02. He lay on his back, staring into darkness, and envisioned the deal taking place above Shane's less than four hours from now—and the things that could go wrong. He pictured Maurice downstairs by the entrance, listening. If the buyer pulled a weapon and tried to steal the bag, Freeman would... what? The thought made him uncomfortable, but he'd go along with the deal, knowing that the bodyguard waited at the exit.

He got up, sat at the edge of the bed hunched over, and thought again about what the woman had said earlier today. She must have been talking about something like that; or was she just warning Freeman not to try anything? Again, he tried to figure out what she'd meant, then realized that he never would and was wasting his time thinking about it.

He went to the window and parted the curtain; steady rain fell on houses across the street and on parked cars during this, the night's most peaceful hour. He wondered about whether or not Simone missed him. Was it over? Was someone with her now? Did it matter? Her words from a couple of nights ago came like a slap: "...dumb ass, Freeman. Watch, you're gonna fuck it all up." That challenge had made him hire a bodyguard because he wanted to prove her wrong by getting it right. But doing that had validated the idea underneath what she'd said, that he couldn't do it by himself. He thought about Maurice's mocking tone during their conversation that afternoon in the bodyguard's car: Maurice laughing, thinking that Freeman didn't know what he was doing and that Freeman's way couldn't work.

Freeman released the curtain and went back to bed. Part of him wanted to forget the whole thing, but another part wanted to do it his own way and prove them wrong—and to prove something to himself. If the guy pulled something this morning, he just pulled it; whatever happened, Freeman would have faced it on his own terms. He realized the danger, but he'd wanted to do it by himself from the beginning. Going it alone felt right.

So Freeman chose to go solo. He'd have to leave before Maurice arrived; he set his alarm for half-an-hour earlier and fell right back to sleep.

Chapter Eleven

June Rain

Henry kept his cell on vibrate, and when it finally woke him early on Saturday morning, he realized that it had been going off for a while. He had a brutal hangover. He checked the phone: Redda had called, twice. What time was it? Shit! He was supposed to be meeting him right now to take the package from Simone's boyfriend in southeast!

Henry called back and said, "I just woke up."

"What?" Redda sounded shocked. "What's going on, man? What's happened to you? I could see something was wrong last night."

Henry could hear in the background that Redda was driving. He scratched his head and spoke with eyes shut. "Where are you?"

Redda said, "I'm on my way to meet the guy now."

"I'm going to be a few minutes late," Henry said. "Try to hold him there. We can still do it."

Redda sucked his teeth. "Look, I can't wait. If you're there, you're there. I'm going ahead." He clicked off.

Henry struggled to his feet and stumbled to the shower. Not until he came out dripping ten minutes later did he remember vaguely that a woman he'd called after getting to his room last night had slept with him and left. He sniffed the pillow next to his and smelled her perfume.

He checked for his wallet and found it intact in his pants pocket. Half wet but relieved, Henry threw on clothes. Redda had given him a .45 for what they'd planned to do with Simone's boyfriend. He slipped it into his waistband in the small of his back under a shirt, put on his hat, and rushed out into the rain.

———

Maurice pulled up to 67 Gersi Place, Freeman's house, around six-twenty. The building showed no sign of activity. He called Freeman's number and went straight to voicemail. He guessed that Freeman might be running late and taking a shower or something and called again two minutes later. When he got the same result, he went to the front door and rang the buzzer. Still no response. He faced the street and stood with hands on hips. What the fuck was going on? He called a third time, and Freeman answered.

"I'm outside waiting, man," Maurice said. "You ready?"

"I ain't there."

"What?"

"I ain't there for real," Freeman repeated.

"You ain't here? What you mean you ain't here? Where the fuck are you?"

Maurice hesitated and tried to stay calm. "You're bullshitting me, right?"

"No. I ain't there."

"You out your goddamn mind? You make me come all the way out here..."

"Hey look, I'm sorry 'bout all that. Something came up at the last minute."

Maurice yelled into the phone. "What the fuck you mean, 'something came up'? Something comes up, you supposed to call me. I drove up here from Virginia..."

"I was rushing to get out the house. I'll give you something for your time, yo. Don't worry. It's gonna work out. Look, I gotta check you later on."

Maurice said, "Listen ..." but Freeman clicked off.

Maurice couldn't believe it. He wanted to kick Freeman's door in, but that wouldn't solve anything. He shook his head and walked back to his car, thinking that Freeman was one strange dude; but he was a musician, and most of them were that way. Anyway, the good thing was, whatever was going on, Maurice could go home and get some more sleep.

He got behind the wheel and put the key into the ignition, but he didn't start the car. He'd once seen a drug deal go bad where two guys got shot and another got his throat cut. Freeman was naïve, and the bodyguard pictured him at this moment, on a bus with hardly anybody else on board this early on a rainy Saturday morning, carrying drugs or whatever it was he was trying to sell, heading for trouble. Maurice believed that people should lie down in whatever beds they made, but it sounded like Freeman was playing out of his league and could get hurt—at least. So, despite being pissed, Maurice decided to go to Shane's.

He started the car and switched on his headlights and windshield wipers. As he began to pull out, somebody knocked on the passenger window. Maurice hadn't seen anyone approach. He started to ignore the guy, but, through raindrops running down the glass, the young brother looked like he needed help, maybe directions. When Maurice lowered the window, the man pointed a Glock at Maurice's eye.

"Open the goddamn door," the man snarled. Maurice did, thinking carjack. The man got in, kept his aim, and said in a southern accent, "Close the window and don't try no bullshit. Now what the fuck is going on?" He was slim and had a tiny gold and black knife hanging from a chain around his neck. Fire burned in his eyes, which were popping out of his head like he was wired off something. But he knew how to handle the gun.

"What's goin' on where?" Maurice kept his hands in plain sight because he thought anything would set this guy off. "What you talking about?"

The guy spoke without blinking: "Nigga I ain't playin'. You tell me right now what's goin' on with homeboy in there, or I'm gonna light your motherfuckin' ass up. Talk, goddamn it!"

Maurice had a gun, too, an old .38 revolver, oiled and ready, in a holster above his ankle. He cut off the engine and told the man what he knew, all the time looking for the right moment to make a move. This guy looked crazy, and a crazy man's unpredictability made him the most dangerous. But all Maurice needed was for the man to look away for an instant.

"Where the deal gonna be at?" the man asked.

"About twenty-five minutes from here, upstairs from a store, Shane's, in southeast." Maurice pointed, trying to distract him.

The man stayed focused. "It's supposed to be at seven?"

"Yeah." Maurice glanced at the dashboard clock hoping that the man would do the same. He did. Maurice went into action.

—

Tommy awoke wide-eyed to rainy early daylight. The dashboard clock read 6:14; when he realized that he'd slept in the car for eleven hours, he knew that he had to see a doctor. He looked at 67 Gersi Place, thinking that he'd waited much too long to make a move. He got the .45 from under the back seat and tucked the weapon into his waistband, under his lightweight jacket. He was about to go to the house when a white Acura, just like the one he'd seen yesterday outside the music store, cruised by and parked across from number 67. Two minutes later, a dark-skinned, weightlifter type, wearing a black t-shirt, jeans, and boots got out and walked to the front door. No one responded when he rang the buzzer. He made some calls, got angry about something, then walked slowly back to the Acura shaking his head.

From the way this dude acted, the dreadlocked guy wasn't in the house. Tommy held the gun, thinking for a second that the Acura might lead to him and considered following it. But he'd done enough following, watching, and waiting. He made sure the gun was hidden, got out of his car, and strode to the Acura. As it started to pull out, he reached it and knocked on the window.

Once Tommy aimed the gun at the guy and sat inside, the muscle-bound dude told him about the dreadlocked guy selling something—probably Tommy's merchandise—in about half-an-hour. Tommy realized that he'd been following the right guy all this time. He looked at the dashboard clock. The moment he did, the man moved, like a cat. He grabbed Tommy's gun hand and twisted it, almost breaking Tommy's trigger finger. Tommy yelled and dropped the gun. A sledgehammer-like blow to the temple smashed his head into the passenger-side window, which broke. The man reached across, opened the door, leaned back, and kicked Tommy hard. Tommy flew out of the car, semi-conscious. The door slammed, and the engine started. The Acura peeled out, sped down the street, and skidded around the corner.

Tommy regained his senses after several moments. His head hurt on both sides, and rain fell on his face as he lay on his back, arms outstretched. Finally, he stumbled to his feet and massaged his head despite his aching trigger finger. He couldn't believe the guy's speed and strength. He got his bearings and, brushing bits of glass from his hair, face, and clothes, staggered to his car.

—

Freeman's anxiety grew with each of the five blocks that he walked from the train station to Palletta Road. He was soaked by the time he reached Shane's Sporting Goods and unlocked and opened the inner and outer doors next to it. He went up a flight of stairs and entered a large room above the store. It contained a dusty wooden table and a metal folding chair, and the only light came from a row of windows facing the street, each with its bottom half blacked out. The vibe suggested that no one came up here. He left the overhead light off to avoid attention and removed from his back a brown leather satchel, which he lay on the table.

He walked to the windows and tried unsuccessfully to control his anxiety—no sign of the guy he was supposed to meet, or anyone else. He went back to the table, walking deeper into shadow as he moved further from the windows. He reached into the satchel and removed several books that he'd brought to cover up the package, then, from the bottom, the heroin itself.

Freeman held it in the palm of his hand, thinking that he was holding a bag of death itself. "You gonna kill anybody here today?" he whispered. "You gonna kill me?" He wiped dust from the folding chair, sat, shut his eyes, and tried again to relax. But he couldn't. He wound up pacing the room and checking his watch every few minutes.

At 6:59, the doors downstairs opened, and a sudden burst of adrenaline shot through Freeman's stomach. Footsteps ascended the flight of stairs leading to the room, each accompanied by the "clack" of someone pulling something up. He shoved the package back into the satchel, threw the books on top of it, and leaned against the desk with his back to the satchel in a pose meant not to betray his tension. The door opened. Redda entered, rolling a black traveling case on wheels. He said, "Hah. June rain," as he shrugged water from his waterproof tunic and shook a full-sized umbrella.

Freeman's knees felt as if they'd give out from nervousness. He managed to say, "Okay. I'm ready."

Redda chuckled and said, "All right, all right. Take it easy. Let's just get set up here. Let's see . . ." He looked around. The room had three doors at the far end, two leading to closets and one to a bathroom, and he went to each, opened it, and looked inside. Satisfied that he and Freeman were alone, he came to the table and said, "I've got to search you. That's how I do business."

"For what, a gun?" Freeman asked, raising his arms. "Go ahead. I told you I wasn't bringin' nothing like that."

After Redda frisked him, Freeman said, "Okay. Now I've got to search you." The buyer complied.

Once Freeman had finished, Redda patted himself as if he'd lost his keys and finally pulled a nail file from his jacket's breast pocket. "Where is it?" he asked.

"Right here," Freeman said, putting his hand on the satchel.

Using both hands, Redda carried his bag to the table and poured out bills stacked in rubber bands, much too much to count. "Check it, brother. I had to throw in some twenties, but it's all there."

Freeman had never seen anything like it; how could the guy have gotten this much cash so fast? Staring at the heap of money, he groped around in his satchel until he found the package, which he handed to Redda. The buyer took two small vials from his traveling case. He used the nail file to scoop a tiny amount of powder from the plastic bag and performed the same test that he had two nights earlier; but before emptying the first vial into the second, he paused for a moment and listened closely, as if he'd heard something downstairs. He continued, and when the liquid turned blue-ish, he nodded. "Are we okay?" he asked.

Freeman, thumbing through each stack as he put the money into his satchel, said, "I am, yeah."

"All right. Good. It's good to do business with you, brother," Redda said as he slipped the heroin, vials, and nail file into his bag.

Freeman hadn't figured on how much the money weighed. His satchel probably wasn't going to hold all of it, and if it did, he wouldn't be able to carry it; they'd have to switch bags. But it had all been so quick and easy, going back to the meeting at Ellingwood...

"Oh. One other thing," Redda said. He unzipped a pocket on the bag and took out a black gun that he pointed at Freeman's chest. "Put your hands up and move away from the money. Get over there by the wall. Hurry up."

Freeman's anger paralyzed him; he would've given his life to get his hands around the man's throat. If he survived, he'd find some way to make Chandler pay for introducing him to this motherfucking son of a bitch...

"Over by the wall," Redda repeated, raising the gun. "I'm not going to tell you again." Still stunned, Freeman glared at the man. He raised his hands slowly and started to back up. If only he'd waited for Maurice this morning, this stinking bastard in front of him would get what he deserved as soon as he tried to leave.

Just before Freeman reached the wall, something heavy banged hard against the store's metal gate downstairs; seconds later, it banged again. Something was happening on the street. Redda kept his aim on Freeman and stepped toward the window to look.

—

Maurice glanced in the rear view mirror at the guy he'd just kicked out of his car, then picked up the gun and slipped it into the glove box as he sped southeast toward Shane's. He had a bad feeling about Freeman's deal; the guitar player wasn't the type to handle anybody else like homeboy stretched out in the middle of the road back there. No, that was Maurice's specialty.

The bodyguard arrived on Palletta soon after seven. Few people were on the streets in this weather on a Saturday morning. Freeman had told him about a vacant second floor above Shane's. Its windows had no curtains; he drove past the store so he could approach it on foot on the same side of the street without anyone inside seeing. After parking around the corner, he got out of the car and walked to the unlocked door next to the sporting goods store. He entered the building and opened an inner door slowly. About twenty steps with a wall on each side led to another door on the right. Maurice pulled a gun from his ankle holster and took every step in super slow motion so his two-hundred-and-seventy pounds wouldn't make the stairs creak, but one of the first ones did anyway, enough to make him pause before continuing.

As he passed the halfway point, a muffled voice, not Freeman's, came from behind the door up ahead. Maurice took the next step, thinking that he didn't want to enter the room because he had no idea what was happening inside. Maybe the deal was going smoothly. Freeman had wanted him to stay out here anyway, but the guy Maurice had just encountered outside Freeman's house had made Maurice reconsider everything. He heard the voice again from inside the room, the tone as if giving an order.

He reached the top a minute after starting up. No sound came from the room, and he was about to put his ear to the door when two men spoke on the street, directly outside the outer door. Maurice looked downstairs toward the voices. He hoped the men weren't coming in, and he hoped to God they weren't cops.

Outside, something smashed against the gate covering the store next door, and again. Maurice wondered what was going on. He started back downstairs to find out, trying again not to make the stairs creak.

—

The plan had been for Redda to bring the money and have Henry walk in on the sale on the second floor and "steal" the cash and the drugs. Henry couldn't see any reason for Redda to bring all that cash, but Redda said that once Simone's boyfriend had seen it, he wouldn't know that Redda had robbed him; plus, if anything went wrong, Redda could still make the buy and turn a good profit.

Redda had given Henry a gun. It sounded simple enough, and Henry was supposed to get a hundred thousand dollars for his work, then drive out west. But he'd woken up late. He had no idea what Redda was thinking, but all Henry could do was go ahead as planned.

In light steady rain, he turned on to Palletta and approached the door leading to the second floor. A slim young black man, the only other person in sight, approached from the other direction. This couldn't be Simone's boyfriend; she'd mentioned his weight problem more than once. Redda had said that the store didn't open until late and that no one used the building's second floor, so Henry assumed that the guy would keep walking past the door, but when Henry was about to enter, the guy did, too. This guy had nothing to do with what was going on inside. Henry stopped in front of the door and asked him, "Where you going?"

The man walked right up to him and said, "What?"

Henry said, "You got no business. Go on. Get the hell out of here."

The man pushed Henry hard. Henry reached back for the gun...

———

Tommy had made two wrong turns while following his GPS's instructions, but he saw the sign for Shane's Sporting Goods soon after he reached Palletta Road. His head was killing him. The man who'd hit him said the deal was supposed to take place on the second floor, above the store. Tommy had no plan and no weapon; he'd have to make it up as he went along.

A Spanish guy wearing a white hat and carrying no umbrella neared the building from the other direction. He had nothing in his hands, so he probably wasn't part of the mix. But Tommy knew something was up when the guy stopped outside the door and asked who Tommy was, then cussed him, with an accent.

Whoever this was, Tommy had had enough; if he still had his .45, he'd empty it into this motherfucker, right there, and go on about his business. Tommy pushed Henry with both hands, sending him flying into the metal gate covering the store. Henry reached for something. Tommy lunged forward and grabbed him. Henry grabbed back, and they scuffled until Tommy again slammed Henry into the gate. With his arms pinned, Henry couldn't reach his weapon. He brought his knee up hard to Tommy's groin but didn't land squarely. Tommy groaned and slumped, and they fell away from the gate. Henry's gun hit the ground. His eyes wide, he raised his hands to Tommy's throat and shouted as he started to choke him. Tommy tried to break Henry's grip but couldn't. He raised his thumbs to Henry's eyes and squeezed. In those positions, they wrestled each other across the sidewalk until they banged against a parked SUV.

Heavy gunfire sounded from inside the building. Henry flinched, and Tommy shoved him off. As if he'd practiced it a thousand times, Henry leaned onto the SUV and rolled off holding its antenna. He swung it fast, like a whip, forehand and backhand, grunting every time. Cuts opened on Tommy's face, ear, neck, and hand. Tommy crouched and raised his arms for protection. He glanced to his right, saw no cars approaching, and backed into the road, trying to escape the blows. Henry kept swinging until Tommy tripped on the raised median and fell backward. Henry jumped on top of him, and they rolled around in the middle of a westbound lane.

A cab stopped forty feet away, its driver leaning forward in disbelief. When Henry looked toward it, Tommy punched him in the jaw. Henry punched back, and Tommy's head bounced off the ground.

Again, Tommy's thumbs went for Henry's eyes. One thumb slipped in under an eyelid, and Henry yelled. He stood and staggered slowly to the sidewalk with a hand covering an eye, looking for the .45 lying near the gate. Tommy got up and followed. As Henry neared the gun, Tommy tackled him, and they collapsed in a heap. Exhaustion slowed them as they struggled to their feet. Clutching Henry's shirt, Tommy swung hard and sent Henry sprawling.

Tommy was woozy. Blood dripped from his injuries as he walked slowly toward the gun and picked it up. The door to the building opened to his right. The muscle-bound guy emerged, hunched over, bleeding from an unseen wound, holding a .38. Tommy aimed at him with both hands, but Maurice turned away and hobbled down the street.

Tommy aimed at Henry, who stood straight and raised his hands. This guy had just kneed him in the balls, choked him, and cut him up with an antenna. Tommy wanted to shoot, but as he'd been doing all week, he reminded himself that he'd come for his merchandise, not a murder charge. He stepped toward Henry and asked, "Who are you?"

Henry said nothing, and Tommy hit him on the head with the gun's handle. "Who are you motherfucker?" Henry remained silent.

Tommy didn't have time for this. Once more, he resisted the urge to shoot and said, "Get your ass out of here. Go on. Don't let me see you again, anywhere." Henry stood still long enough to show that

Tommy didn't scare him. Then, he retrieved his hat and walked away. He looked back twice.

Cops would be here any second, Tommy thought, and he still didn't have what he'd come for. Weary, wet, and wounded, Tommy entered the building to look for the package.

—

Up on the second floor, Redda pointed the gun at Freeman while walking to the window to check the banging noise from outside. He looked down to the street: Henry had his hands around a black man's throat and was pushing him against a black truck. Redda wondered, "What the hell…?" He turned to Freeman and said, "Get in the bathroom, quick."

Freeman walked to the first of three doors at the other end of the room and went inside. Redda propped the metal chair behind it. He picked up both bags—one containing the heroin and the other money—and slung each over a shoulder. The money weighed a ton; he couldn't carry it and would have to wheel it to his car. He grabbed his umbrella, yanked open the door that led downstairs, and froze: a huge black man, wearing a black t-shirt and holding a gun, was tiptoeing down, trying to be silent. The man heard Redda open the door and whirled toward him. Redda raised his gun but hesitated, wondering, "Cop?"

—

At the top of the stairs, Maurice heard banging from outside and started back down to see what was happening, but he moved slowly; he didn't want the steps to make any noise. As he neared the bottom, someone came out of the room upstairs. Maurice whirled. A surprised-looking Middle Eastern man with two bags stared at him open-mouthed, then raised a gun. Maurice crouched military style and fired six times. The man collapsed, his gun going off as he fell, spraying bullets in all directions. One zipped past Maurice's ear before another smashed into his ribs, causing him to yell and double over.

The man on the steps looked dead. Grimacing, his eyes watering, Maurice cupped his hand to his mouth and called Freeman's name twice. No answer. He imagined what the man's two bags contained. He wanted to take them, but the burning in his ribs and chest was making it hard to breathe. He couldn't carry either bag. Maurice knew about torso wounds; he could easily be bleeding to death internally. He had to get to a hospital.

He staggered outside, both hands covering his injury. The man he'd kicked from his car an hour ago stood there holding a gun on a Spanish guy. Maurice ignored them and, wincing with each step, tried to make it to his car.

—

When the man had told Freeman to get in the bathroom, Freeman thought it was time to die. He walked numbly to the other end of the room on legs that had turned to jello and opened the door. Some relief came when the man closed it from outside, propped something behind it, and walked away. Nausea made Freeman close the toilet's lid and sit on it with his head lowered.

He was trying to compose himself when about ten shots sounded from within the building. Seconds later, he thought he heard someone call him twice. Maurice? The voice was muffled and weak, and Freeman wasn't sure. He remained in the bathroom for a while longer. But with shooting and drugs and whatever else, police would be here soon. This wasn't the place to be.

The building was silent. He tried to open the door, but something was blocking it. He stepped back, barged into it, and forced it open.

He walked warily to the door that led downstairs and opened it two inches. The man who'd just tried to rip him off lay face down on the top steps, not moving. Blood ran from his body toward the gun he'd dropped. He looked dead; who the hell had shot him? Freeman thought, "Another corpse. Damn." Slowly, he opened the door wider and, trying not to touch the body, picked up his brown satchel. The dope was still in it.

Someone opened the outer door downstairs. Freeman dropped the satchel and grabbed the other bag—the black one, the one with the money. He went back inside and into the bathroom, trying to avoid whoever was coming in.

—

Tommy entered the building and aimed at the body lying face down at the top of the staircase until he saw the man's gun near the bottom step. Using the handrail and wall for support, he made his way up. It took a while, but once he got to the top, he prodded the man with his foot: dead. A brown leather satchel lay on the corpse. Could it be? Tommy emptied the bag onto the floor: five books fell out, then his green, plastic, duct-tape-wrapped package. Tommy picked it up and sniffed it. Despite hunger, a splitting headache, a sore groin, bruised knees and knuckles, and stinging cuts on his face, neck, and hands, he smiled. He threw the package back into the bag, which he slipped onto his shoulder. He opened the door to the musty, dimly lit room and looked inside: empty. Tommy started to leave but noticed three closed doors to his left at the shadowed end of the room. The nearest had a chair propped against it.

Cops would be here any second, but someone could be behind those doors, or maybe Tommy would find something good, something like money. He entered the room and walked toward the first door. Subconsciously, his hand went to the miniature stiletto hanging from his neck. It wasn't there! Tommy froze; he must have lost it during the fight, or maybe the chain had broken when he'd fallen out of the Acura back on Gersi Place. A corpse lay a few feet away. If the chain was here and the cops found it, it would connect him to a homicide. Shit!

Carrying the brown satchel, he traced his steps past the body on the stairs and outside, looking for the gold chain the whole way. He went to the gate that covered the store and looked along the sidewalk but didn't see the chain or the stiletto. To his right, rain was washing away drops of the muscle-bound guy's blood from the street; a siren sounded in the distance.

Tommy didn't have time, but he couldn't leave the chain. He kept looking, hurrying from the gated storefront to the SUV to the doorway to the middle of Palletta Road and back to the front of the building, with the cop car getting closer. He had to get away. But where the hell was the chain? Crouching and scanning the ground, Tommy went again to the SUV where the Spanish guy had gotten the antenna. The chain lay there, on a grating in the gutter, behind the front tire. He picked it up and dropped it into his pocket.

Tommy felt as if he'd been in a bad accident; he had aches, cuts, and bruises from his head to his knees. The approaching cop car's lights flashed in the distance. He didn't remember where he'd parked, but he headed west. He ducked around a corner and did his best to hurry from the murder scene.

—

Freeman heard the door close. He took a minute to compose himself; then he left the bathroom and wheeled the black bag containing the money to the steps leading down. Someone had taken his satchel, but the books that he'd brought to hide the bag of dope inside it were next to the body. He scooped them up and while slipping them into the traveling bag, heard a distant siren. He stepped gingerly over and around the dead man, carried the bag downstairs, opened the two doors, and peeped outside. The street appeared normal. He stepped out and rushed from the building. He thought about a cab but decided against it: right now, the fewer people he interacted with, the better. Head down, he carried and rolled four-hundred-thousand dollars to the train station. He didn't look at any of the three squad cars that passed him on the way, their lights flashing and their sirens wailing.

—

Henry picked up his hat and walked away looking in the gutter for a good piece of glass. Anger clouded his vision; more than anything, he wanted to go back and, if the black guy he'd just fought went into the building, wait outside and cut his throat when he came out. But cops would be here soon.

One of his eyes was puffy and sore; both had scratches and bruises. He figured that something bad had happened to Redda inside the building, but fuck him. Fuck him, fuck Simone, fuck the boyfriend, and fuck D.C. Fooling around with drugs brought bad luck anyway. And add that to how many blacks were in this town, and he should have known something crazy was going to happen.

He got into his car and drove to the hotel. After a shower, he changed his clothes, iced his bruises, packed, and went to the airport. He had no plans to come back anytime soon.

Within three hours, Henry was airborne, headed to Las Vegas via St. Louis.

—

When Freeman got home, he flopped into his armchair and stared at the wall. His fingers and legs were trembling. Ten minutes later, he went upstairs and took a shower. After drying off, he came back down to the living room and the black traveling bag. He left the curtains closed and poured the money on the same living room table where he'd put the green bag of heroin the first night he'd found it. He sat in his armchair and eyed the loot, but the previous hour's events kept replaying in his mind.

Who'd killed the buyer? Maurice? Freeman would have to talk to the bodyguard to find out. Could anyone connect Freeman to the murder? Only Chandler and the woman who'd come to Sound Value, warning Freeman to be careful. Chandler hated cops, and what could the woman do—tell the police that her boyfriend or husband or whoever the guy was had been killed trying to buy a pound of heroin? Freeman had no idea who'd been shooting on the stairs, but he didn't see how anyone could pin anything on him.

Still, he couldn't relax. The adrenaline rush he'd felt back on Palletta, when the downstairs door first opened and the buyer entered the building, had intensified when the son-of-a-bitch pulled a gun, and it flew off the scale when the shooting started. Freeman was still wired. Cops could come knocking at any time—now, next week, next year; he'd have to think of what to say if they did. Maybe he should just leave town, but he loved the District…

His tension felt like an electric current running from head to toe and back up again, but along with it came relief and a sense of freedom. He no longer had the drugs, and he'd proven Simone wrong: he knew he'd been lucky, but Freeman had faced a guy who'd tried to rip him off—and maybe intended to kill him—and come away with the money.

Freeman re-focused on the green stacks in front of him. He'd been so nervous that he hadn't planned what he'd do with the money. He got up, threw the cash back into the bag, and took it down to the basement to find a good place to hide it. Then he came back up, he went upstairs, lay in the bed, and stared at the ceiling. The band had a show tonight, but that was the furthest thing from his mind. Today was his day off, and he had plenty of thinking to do.

JUNE RAIN

—

Tommy's cuts from the antenna were superficial, but they stung. Back in his motel room, he treated them with iodine and Vaseline after brushing his teeth and taking a long shower. He got his things together and hit the road for 95 South with the green plastic bag in the trunk beneath the spare, along with the gun that the Spanish guy had dropped. He didn't worry about the car being stopped and searched; he had his papers in order and had no intention of driving in a way that would draw attention. He looked forward to getting back to Miami's sunshine, finishing his deal, and seeing Gabrielle. Once he reached Florida, he'd have accomplished his mission.

But even though he'd gotten what he'd come for, it seemed to be a hollow victory; Tommy would never again see his friend, Edgar.

CHAPTER TWELVE

ROSITA

Simone punched out from Lapham Bros. at seven and, under an umbrella, headed across the parking lot toward her Volvo. Earlier, she'd accepted a friend's invitation to hit a club at around ten tonight, and she wanted to go home and get ready. This time last week, she'd been dealing with two men; now, she was in neutral with both. How was Freeman doing? The more she thought about it, the harder it was to see anything good coming out of him getting involved in drugs. Safety was part of why she'd wanted him to deal with Henry, although she wasn't even sure about that anymore. And what *was* the deal with Henry? She hadn't heard from him all day, and he was supposed to leave tomorrow. She pulled up his number on her cell and called—no answer. Strange. She left no message.

As Simone walked toward her car, a red 4Runner pulled up beside her. A movie-star-handsome Latino in his late twenties lowered a tinted window, smiled, and said, "Hey, baby, what's up with *you*?"

"Not much."

"What's your name?"

"Simone."

Still smiling, the man leaned out further and said, "You're the best looking girl I've seen in a while, Simone. My name's Ricardo. You live around here?"

"Not far."

The 4Runner continued to roll beside her as she approached her Volvo. He said, "Nothing much going on, huh? Well let me talk to you for a second. Check this out…"

—

Alex Kirby was waiting outside an Ethiopian restaurant in Silver Spring when Hazel Royce arrived at 8:00 p.m. The rain that had been falling for almost twenty-four hours was now a light mist, barely visible against the beginning of a soft yellow sunset. Royce and Kirby smiled when they saw each other. They entered the cozy, aromatic eatery; each table had a set of tiny candles that helped create subtle lighting. A host escorted them upstairs. They ordered, and while the chefs prepared the food, Kirby did most of the talking: "I got married right out of college. It lasted eight years. We'd known each other since ninth grade, but it was like we knew each other better than we knew ourselves. She was a good person. She *is* a good person. We just weren't anywhere near ready for marriage, you know? Nowadays, it's a mistake before, say, thirty, thirty-five. No, we didn't have any kids."

And during the meal: "I was in the navy, on submarines. Loved it. You have to get used to the military at first, but I got a lot out of it. It helped me grow as a person. You've traveled, right? You know how you see things differently whenever you come back to this country? We take lot of things here for granted. People complain a lot, but our poor folks have it better than ninety percent of the people in the world. I mean, I've seen poverty—people who are born, live, and die in it—average American doesn't know what the word means. That's why you've got people actually killing themselves every day trying to come here. It's not perfect, but no place is."

And afterwards, when they sat on a lakeside bench after a twenty-minute walk from the restaurant: "Real Estate just came naturally to me. I'd studied it in college, and I knew about contracting, so managing property was a good fit. I started out doing it for a guy who made money in the stock market. I did okay on that, but he was doing better than okay, so I branched out and bought a couple of buildings. I did pretty well with them. Still do. I like what I'm doing now, too, with the cottages in northern Virginia. I wouldn't mind having your gig, though, F.B.I. Ever shoot somebody?"

They took his car to a small nearby theater and saw a movie called *Panic*. The conversation resumed afterward as he drove her to her car. Royce enjoyed the talk, and she sensed good chemistry between them. As their evening ended, he kissed her cheek and smiled before she unlocked her car and got in. In the rearview mirror, he waved, tall, well-groomed, nice-looking, smiling. Royce didn't want to get too excited. "Good guy," she thought just before he faded from view. "Almost too good."

—

Near midnight, Tommy drove onto an unpaved driveway and parked in front of a small, two-story house that stood fifty feet from the dirt road. He'd never been there before. Overhanging trees and thick shrubs surrounded the wooden building, which had vines climbing up its sides. This part of Georgia had few streetlights, and he saw no other houses. Tommy got out of the car and looked up. The air was humid and seemed different, somehow. Stars seemed nearer and brighter; they lay across the sky as if sprinkled there. Thousands of crickets created a wave of noise that pulsed through the night.

Tommy stared at weak yellowish light, the house's only one, from a second floor window as he walked to the front door and knocked. After a minute, Iris opened it. A short stout woman with honey-brown skin and warm eyes, she was twenty years younger than Leon, not much older than Tommy; she'd stayed with Leon for the two years that he'd been sick. Tommy had called in the afternoon, so she expected him.

"Come on in," she said, looking him up and down. "So you his son, huh? Tomaas?"

"They call me Tommy. Yep. I'm the only one. I think."

"He's upstairs." As Tommy stepped inside, she noticed his cuts. "What happened to you?" she asked.

"Tell you the truth, I don't know, my damn self. Some guy started a fight."

"Oh. You got to be careful out there."

"Yeah, I know." Tommy followed Iris along a narrow, dimly lit corridor and up a flight of stairs. They paused outside a closed door, and she spoke quietly: "I told him you were coming. He can't talk much, and you know that's not him. He's in and out of sleep."

Tommy smelled death as soon as Iris opened the door and led him in. The room where his father lay was warm and contained several mid-sized plants. A low-watt bulb shone from a shade-less lamp near the foot of the bed. Iris turned on another lamp on a nightstand and left, closing the door behind her. Tommy braced himself and approached the bed. At first, he barely recognized the skeletal figure with paper-thin, almost transparent skin lying under white sheets. Little of Leon's full head of hair remained, and whitish crust covered and surrounded his nostrils and cracked lips.

Tommy pulled a chair up close. Leon turned slowly and asked "That you, son?" in a raspy voice, his sunken eyes burning brightly, then, "What the fuck happened to you?"

"What the fuck happened to you?" Tommy asked back.

Leon smiled weakly. "Goddamn needle just about finished me off. But that's what that shit'll do to you. Can't think straight once you start foolin' with it. I knew what I was gettin' into, though."

Tommy wondered about what to say to a dying man. "Well, we all gonna go some day. You ain't got no regrets, I know."

"Not a one. Nobody got time to be worryin' about the past," Leon said. "Live your life, Tommy, you hear?" He coughed and struggled painfully to clear his throat. "*Live* it. Do what's best for yourself and whoever you got with you, and don't look back."

Tommy nodded as Leon continued: "That's what I'm tellin' you. Don't be feeling bad for me." He paused and measured his breathing. "Rough times put everything in perspective. I slept homeless on park benches, and I slept in mansions. I done eleven months in solitary, and I seen the pyramids. Been to Paris and Tokyo. Had some of the finest women. This one here, she a good one." He nodded as best he could. "You got to grab a hold of life with both hands while you got time. Squeeze the shit out of it. Don't lay back wastin' time, feelin' sorry, especially for yourself, hear? Whatever you got goin' on, you focus on what's up ahead ..." His voice trailed off, and he closed his eyes.

Had he fallen asleep that fast? Every breath seemed quick and too shallow, and Tommy leaned forward, wondering each time Leon exhaled whether or not he'd inhale again. After a couple of minutes, Tommy stood. As he reached to turn off the bedside lamp, his father asked with closed eyes, "What happened with that deal you was setting up from Thailand?"

Tommy was surprised he remembered. "It's okay so far. Had a little trouble with the last shipment."

"Oh yeah? That how you got them marks on your face? That's an antenna did that, right?'

"Something like that."

"You a good boy," Leon said. "You handle yourself all right. You gon' make it." Again, a faint smile.

Tears formed behind Tommy's eyes. He held them there and said, "I got to go. I got a lot happenin' the next couple days."

"All right." Leon extended his left hand, the one closest to his son.

Tommy held it and applied gentle pressure. "Bye, dad," he said.

Leon held on to Tommy's hand and tried to pull him closer. He said something that Tommy couldn't make out. Tommy leaned closer and said, "Huh?"

"I'm sorry…about your mother."

Tommy nodded. "That's the past. I don't even think about that no more," he lied. Leon released Tommy's hand, groaned, and slumped back.

Tommy switched off the lamp, left the room, and went downstairs, where Iris sat in the kitchen. "You staying overnight?" she asked.

"I got to get back on the road."

"You okay driving? You look like you need rest."

"I be all right," he said as they shook hands.

Tommy left the house and walked to his car. He sat behind the wheel and stared into darkness that lay beyond the house. The cuts on his face, neck, and hand stung and throbbed, and his father's approaching death coupled with Edgar's murder weighed heavily on him.

He couldn't believe how disease had devastated his father, robbing him of the off-the-wall energy that had made him who he was. Tommy would never forget how his father had looked, sounded, and smelled while making the first apology that Tommy had ever heard from him.

Then, he remembered what Leon had said about focusing on the future. He looked at the clock: Tracy Whitlock, the D.C. cop, would be getting off duty around now. He called her number and went straight to voice mail. He left a message: "I'm gone. I got what I came up there for. Jake take care of you."

Tommy clicked off and looked at the weak light coming from a side window on the second floor, the window to his father's room. He made himself start the car.

—

Freeman woke early on a breezy Sunday morning and went for a walk in Clemente Park. The night before, Vortex had had the crowd jumping at a club in Laurel, Maryland. When live music connected, it was like good sex, with the band and the audience feeding off and elevating each other. He'd gone to an after-party with the others and had a drink, but he left as soon as he could get a lift back to D.C.

Now, he crouched near a boulder by a pond and threw out breadcrumbs for ducks. He should be nervous, considering what had happened the previous morning—and what could happen in the future—but for some reason he wasn't. Again, he wondered about Maurice. He'd called twice yesterday but gotten no answer. Was the bodyguard ducking him? Freeman would call again later.

He'd decided what to do with the money, for now. He'd wait a couple of weeks; then, two safe deposit boxes should handle part of it—the hundreds and fifties, at least. The rest he could keep at his place. The smart thing would be to invest it. But for now, the important thing was to draw no attention to himself and what he had.

Ducks approached warily on the water. Freeman stood and left the park; he had to put in six hours today at Sound Value. He didn't feel like work, but he wanted to behave normally.

—

Gabrielle got up a few minutes before nine and jumped when she went to the kitchen: Tommy was sitting at the island, eating a sandwich. They smiled at each other. She went to kiss him but froze when she saw two cuts from behind his left ear to his eye and another on his neck and along his jaw. "What the hell happened to you?" she asked.

He drank some apple juice and, without being specific, told her about his fight in D.C. while trying to get back something he'd lost.

"Tommy, something like this happens, I get real nervous. I ain't trying to change you or nothin,' but right now I'm wishing you did something different."

Tommy rolled his eyes. "Look, I just got here. You gonnna start that shit again? Different like what? You mean get a job? We got bills. What kind of job I'm gonna get?"

Gabrielle saw how tense he was. "Take it easy," she said. "I'm just sayin', this hard on me. I worry when you're gone. It's crazy out there. I know you doin' what you got to do, but it's getting to me. It ain't supposed to be like this. Not for us."

"You sounding like I'm too dangerous for you now. You want to leave? Go ahead. Get the fuck out."

Gabrielle remained still, thinking she didn't want this discussion now; she walked to Tommy, held him tightly, and peered in through the windows to his soul. "I ain't goin' nowhere. I'm *your* girl, Tommy," she said, her voice heavy with desire. "Know that."

He stood and kissed her. Forgetting his aches, Tommy picked her up the way he used to. He carried her to the bedroom. They started to make love, but Tommy, exhausted from the last few days, rolled onto his back and closed his eyes. Gabrielle's remained open as she considered whether or not this was the time to tell him what she had to say.

They lay there for several minutes until finally, she said, "There's something I got to talk to you about. It's important."

He seemed about to doze off. "Hm. I got something to tell you too. Go ahead."

Gabrielle sat up with her back against the headboard. She gathered herself and said, "There's something I never told you, never told anybody." She hesitated again for a second before saying, "I got a kid, a daughter, going on six."

Tommy opened his eyes. "What?"

"Her name's Jasmin. I gave her up for adoption right when she was born. She lives with a couple in Ridgemont. I'm supposed to go see her in a couple days." She explained the "mistakes" she'd made in her teens, the sudden curiosity that had arisen over a year ago about the girl, her contact and follow up with the adoption agency, her meetings with the Briscoes.

Tommy sat up and stared at her. "You bullshittin', right? This a joke."

"No, Tommy. No joke"

He looked at her for a long while without blinking, then said, "How we gonna be the way we been for the last four years and you don't tell me something like that? We supposed to be straight up with each other, right? I'd never keep nothin' like that from you. What I'm supposed to think?"

"Look, I didn't tell you because I didn't even tell myself. I just shut the whole thing out. Then, you and your dad went to Asia a year-and-a-half ago to work on some business deal you were setting up. I was sitting around here by myself one day, and it just hit me: I had to face the truth. But 'til then, I never even thought about it."

"I don't believe this shit," Tommy said, shaking his head as if stunned. "What else you ain't telling me?"

"That's it, Tommy. It's nothing else."

Tommy threw off his sheet. He got out of the bed and walked toward the door.

Gabrielle said, "Don't be mad, Tommy, okay? Try to understand."

He stopped and turned to face her. "You been lying to me from the first day I met you. I understand that."

He left the room. When he returned twenty minutes later, he'd taken a shower. He dressed in silence, ready to go out. As he left the bedroom, Gabrielle said, "You said there was something you wanted to tell me."

At first, Tommy didn't respond. Then, as he walked into the living room, he muttered, "Edgar's dead."

"What?" Gabrielle got up from the bed and followed Tommy to the front door.

"What do you mean 'Edgar's dead'? What happened?"

Tommy stopped with his hand on the doorknob. He turned his face to show his profile and said, "They shot him up in New York a couple days ago." He opened the door and left.

Gabrielle locked the door and leaned against it. Edgar had been like a brother to Tommy. He and his ex-wife, whom Gabrielle was still in touch with, had gotten together socially with Tommy and Gabrielle several times, and Gabrielle considered him a loyal friend.

She walked to a nearby table, put her hands on it, squeezed her eyes shut, and lowered her head.

—

That afternoon, Freeman prepared dinner after he got in from work. A Burning Spear CD played in the living room. As he went to the dining room to eat, someone knocked on the door. Surprised, he peeped through a window and saw Vaughan Chandler standing outside. He opened the door, and the singer stepped into the house without waiting for an invitation, saying in his Jamaican accent, "What the fuck happened, man?" His movements and tone showed agitation.

"What you mean, what happened? You hooked me up with a ripoff artist. That's what happened."

Chandler stood with his hands on his hips. "What you talkin' about?"

"No," Freeman said. "I want to know what *you're* talkin' about."

"You shot him?" Chandler asked.

"Hell no! Man, I never touched a gun in my life," Freeman said. "Don't know nothing about shooting nobody."

Chandler stared at him. His voice turned cold: "It real easy. You ever hear of a trigger? You pull that. The man's girlfriend call me last night talking about 'he dead, he dead.' She tell me is you kill him."

Freeman sucked his teeth. "I didn't kill nobody. How long you known me? I'm gonna kill somebody about some drugs? You know me better than that."

"It's so I tell her. Twice she call me. First time she cryin'."

Freeman said, "C'mon in, man. I just fried up some fish. I got extra."

Never one to refuse food, Chandler followed him in and sat down. Freeman brought out another plate and opened two beers. They started to eat, and Chandler asked, "What happened?"

Freeman told him. "I come out the bathroom, and the guy's laying on the stairs, dead. Whoever shot him must've taken the money and the drugs, but I didn't care; I just wanted to get out of it without getting killed my damn self."

Chandler said, "That's a tough one to sell right there. Only way I believe you is 'cause I know you. I tell her you don't know nothin' bout no guns. I tell her you scared of them. You not the type to go shoot nobody.' I tell her, 'Let me talk to him see what happened.' It's so I tell her."

Freeman asked, "Who was the guy?"

"Redda, from Syria or Lebanon or some place like that. He had money. That's what he did, buy and sell, just like what he did with you."

"Oh yeah? Well what he tried to do is rip me off. When he told me to get in the bathroom, I thought he was gonna kill me. How long you know him?"

"Couple years. You remember the house where you stayed Monday night when you come to Chicago? The guy who own that house, Dougie, it's he introduce me to Redda."

Freeman finished his food and downed half of his beer. "What about the woman?" he asked.

"She used to own a big place here in the city where they did women's hair. Something happened there, taxes or something like that, and she don't own it no more. She was with Redda for about a year. Her name Lucinda. She smart."

"Yeah, well, you talk to her again, you tell her I didn't shoot him, and I didn't see who did. I never touched a gun in my life. Anyway, he needed to get shot. But don't tell her that." He finished his beer.

Chandler downed his, broke out a joint, and lit up. Part of the way through it, Freeman asked, "You remember a dude used to work security for the band couple years ago named Maurice?"

Chandler filled his lungs and exhaled smoke through his nose before saying, "Uh uh. That must've been just before I joined up, but I know the guy. Dark-skinned, bodybuilding brother."

"Yeah. You know where he lives?"

Chandler shook his head no. He toked again and said, "Ask Charles. Charles know everybody."

Freeman nodded as Chandler passed the joint. He'd call Charles, Vortex's drummer, when Chandler left. Describing what had happened had gotten him wound up again, and the smoke would help him take the edge off. After two more hits, he played air guitar to the reggae coming from the other room.

—

Every November, Tommy paid a year's rent on a four-hundred-dollars-a-month studio apartment in an out-of-the-way complex in Kendall. Nobody else knew about it. He used the place and its small, basement storage area to stash items, and once in a while he'd go there just to cool out. When he'd hit Miami that morning, he stopped there before going home and left the bag of heroin. Now, disgusted by Gabrielle's deceit, he rode his motorcycle there.

He opened the sofa bed and tried for twenty minutes to get some sleep, but he couldn't. He walked to the window and lit a cigarette. His thoughts went to a time that they rarely visited, the afternoon seventeen years ago when the chaos that he couldn't escape, no matter how hard he tried, had begun...

Tommy was a short, thin ten-year-old who lived with his parents in a ranch-style house in Allappatah. As usual, his dad was often not home, and his dad's sister, Doris, was staying with them in a spare room for a few days. Tommy's mom, Rosita, usually picked him up from school, but this Tuesday afternoon, Leon and Doris were waiting for him outside the school gate in Leon's Jeep. Tommy learned from their talk that his aunt wanted a set of cushions from Macy's. After shopping, they ate at a food court, and Leon dropped them back at the house, where Tommy's mom was housecleaning.

As Tommy and his aunt walked along the pathway that led to the front door, a dog started barking wildly in the distance. Doris fumbled in her purse for her keys. Finally, she opened the door, and she and Tommy stepped into a ransacked living room. Tommy's aunt stood still; the place was silent. She put her arm across his chest and whispered, "Don't move." When she called out, "Rosita!" twice but got no answer, Tommy began to worry about his mom. Doris took a can of Mace from her bag and walked slowly toward the kitchen. Again, she called for her sister-in-law.

Everything was overturned or broken. As Doris disappeared from view, Tommy sensed something bad; terrible fear stirred within his stomach. The front door remained ajar behind him. He took a backward step and opened it wider; he wanted to go, but his aunt had said to stand still, so he did. Something fell in the kitchen, and his aunt screamed the most awful sound he'd ever heard or ever would hear: "Ooooooooooh!! Oh God! Oh God! Oh God!..." Doris sprinted from the kitchen, eyes bulging from a face about to burst with horror. Tommy started to cry, and she scooped him up and rushed outside. As she dashed along the pathway toward the street, his arms reached back toward the house's gaping door. He cried out, "Mommy..."

He went to her closed-casket funeral eight days later. Leon didn't. In fact, Tommy didn't see his father much for weeks after that, and when he did, Leon seemed different, subdued. No one ever told Tommy directly what had happened to his mother that day, but as he got older, he put together enough bits of information to figure out that Leon had owed drug money to two men who'd tortured Rosita before nearly decapitating her, all to punish her husband.

Things changed drastically for Tommy after that. He was shuffled from one relative to the next, one school to the next, with Leon popping up now and then, always going somewhere, always having something to do. Twice, as a teen, Tommy asked his dad about the men who'd murdered Rosita; the first time, Leon looked at him hard and said, "Don't worry about it. That ain't nothing to be talkin' about." The second time, two years later, Leon muttered, "I told you, don't ask me about that. I done took care of it."

Anger simmered within Tommy, but once he, too, began to hustle, he learned about how Miami's streets had everything but mercy; one bad move, one bad break, and he could suffer the same fate that his father had on that Tuesday afternoon.

Mindful of the cause of his mom's death, he avoided dealing in drugs while selling every other type of contraband he could get his hands on—until Leon convinced him to set up this Thailand to New York to Miami operation. Profit from his first run had more than covered the cost of setting it all up, and if this shipment and the remaining two went through, he'd clear his three million and walk away, as planned. None of it was worth Edgar's life, but he was in it now and had a scheduled meeting with his buyer tomorrow night.

Time to think about something else. Tommy turned away from the window and went to the TV. He popped in a DVD and flopped onto the sofa bed to watch it, but he couldn't concentrate.

—

Hazel Royce's two teenaged nieces had driven down from New York, and Royce spent the afternoon and early evening with them. Once they'd left her house, she did something that she'd never done before. She liked Alex Kirby, and felt excited whenever she thought about their date last night. But she found herself wondering about whether or not he was as he appeared. Her naturally questioning nature had turned to suspiciousness during her years in the F.B.I., years that had shown her, among many other things, how often and easily people committed crimes in one state and adopted a new identity and/or a new life in another. She wondered—was he as good as he seemed? So Royce went to her laptop and logged on to VIDANT IV, a highly classified, personal information database available only to certain members of the law enforcement, legal, and intelligence communities.

She clicked on the "auto" link and typed in "POE 3934," the number on Kirby's silver Audi. An enlarged copy of Alexander Haywood Kirby's driver's license, complete with his date of birth and social security number, appeared. She scrolled past links that would list his credit card transactions, Internet use, and phone records by day, week, month, or year. She stopped at his marriage, in Los Angeles at age twenty-two, to Frances Carol Allen and their divorce eight years later. They'd had no children. She scrolled down further, skimming through his years in college, his time in the navy, his jobs in business and real estate.

Kirby had excellent credit. Royce clicked on "legal record" and saw that he'd never been arrested and had no child support issues. She clicked out of the program and logged off. Kirby's background appeared to be as he'd said; nothing indicated that he'd lied to her or changed his identity or done anything else wrong. Royce nodded, a trace of a smile tugging at her lips.

—

Freeman had Monday off. After going for a walk, he went to his basement and, with pen and paper, spent over four hours counting and recounting the money. Each time, he came up with around $372,000, $28,000 short of the price he and the dead buyer had agreed on; the guy Redda was going to rip him off either way. That was okay. Freeman wrapped the half of it that was in hundreds and fifties in plastic shopping bags. One went into a knapsack and the other into a leather book bag.

He carried them outside and got to the bus stop five minutes before the number sixty-five arrived. He rode the bus a few blocks to his bank, Franklin Federal, smiling at one point at the thought of carrying this much cash around in Washington. Once he got there, he filled out a couple of forms and put the bags containing the money in three safe deposit boxes.

Outside the bank, Freeman called Maurice for the fifth time since Saturday morning: again, no answer. Freeman went to a nearby car rental agency, got a Hyundai, and drove west to Durham Drive in Germantown, where he'd been told Maurice lived.

—

Shafts of sunlight beamed through yellow poplars that surrounded Maurice's two-story house. Freeman rang the doorbell twice and waited. After a long wait, he heard movement inside. Maurice opened the door and eyed Freeman. He looked up and down the street before asking, "How you find me?"

"Charles, the drummer for the band."

A black and white Akita came from within the house to stand beside Maurice. The dog looked at Freeman and barked once. Maurice held its collar and said, "Quiet, Zak." Then to Freeman, "He's cool, as long as he sees me talking to you." He scanned the street again and said, "Come on in."

The hulking bodyguard wore a Raiders shirt and gray, knee-length shorts. He walked gingerly, as if every movement caused pain in his midsection. Freeman followed him to a simply furnished, Japanese-style living room, where they sat on low canvas chairs. The dog sniffed Freeman, wagged its tail, and ran to the basement as Maurice asked, "So what happened on Saturday?"

Freeman told him but said nothing about having the money. He asked Maurice, "Was that you on the stairs shooting?"

Slowly, Maurice lifted his t-shirt. Bandages covered his torso. He pointed to his ribs and said, "The guy you saw laying on the stairs got me right here. You didn't hear me call you, yo?"

"I heard somebody, but I didn't feel like walking into the middle of a gunfight, you know what I'm sayin'? That was crazy. So it *was* you shot the guy."

"It was gonna be either him or me," Maurice said. "You say the money and the drugs were gone when you came out the bathroom?"

Freeman nodded. "I figured whoever shot the guy—you or whoever—took whatever was there."

"All I took was this bullet," Maurice said. "Must've been one of the guys fighting on the street took them."

"Fighting on the street? Who was fighting on the street?" Freeman asked.

Maurice explained about his confrontation with a slim young man outside Freeman's house half-an-hour before the deal was supposed to take place. "While your buyer was pulling a gun on you, the same guy I saw and some Spanish-dude were fighting on the street. That was the banging sound that made the buyer look out the window when he told you to get up against the wall."

Freeman wondered who the slim guy was and what he'd been doing outside Freeman's house when Maurice first saw him. He probably had the drugs; was he someone to worry about? He was already concerned about the woman who'd come to his job to tell him to be careful; she seemed like the type who might do anything. But it was best not to worry about her or him or anything else. He asked, "You had to get that bullet cut out, right? Who paid for that?"

"Me. I got my own insurance. It still cost me, though."

Freeman appreciated Maurice coming to help on Saturday morning. He thought about telling the truth about the money and giving the bodyguard the fifteen thousand that they'd originally agreed on. But, not wanting *anyone* to know that he had the cash, he decided to wait. He asked, "How long the operation last?"

"Two-and-a-half hours. The bullet busted a rib and nicked a lung. They said they don't know how it missed my heart. They wanted me to stay longer, but I walked out this morning."

Freeman asked him to describe the men who'd been fighting, and he did. A few minutes later, Freeman shook Maurice's hand, thanked him, and got up to leave.

Maurice followed him to the door. He watched him walk to a small blue car and asked, "You finally break down and get a car?"

Freeman looked back and said "Rental."

Maurice believed that the buyer of the drugs, if the fight on the street hadn't distracted him, would have killed Freeman. As the car left and the bodyguard re-entered his house, he wondered why some people were so lucky.

—

With no Edgar, Tommy called Armando Catera and Lonnie Burdon, guys he'd known for years, and arranged to meet them at noon behind second base in Marley Park's baseball field. He arrived ten minutes early and saw no one else in the park until Armando walked toward him from centerfield; soon, Lonnie came from left. The three of them stood there in the sun, where no one could hear them as Tommy explained the deal: he'd sold his previous two shipments to a short, muscular, hard-looking man known as Mingo, whom he recognized from someplace, in the back of a van. (He hadn't remembered where he'd seen Mingo before until a couple of weeks later: they'd both done time at the Dorsey home.) He needed someone to cover him tonight when he'd meet Mingo again on Morton Terrace. Armando and Lonnie agreed to two thousand apiece for twenty minutes work; they shook hands with Tommy and went their separate ways.

—

That night, just before Hazel Royce went to bed, Alex Kirby called. "Hope this isn't too late," he said.

"No, I can talk a bit." They spoke about the movie they'd seen on Saturday. They had similar taste and discussed other good ones they'd seen. She read often, he occasionally. They'd both traveled a lot, especially Kirby, and the conversation eventually shifted to people, cultures, and experiences in countries they'd visited—Singapore, Ireland, Morocco, Germany, Spain, Japan. They talked about his ex-wife and other relationships he'd been in, and she told him about previous boyfriends, including her ex-fiancé.

As their discussion approached its fourth hour, she said, "Alex, it's been great talking with you, but I'm an early riser. I've got to turn in."

"What time is it?"

"After one."

"Wow. Well, I enjoyed talking to you, too." he said. "You busy tomorrow night?"

"I don't have any plans, no."

"How about dinner?"

"Sounds great," she said. "What's a good time?"

"I'll be off at five," he answered.

Royce said, "How about if I meet you at your job? We can go straight from there."

"Works for me. See you then."

They clicked off, and she went straight to sleep.

—

Widely spaced streetlights cast a blue-ish fluorescent glow onto Morton Terrace, a four-lane street lined on both sides by royal palm trees, west of Carol City. At 2:10 a.m., Armando Catera parked near one of the lights, a block south of where the deal was to take place; Lonnie was a hundred-and-fifty yards north.

The night was warm and humid, and no pedestrians were in sight. Within minutes, the white van Tommy had told them to look for turned onto the block, cruised halfway down it, and parked on the left, by an empty playground. A large, dark, modern-looking commercial building stood across the street from it.

Armando figured Mingo had people out here too, maybe in the playground, maybe around the building, people who were watching everything. Fine; as long as Mingo and his people didn't start trouble, there wouldn't be any, but if they did, Armando and Lonnie were ready to turn this quiet June night into a Fourth of July fireworks show come early.

Armando focused night vision binoculars on the back of the van, pausing every few seconds to look around and in the rear view mirror. Just before 2:30, Tommy walked onto Morton Terrace and toward the van, smoking a cigarette and looking in all directions; a knapsack hung from his shoulder. He was wearing a plaid work shirt, worn jeans, and boots, dressed not to draw suspicion. As he neared the van, its passenger door opened. He dropped his smoke and got in.

Armando remained alert for anything unusual or suspicious. Ten minutes later, Lonnie, summoned by a phone call from Tommy, drove a gray Buick LeSabre onto the street and parked behind the van. Immediately, Tommy came from the van's rear door without the knapsack, dragging a green military duffel bag. He and Lonnie dropped it into the Buick's trunk and got into the car. They drove off, and Armando called Tommy. "Everything cool?" he asked.

Tommy sounded tired. "Yeah, short and sweet. Meet us at Lonnie's basement."

"Okay." As Armando clicked off, the van pulled out and drove away. He opened the glove box and flipped the safety on a Mauser semi automatic that lay there. He dropped the gun into a nylon gym bag, along with a Tec-9 fitted with a red dot laser scope that he'd hidden under the passenger seat. The bag went into the trunk. He started the car and drove toward Lonnie's house to get his money.

CHAPTER THIRTEEN

MIRROR IMAGES

At 1:45 on Tuesday afternoon, Gabrielle sat in her living room, still dealing with the news of Edgar's death. She was also disappointed by what had happened with Tommy but excited about what was about to happen today. Two things bothered her—not having seen Tommy since he'd left on Sunday and his unwillingness to understand her reason for keeping her secret. Where was he? He wasn't somewhere with some teenage girl, was he? Despite their disagreements, Tommy had always treated her in a way that made her never question his loyalty. But he was a man, so you never could tell for sure, and the way these young girls acted nowadays, especially when they saw a good-looking guy with a little money...Well, he'd *better* not, for his sake...

What would happen next? She'd missed him a lot last week while he was out there trying to find whatever it was he'd lost, and when he finally came home, she angered him by telling the truth about her daughter. Mistake? Maybe, with the timing. Her plan had been to tell him after sex, when they were closest; now, she hadn't seen or heard from him in two days...

The buzzer sounded—Ann Claiborne-Strauss. Gabrielle didn't bother to check. She went to the elevator, rode down, and walked out into the heat to where Miss Ann waited in a blue Chrysler. Gabrielle got in, and they drove northwest, mostly in silence.

The Barbara Mabrity Academy was a red brick structure that looked more like a statehouse than the private school that it was. Gabrielle's anticipation increased once Claiborne-Strauss parked across the street, behind a number of white, chartered buses there to carry students home. Claiborne-Strauss smiled and asked, "Nervous, right?"

"Not really," Gabrielle replied. "Excited, more." Early yesterday, the caseworker had called to say that she thought that it would be a good idea for her to go with Gabrielle today, partly because Jasmin's stepmother still seemed a bit uncomfortable. Gabrielle preferred to go alone and didn't quite understand the logic, but she agreed.

Now, near the school's entrance, scores of mothers, none of whom she recognized as Erica Briscoe, and a few fathers gathered, waiting for school to let out. Someone held a set of pink, green, and purple balloons that said "Happy Birthday!!" Gabrielle and Claiborne-Strauss sat quietly until a bell rang inside the building. Within seconds, the first child emerged, then another and another and another until they flowed out like grains of sand from a cracked hourglass, rushing to their parents and to the buses.

A pink birthday balloon floated from the noisily dispersing crowd, above the school's roof, toward the sun. Gabrielle still didn't see Mrs. Briscoe, and, as mothers started to lead their children home, she wondered if Jasmin's stepmother had decided to back out at the last minute. Gabrielle scanned faces until Claiborne-Strauss said, "There they are. Over there. Look."

Gabrielle followed the direction of Claiborne-Strauss's voice and looked to her left. There, Erica Briscoe was leading a short, chocolate-brown girl by the hand toward the car. The girl wore the Academy's uniform—lemon-yellow blouse under a knee-length navy blue dress that had shoulder straps, white socks, and black patent leather shoes. Yellow ribbons decorated two thick braids that hung from her head.

Gabrielle shifted in her seat as this small reflection of her, this piece of her, approached. Jasmin looked well cared for. She was a bit bow-legged and had big brown eyes and Gabrielle's smooth complexion. Mrs. Briscoe led her to within five feet of Gabrielle and stopped to adjust the girl's shoulder straps. As she did, Jasmin glanced into the car at her birth mother and the caseworker sitting beside her; Gabrielle tried not to show too much emotion as their eyes met. A few seconds later, Mrs. Briscoe led Jasmin away.

Gabrielle felt as if her heart would burst. Her hand rose to cover a smile, and tears clouded her vision. She blinked them away and turned her head in time to see Jasmin and Briscoe enter a tan SUV parked six car lengths back.

Claiborne-Strauss asked, "Okay?" as her hand fell onto Gabrielle's. For now, excitement—and sadness—had overwhelmed Gabrielle so that she couldn't speak. She nodded, and Claiborne-Strauss started the car's engine.

When Gabrielle got home, she understood why the adoption worker had accompanied her: from the time Jasmin had left Gabrielle's sight, Gabrielle had seen nothing else.

—

At his studio apartment, Tommy slept all day. After six, he awoke feeling drowsy and lay in bed for forty minutes before calling his cousin Monet. She didn't answer but called back twenty-five minutes later, after he'd showered. "How you doin'?" Tommy asked.

"Fine."

"How's your mom?"

"Okay, I guess. The same."

"Where you at now?"

Monet said, "Work. You know Duvall's shoe store in Hetison Mall?"

"What time you get off?"

"Eight thirty."

"How about I give you a lift home?"

"On your motorcycle?"

"You all right with that?"

"Yeah. I've been on it before, remember? I come out an exit near Sears."

"I'll meet you there."

—

Two hours later, Monet was crouched, hugging Tommy's back as they zoomed south through traffic along Biscayne Boulevard, the sun setting in all shades of gold and gray to their right. Tommy stayed mostly in the middle lane. To Monet, apart from the engine's roar, the ride's speed and excitement felt like being in an amusement park at twilight; wind felt as if it were passing through her, and the city's multicolored lights shot past as neon blurs through her helmet's tinted visor. His white shirt flapping, Tommy dipped in and out of traffic as they flashed by parks, shopping centers, run down motels, upscale apartment complexes, office towers, and luxury hotels. Monet loved every second.

Tommy pulled up outside Lazaro's, a small Mexican-American restaurant near the water. He cut off the engine, removed his helmet, and looked back at her. "I thought I told you to hold on tight but relax," he said.

"I did."

"No, I said '*Relax.*' You done collapsed my damn chest," he said, pretending to stagger from pain while dismounting the bike.

"Uh uh," she smiled.

They sat at a sidewalk table. Tommy ordered a salad, two burritos, and a beer. When she said that she wanted a beer too, he frowned and said, "Yo, hold up. How old are you, again?"

"Eighteen," she lied.

"Tell the truth."

"Eighteen. Next December."

"Um hm." He looked to the waiter and said, "She'll take a Sprite."

Monet said, "Awwwwww, man..."

"See, listen to you. You a kid. What you know about beer, anyway?"

"I know enough."

"Oh, yeah? What would your mother do to me if she found out I was letting you drink beer?"

"She ain't got to know."

"Right. This time next year, I'll buy you a beer," Tommy said.

"Maybe."

He waited until the waiter had left to ask Monet about her mother. The girl said that Vonetta remained in the deep depression she'd been in since her son had been murdered, depression that had worsened with the accused killer's acquittal. "Be honest, I feel kinda the same way she does," she said. "I just try to handle it. Last time I saw Anthony was at school. He was with some people walking down a hallway. He looked back and told me I was gonna pass a test I had to take later that day. And that was it. Next time I see him, he's in a casket."

Tommy remembered Monet sobbing quietly throughout the funeral.

"I still can't believe he's gone like that, you know?" she continued, shaking her head. "It's like I just can't accept it. For him to get *shot* like that, type of person he was…" She gazed over Tommy's shoulder into the distance, her mouth hanging open as if she were still in shock.

Tommy stared at her hard, nodding slowly. Pain and anger from his mother's murder bubbled to the surface though he didn't acknowledge them as such. He said, "The boy who shot your brother. Mark. You know about him, right? Where he live, who he hang with, where he go…"

Monet nodded.

The corners of Tommy's mouth turned downward as he leaned forward. He put both elbows on the table and said, "I'm listening."

—

The next day, a dreary Wednesday, Freeman got to work late because the bus had broken down en route. When he arrived, Lynnette, the manager, was by herself, and as soon as he got set up, she asked him to man the counter while she drove to Georgetown on an errand. "Errand," he thought. "Probably brunch."

Twenty minutes later, the phone rang. He picked up and heard a woman's soft pleasant tone: "Mr. Freeman?"

It was the woman who'd been with the buyer at Ellingwood, the one who'd come to warn him. Freeman said, "Speaking."

"You know who this is, right? I have to talk to you."

Freeman said nothing; knowing what had happened to the woman's partner, he wanted no part of her.

"I'm not going to do anything to you. I just need to know the truth."

He heard a note of desperation in her voice, as if she really did need to know. He said, "I'm supposed to get a break at 1:30 today."

"I'll be there."

Freeman started to say that some other worker would have to show up before he could leave the counter, but she'd already hung up.

—

At 1:30, with Lynnette back in the store, Freeman walked outside and looked around. Directly across the street, the tinted, driver's side window on a blue Infiniti lowered to reveal Lucinda Williams' eyes. Freeman jaywalked to the car. The passenger door opened, but Freeman didn't get in. "What do you want?" he asked, checking to make sure that no one lurked in the back.

"Get in," she said. "I just want to talk."

Freeman remained outside the car. "We can talk fine right here. Or we can walk somewhere."

She showed her empty hands. "Look, you think I'm going to shoot you here, in the middle of D.C. in broad daylight with all these people around? Get in."

Freeman hesitated, then thought about how she'd come to warn him about the buyer. He entered the car warily.

Lucinda raised her window back up, and they faced each other in the car's air-conditioned dimness. She looked at him as if trying to shine a flashlight into his soul. Freeman asked, "How do you know me? How did you know I work here?"

"You play music, right? It's not hard to find you."

He said, "Okay, look, first off, I didn't do anything to your boyfriend or husband or whatever he was. I want to get that straight."

"Um hm. If you didn't do it, who did?"

Freeman shrugged. "I don't know. You know him and me were supposed to make a deal. He checked to make sure I didn't have a gun, then he pulled one on me. He tried to steal what I wanted to sell to him. Then something happened out on the street. He told me to get in the bathroom and locked me in. Next thing, shooting: boom, boom, boom, boom, boom. Don't ask me who, why, how, what it was about. I guess somebody robbed him same way he tried to rob me. All I know is when I came out, he's laying there dead. Drugs gone, money gone. But I wasn't thinking about any of that. I was just glad I was still breathing."

Her unblinking eyes continued to search his. "You're not telling the truth," she said.

Did she know something? Did she know he had the money? When he'd taken it, Freeman had looked around while leaving the building. He hadn't seen this car he was sitting in, nor the van she and the buyer were in when Freeman had met them on Thursday night; he'd seen nothing suspicious.

He decided she didn't know anything. "You know what?" he said, his voice rising in anger. "I'm sorry for your loss, but *he* tried to steal from *me*. I'm not the one who pulled the gun. I'm not the one who lied. I held my end of the deal. Like I said, I didn't shoot him, but if I did, he'd have deserved it!" Freeman didn't want to say the wrong thing, but he could feel himself losing it. "He didn't carry himself right," he said. "You know it. That's why you came here last week and told me to be careful when I was dealing with him. Now you come acting like *I'm* the one who was out of line."

Freeman opened the door and said, "I understand you want to know what happened to him, but, like I said, I can't tell you. Who knows, maybe if he hadn't have done what he did to me, he'd still be alive. But right about now, I'm thinking your old man was looking to take me out, and I feel like I ain't got nothing else to say to you." He got out, half-slammed the door, and walked back across the street, thinking that he had to get his blood pressure checked and that he'd never again get involved in anything like this.

He returned to Sound Value and remembered that he was on lunch break. When he went back outside to get something to eat, the woman had left.

—

That evening, Alex Kirby took Hazel Royce to Courtney and Cress, a sixty-year-old, four-star restaurant in Georgetown. Kirby was a talker—he chatted with the valet and the waiter—but tonight, over appetizers, chablis, entrees, and dessert, Royce opened up more than she had on Saturday.

After eating, they enjoyed a long walk, and when it was time to say goodnight, Kirby kissed her twice before she got into her car. She felt upbeat and optimistic while driving home, as if things were going to work out well for them.

And they did. Within seven months, they were married. They remained together for over forty-one years.

———

As Kirby kissed Hazel Royce, Lonnie Burdon steered his Buick onto Crescent Boulevard and cruised toward the Perkins Recreation Center; Tommy, in the passenger seat, described to Lonnie the boy who'd gotten away with murdering Tommy's nephew: "About as tall as me, fat, brown-skinned, always got his hair in corn-rows, got a little peach fuzz mustache and a scar near his eye. Talks a lot."

Lonnie parked and went inside the center. Ten minutes later, he returned to the car and said, "Yeah, he in there playing ping pong, running his mouth."

For an hour and a half, they waited, until finally, Lonnie said, "Here he go."

Mark Wilkerson came out with a taller boy about his age. Both wore white t-shirts and cargo shorts. The other boy went one way, and Mark lit a cigarette and walked toward the Buick.

Tommy flipped his own cigarette out the window and drew a .45 from his waist. As Mark passed the car, Tommy got out, walked up behind the boy, pressed the gun's muzzle against his spine, and said, "Turn around."

Mark said, "What the fuck…" Despite being bigger than either man, he had a boy's voice.

Tommy hit him hard behind the ear with the gun's handle. Mark yelled. He raised his hand to his head, staggered, and almost fell.

Tommy said, "Shut the fuck up and turn around."

Mark did so, and Tommy pushed him toward the car. Once they reached it, Lonnie got out and patted the boy down. Satisfied that Mark had no weapon, he opened the rear door. Tommy pushed the boy in and sat next to him. Lonnie got behind the wheel, started the car, and drove off.

Mark scoffed, "What is this shit? You all niggas crazy? You know who you fuckin' with?"

"Shut up, punk ass."

Mark chuckled. Smiling, he folded his arms, leaned back, and said, "You know who my uncles is?"

Tommy smashed the gun into Mark's mouth and felt teeth loosen. He said, "I told you to shut the fuck up. Say one more word I'm puttin' six holes in your fat gut." He pointed the gun toward the boy's midsection. "Say somethin' else. Go 'head." Mark grimaced while straightening from the blow; he covered his bleeding mouth with his hand and aimed twin beams of icy hate at Tommy.

Lonnie drove to a commercial area that housed old factories and van-filled lots, and turned onto a dim, deserted, dead-end street. Two blocks away, a white building loomed, the once successful nightclub The CasBar, now closed down and boarded shut. Lonnie parked in front of a small, abandoned warehouse. He got bolt cutters from the trunk and disappeared into shadows that cloaked a door. A few seconds later, he clenched a mini-flashlight in his teeth and opened the lock with a master key.

Tommy said to Mark, "Get out." The boy did and walked to the building's entrance. Lonnie gave Tommy the light and went to the car while Tommy pushed Mark forward and followed him into the warehouse.

The humid, moldy-smelling place was in total blackness except for the flashlight's beam. Rats, unused to company, scurried in the corners and ceiling. Tommy looked around. Cobwebs were everywhere. Several steel girders stood from ceiling to floor, and two dusty wooden work tables were among aging machinery at the far end. Debris covered the floor, and paint had cracked and crumbled to show rusty pipes in holes in the walls. Lonnie entered, carrying a rope, and closed the door.

Still aiming the gun at Mark, Tommy pointed the light at a steel girder and said, "Get over there."

Scowling, Mark mumbled through his injured mouth, "I ain't walkin' in all this shit."

Tommy shot him in the knee. Mark went down, yelling.

Tommy aimed again and said, "You wanna keep runnin' your mouth like a little bitch? Go 'head. It's five more in this piece. The whole building soundproof. Can't nobody hear you no goddamn way."

The fetid air had the three of them sweating. Tommy pointed the flashlight at Mark's agonized face.

He stepped toward the boy, picturing his nephew's murder the way it had been described at the trial: Anthony, his mother's favorite, lying on the ground, wounded, the way Mark was now, and Mark standing over him, firing into the fallen body again and again and again.

Squinting and clutching his leg, Mark sneered, "Fuck you, punk motherfucker. I ain't scared of you. Do what you gonna do. You gon' pull the shit, use it." He spat blood onto Tommy's shoe.

Tommy's mouth twisted. Anger pumped through his veins and into his brain like firewater. He clenched his teeth, aimed at the boy's head, and started to squeeze the trigger.

But he hesitated. At eighteen, Tommy had been just like Mark—no guidance, wild, mad at everybody, high half the time; he'd shot three people by that age, almost killing one. Now, he wanted to even the score for Anthony, for Anthony's mother, for Anthony's sister, for himself.

Dizziness and nausea swept through him; sweat dripped from his face. He stood still for several seconds, blinking fast, barely hearing Lonnie behind him say, "Yo, man..."

He turned off the flashlight, pointed away from Mark's head, and fired five times into the floor, yelling as he squeezed the trigger. Sweat soaked, his ears ringing from the gunshots, he left the boy writhing on the floor and cursing. Tommy was still gritting his teeth and blinking heavily as he and Lonnie jumped into the Buick and sped away.

Chapter Fourteen

THURSDAY KARMA

Percocet that Maurice was taking to ease the pain of breathing made him sleep heavily, so on Thursday morning, when his dog, Zak, started to bark downstairs, it took him almost two minutes to wake up. Finally, he did and went down the steps very slowly, the way he did everything now. Zak was at the front door, still making noise, near a sealed envelope that had just been slipped in through the mail slot. The unstamped envelope had been hand addressed simply to "Maurice." The bodyguard picked it up, held it to the light, and opened it. It contained an unsigned, hand-written note: "Check the bush on the left by the back door."

Wondering what the hell was going on, he opened the front door, looked around, and saw no one. He went to the back door and after doing the same thing, peered under the bush. Hidden there was a small cardboard box taped shut in two plastic shopping bags. Confused, he eyed the parcel for a few seconds. Maurice had enemies, and his first thought was that this could be a bomb. He picked it up, slowly and painfully. He listened to it, smelled it, shook it gently, and took it inside the house, where he used a kitchen knife to open it.

The box contained about two-dozen thin stacks of hundreds and fifties. Maurice couldn't believe it. He stood there with his hands on his hips, then returned to the back door, poked his head out, and looked around again. He saw no one.

He went back inside and counted twenty-five thousand dollars out onto the table. For a second, he stood in shock, trying to figure it out; then, he stroked his chin and thought, "Freeman." He smiled.

—

Freeman wasn't on Simone's mind, and neither was Henry as she walked a quarter mile to the post office, seeing D.C. through plum-tinted shades. She felt great, mostly because of Ricardo, the guy she'd met while getting off work on Saturday evening. He'd driven beside her until she got into her car, and she stayed there, talking to him for twenty minutes; among other things, he convinced her that he wasn't a Lapham Bros. customer stalking a pretty employee, and, eventually, that she should go with him to a house party near Georgetown University in a couple of hours.

They had a good time that night. He was tall and broad shouldered, as fancy a dancer as she, and he kept her laughing until early morning, when he dropped her off at her car. She had dinner and drinks with him at a candle-lit, Italian bistro in Arlington on Tuesday and enjoyed that, too. Ricardo's calmness and steadiness made it seem as if everything was under control. A native of Albuquerque, he'd have an international law degree from Georgetown in six months. The best thing, though, was his looks—the jet-black hair, that bright smile, those clear long-lashed eyes that left no doubt about how he'd be in bed.

Simone had been thinking about that a lot, and she couldn't wait. They were supposed to get together again that night, and she'd decided to sleep with him then. She was just getting to know him, but as long as he was anything like the way he seemed, she had plans for him...

She reached the post office and got on line behind a young man and a middle-aged one, feeling as if she were standing on a cloud...

—

Tommy had a headache and was watching TV at his studio apartment early on Thursday when Iris called to say that his father had slipped into a coma overnight and been taken to a hospital. Tommy continued to watch the screen, but his mind was in Georgia. He'd accepted the fact that Leon's life was basically over, but that didn't make him feel any better about it. When he tried not to think about that, his thoughts drifted to Gabrielle. He hadn't had time to figure out how to respond to what she'd said about having been a mother all this time, and he still didn't want to see her. To him, it was a betrayal of trust by the person he'd trusted most, and he thought that their relationship had changed permanently.

But his mail went to the condo, and that was where his possessions were, so around noon, he got dressed and returned there.

When he walked inside, she was in a hurry, wearing a navy blouse and white skirt, about to go somewhere. She looked at him closely and said, "Hey, Tommy."

He said, "Hey."

"You still mad?"

"We'll talk about it later," he responded, not looking at her.

She went to the bathroom briefly, and as she was leaving, she said quietly, "Two cops came here this mornin'. They haven't found who killed Edgar. They said he had you down as an employee at his contracting business, and they just wanted to ask you if you knew anything or why he was up in New York. That's what they said. Left a business card. It's in the living room next to the lamp."

Just what I need, Tommy thought, *cops coming here*. He nodded and said nothing. When Gabrielle left, he sat in the living room, squeezed his eyes shut, and leaned his aching head back. After a minute, he noticed an odd feeling—beside the pain, pressure on his skull from all sides. Strong panic took over his thoughts, as if something terrible were about to happen. His hands began to tremble and wouldn't stop. His body tensed as his hands continued to shake uncontrollably. He reached for a cigarette to calm himself but couldn't grasp the pack. He went back to the chair and waited, his body tense.

Finally, the trembling stopped. He went to the liquor cabinet and poured a shot of bourbon, which he downed in one gulp. He lit a cigarette and smoked it with hands that still weren't steady, wondering how much longer he could continue this way.

—

In Las Vegas, Henry sat in a poolside umbrella's shade on the Bellmonde

Hotel's roof twenty-seven floors above street level. He was wearing all white—wide-open Guayabera shirt, knee-length shorts, patent leather slip-ons, and Panama hat—and an unlit, partially smoked cheroot hung from his lips. The sun was scorching, the way he liked it. Sunglasses covered the eye he'd injured in the fight in the rain last week, but it was no longer swollen, and it didn't hurt much; he could see well enough out of it to watch tomorrow night's championship boxing match, so he figured it'd be normal soon.

He wanted to talk to a girl in a pink-and-black, two-piece bathing suit who sat across the pool from him, getting a tan. She had good legs and tits and appeared to be alone, but she'd gotten him aroused, so he had to wait a while before standing. She was young and tall enough to remind him of Simone, and as he'd done repeatedly since Saturday, he wondered about the mistake he'd made in D.C.

Simone knew about him, not much, but enough—that he was here, for instance. For some reason, government agents had been looking for him recently. If they'd seen him with Simone, they could question her, maybe already had. And she'd shown that she didn't mind running her mouth…

Henry shook his head, cursing whatever had made him admit to her that he was a professional criminal. Again, he thought about heading back east and making sure that she'd never tell anyone his business. He knew where she lived and could go there late one night and do it easily. But was it worth the risk, especially now? He'd have to think.

The girl across from him turned onto her stomach, giving him a good view of her ass. Slouching slightly to hide his erection, Henry went to talk to her.

—

On workdays, Tracy Whitlock liked to get to the stationhouse fifteen minutes early, but this morning she'd gone back to sleep after her stroll through the neighborhood and was now a few minutes behind schedule. She threw on her police uniform, grabbed her bag, and rushed past the sunlight-filled kitchen to the door that led to the garage.

The front doorbell rang. "Shit," she thought, "I don't have time. Who the hell is that?" She continued to the garage and got into her Wrangler. Once she'd driven outside, she stopped. Birds chirped all around, as if happy. At the front door stood a tall, well-built Hispanic in his early thirties, wearing a herringbone blazer, navy shirt, black pants, and cream-colored tie. He walked around a hedge and toward the SUV, gazing at her with unblinking eyes that smiled as if he alone knew some humorous secret.

"Tracy Whitlock?" he asked as he approached her lowered window.

Tracy raised her sunglasses atop her head. "Yeah. What's up?"

The recently transferred detective reached into his breast pocket, pulled out a badge, and identified himself: "Cisco Bermudez."

She'd heard that name before…Beck had mentioned it more than once. Sensing something weird starting to happen, she leaned forward. "You were there with the chase of the drug dealer who smashed into a squad car and killed the lieutenant."

"Um hm." Bermudez saw her glance at her watch and said, "I'm with Internal Affairs now, chasing dirty cops. I know, I caught you at a bad time, right?"